Outside, the Trade Winds Rustled the Palms Seductively. . . .

Fiftul shadows raced across the moon. The night air from the Caribbean was filled with magic.

It was then that Kells strode in.

Carolina had heard his step in the hall and tensed, expecting his knock. But she was unprepared for the sudden way her door burst open. She was caught standing there clad only in her thin chemise—more than sufficient for the heat—before her dressing table. She had been about to comb out her long fair hair, but as the door opened she whirled and dropped the fan with which she had been cooling her damp skin.

"Get out!" she cried, outraged. "Can't you see I'm not dressed?"

"Indeed I can see that." Kells's raking gaze passed over her, but he made no move to go. . . .

Lovesong

by *New York Times* Bestselling Author

Valerie Sherwood

"ONE OF THE TOP FIVE MOST WIDELY READ AUTHORS IN THE UNITED STATES TODAY."

—*Winston Salem Sentinel*

Books by Valerie Sherwood

Lovesong

Available from POCKET BOOKS

Coming Soon

Windsong (May 1986)

Nightsong (December 1986)

Valerie Sherwood

Lovesong

PUBLISHED BY POCKET BOOKS NEW YORK

Distributed in Canada by PaperJacks Ltd., a Licensee
of the trademarks of Simon & Schuster, Inc.

Another *Original* publication of POCKET BOOKS

POCKET BOOKS, a division of Simon & Schuster, Inc.
1230 Avenue of the Americas, New York, N.Y. 10020
In Canada distributed by PaperJacks Ltd.,
330 Steelcase Road, Markham, Ontario

ISBN: 0-671-49837-1

First Pocket Books printing September, 1985

10 9 8 7 6 5 4 3 2 1

POCKET and colophon are registered trademarks
of Simon & Schuster, Inc.

Printed in Canada

WARNING

Readers are hereby warned not to use any of the cosmetics, unusual foods, medications or other treatments referred to herein without first consulting and securing the approval of a medical doctor. These items are included only to enhance the authentic seventeenth century atmosphere and are in no way recommended for use by anyone.

DEDICATION

To the memory of wonderful Fuzzy, our beautiful long-haired English tabby, who came into our lives walking across a stone footbridge at mother's antebellum home "Sunset View" and chose to stay, unforgettable Fuzzy making his leisurely descent down our grand staircase at Dragon's Lair, plumed tail waving—or his hopping ascent up those same wide stone stairs because his wide-pawed furry legs were too short to walk up conveniently! Fuzzy the philosopher, the wonderful traveling companion, Fuzzy, who could be sound asleep beside us in the car after a journey of hundreds of miles and yet would always wake up and stretch two blocks from home! To charming Fuzzy, content in town house or brick-walled garden, but perhaps happiest on the wide lawns of Thorn Hill near Charles Town, Fuzzy the gallant who fought back death so bravely, to dear unforgettable Fuzzy, loved companion of other days, this book is affectionately dedicated.

AUTHOR'S NOTE

Although this story of reckless Carolina Lightfoot of Virginia's celebrated Eastern Shore and her stormy love affair with her buccaneer lover—and indeed all the characters and events in this novel save those noted here—are entirely of my own invention, I have tried to give an accurate picture of the times in which young Mistress Lightfoot lived—the glorious and exciting 1600's.

However, certain delightful incidents are indeed based on fact:

Matelotage—taking a wife "sailor fashion"—really was a custom among the buccaneers.

The Marriage Trees on the border between Virginia and Maryland really did exist—and lovestruck runaway couples dashed for that border and the parsons who waited beneath the branches just as in a later century in Scotland runaway lovers would dash for Gretna Green.

And the remarkable scene where Fielding Lightfoot and his headstrong wife Letty clash so violently during a carriage ride, according to Eastern Shore tradition actually happened—but it was that "gallant whip," the fourth John Custis of the great house called Arlington, who drove the carriage (his son was the first husband of Martha Dandridge, who later married George Washington) and it was his own wife Frances who gave such a famous rejoinder to his astonishing statement. Their quarrels—like those of the Fielding and Letitia of my story—were legendary and well documented in court records (they were said to pass long periods without speaking except through the butler and when at last they did speak, it was to revile each other). Indeed he had mention of it engraved upon his tombstone!

For the first home of the stormy Lightfoot clan I have therefore, with suitable adjustments for my story, chosen historic Arlington's setting on Old Plantation Creek and renamed it Farview.

Beautiful Level Green, the "new" home Fielding Lightfoot builds for his family, will at once be recognized by those who love old Tidewater houses as famous Rosewell, home of the Pages, the largest (and perhaps the finest) house in Virginia in that early day. Many years later young Thomas Jefferson, a frequent guest at Rosewell, is said to have penned a draft of the Declaration of Independence in one of its turret rooms.

The name of neighboring Fairfield, later to be re-christened Carter's Creek, I have left intact along with its setting. It was the home of the Burwells, and both it and Rosewell furnished governors and lieutenant governors to Virginia. The two families, Page and Burwell, intermarried. Indeed a Burwell daughter by the name of Rebecca refused the hand of young Thomas Jefferson and nearly broke his heart.

Although both Rosewell and Fairfield may have been built slightly later than the period of my story (Rosewell is said to have been begun in 1725 and Fairfield's date is disputed; it may have been built as early as the 1650's or as late as 1692), they admirably fit my story. But I chose them for another reason as well—in honor of my first cousin, Page Nelson Welton, whom I hold in affection. For Page is a lineal descendant of these Pages and these Burwells—as well as the Nelsons of Nelson House in Yorktown.

In the same manner, I could not resist whimsically renaming Rosewell to Level Green in honor of that other lovely Level Green in Hardy County (then in Northern Virginia), the home of my maternal great grandfather, Dr. Jacob Kinney Chambers, where my grandmother, a reigning belle of the Old Confederacy, was given in marriage to my grandfather, Joseph Daniel Heiskell, a gallant officer who had reluctantly surrendered his sword at Appomatox (and whose people in Hampshire County in the aftermath of the war were said to be the first to erect a monument to the Confederacy). It was from that same Level Green that grandmother rode with him to Texas.

Rosegill, where my heroine schemes her escape, also is authentic. It was built in 1650. As with Fairfield, it is peopled in my novel with the original owners, in this case Ralph Wormeley, in whose famous library my heroine and her sister discuss the disadvantages of being a reigning belle.

Although I was not able to discover the actual publication dates of those much maligned "trashy" novels so dear to the hearts of Colonial wives and daughters, *The Nunnery of Coquettes*, *Wife to Be Let*, and *Harriot, or the Innocent Adulteress* were all very early and were extremely popular—despite the sighs of Colonial gentlemen who felt their womenfolk would be better occupied in perusing *The Compleat Housewife*.

Readers might be interested to know that Virginia's doll, Nan White, over which Carolina agonizes, is a faithful representation of Letitia Penn II, a doll that has been called "the oldest and most famous doll in America." Letitia Penn II was purchased by William Penn and named for Penn's daughter Letitia, who had selected the doll as a gift for a child in Philadelphia. Together, twenty-inch-tall Letitia and her famous purchaser in 1699 crossed the seas in the good ship *Canterbury*—and when last I heard of her she was residing in Montgomery County, Maryland.

And that dainty little seven-inch doll with the bisque hands and feet and composition head and black painted coiffure that Aunt Pet gives Carolina is a true replica of what has been labeled the "oldest known doll in Virginia." With her kidskin body still dressed in its original pantalets and delicate gauze gown, now yellowed with age, she was, when last I heard, in residence at Little Berkeley, in Hampton, Virginia. Though it is of somewhat later vintage, I thought this tiny doll reminiscent enough of the times to be appropriate to my story.

I would note in reference to the famous couplets chanted by generations of English schoolchildren, which begin with the "oranges and lemons" peal of St. Clement's, that both St. Clement Danes and St. Maryle-Bow, Cheapside, are quite ancient—they long pre-dated Carolina's time—but that St. Martin's and possibly some of the others mentioned are of slightly later vintage. Still, I have included them because they are so beguiling.

As for Carolina's buccaneer lover, let me say that England holds the West Indies today by courtesy of the buccaneers, who paid for it in blood in the long wars with Spain over who had the right to sail the Western Seas, the right to colonize the Americas. Rightfully these men should have been called privateers, for privateers they were—many licensed by their governments, many others unlicensed but approved. They were callously used for political expediency, hanged without mercy to placate Spanish might—but they were redoubtable men, these renegades from many lands.

And it is of an English buccaneer and his fiery lady that I write. Let it be known that wherever I was able to find historical fact about the buccaneers, I have hewed to the line (and much is known of the articles they signed before "ventures," of their generosity in providing fallen comrades with what amounted to a forerunner of today's Social Security system, and of their gallantry toward women—including the ladies of their enemy Spain). Where history seems lacking, I have perforce embroidered events with my imagination.

In my view, these much maligned buccaneers who held their strongholds of Tortuga and Port Royal at such cost are not to be confused with pirates who attacked any weaker vessel afloat. *These* men, without any real official backing and no government guns to aid them, took on the greatest foreign power of their day—Spain—and backed her to the wall. *I* think they are to be revered.

Perhaps I can sum up in verse my feeling for the buccaneers:

Where the sunken treasures lie, where golden
    galleons came to die,
Mid coral reef and whited dune, a gull's cry echoes
    to the moon,

And who can say that in its light they do not now still
　　sail the night?
Let us toast them all once more as we reckon up the
　　score
And ferret out their faults and list their sins.
Did they never count the cost, those who
　　fought—and often lost?
Did they balance off their losses with their wins?
Do we honor them too much, all those English,
　　French and Dutch
Wild fellows who took on the power of Spain?
No, I say that we do not, and here now and on the
　　spot
Let these firebrands and their ladies live again!

　　　　　　　　　　　　　　　　Valerie Sherwood

CONTENTS

PROLOGUE
THE ISLAND OF TORTUGA

Summer 1688

Entice him, tease him with your lips,
Your sultry sidewise glances,
But if you drive a man too far
You then must take your chances!

Fitful shadows raced across the moon. The night air from the Caribbean was filled with magic. The lean buccaneer took a step toward her.

"Kells," she warned him, "go back."

He paused and the moonlight that poured through her bedroom window in a pale golden shower struck full upon his face, etching the hard lines and the steady narrow gray eyes. He cut a handsome figure, tall and dark, with his white shirt with its flowing sleeves open to the waist, cutlass hanging carelessly from his belt and slapping against his lean thighs in their dark trousers. But his saturnine countenance, deeply tanned from the tropic sun, did nothing to reassure her.

"And why should *I* be left out?" he demanded insolently. "Why should I not share you too? Since you promise yourself so recklessly to others?"

For a moment she forgot that she was standing there clad only in a thin chemise and gave him a bewildered look. "What are you talking about? I have promised nothing."

"What of your dealings with O'Rourke and Skull? They have tossed coins for you!"

Her color heightened at the way he said that and she answered with heat. "They tossed coins only to decide which one would take me where I wish to go. Since *you* will not!" she added bitterly.

He had taken another step toward her now and she retreated warily across the stone floor. His face was again in darkness but she could see the gleam of his strong white teeth, flashing in a smile that held no mirth.

"Kells, you cannot blame me!" she cried in sudden panic at the looming anger she saw in his face. "They promised to take me wherever I wished to go."

"Promised to take you. . . ." he murmured. *"And you believed them?"*

Her heart was hammering harder in her chest. Not only his commanding presence but something dangerous in his tone frightened her.

"Should I not?" she asked stiffly.

"You agreed to accept *matelotage* from them!" he exploded. "Don't you know what that means?"

In truth she did not, but she would not have admitted it for worlds. "Of course I know." She tossed her fair head and the moonlight struck it into a cascade of spun white gold that poured down upon the rounded gleam of her shoulders. "It is—oh, some Spanish word that means 'to share metal' or some such. I had promised them gold—"

"Whose gold?" he cut in.

"Why—why, Doña Hernanda's, of course!"

His expression grew incredulous.

"She may not have it, but she can get it!" She had hastily retreated behind a big carved chair at his advance and now her lovely face stared back at him indignantly from over the chair's tall back. "And since they had both offered, they felt entitled to share the gold—to share the metal, I suppose," she added lamely. She was wishing with all her heart that when

2

O'Rourke had mentioned the word *"matelot"* on the quay that she had asked him what it meant instead of so blithely assuming its meaning.

"Share metal . . ." he murmured and for a moment she thought his expression was bemused. *"Matelotage* is a French word, Christabel, not a Spanish one," he informed her grimly. *"Matelotage* is an old custom among the buccaneers, who have long suffered from a shortage of desirable women. It means to take a wife 'sailor fashion.' Two buccaneers toss a coin as to which one will marry the wench, and the loser goes through with the ceremony."

It rang now in her head, Skull's snorting laugh, *"Ye've lost!"* and O'Rourke's triumphant, *"No, damme, I've won!"* as he pocketed the coin he'd tossed—and all the while his hot green gaze had roved over her lissome body in the low-cut red silk dress she'd worn down to the quay.

She was looking at Kells now, dazed. Dear God, did these buccaneers think she had actually promised to *marry* one of them?

He returned her gaze coolly. "I see you still do not fully understand, Christabel. When two buccaneers desire the same woman and that woman is willing, one will wed her and stay with her for a time whilst the other is at sea. The other then returns and takes the husband's place and lives with the bride as if *they* are man and wife—until the husband returns, when they trade places again. The one to whom she is *not* wed is called the *matelot.* It is a custom time-honored among the buccaneers."

As the full import of what she had gotten herself into, down on the quay, sank in on her, she thought her knees would buckle. Those two buccaneers believed she had promised to—! She clung to the chairback, staring at him in horror. "Oh, I never intended—I did not understand."

"You are hot to depart with O'Rourke or Skull—and they intend to share you."

"But they cannot!" she cried. And it was Carolina Lightfoot, the reigning Colonial belle, who was speak-

3

ing, and not this other self she had become—Christabel, the Silver Wench of the buccaneers.

"Who is to stop them?" he asked softly.

Her breath came shallowly. It was hard to keep her voice steady. "You mean—you would not stop them?" she whispered. "Oh, Kells, you would not let them take me?"

A muscle in his hard jawline worked for a moment as his steely gray eyes considered her. She felt she saw doom in their hard glitter, but she could not know the torment within him. *Let them take her? They would have to cut him down first!* Indeed, for her sake he would chop them both down like trees—but she was not to know that, for it would give this arrogant Silver Wench a power over him that he did not wish her to realize she possessed.

He fought for control and when he spoke at last his answer was cool. It was flung in her face and it struck her like a slap.

"You are saying that you are mine?" His hard gaze swept over her.

"No—no, of course I am not saying that!" She was suddenly terribly conscious of her state of undress, that she was standing here in the tropic night in her bedroom, clad only in her chemise. "I am saying—" She swallowed nervously. "I am saying that you could *pretend* that it is so."

"I will not pretend." The words rang like metal cast upon stones. "If I do this thing, it will be *true in fact* that you prefer my bed to theirs. Make your choice, Christabel. It is to be them—or me. I am telling you that I will deal with this pair on your behalf—but only if you come willingly to my bed."

She recoiled. He would let this terrible thing, this *matelotage,* happen to her if she did not agree—he would! She felt blind terror surge through her.

"I will do as you ask," she said faintly.

Around them the stillness was suddenly deafening. It was broken only by the sound of the sea breaking over the beach. The moon, being old and wise in the ways of lovers, with sudden delicacy retired behind a cloud and

4

left them alone in scented darkness in that wildest place of all—Tortuga, stronghold of the Brethren of the Coast, the buccaneers.

Dear God, she asked herself in silent wonder, *how could I say that? After all that has happened?*

And for a brief tense moment as the lean buccaneer captain reached out and touched caressingly her shrinking bare shoulder, her past flashed before her as vividly as if she were living it now—and she was Carolina Lightfoot once again, fourteen and safe and careless and living in the American Colonies on Virginia's Eastern Shore.

BOOK I

The American Beauty and the English Lord

His siren song pursues her down the street,
His sins are legion but—his voice is sweet
And she, caught up in rapture, standing there
Is tempted to embrace and love and dare. . . .

PART ONE

The Colonial Minx

Let your skirts lift in the breeze!
And we'll away to the Marriage Trees!
Twenty miles deep and twenty miles wide,
A forest fit for lovers to hide!

FARVIEW PLANTATION
OLD PLANTATION CREEK
VIRGINIA'S EASTERN SHORE

1685

Chapter 1

Carolina Lightfoot paused in her task of helping the servants gather in the laundry before the fast approaching storm, and her questing silver gaze flitted treacherously to the north. Toward the Marriage Trees. Up there somewhere past the flat meadowland, past the blue-green pines whipping in the wind, past the horizon where fluffy gray clouds whizzed by in puffs, Carolina knew, was that line of ancient gnarled oaks that marked the boundary between Virginia and Maryland—and beneath their heavy branches on the Maryland side sat Maryland parsons and justices ever waiting for run-away Virginia couples eagerly making the dash north across the border to be wed.

At this very moment Carolina's older sister Penny was riding hard for that boundary—riding the best horse from her father's stables, with a lanky young fellow by her side whose mount would have a hard time keeping up! Wistfully Carolina imagined Penny, who had slipped out of the house before dawn clad in her best yellow silk dress, taking with her naught but a light shawl and a basket of lunch. "Emmett and I will buy what we need," she had declared blithely, and indeed all her sisters had contributed their pocket money to the venture.

All through the day the younger Lightfoot sisters had been covering up for Penny, but eventually her absence had been noted, the house and grounds thoroughly searched, the worst suspected (for hadn't her own parents eloped by way of the Marriage Trees?). And even now Carolina's glowering father, Fielding Lightfoot, and all the men of Farview Plantation were thundering after the runaways, galloping on lathered horses up the narrow peninsula that split the Chesapeake Bay from the Atlantic Ocean.

Carolina felt a stab of hope that Penny and her Emmett would make it to the Marriage Trees, gasp out their vows and disappear somewhere into the wilds of Maryland before Father caught up with them. He would at the very least horsewhip Emmett, for his temper was notorious and red-haired Penny was his eldest—and favorite—daughter.

For a treacherous moment she wished that it was she and not Penny out there making the dash for the Marriage Trees. For Carolina was growing up, losing her coltishness. She who had scoffed at men was beginning to look at them more critically. And sometimes, lately, when the moon poured its pale radiance over the Eastern Shore, her heart had seemed to catch at the beauty of the night that turned familiar landscapes to magic. Although she was only just starting to be aware of it, sweet feminine stirrings, older than time, were calling to her like a siren song.

Like a fortnight ago when she had fallen asleep in a hammock in the afternoon heat—partly because she'd been sleepy from staying up late the night before, avidly reading *Wife to Be Let*, one of the "trashy" (and tremendously popular) novels she had borrowed surreptitiously from her friend Sally Montrose, who had got them while attending school in London. The hot afternoon had drowsed on, the plantation's noises had dimmed, and Carolina, with her damp fair hair spread out over her arm, and her thin, rather childish blue

voile dress falling over her young body like wilted
flower petals, had fallen fast asleep.

And while she was sleeping she had dreamed. Not
the rousing adventurous dreams she sometimes had.
This dream was different.

She dreamed she was swimming alone and naked in a
warm sea of boundless blue. She came up out of the
water to dry herself on a white beach littered with pink
conch shells. Her dress had blown away somewhere,
but it did not seem to matter. As the sun dried her wet
nakedness she slipped into an almost transparent chemise and sat down on the beach, digging her toes into
the hot sand. Palm trees waved from distant purple
cliffs and a flight of brown pelicans flew over in a wavy
line, the lead bird diving down into the water for a fish.
Nearby a hermit crab tottered toward her. But she was
not to be diverted by the denizens of sea or beach.

For in her dream a man had just stepped ashore and
she had eyes only for him. He was as unlike her father
as could be—not over tall and slightly built—but he
dropped over the side of a ship's boat, beached it, and
came confidently toward her over the sand. The sun
glinted on his fair hair, turning it to glowing gold that
haloed around his face, and the eyes that looked upon
her were a merry burning blue. He was rakishly dressed
in bronze satin, his coat laced with gold, and a single
pearl earring dangled fashionably from one of his
well-shaped ears. But she was not surprised by his
elegance in such a setting any more than by her
nonchalance at her own near nakedness in the thin
chemise, because in dreams, all things seem natural and
right.

She came to her feet as he strode up to her and stood
for a moment bedazzled by him, feeling the hot sun
caress her back even as his hot blue gaze wandered
fierily down her feminine body.

"I thought I would find you here," he said hoarsely,
and she had no answer for him although her heart was
near to bursting.

Silently she held out her arms.

And he went into them as if by right. His arms

12

encircled her fiercely, his mouth trailed over hers and down her throat as his lips sought her firm young breasts. His impatient fingers were loosening the riband that held her chemise. She shivered as she felt the light material slide from her shoulders and a soft tropical wind stirred the sea and blew the thin fabric between her thighs as it glided down her back to fall unnoticed around her feet.

"I waited for you," she heard herself gasp and knew, with a certainty as loud as trumpets sounding, that this man was destined to be her lover, and that the tingling expectancy that invaded every secret part of her was Love.

"Carol!" It was Virginia's voice calling, filtering through her dream. "Carol, where are you? It's almost time for supper."

Carolina had come to in a kind of shimmering haze. She hated to move from the hammock for she was still under the spell of her wondrous dream.

She had lain there for a long time thinking. About life. About love. About what the future might hold for her. About the man who had come from the sea to find her.

A perfect man who, she was suddenly certain, was out there somewhere looking for her, searching for her—and who would someday find her and make her life complete.

And after that, whenever she thought about that dream man—and she would think about him secretly for a long time to come—she always called him The Golden Stranger.

For a moment last week—while that vivid dream was still very fresh in her mind—she thought she had seen The Golden Stranger at the Radcliffes' ball in Yorktown.

All the family had gone. Carolina's beautiful mother always went to Yorktown with glinting eyes and a very stiff back for Yorktown was where her husband's people lived, or at least *had* lived until his parents had died. Fielding Lightfoot's family had never really accepted wild young Letitia Randolph and in turn Letitia

13

had chosen not to be civil to her in-laws. They had all ended up not speaking and when Grandfather Lightfoot had died last winter—following his wife to the family burial plot by one week—he had delivered the final blow. He had left everything he owned to his younger son, Darren, and had cut his elder son, Fielding, off with a shilling. Carolina's mother's feud with Fielding's younger brother Darren was celebrated and much talked about, for even at social gatherings spirited Letitia always cut Darren dead, lifting her aristocratic chin high and passing by him in a whirl of taffeta and lace as if he did not exist.

It had been at such a moment that Carolina, following in her elegant mother's wake, thought she had glimpsed The Golden Stranger.

Through a sudden break amid the close-packed satin-clad guests she had seen a golden head, and suddenly all the light in the room had seemed to gather around him so that his hair was haloed by the candlelight.

It had been a dazzling moment and Carolina had caught her breath. But then he had turned and it was only gangling Jimmy Radcliffe, who stumbled over his own feet and was always tongue-tied in the presence of ladies.

Carolina had sighed and gone looking for a glass of cool cider or fruit punch, always refreshing on such a hot night in such a crush.

But drinking the cider she had known a stab of deep regret. Someday, she had promised herself gloomily. *Someday* . . .

Across the room Carolina's mother had danced repeatedly with her old flame and distant cousin, Sandy Randolph, and Carolina's father had noticed that and was drinking too much and glaring at them both. Nearby Penny had slipped through the open door into the garden to meet Emmett somewhere down a dark path and make final plans for their elopement. And Virginia could be glimpsed sneaking down the hall with a plate piled high with little cakes despite her mother's

14

stern warning that she would soon become so fat she'd burst her seams.

All of it had escaped Carolina, lost in her thoughts of The Golden Stranger.

He had still been haunting her thoughts when, the next day (for they had stayed overnight at the Radcliffes'), she had stood watching her mother, who at the time was sitting before a dressing table in the Radcliffes' blue guest room, carefully arranging the shimmering dark honey hair that, except for its darker hue, could have been Carolina's own, so thick and so softly waved.

"Wasn't that the door knocker I just heard?" Her mother had lifted that elegant head to listen. "Yes, I'm sure it was." She gestured with her hairbrush. "Would you run down and see who it is, Carolina? Nobody seems to be answering the door and Sandy Randolph promised to stop by and take me for a drive today. Wasn't that nice of him?" The words were spoken carelessly. "I told him how seldom I get out of late."

Carolina had run downstairs to tell elegant, smiling Sandy Randolph (who had a mad wife back home at Tower Oaks but was said to be in love with her mother all the same) that her mother would soon be ready. And the words were hardly out of her mouth before her mother, attired in glowing green silk, drifted down the stairs and greeted him warmly.

Once in Williamsburg when she was very young, sitting beside a front window in Aunt Pet's green-painted living room, Carolina had heard Aunt Pet mutter behind her fan to a caller that Letitia's family never should have pushed her so far that she had flown into marriage with Fielding Lightfoot. By their loudly voiced displeasure, by trying to force Letitia onto that old widower, they had turned her simple schoolgirl passion for her glamorous Cousin Sandy Randolph into open rebellion—and everybody had suffered for it. Why couldn't they have let time take its toll, let beautiful Letitia tire of her attraction to a married man? Indeed, whomever she wed, Letty should have

15

certainly left Fielding to that Bramway girl who was so mad about him. Headstrong Letty would have made many a planter an admirable wife—but not Fielding, who wanted a clinging vine, someone who would bob her pretty head "yes" at everything he said, instead of a spirited woman like Letty who would insist upon arguing the point if she didn't agree. Mismating, that was what it was—two strong wills opposing each other. It was no wonder they did not get along, they were each so determined to lead!

On that day in Williamsburg, Carolina had turned her young gaze thoughtfully to Sandy Randolph, just riding by the windows on a big gray horse. He was tall and arrow straight in the saddle and he had a fencer's lean grace. His real name was Lysander—his mother, a learned woman who read Greek and Latin, had named all her sons for the heroes of ancient Greece. And like those heroes, all were now dead, victims of Indian uprisings that had burned their homes and slaughtered their families along the raw Virginia frontier. She was gone too, and all the family. Only Sandy remained—so nicknamed for his hair, so pale in his youth that it resembled the white sand of beaches, now gleaming, as he rode by, like a helmet of white metal in the sun.

She saw him glance toward the house and then doff his hat to someone beyond her vision—perhaps to her mother, who had strolled out into the garden to walk amid the fragrance of the morning flowers. *Would* her mother have been happier with Sandy? she wondered. Certainly Letitia Lightfoot seemed to release a kind of pent-up excitement whenever she was in the same room with him. Her dark blue eyes sparkled, her slim body had a taut vibrancy and she carried her honey blonde head even more rakishly than usual.

And to Carolina's childish mind her mother's choice of a mate had somehow got mixed up with the color of his hair. If her blonde mother had chosen a blond man, all would have been well. If dark-haired Fielding had wed the striking brunette, Amanda Bramway, who was "so mad about him," all would have been better. None

16

of this turmoil between her warring parents would ever have come about.

The thought had been fixed in her mind so deeply that, without being aware of it, Carolina had turned against *all* dark-haired men. And so her dream of a golden lover had come quite naturally, the result of hours of brooding over the plight of her parents, tied to each other for a lifetime and fighting it every step of the way.

Fielding Lightfoot had come in just in time to witness that warm greeting at the Radcliffe house, to see his wife breeze by him, to view with fury her lighthearted wave as she drove off with her handsome cousin in a carriage built for two.

The elder Lightfoots had quarreled about that drive after Letitia had returned, pink-cheeked and laughing, and Sandy had driven away looking more than ever like the villain in a play.

"You're becoming a scandal, Letty!" Fielding had growled at her as he went upstairs. He brushed roughly by Carolina who was just then making her way downstairs. Indeed he averted his gaze from the young girl as if he could not bear the sight of her and Carolina shrank back, bewildered. Her hurt gaze fled to red-haired Penny who was frowning upward from the living room door. He had not looked so at Penny when he passed her and *she* was the one about to run away! It was one more gratuitous rebuff from the father she had tried so hard to love. Her soft mouth trembled as she turned to stare after Fielding, to hear him bawl, "At the Raleigh Tavern today conversations were hushed when I came in—and I've no doubt they were all discussing you and Sandy riding about town together!"

Letitia's cheeks had grown very pink. It was perfectly true—and she could not help but know it—that while great events were happening in the outside world (Charles II had died suddenly in February and his illegitimate eldest son, the wild young Duke of Monmouth, was expected momentarily to sail from Holland and mount a rebellion against his uncle, the newly

17

crowned James II) Williamsburg gossip was generally focused on the tempestuous Lightfoots.

"Surely you cannot fault me for riding about in broad daylight with my *cousin!*" she cried in her imperious voice.

"You were a bit more than that," he flung bitterly over his shoulder, "when *I* had the misfortune to meet you!"

"Misfortune?" Her indignant voice followed him up the stairs. "Indeed 'tis a deal more likely the gossips are discussing *you* and the way you fawn over that Roland girl!"

"Young Mistress Roland has admirers aplenty without adding *my* name to her list!" roared her husband from the landing. "You're only trying to divert my attention from your behavior, Letty!"

Carolina had now gained the first floor. She and her older sister Penny watched, fascinated, from the living room door, as Letitia gathered up her skirts and charged past them. She ran up the stairs and began pummeling her husband on the chest with her fists. "I won't have you speak to me like that!" she had cried, almost sobbing. "I stayed with you through the worst times! I've been a good wife to you—*I have!*" He had dragged her into the bedroom from which angry voices had erupted in bursts—and Fielding had ended up taking them all back to Farview Plantation a day earlier than had been intended.

"I'll be glad to be out of it," Penny had muttered shortly before leaving with Emmett for her mad dash up the peninsula to the Marriage Trees. She had tossed back her cloud of red hair. "All this constant bickering, all this hatred, I'll be glad to leave it all behind me!"

It wasn't so much hatred, thought Carolina, as rage. Rage that they should have been tied together in the first place, she supposed, although theirs had been a runaway marriage. Letitia had had a falling out with her illicit love, Sandy Randolph, Sandy had gone away, and her parents had seized upon his absence to betroth rebellious Letitia to a doddering old gentleman—and she had suddenly run away with Fielding Lightfoot instead.

It hadn't worked out. Everybody agreed on that. They both had combustible tempers and sharp tongues.

"And *you* must go too, Carol." Penny had given her younger sister a troubled look. "Oh, *promise* me you will—just as soon as you get the chance! You mustn't stay here any longer than you have to."

Carolina had been startled by her older sister's vehemence. "But—but I haven't anyone to run away *with!*" she had objected.

"You will have." Penny sighed. "And when you do, don't waste a minute—*run.* You can never be happy here. Don't you see that Father—" She broke off.

"No, I don't see," said Carolina sturdily, for something in her sister's tone alarmed her.

"Well, I mean—" Sophisticated Penny gave her a worldly look that suddenly took in her youth, her innocence. "I mean all this—this trouble between them. We seem to fire it up, don't we?"

"*You* don't, Penny," Carolina had said truthfully. "But *I* certainly seem to." And she had fallen silent before her sister's muttered, "Poor little Carol," and her sudden suffocating hug.

They had not spoken further about it. They had all gone back to Farview—the girls agog with plans.

Ordinarily her parents' bickering and long silences worried Carolina—as if *she* were somehow to blame. But not this time. This time she had been too excited over Penny's impending elopement.

Now, holding a wet sheet cradled against her flushed face to keep it from whipping away from her in the wind, Carolina drew a deep heartfelt sigh. If only *she* could be riding toward the Marriage Trees today—not with someone dull like Emmett, of course, but with The Golden Stranger of her dream!

"Oh, *do* come along, Carol!" Virginia's impatient voice interrupted Carolina's reverie, even though the sound of that too was almost blown away by the wind. "That's the last sheet you're clawing at there. Snatch it

19

up and *don't* stand there staring toward the north—
Mother will see you and be furious. She's already
broken half the dishes over finding Penny missing!"

Galvanized into action by the sudden mention of her
mother, whom all five Lightfoot daughters secretly
feared—although somewhat less than they feared their
tall handsome father with his violent temper and his
forbidding expression—Carolina made a snatch for the
sheet, which had just blown away from her, and gasped
as a sudden gust of wind tore away her blue hair riband,
seized her long fair hair to send it flying, and whipped
her sky blue linen skirts and frosty white petticoat up
above her knees. Even as she was fighting those skirts
down—for her mother might be watching from the
dining room window and her mother vastly disapproved of Carolina's lightsome ways, which were too
much like her own as a girl—that last damp bedsheet
from the wind-whipped laundry slapped her in the face.

Penny had certainly chosen a day of terrible weather,
thought Carolina, to elope. But of course it had all
been planned ahead—indeed schemed over for weeks
by the three older Lightfoot daughters. And the Great
Laundry, which took place in large households like the
Lightfoots' every two months, had been unanimously
chosen as the time that fleeing Penny was least likely to
be missed. But the weather had turned out to be as
tempestuous as Penny's young heart. All along the
Virginia Capes it had been a day of wild weather.
Carried on the leading edge of a storm that was howling
out of the Caribbean, gale force winds had ripped into
the Carolina Capes, and from Hatteras to Nag's Head
great seas were even now crashing into the grassy
dunes.

The long peninsula where Carolina stood—which the
Indians called Accomack meaning "the other-side
land" but which Virginians called "the Eastern Shore"
—was beginning to feel the brunt of the approaching
storm. At the ramshackle wooden plantation house on
Old Plantation Creek, built frighteningly near the
water and in bad repair (After all, why repair it?
They'd soon be abandoning it to occupy the fine new

20

brick house for which Fielding Lightfoot had already laid the foundation near Yorktown!) the enormous laundry the servants had hung out to dry late yesterday had almost all been taken in—along with such clotheslines as had not already been blown away.

Carolina, with her mind still on Penny's fate and with the damp bedsheet clutched in her arms, was the last to make the trek to the big attic where the sheet would join its fellows, all neatly hanging on lines where they were least likely to mildew. On her way up she passed the servants coming down, and found only Virgie waiting for her in the dimness of the rough-beamed attic.

"Isn't it exciting, Penny eloping like this?" giggled Virgie. Virgie was two inches shorter than Carolina and considerably plumper; her hair was somewhere between Penny's true red and Carolina's shimmering pale silver-gold. She was a strawberry blonde with her mother's dark blue eyes but without her fire—indeed her placid unremarkable features resembled Aunt Pet's and looked more in keeping on the older woman than on a girl. She took a deep longing breath. "I wish *I* were running away to the Marriage Trees!"

"But you haven't even selected anyone yet!" objected Carolina, giving her older sister a startled look. She and Virgie and Penny had always been closer than the other two Lightfoot daughters, who had straggled along years later.

"I know. Still—I'd run away from here in a minute! Did you hear all those dishes breaking? There won't be a plate left to eat on, we'll be back to pewter!" The wind sang eerily around the eaves, seeking to find a chink in the roof that would let it in. Virgie cocked her head, listening. "At least these wind gusts should slow down the horses so maybe Father won't catch up with Penny and Emmett!"

"Penny and Emmett are battling the same wind," pointed out Carolina.

Virgie shrugged. "Yes, but Penny and Emmett started out early and it wasn't nearly so bad then." She leaned over to help Carolina pull the last damp sheet

21

taut on the line. "There's no chance Father will be back tonight unless he gives up the chase—and you know Father, he'll never do that!"

Somewhat sobered by that thought, both girls picked up their voluminous skirts and hurried downstairs.

They had almost reached the lower hall when their mother's imperious voice called to them. "Carolina, Virginia, come here." And the two girls went into the dining room where their younger sisters, little Della and Flo, already stood in awed silence against the paneled pine wall, staring first at their mother and then at the broken dishes that littered the floor.

Letitia Lightfoot, tall, slender and formidable in her fashionable sprigged calico gown, stood at gaze as she surveyed the new arrivals. Her thick honey hair, unfaded by bearing five children, shimmered like Carolina's though in a deeper hue, but her long fierce blue eyes would never match the calmness of Carolina's silver gray ones which turned to tarnished silver when she was angry. Carolina returned her mother's raking gaze innocently.

Where have I gone wrong? Letitia Lightfoot was asking herself as she surveyed what she had wrought. *Why would a daughter of mine run off like that? And with a totally unsuitable boy!*

But perhaps the situation could still be saved. Perhaps the girls knew something. Even if Fielding failed to arrive in time to prevent the marriage, there was still such a thing as an annulment if he did but arrive before the consummation had taken place. And perhaps Pennsylvania—for Letitia never called her daughters by the nicknames they used for each other—had plans to marry over the border and then circle back to Williamsburg where Emmett was employed as a clerk.

"Virginia," she said, addressing her second eldest. "I want you and Carolina to tell me all you know about your sister Pennsylvania's elopement. Delaware and Florida"—she nodded toward the two solemn tots standing against the wall—"have already told me all they know."

The two older girls winced at this use of their given names. Even garrulous Aunt Pet had wailed at her niece Letty's decision to name her daughters for an assortment of colonies instead of decorously christening them "Petula" for her and "Samantha" for Fielding's mother and so on. To the Lightfoot daughters it was too much to be borne, and they had promptly nicknamed themselves Penny, Virgie, Carol, Della and Flo—but to their mother they remained Pennsylvania, Virginia, Carolina, Delaware and Florida, and she never called them anything else.

"I don't really know anything, Mother," said Virgie nervously.

"Nonsense, of course you do!"

"We know that Penny and Emmett rode off to the north," supplied Carolina serenely.

Their mother's face hardened. "You knew they were eloping then!" she surmised with remarkable calm.

"Why, Mother, how could *we* know?" quavered Virgie, who had not Carolina's stamina.

Carolina gave her older sister a scornful look. Virgie always folded under pressure. "*I* knew they were eloping," she announced with a calm that matched her mother's. Virgie gave a squeak of fright at this admission.

"And you did not choose to inform me?" Those fierce blue eyes pinned Carolina and the girl felt a shimmer of fear go through her.

"You were very busy," said Carolina in a moment of inspiration.

"Busy?" Letitia Lightfoot sounded amazed. "You thought I was *too busy* to be told my daughter was eloping?"

"You were quarreling with Father," supplied Carolina uneasily.

"Nonsense, I am *always* quarreling with your father," said her mother in a quelling voice. "His ways would try the patience of a saint! Tell me, why did you not interrupt this quarrel with news of such importance?"

"But Mother, we could hear you all the way to the stables," interjected Virgie, seeing a possible way out. "We were afraid to interrupt."

"Carolina was not afraid," interrupted her mother, her eyes never leaving Carolina's face. "Carolina is like me—not afraid of anything."

Carolina regarded her steadily. She wondered what would happen this time—a switching, boxed ears?

"So tell me, Carolina, what are their plans?"

"I don't think they have any," said Carolina, unhelpfully but with perfect truth. The young couple's plans reached mainly to the Marriage Trees and getting the knot securely tied. After that they would plunge into Maryland and lose themselves before a furious Fielding Lightfoot could get his hands on them.

Her mother frowned and turned suddenly upon Virginia, who flinched. "And you, Virginia? What do you know of their plans?"

"Nothing," bleated Virginia. "It's the truth!" She was almost sobbing.

Letitia studied both her daughters for a long while. Then, "I believe you," she said in a softer voice. "You will stay in the house—it is dangerous outside, I just saw a tree limb fly by. And you, Carolina and Virginia, will go to bed this night without supper. And you will pray on your knees that Pennsylvania is found and in time."

Carolina dropped her silver-gray gaze to the random-width oak floor boards lest her mother see the rebellious light in her eyes. If she prayed at all, it would be that Penny and Emmett forever eluded Fielding Lightfoot!

Chapter 2

All five girls trooped out, picking their way over the broken china, and Letitia Lightfoot turned to gaze out the window at a bit of clothesline flying by. Of them all, she told herself, only Carolina was truly like her. Not in looks but in the way she met life—head on and unflinching. She sighed. It would bring her nothing but disaster of course.

It was very hard having all daughters. She remembered Aunt Pet's plaintive comment when she had borne her last child: "It's *too bad* you didn't have a boy—Fielding would have been so pleased. I really think that's the reason you don't get along."

Letitia, lying in the big feather bed nursing her newborn daughter, had given her aunt a wry look. She *knew* why they didn't get along but she had no inclination to discuss it—with Aunt Pet or anyone else.

"Oh, well," Aunt Pet had sighed, seeing that expression. "Perhaps you'll have a boy yet!"

Letitia doubted it.

Her first two daughters, arriving barely a year apart, had been born during the years when she and Fielding had gotten along, those first years when, after an ill-considered runaway marriage, she had tried so desperately to love him. Looking back, her gaze turned wistful. The lad from the York and the girl from Jamestown should never have married. Indeed she had only turned to him in desperation when she had quarreled with Sandy and he had left in a huff, sailed away to God knew where. Her parents—already furious that she should be in love with a married man, had seized upon Sandy's absence to betroth her to elderly Martin Spalding, a widower with nine children, whose holdings bordered Tower Oaks, the Randolph estate along the James River, where Sandy Randolph had grown up.

Fielding Lightfoot's parents had planned for him to marry dark lovely Amanda Bramway, heiress to the adjoining plantation. Indeed there was bad blood between the Lightfoots and Letitia Randolph's parents—a trivial matter over a horse race that had rankled and been blown up much bigger than it should have been—so any match between the Lightfoots and the Randolphs would have been frowned upon. Desperate at the prospect of being tied to an elderly man who hobbled around with gout, young Letitia had turned her fiery dark blue gaze upon the likeliest of the eligible young bucks—Fielding Lightfoot.

They had met in secret, pledged their troth in secret, and it had all culminated in a whirlwind—though carefully planned—visit to a friend's house on the Eastern Shore and a wild dash for the Marriage Trees where a tipsy justice of the peace had performed a ceremony that had chained them together forever.

Yet they had been happy during those first years, spent in Philadelphia, and Letitia had named her first daughter Pennsylvania in celebration of that happiness, and her second daughter Virginia for the home she missed. But then things had begun to go wrong. Fielding's ventures into the mercantile world were failing, for he was at heart a planter, not a merchant. Too proud to tell his young wife they were near ruin, his temper grew short and he bitterly criticized everything

—her friends, her housekeeping, even the clothes she wore. Spirited Letitia, not understanding, fought back and their quarrels lingered for days. Finally it was too much. She packed up and left him—took her two children back to her father's house in Virginia. But eventually, as Aunt Pet put it, she had "come to her senses" and returned to Philadelphia.

Whether she had come to her senses or not, Fielding's tired words, "We're ruined," that greeted her when she arrived had certainly galvanized energetic Letitia into action. She had been a tower of strength in moving their little family back to the Tidewater country —and a temporary home with Fielding's people. There family quarrels had erupted for Letitia was outspoken and Fielding was blunt—diplomacy was needed and none was to be found. By the time her third daughter was born Letitia was heartily sick of all her husband's blood relations and she once impulsively told Aunt Pet that she had named her third child Carolina out of an ardent wish to fly away south.

That was the beginning of the worst years when Fielding, no longer welcome in his father's house, had settled (with funds his ailing mother had managed to scrape up) into a deserted plantation house on Old Plantation Creek which Letitia named Farview for its long vistas but which was promptly rechristened Bedlam by the wags in Williamsburg, when they heard of the wild goings-on there.

Baffled and angry at what seemed to them a comedown in their way of life, the hot-blooded young Lightfoots had turned upon each other with scathing scorn. Fielding frequently dashed from the house and spurred away in fury while an enraged Letitia ripped to shreds a favorite ballgown or smashed the crockery. There had even been one wild fray Williamsburg would never forget. It had taken place over dinner at the Raleigh Tavern. Letitia had taken offense at something Fielding said. Trembling with fury, she had risen to her feet in the crowded room and onlookers had reported that her dark blue eyes had glittered as brightly as the brilliants on the bodice of her deep blue velvet gown.

27

"Damn you, Field!" she had choked—and with the words had hurled her wineglass at her husband. He had dodged. The ruby port had splattered his white shirt but the glass had missed him and crashed upon the hearth. With a curse, Fielding had gained his feet. He had lunged across the table and dragged his Letty away through the crowd by her long thick hair as she clawed at his sleeve in an effort to free herself. People had rushed outside to observe him throw his young wife summarily into his carriage and sit on her to hold her down while she beat her fists and screamed. They drove away amid laughter and light applause toward the boat that would carry them home to "Bedlam."

That they had had two more children after such an event was, to Williamsburg, a marvel. But someone with a near view might have understood. They loved each other in their fashion, did the young Lightfoots, but their love had sharp edges and their anger made them wield it like a sword. *She* could not forgive *him* for bringing her to this barren coast, where she seldom saw anyone; *he* could not forgive *her* for having so alienated his father with her sharp tongue that his younger brother had inherited all the property when the old man died while he, the elder and once favored, had been cut off with a shilling. And then there was the big underlying quarrel, the wound that would never quite heal, to which they never alluded. . . .

They would rage at each other and then not speak for days, perhaps weeks, conversing only through the servants or one of their daughters. And then their anger would erupt again over some small thing and Fielding would do something desperate: He had once seized Letitia and held her suspended over the well, howling that he would drop her in it and be rid of her once and for all! But at the last moment, hanging upside down with her long hair streaming downward toward that glint of water far below, Letitia—who was fighting her voluminous skirts so that the servants would not see her silk-stockinged legs—had been overcome with sudden mirth at how ridiculous they must look, snarling above the well while the servants ran

28

about bleating in fright. Glaring down into her unafraid laughing face, Fielding had begun laughing too. He had set her back upon her feet and they had both leaned against the low curving brick wall that surrounded the well, rocked by gales of laughter. Still overcome with mirth, they had tottered arm in arm toward the house and halfway there the amazed servants, who were trying to comfort the crying children, had seen Fielding sweep Letitia up and carry her triumphantly indoors. He carried her all the way up to the bedroom they shared so seldom—for he preferred to spend his nights on the long sofa before the living room hearth rather than having his wife ostentatiously turn her back on him in their big square bed. And that night had been like the early days of their marriage, full of laughter and sighs, of silken caresses and moaned responses, a night of passion and yearning that reminded them of all that once had been.

A night that had resulted in Delaware being born nine months later.

It was the same with little Florida. Only that time had been in a boat. Fielding and Letitia had been returning from a funeral in Yorktown in weather so calm the bay seemed like glass. They had quarreled heatedly all the way over, simmered during the funeral service, almost choked on the wine offered afterward, and now on the way home, hostilities had commenced anew. In sudden rage that their light skiff should be becalmed due to lack of wind, thus trapping him with this maddening and beautiful woman, Fielding had snatched up his wife and dropped her over the side. In fury she had floated there, held up by her big black taffeta skirts, screaming at him. Grinding his teeth, Fielding had tossed her a line and after he had pulled her aboard, drenched, she had struck him such a blow as had caused him to trip and fall backward overboard.

"Throw me a line, dammit!" he had yowled, for his boots were fast filling with water and he was in imminent danger of drowning.

His wife tossed him the same line that had brought her to safety and pulled him in. When he came over the side, tearing out the seams of his satin coatsleeves as he did so, she collapsed in wild laughter, gasping so that she could hardly breathe. Her husband, trying to work his way out of a tight wet coat, gazed at her in astonishment.

"Oh, Field!" she had gasped, holding her side and shaking with mirth. "How we must look to that sloop over there!" And he had followed her gaze across the placid blue water to a green rowboat that had been approaching whilst they quarreled and in which two buckskinned men sat, watching round-eyed the doings in the boat.

The humor of the situation now struck Fielding and he began to laugh too, the rich deep chuckling laugh that had so endeared him to her in their courting days. And suddenly he had seized her with an amorous light in his eyes and before the gaze of the fascinated watchers they had disappeared into the bottom of the boat, from which a flailing foot and a trim silk-stockinged ankle had signalled the storm that had come upon them.

And that incident had brought on little Florida nine months later.

They were a scandal, were the Lightfoots. And the doings of handsome Field and his beautiful unmanageable Letty were duly reported on and guffawed over at the Raleigh Tavern and across all the aristocratic boards of the Tidewater. "What's doing over at Bedlam?" was a common greeting and it was always met by gales of laughter for the elegant young Lightfoots never did anything small, or anything halfway. They were like a pair of showy peafowl fluffing out their ruffled feathers. The Tidewater would have missed them had they departed.

None of this was clear to Letitia Lightfoot as she stood there frowning, surveying the windswept lawn. But she was guiltily aware that during these latter years she had so concentrated on her never ending war with her husband that she had given her daughters, growing up in this atmosphere of turmoil, very little thought.

And now Penny had run away.

It was, she supposed wearily, on her own head. For having married Fielding—a man with whom she would never get along. And he was so intolerably jealous of Sandy! Why couldn't he understand that Sandy was her past and *he* was her present and her future?

For a moment her shoulders drooped and she felt very sorry for herself. Then with characteristic energy she lifted her head, straightened her back, and went out to give orders to the servants. There was a storm to be lived through—and on this low-lying coast that could be tricky. And a rebellious daughter to be dealt with if Fielding could get there in time.

In short, a lot to do.

Letitia Lightfoot, completely oblivious to the fact that her daughters needed her, that they were young and frightened of the storm and felt abandoned, turned her mind to her household help and—as always—to what she would say to Fielding when he returned. Penny's misalliance was all his fault! He should have known better than to hire such a handsome clerk as young Emmett—even temporarily!

Oh, she would have a word with him, all right!

The day wore on, the wind increased in volume and the sky darkened. Fielding did not come home and evening found his daughters Carolina and Virginia hungry and restive in their nightclothes—and annoyed that the two younger children could sleep placidly in their trundle bed with all the noise and the house fairly swaying as the storm worsened.

"Do you think it will be as bad as the Great Storm?" Virginia rolled her eyes toward Carolina.

Uneasily, Carolina listened to the moaning of the wind. The Great Storm was long gone but not forgotten. It had nearly knocked the house down and they had spent months at Aunt Pet's in Williamsburg while it was being repaired. That was when Emmett, newly hired as a clerk at the apothecary's shop after his brief stay as clerk at Farview, had got so thick with Penny. As the oldest, Penny had been sent frequently to the apothecary shop to pick up various nostrums demanded by Aunt Pet, and one thing had led to another.

31

So in a way the Great Storm could be credited with Penny's elopement.

The Great Storm could be credited with something else. It had brought Ramona Valdez into their lives. Ramona was the sole survivor of the wreck of a Spanish galleon that had been driven into the Chesapeake during the worst of the storm, and she had ended up, more dead than alive, among the wreckage washed ashore near Farview. The Lightfoots had promptly taken Ramona in and she had lived with them until she could be returned, via the Spanish ambassador in London, to her native land. As a result of her long sojourn with them, all the girls had picked up a smattering of Spanish and Carolina, to whom languages came easily, had become quite fluent. Ramona and Carolina had become good friends and Carolina missed the Spanish girl. She had heard from Ramona only once and that letter had been a heartbroken one. *"A marriage has been arranged for me to the new Governor of Havana,"* Ramona had written through an English scribe. *"I am told he is handsome—and twice my age. I suppose I will never see any of you again."* Reading the letter, Carolina had ached for her friend.

So the Great Storm which had swept Ramona onto their shores had brought change to them all. Carolina wondered what changes *this* storm would bring in its wake.

Another gust of wind shook the house and rattled the windows.

"Oh-h, listen to it!" shuddered Virginia, and both girls jumped as a flying branch, borne on the arms of the wind, struck the house a heavy blow.

Their alarm was in no way lessened when their mother appeared in the doorway wearing a surprisingly genial expression—Letitia was always at her best in time of trouble.

"You may dress and come down and have a bite of supper," she told her astonished daughters graciously. "I will get the younger children dressed. Hurry down and eat what is on the table." By way of explanation, she added, "I do not like the sound of the wind. It is rocking the house and I think the roof may go—I never trusted the repairs your father had made after the Great Storm—so I would prefer to have you both on the first floor. And once downstairs you are not to return to the south wing. These timbers are old and it may go too."

Virginia came to her feet and began to dress with shaking fingers. This very room was in the south wing! But Carolina sprang up with eyes as bright as her mother's. "Can I help?" she demanded, absorbed by the drama of a situation which might see them homeless by morning.

"By doing as you're told," said her mother dryly and turned with that quick light step that was so like Carolina's, to wake and dress her youngest.

Some of the glow went out of Carolina's silver eyes. Her mother was brave and she was beautiful, and as a young girl she had undoubtedly swept all before her. But it was very hard to love her.

Hardly had the girls eaten the hasty repast of cornmeal mush, leftover stew, and spiced crab apples set before them on the long dining table than they were whisked away to the kitchen where they saw with astonishment that the fire in the big brick fireplace had been put out and all of the iron implements that normally reposed there had been removed and the whole swept clean. The servants, scared by the din outside from wind and pounding rain, were still looking resentful over the fire being put out, for fires in colonial houses were rarely extinguished, but kept going winter and summer because it was such an arduous task to get one started again.

"Girls, get into the fireplace," instructed their mother brusquely.

Four pairs of young eyes turned on her reproachfully.

"I mean it." She spoke calmly. "This fireplace is the strongest place in the house. It will form a bulwark against the wind that may be coming. In case the house is swept away, you will have a chance here."

At the suggestion that the house might be swept away, Virginia blanched and all four girls quickly

33

scrambled into the fireplace, so large that it easily accommodated them all. They crouched together, fastidiously trying to edge away from the darkly burnt brick sides.

"Now fetch me the table from the dining room and we will shove both it and the kitchen table against the fireplace and everyone else will crouch under that—it will provide protection against falling beams."

The frightened servants obeyed and soon the two heavy tables were pressed against the now cold bricks of the fireplace. The heavy cook groaned with effort as she crawled under to join the more nimble maids.

"I wonder where Penny is," whispered Virginia.

And Carolina thought, *Perhaps Penny and Emmett never made it to the Marriage Trees. Perhaps a tree crashed down and pinned them as they rode under.*

"Safe, I hope," she said quickly and turned to comfort little Flo, who had squeaked with fright as something heavy—probably a tree limb—crashed and grated against the roof.

That night was a test of everybody's nerves. The rain beat against the house like gravel. The wind screamed defiance in the chimney and under the eaves. And beyond and over the incessant screech and patter was the menacing roar of an angry ocean, lashed to fury by the storm.

Twice shutters came loose and Letitia and two of the servants crawled out from under the tables to secure them. Her daughters sat crouched together fighting the cinders and soot that filtered through the closed damper, sifting down upon their hair and smudging their faces and clothes. Just as everybody resumed their places after the second shutter closing, a terrible roar shook the house, culminating in the agonized sound of straining timbers being ripped apart.

"That will be the roof of the south wing," said Letitia calmly and Carolina, being clutched by a terrified Virginia with fingers that bit into her skin, could not but admire her mother's cool courage. The bedroom Carolina shared with Virginia and the smaller children was in the south wing and she imagined the rain pouring through the torn off roof and descending in buckets onto the big feather bed in which she and Virginia would even now have been huddling, had her mother not perceived the danger and ordered them downstairs. The sound of the storm was now so loud that it interfered with coherent thought. Devils seemed to be chasing each other through the murk and rain of the wind-driven night sky, demons of sound and force and fury that made her feel isolated and small and insignificant. Great forces were out there battling for supremacy—the sea pounding against the land, the wind sending its missiles, the rain battering everything. She realized her clothes and Virginia's, upstairs in the big press, would be ruined—if indeed they were not blown away to disappear mysteriously into Chesapeake Bay! She had a slight pang that she had not thought to bring along her favorite hair ribands, but she felt that moment of regret in a detached, impersonal way. The storm had made her feel she was a disembodied thing floating halfway between heaven and hell.

The storm's fury mounted. Unidentified objects were blown with crashing force against the house, one hammer blow after another. The very foundations seemed to tremble and shake. But in the midst of the battering, as she comforted the younger children who crowded against her, shivering and crying, while on her other side she could feel Virginia cringe and jump with each new assault, she envisioned those others out in the storm. Her father and the men from the plantation were doggedly fighting their way up the peninsula, while Penny and Emmett were probably lost somewhere, blinded by the wind and rain—or perhaps already among the Marriage Trees with great tree limbs crashing to earth about them as they sought for a preacher who was bound to be tucked away behind his shutters on such a wild night.

Her thoughts were interrupted by a wild scream from Virginia and a new burst of tears from the younger children as an even more horrendous sound seemed to come from the direction of the south wing. It was followed by a mighty earthshaking crash that left even Carolina's stout heart shaken.

"That was the south wing's walls collapsing," shouted her mother, her voice barely reaching Carolina above the tearing wind. "We're all right, girls, the house will hold." And then as a series of minor crashes followed, she added with a reassurance that nobody else felt, "I think the worst is over."

It was. Hours later, stiff with fatigue, they all crawled out to assess the damage. The roof of the south wing had indeed blown off and the entire wing had collapsed, leaving a sodden rubble of splintered timbers and broken furniture and ruined bedding. A corner of the roof of the main house had also blown away, allowing rain to pour in over the cupboard just below.

In the wild dawn, with its scudding gray clouds and frothing sea, Letitia instantly took command. New clotheslines were to be rigged, all the bedding and clothing hung out to dry.

She straightened up suddenly and for a moment a startled expression played over her beautiful face. "That's your father," she muttered. "He can't be home yet!" She fled toward the door to the muddy driveway where Fielding Lightfoot, riding ahead of his men on a lathered horse, was just coming out of the saddle in a bound. He met his wife just emerging from the house with her rich honey hair bursting free from its pins and making a golden halo around her head.

"What has happened?" she cried, as the girls watched from the doorway. "Why are you back so soon, Field?"

Fielding Lightfoot breathed a deep sigh of relief at sight of her. Amid that howling storm last night he had thought the house might be swept away—and Letty and the girls with it. All the way down the peninsula he had been harried by the thought that he might never see his wife again. Now he drank in the sight of her. "I turned back when I saw how bad the storm was."

"You turned back?" There was anguish in her voice. Once started on such a mission, Letitia would have

36

ridden on to hell. "But what of our daughter? Where is she?"

"Safe, I hope, somewhere beyond the Maryland border."

"She made it," breathed Carolina. "Penny made it!"

Fielding heard that and his dark head swung round. His gaze fixed on Carolina, standing there tired and disheveled in the dawn, and a mixture of emotions crossed his face—resentment, frustration, rage even. That storm was quickly gone and he turned an expressionless countenance back to his wife, but Carolina felt devastated by it. That look had not included Virginia, who was standing nearby just as glad about Penny as she was—it had been meant for her alone. Whoever else he was glad to see, Fielding Lightfoot was not glad to see *her*. She felt a sudden wash of loneliness, and a kind of inner weeping for herself, the only daughter her father could not seem to love.

Dully, she heard Letitia's contemptuous voice ring out. *"Safe!* Safe, you call it, Field? Your daughter is off marrying a lad with no money and no prospects and you call her *safe?* She will end up taking in laundry!"

Fielding Lightfoot, so blazingly glad to see his wife a moment before, now gave her a lowering look. "I'm hungry," he announced. "And the horses must be attended to. Is there some hot broth about for the men?" When his wife did not answer him he brushed past her and the girls melted away before him as he strode toward the kitchen. "Why, what is this?" he demanded, amazed. "The fire's out!" He realized suddenly how bedraggled his daughters looked, hovering nearby with their faces and clothes smudged with soot. "And you're all filthy," he cried, and turned on his wife, just now coming through the door behind him. "What were you thinking of, Letty, to let the fire go out? And to let your children run about in this condition?"

"I was thinking to save your house," she shot at him. "And the girls spent the night sheltering in the kitchen fireplace—while you were fruitlessly galloping about the peninsula!"

Fielding's expression, which had softened as her explanation sank in on him, hardened again at that last remark.

"Cold food will do," he said harshly. He turned to the servants. "And be quick. My men are like to fall off their horses from exhaustion after fighting that wind and rain all day and all night."

Carolina, watching, thought she had seen the spark that might have united them when he returned flicker and die. They were at odds again, this handsome warring couple.

Her heart was still aching from that cold implacable look her father had given her, a look she ascribed, in her innocence, to the part he believed she must have played in Penny's plans for a runaway marriage.

Ardently, like Penny before her, she wished herself someplace else.

Chapter 3

Carolina turned away from the combatants and wandered into the damp world outside. There was work to be done, but at the moment she did not want to gaze upon either of her parents, hero and heroine though they might be. In the wake of the storm she wanted to see happiness around her—and if she could find no real happiness, then she would imagine it.

She would imagine her father's homecoming as it should have been—as it *would* have been, she told herself staunchly, had *she* been in her mother's shoes. Her mother should have run to him, clung to him, told him how glad she was that he was safe—and he would have responded. He would have run his long fingers through the halo of her hair and hugged her to him and thanked God they were all safe—even if Penny had eluded him.

Her foot caught on something and she looked down. Why, it was a doll! It had once been Virginia's doll and she herself had named it Nan White for a beautiful legendary ghost the servants muttered about. How could it have gotten out here, bedraggled, face down and covered with mud? She picked it up and saw that its painted face was ruined, its once trusting and innocent expression oddly distorted by cracks and hard knocks, its soft kid-covered body soaked beneath its tattered clothing. The two younger children must have been playing with it and carelessly left it on the ground when they had been called indoors yesterday. . . .

She held the doll up and to her its battered face was still sweet. Her gray eyes clouded. *Oh, she had memories of Nan White.* . . .

Fielding had brought the doll home from Williamsburg one day. He had tossed it onto the little blue velvet sofa and gone striding out to find Letitia. But little Carolina, who had observed his entrance from the next room where she had been playing quietly, for Penny was away visiting and Virginia in bed with a cold upstairs, had come running in after he had left and seized the doll rapturously.

This must be the dolly her mother had promised her! It had to be! And oh, wasn't she wonderful with her slim waist and her hair drawn back from a full high brow? And look at her gown—a magnificent court dress, its flaring skirt held out by a real hoop! Blissfully, little Carolina had rubbed her childish cheek against the softly tinted velvet and striped brocade of the doll's gown and determined then and there that she would christen her Nan White.

She had been about to dash upstairs to show her wonderful new doll to Virginia when she heard angry voices approaching and paused.

Her parents were quarreling when they came into the room.

Letitia swept in first, stiff-backed in her swirl of purple damask skirts. "I had every right to demand full payment for the mare!" she was insisting. "You were not here and—"

"But I had told Cart he could have time to pay for her!"

"How was I to know that? I thought he should—"

"Damme, Letty," exploded Fielding. "Why can't

you let me run the plantation while you occupy yourself with women's pursuits?" His glance suddenly took in little Carolina, cradling the doll.

"I've named her Nan White," the child announced. She clutched the doll to her in sudden fright as if she sensed that this angry man might wrench it away from her.

For a moment Fielding glared down at her and the child stepped back before the anger in that look. Then he swooped down and tore it from her grasp. "I bought that doll for Virginia—not you!" he said, anger at his wife harshening his tone. "*She's* the one who's sick upstairs!"

Indignation made little Carolina cry out, "But Virgie already has a doll—and I haven't any!" She made a desperate snatch for the departing velvet and striped brocade of the doll's dress. When she missed, she turned to her mother with a wail.

"Oh, *do* be quiet, Carolina." Intent on settling the matter of the mare, Letitia pushed the child away impatiently. "Aunt Pet will bring you a doll—she promised!" She turned with a swirl of purple brocade to follow Fielding up the stairs. "You must understand, Field, that when you are not here, the plantation still must be run, and I have no intention of standing by and watching everything go to wrack and ruin!"

Their quarrel raged on, taking itself elsewhere, but to the flaxen-haired child standing there amid the ruin of her hopes, it was only sound and fury. Sick at heart, her knees gave way and she collapsed weeping by the blue sofa. And then, hearing their footsteps coming down the stairs, she scrambled up and ran blindly from the house—and kept on running with tears streaming down her face until she collided with a tree and knocked herself backward upon the grass. At that point, she had wept from pain as well as grief.

Penny, returning, had had a difficult time coaxing Carolina back in and she had refused to eat her supper, even though her nurse had given her a couple of sharp whacks on her backside for her stubbornness. She had crept woefully into her trundle bed that night, feeling her life was over. Over before it was begun.

Enthroned in the big bed high above her, still flushed and feverish from her cold, Virginia was clutching the lovely new doll to her and murmuring in her sleep. But lower down in the trundle bed with the white moonlight pouring in through the dormers and spilling over the blue coverlet, little Carolina fought back another surge of tears.

It wasn't fair that Virginia should have two dolls and she should have none! And when Aunt Pet, true to her word, had on their next visit to Williamsburg presented her with a doll, Carolina had dutifully curtsied, she had thanked Aunt Pet perfunctorily and put the doll on a shelf, never to be played with. For Aunt Pet's dainty gift was more a doll for display than for a child to treasure. Aunt Pet's doll had bisque hands and feet, a kid body and a composition head with a black painted coiffure and an intricate gown of delicate gauze. And it was seven inches high—a "doll in a teacup" as it were, not the twenty-inch glowing wonder named Nan White that Virginia, well and running about again, was hugging to her breast.

When Virginia politely admired Carolina's new doll, exclaiming over her gown, "Isn't it beautiful?" Carolina responded with, "If you like her so much I'd be glad to trade her for Nan White."

"Trade her for Nan?" Virginia squealed, for she had kept the name Nan White. "Oh, no!" She hugged the big doll to her. "Nan's twice as nice!"

Carolina thought so too. Indeed in any fair world Nan White would have been *her* doll—and Nan White was the only doll she wanted or would ever want.

But Nan remained Virginia's doll, closely guarded. And even though Virginia graciously offered Carolina her old doll, Carolina refused.

She never played with dolls again. In a way she had grown up a little that terrible afternoon when Fielding had glowered at her for daring to touch his gift for precious little Virginia upstairs. Hurt and disillusioned, Carolina had reached that day a vague glimmering of what life was going to be like for her in this tormented household.

Having Nan White snatched away from her had been her first real inkling that her father did not love her. It was a blow from which she had never really recovered.

Now in the aftermath of the storm Carolina looked down at a ruined and battered Nan White, carelessly tossed away by children who did not love her as she would have, her once pretty face cracked and damaged by the storm—and abruptly she burst into tears. Hugging the muddy doll in its tattered brocade and threadbare velvet to her breast, she ran in sodden shoes down to the beach where the waves had surged so violently last night, where they were still rough and dangerous. Out of breath, she paused and looked through tear-blurred eyes out over the choppy waters of Chesapeake Bay.

There was not a soul in sight, not a single sail upon the water. She might have been alone in the world.

Unwatched by anyone, she sank down on the wet sand and in a childish gesture, Carolina, the rejected child, cradled the ruined doll to her. Virginia had thrown Nan White away, little Flo and Della had other handsomer dolls—they threw poor Nan back and forth between them like a ball and sometimes, laughing, bounced her against the house.

Well, none of them would ever harm Nan again!

Silent and in desperate haste, driven by some instinct older than time, Carolina dug a hole in the sand and buried the doll. And with it she buried her childhood—and the last of her hopes that her father would ever love her.

She stayed there for a long time, with a lump in her throat, looking at the piece of driftwood she had thrust into the white sand to mark Nan White's grave. And then she got up and stretched and looked out toward the bay where already the water was calming. Life, as she knew it, was beginning all over again—and the glint in her silver gray eyes was very like that in her mother's dark blue ones. Resolute.

She had survived Nan White being wrenched from

43

her, she had survived the storm—she would survive whatever came. As she turned and trudged back toward the house, a slight figure in a sooty dress, with soot-smudged fair hair and face, she looked like a chimney sweep. But her heart, with the bright resilience of youth, was already burgeoning with hope. The storm was over—this was a new day! Penny would not be the only one to find a lover, and a new life far from here. Somewhere out there, there was a man for her too.

A man quite unlike her father. Her father was handsome, true, in his dark debonair way, and quite dashing. But seeing his anger erupt all these years had turned his daughter against all tall dark men. *They were overbearing and dangerously jealous—indeed they were not to be trusted at all,* of that she was very sure. And they would not continue to love you—of that she was certain as well. *If they ever loved you at all.* . . .

No, the man she chose could not be domineering like her father, for all that she frequently admired the way he handled men. He must be more . . . pliable, more charming, more like everybody else. Preferably blond. And smiling. Like the man in her dream.

None of the lads she had thus far found seemed to quite fit her judgment of what a proper man should be. Men like . . . Sandy Randolph, for instance. Only younger of course. Sandy as he might have been when her mother had first met him and fallen desperately in love.

A young lord perhaps, fresh out of England with jingling gold to buy a great plantation. Or a merchant's favorite son, who would inherit an empire of ships and trading posts and take her to faraway exciting places that smelled of spice and danger. But whoever he was, he must be softspoken and charming and given to long meaningful looks and have a deep powerful timbre in his voice that would move and excite her, that would make her feel like a woman!

Lost in her reverie, she hardly noticed the time.

By the time Carolina got back to the house, all had

been decided. Until Farview could be properly repaired, Letitia and her daughters would go to Aunt Pet's in Williamsburg.

"Again?" Fielding was saying ironically as Carolina strolled up. He was standing on the muddy driveway and Letitia was facing him.

"Of course! I realize we stayed there a long time after the Great Storm, but Aunt Petula will understand."

Around them the exhausted men who had ridden north with Fielding had cared for their equally exhausted horses and were now drifting away to throw themselves down in any convenient spot to sleep.

"I suppose she will understand," he said, but he sounded reluctant. He moved his big shoulders in his white cambric shirt restlessly, for he had discarded the wet coat in which he had begun his ride north. He was a handsome man, a determined man, was Fielding. And as Carolina looked at her father, saw him tossing back his dark hair with an impatient hand as he once again studied, without much hope, the ruins of his home, she felt very sorry for him—a feeling which was promptly dispelled by his next words. "I suppose you'll welcome a round of balls with your old flames, Letty."

His wife, who had survived this recent ordeal by storm so splendidly, straightened up and gave him a level look. "I *promise* to enjoy it," she said in a voice of menace.

Carolina exchanged uneasy glances with Virgie, who had come out now. All this trouble, which should have brought Fielding and Letty together, was rending them apart again.

To Williamsburg they went, to Aunt Pet's two-story house on Duke of Gloucester Street. The house was of rubbed brick set in a checkerboard pattern. Its steeply pitched roof had clipped gables set with five dormers which housed the bedrooms. A pair of handsome tapering brick chimneys towered over each end, and neat clipped boxwood flanked the front steps which Aunt Pet bragged "had been brought over from England, stone by stone."

45

Aunt Pet's was a favorite place of the girls, for past the wall and the smokehouse and the tiny dairy was an attractive small garden which was their aunt's pride. It boasted fruit trees and a sunken turf panel in which had been carefully sculpted corner seats shaded by big lacy-leaved locusts, and all of it edged with deep green boxwood and a hedge of carefully clipped live oaks.

Carolina might have been lonely in Williamsburg had not Sally Montrose from upriver been visiting her great aunt who lived across the street. For Virginia had discovered the miller's son and was always off to the windmill to buy meal. This was at least three times a week, for colonial meal was unrefined and unbleached and did not keep well. Aunt Pet was adamant about using fresh meal and delighted that Virginia had taken this task upon herself. She would have blanched had she known of the flirtation that was going on at the awkward-looking post mill, the whole superstructure of which revolved atop a single post. While the windmill's great sails flailed noisily in the wind, Virginia would stroll through the upper chamber which contained the millstones and the main shaft, talking pertly with Hugh Clemens, the miller's tall blond son.

"Hugh kissed me today," she would report excitedly to Carolina when she returned home. Or, "Hugh says he does not believe in long betrothals," she would say, blushing. Or, "Hugh says there is need of many good mills in Virginia and that he would like to establish a whole chain of mills, if only he had the backing." On and on.

Carolina realized as time went by that this was no summertime flirtation, that Virginia was actually falling in love with Hugh—and wondered uneasily how her mother would take it. Very badly, probably, for Hugh was but one of seven sons of the miller and unlikely to inherit more than a pittance. And for all his blond Viking good looks he had no education, could not even write his own name. Oh, no, Letitia Lightfoot would not approve of Hugh as a son-in-law!

Her mother was holding up very well during this enforced leave of absence from home. As Fielding had predicted, she was engaged in a perpetual round of balls. Usually she took her two older daughters, eager to dance in their newly stitched up dresses which were of coarser materials than their mother would have liked but which Aunt Pet insisted were the best they could afford "at such a time as this!"

Carolina was just on the brink of becoming the blazing beauty her mother before her had been, but at the moment her figure was a bit coltish and awkward, her silver-gold hair considered too "theatrical" for one so young—in short she was not the fashion, but she had plenty of time to watch the older Virginia flirt coquettishly with young upriver planters come down the James to enjoy the social life of Williamsburg.

Somewhat to her regret, the repairs to Farview were accomplished speedily, a new south wing went up to replace the old, and Letitia and her daughters were home again before the summer was entirely gone.

Virginia had been desolate at leaving.

"Oh, Virgie, you'll see Hugh again." Carolina had tried to console her sister. "It isn't as if you were off to New York or Boston, you know!"

"I know, but it isn't like being just—just across town from him either," sobbed Virginia, to whom tears came readily these days and whose face would suddenly become still while her gaze sought distant vistas. "Virgie's in love!" Sally Montrose was fond of whispering to Carolina with a smothered giggle, for Sally had assumed a certain loftiness about other girls' love affairs ever since returning from that overstrict school, Mistress Chesterton's, in London.

Virginia had cornered Carolina just before they left Williamsburg. "Oh, Carol, Hugh is going to come calling at Farview—he promises he will, and so far Mother does not have wind of a thing—I can tell by the serene way she looks at me. And she mustn't find out!"

"How will you manage that, when Hugh comes calling?"

"Oh, she won't find out—if only you will help me," Virginia pleaded.

47

"I will," Carolina promised, bewildered. "But what do you want me to do?"

"Make Mother believe he is your suitor, not mine—then I will be left in peace. Oh, Carol, if you'll do this, I promise I will never ask another thing of you as long as I live!"

Carolina thought that last very unlikely for Virginia was always desperately wanting something that was hers—like her new ruffled petticoat which she had won away from Carolina a fortnight ago and worn to enchant Hugh. "Of course I'll do it," she said dryly. "But she may forbid him the house!"

"Oh, no, she won't," said Virginia instantly. "Because you're only fifteen and have never shown much interest in any special boy. She'll think you're only flirting—indeed she may *encourage* it. She'd believe you're just trying your wings and that it means nothing. But she's already considering a list of possible suitors for me because I'm the oldest now and of marriageable age. I heard her discussing it with Father the last time they were on speaking terms—luckily they fell out over it before they could decide anything and haven't spoken since! But they'll get back to the subject, and if they think Hugh is calling on *me,* they may get back to it right away and I will find myself betrothed to some upriver planter's son and spirited away from Hugh entirely—and oh, Carol, I couldn't bear to lose him!"

"Was there anyone interesting on the list?" asked Carolina, amused, for a death-defying romance with stolid Hugh had always seemed to her vaguely funny.

"I think it included every boy who ever danced with me since we came to Williamsburg," declared Virginia.

"Which must be all of them," laughed Carolina. "For you have the lightest feet in town!"

"Oh, you can laugh," rejoined her sister with a trace of bitterness, "for *you* were not always afraid one of them would become so enamored he would rush up to Father and demand your hand in marriage!"

Carolina went off into gales of heartless laughter. "To tell you the truth, I never thought about it," she agreed when she could speak again. "Mostly I was trying not to get my ball slippers trodden on!"

Virginia gave her an impatient look. "But you *will* do it? Pretend Hugh is your beau?"

"Oh, yes, I'll do it."

"Doing it" proved to be something of a chore, for Hugh seemed to be endlessly resourceful in finding reasons to cross the bay and call at Farview. And Carolina had to manage each time to get him into the garden, or some other secluded place—anywhere it would not be readily apparent that Virgie had dashed down to change places with her, to stroll and talk and laugh with Hugh, and kiss behind the shrubbery.

That first week back there was flawless weather all along the Chesapeake. In the garden of Farview Plantation the boxwoods and big magnolias still showed the effect of the violent storm which had battered them earlier in the season, but the broken branches had been hauled away and cut up for firewood and kindling and the remnants of the roses bloomed bravely in the late summer heat. The younger children were ecstatic at being back, for life at Farview was much freer than at staid Aunt Pet's, but Carolina found she rather missed town and town doings. They had been back six days and she was strolling aimlessly down the drive when she saw a tall blond youth appear on foot and wave to her. Hugh again! He was almost running and Carolina hurried down the drive to meet him. In case her mother should be watching from the window, she greeted him effusively.

"I did not know you were coming today, Hugh," she said.

"I did not know myself, Mistress Carolina," grinned Hugh. "But when I learnt my father was sending a boat over to bring grain from your neighbors, the Whitleys, I volunteered to come. The boat is being loaded now, but I had a little time so I came to see Virginia."

Carolina did not quite know what Virginia saw in this bumbling youth with the overconfident smile, but then love was a funny thing. She had not known what her older sister Penny saw in stodgy Emmett either. They were both so—*tame,* that was it. For herself, she preferred wilder men. Like Sandy Randolph in his youth, she supposed, when he had reputedly always been dashing off on mysterious ventures and had turned up with sudden unexplained wealth and scars he had passed off with a shrug as "dueling scars." Yes, men like Sandy, that you felt were inherently dangerous—and fascinating. She was suddenly frozen at the thought, for hadn't her mother always preferred wilder men, and wasn't Aunt Pet always saying that every day Carolina's ways grew more like her mother's? Aunt Pet doted on Letty so she meant it as a compliment of course, but Carolina considered it a sentence of doom. *She* thought her mother's life was *terrible!*

"I'll tell Virgie you're here," she told the gangling lad hastily.

"No need. She's already seen me from the window—she waved."

"Oh, then I'll just stroll to the garden with you and Virgie can slip out and join us beneath the trees and I'll leave you two alone."

Hugh gave her a contented look. "I'm here to ask your sister to marry me," he confided.

Carolina was thunderstruck. She didn't know why she should be—it had been plain all along that Hugh was in love with Virginia. But somehow she had expected them to drift apart after Virginia got home. Other lads would come calling, Virginia would fancy one of them, the miller's lanky son would be forgotten.

"You do not think she has changed toward me, do you?" he asked nervously when Carolina did not immediately comment. "You think she will favor my suit?"

"Oh, I—I think she might." Carolina felt confused. "But I think you should know that Mother will never countenance it," she added in a burst of honesty.

Hugh sighed and looked glum. "Virginia gave me to understand as much," he said. "I would not like to see her cut off from her family."

"Then—?" A pair of questioning silver gray eyes studied him.

"But what will be will be." He shrugged off trouble with the lighthearted optimism of youth. "Once your mother understands that Virginia and I love each other—"

It will make no difference, thought Carolina gloomily, but she forbore to say so. After all, who was she to blight a lovers' tryst with unwelcome pronouncements?

Dutifully she led Hugh to the garden, wondering if her mother was watching. They had no more than reached the spreading branches of a big oak when Virginia hurried out a side door and ran down the garden path to join them.

"Mother wants to see you inside right away, Carolina," she said breathlessly, and added in a nervous voice, "I think she's angry."

"What about?" Carolina gave her sister an uneasy look.

Virginia rolled her eyes toward Hugh and Carolina understood. She was to be taken to task for allowing the miller's fortuneless son to call on her. Carrying her chin high, she marched inside into the cool, high-ceilinged interior.

"Carolina." Her mother was standing by the long dining room table. Its polished surface gave no indication that it had been used as a bulwark against falling beams in the worst storm of the summer. "This is thrice in one week that the Clemens boy has come here."

Carolina gave her mother a deceptively innocent look. Her mother looked very elegant today—and young. As she always did after her cousin Sandy's visits. And Sandy had been here yesterday and spent a long time with her mother in the cool paneled living room.

"Yes, Hugh has been here three times," she agreed.

"I do not favor him." Letitia came bluntly to the point.

Carolina looked at the elegant woman in lavender silk who stood before her, small-waisted as a girl, beautiful, with her crown of thick honey gold hair. And

51

a frowning expression. "Whatever do you mean, Mother?" she said, choosing not to understand.

"Don't be dense," warned her mother impatiently. She frowned into that winsome face. Carolina was growing up—she was almost as tall as Letitia herself. Her figure was rounding out too. She had counted on that coltish quality to hold Carolina back until she could get Virginia safely wed. It was plain that she had not paid enough attention to her third daughter lately; while she was not watching, Carolina was fast becoming a beauty.

"I am not being dense, Mother," said Carolina plaintively. She was deliberately baiting Letitia, for it was hard knowing your mother rarely gave you a thought unless you did something to displease her. *This* time, she thought wickedly, she would have her mother's full attention!

"Of course you are!" snapped Letitia. "It is plain the lad is pursuing you. I am always finding him wandering about—indeed I wonder how he can cross the water from the mainland so often! His father must miss him sorely at the mill."

"Oh, he is here today on business of his father's," supplied Carolina instantly. "The Whitleys are sending a supply of grain to Williamsburg to be milled and Hugh is to transport it."

"But he is not with the loading party," objected her mother in exasperation. "Instead he is *here*. Again. I saw you meet him on the driveway and disappear with him into the garden!"

"What harm can there be in hearing the gossip of Williamsburg from Hugh?" wondered Carolina.

"You are not to encourage him, do you hear? I forbid it."

For a moment Carolina's teeth caught in her lower lip and there was a rebellious glint in her silver eyes. She was growing up and she did not like her mother's overbearing tone.

"Oh, so you think to defy me, do you?" Her mother read that rebellious expression correctly. "Well, I can tell you that boy has no prospects, and if you think to end up a pauper as your sister Pennsylvania no doubt will do—if ever we hear from her again!—if you think to run away across the border as she did—!"

"Into the Marriage Trees? Why not?" interrupted Carolina recklessly. "After all, you did!"

Her elegant mother paled perceptibly and her lavender silk bodice rose and fell somewhat faster. "If your father heard you speak to me in that tone of voice, Carolina, he would whip you!" she cried. "Indeed, he will do so anyway, when I tell him about it!"

Carolina's resentment spilled over at a mother who, she felt, had never loved her, and who had driven Penny and now most probably would drive Virgie into unsuitable marriages with the first lad who appealed to them.

"But then you aren't speaking to Father, are you?" she demanded waspishly. "And it's unlikely he'll be speaking to *you* tonight—if he gets home tonight—for I'm not the only one in this house who has callers who aren't approved of!"

Two red spots of color appeared in her mother's pale cheeks. "Go on," she said ominously. "Let us hear this accusation you are leveling against me!"

Too late Carolina realized her folly. She had driven her mother too far. She hesitated.

"Well, speak!" cried Letitia in fury.

"Father saw Sandy Randolph's horse hitched outside yesterday and his face changed color and he spurred his horse away as if devils were after him!" Carolina shouted. *"You* drove him away! You did—for you know how jealous he is of your cousin Sandy!"

Her mother's open palm cracked across her cheek and Carolina staggered backward.

"Go to your room," ordered Letitia in a voice gone suddenly wooden. So *that* was why Fielding had not come home last night—he had spied Sandy's horse hitched to the post in the driveway. Someone might have told her, she thought angrily. She should not have had to learn it in this impudent way from her daughter. She turned and her gaze was narrow as it followed Carolina into the hall.

Something would have to be done about Carolina. And soon.

Fielding Lightfoot came home with the evening dusk, when bats were emerging from their dark hiding places to swoop out over the fields looking for the insects that plagued the crops. There was a hum of cicadas on the evening air and the croak of frogs from nearby Old Plantation Creek.

He dismounted gracefully for all that he was bone tired, tossed the reins to a groom who had run out of the stable on seeing him ride up, and made for the front door. There he was met by Letitia who had forgotten their earlier tiff and was bursting to talk about Carolina and the miller's son who—though departed some hours ago—was sure to be back and perhaps would carry her all the way to the Marriage Trees as that miserable clerk had done with her sister!

"It is time you came home," she greeted him in a scolding tone. "For I have a matter to take up with you."

"Indeed?" Sarcasm rang in Fielding's voice; he was slightly drunk. "But perhaps you have already found others to take it up with earlier?" He brushed past her.

Letitia gave him a baffled look. Carolina's "predicament" had washed other things temporarily from her mind. It took her a moment to realize that her husband was speaking of her cousin, Sandy Randolph, and when she did realize it, she turned and pursued him down the hall. "You are imagining things again!" she told his broad back sharply. "There is *nothing* between Sandy and me."

The dark head turned to give her a baleful look. "Then why do we see so much of him?"

"You *know* why!" she insisted impatiently. "He comes here to inquire of his cousin to the north of us, for he hears rumors—in spite of her sending him word that all is well between her and her new husband."

"Then why does he not head north and see for himself how matters are? Why is it always to us that he comes?"

54

Letitia heaved an irritable sigh. Men were so thick-headed sometimes! "Her parents plead with him to ferret out how matters stand because they do not believe her over-cheerful letters. And he stops here because he knows that I would hear things that would not be apparent to him," she explained as patiently as if she were speaking to a child.

"And how is that?" he said ironically.

"You *know* how that is," she cried in a voice of despair. She picked up her skirts and followed her husband up the stairs for he was taking them two at a time. "Maybelle Whitley goes right past his cousin's place twice a week to see her old mother and *she* tells me how things are with Sandy's cousin!"

"Then let him go to Maybelle Whitley!" roared Fielding, disappearing down the hall.

Halfway up, with her voluminous lavender skirts caught up in one hand, Letitia stopped and shook her head. Would he never understand? No, because he did not choose to do so!

"Damn you, Field!" she cried violently, and turned and ran back down the half flight she had just climbed. She was still shaking with rage as she burst into the kitchen, to give the startled servants orders about warming up some dinner for her husband—which was already being done for cook had sharp eyes and had seen him ride up.

Once again the Lightfoots were not speaking. And so Carolina was—for this evening at least—spared the confrontation she had brought on herself by baiting her mother.

She was young enough and foolish enough to think it had all been forgotten. And she went to bed beneath a slender slice of new moon and dreamed again of a lover who would be all that her father was not.

Chapter 4

Breakfast next morning was a silent meal punctuated only by brief exchanges such as Letitia's frosty, "Carolina, please ask your father if he will have more cream," and Fielding's moody, "Carolina, please tell your mother that I have had sufficient." The girls were sensibly silent as they always were when their parents were warring. But they were also painfully aware that their parents might be on speaking terms again had not a messenger arrived just before breakfast with an invitation to the Bramways' ball the following week.

Sandy Randolph was sure to be there. He was sure to dance repeatedly with his beautiful cousin. And Letty was equally sure to encourage him, as if to spite her jealous mate.

Fielding Lightfoot, who had spent the night on the living room sofa, but had come in to breakfast whistling, had heard the message delivered and a deep scowl had covered his features. He had pulled back his chair with such force that he had nearly overturned it. Letitia had tossed her golden head and told the messenger that of course they would all attend the ball—and neither Fielding nor Letitia had spoken directly to each other since.

"Virginia, tell your mother her cousin might as well have told her of the ball when he was here," said her father morosely. "I am told he is often at the Bramways' these days. They could have used him as their messenger as easily as this fellow who called."

"Virginia, tell your father that Sandy didn't know about the ball when he called here!" snapped her mother. "And as for his calling often at the Bramways', you can tell your father as well that Sandy is *not* pursuing Amanda Bramway despite what the gossips will say—he told me so himself."

Virginia, caught in the middle, looked unhappy. Nobody ate much although the poached sturgeon sprigged with lemon thyme and served with butter sauce was delicious.

After breakfast Fielding went upstairs, his wife busied herself with household chores, the younger children were packed off to play and gambol about on the front lawn, and Carolina and Virginia wandered into the garden.

Virginia was very depressed. "Whatever you said to Mother yesterday, it made her furious," she accused Carolina. "She nearly snapped my head off every time I spoke to her! I am afraid she may tell Hugh he is not welcome here."

Carolina sighed. She had behaved badly, she knew, and there was really no excuse for baiting her mother like that. She hoped it would not cause trouble for Virgie and Hugh. "I was—irritated," she admitted.

"You were irritated?" Her sister looked at her in amazement. "The wonder is you are down here in the garden instead of still confined to your room after daring to mention that *she* ran away!" Last night Carolina had told her part of what had been said.

"Yes, I suppose so." Carolina tried to switch the subject. "Tell me, are you expecting Hugh today?"

"No," said Virginia haltingly. Last night she had refused to say whether she had accepted Hugh's proposal. That annoyed Carolina for, since going without supper last night more or less on her sister's behalf, she felt entitled to know.

"The least you could do is tell me what you've decided," she said in a cross voice.

To her astonishment, Virginia burst into tears and ran away toward the house.

She must have said yes, surmised Carolina gloomily. Penny had left and now Virginia was about to fly the coop as well. It would leave her alone on this isolated peninsula with few neighbors, two small children, her warring parents and an uninteresting collection of servants. The prospect was not bright.

But how Virginia would make her escape, only heaven knew, for neither Hugh nor Virginia had any money. Carolina sighed, hoping treacherously that however Virginia chose to resolve her affairs, it would for once not involve *her*. Perhaps they dared not wait, for it was clear that she could not cover up for Virginia forever. The real state of affairs was bound to be found out. Hugh would be banished and another suitor sought for Virginia. Perhaps that was why she had flung away, crying. Carolina realized that something must be done and done now—but how?

She looked up in surprise as she saw the carriage being brought round. No one had told her that anyone was going anywhere today. Curious, she strolled toward the front door where the carriage had come to a smart stop and a smiling groom stood ready to deliver the reins.

A moment later her father came out and both girls gaped at him. Gone were the usual simple broadcloth trousers and plain white cambric shirt in which he rode about the plantation. Fielding was this day splendidly attired in burnished gold satin trimmed in gold braid and gold buttons. A spray of lace edged his cuffs and made startling the big topaz that flashed at his throat. His hair—usually left flying as he rode about the plantation—was concealed by the elegant full-bottomed wig he usually reserved for town, and his boots had so high a polish that you could have seen your reflection in them. He was every inch the gentleman as he turned courteously to his daughter.

"Carolina, inform your mother that I desire the honor of having her ride with me this morning," he said in such a stiffly formal voice that Carolina gaped at him.

A moment later she recovered herself. "Yes, Father," she said quickly, for his dark frown forbade questions. She ran inside, gathering up her green and yellow skirts.

She met Virginia coming woefully down the stairs.

"Something is up," muttered Carolina. "Father is dressed to the teeth and has asked me to convey a formal message to Mother to go riding with him. One would think they were courting!"

Virginia's gloom left her. She was as curious as anyone. But not sparkling as Penny had been. Carolina missed Penny, who had laughed with her at small things, and sometimes tried daring escapades. She sighed. Penny had not surfaced yet. Plainly she and Emmett meant to be firmly established somewhere before they let the Lightfoots know where they were. Which was too bad, because Carolina would have liked to hear from Penny, and none of the Lightfoot emissaries had been able to ferret out her hiding place. Penny was a Master Planner. Carolina hoped that one day she would do as well. She knocked on her mother's bedroom door.

Letitia was usually in her bedroom at this time of day. She would slip up the back stairs from the kitchen the moment she heard her husband's boots clatter down the front stairway, so that she would not meet him. This was the hour when she wrote her letters and read her mail, if any. She looked up as both girls came to the door.

"Well, what is it?" she demanded impatiently.

Carolina swallowed her laughter. "Father requests the honor of your company in driving out with him," she said with a straight face. "He is dressed as if he is on his way to a ball and the carriage is waiting at the front door."

To their delight, Letitia looked thunderstruck. "Has Field taken leave of his senses?" she murmured. Then, recovering herself, she rose majestically. "Tell your father that I will be ready to accompany him in a few minutes," she said tartly. "And that I will be as well dressed as he!"

"Where do you think they're going?" wondered Virginia as she followed Carolina downstairs.

"I don't know," said Carolina. "But I'm going to race to the stable and get a horse saddled while she's dressing. Why don't you come along? We can appear to be out riding and we can follow them and see what they're up to!"

Virginia was amenable, and after Carolina had delivered her mother's reply to her father, who was pacing up and down in the drive beside the carriage with his head bent in thought and his hands folded behind his back, they rushed to the stable and were mounted and walking their horses down the drive by the time Letitia came through the front door.

Into the carriage she climbed, helped in with ceremony by her husband, and the carriage started off. The horse, a shiny black gelding and Fielding's favorite, passed the girls handily.

"Did you see what she's wearing?" murmured Carolina, eyeing the gleaming flash of lilac silk and rose point lace as the carriage rolled by them. "That is her new gown, is it not?"

It certainly was, and both girls were quick to note the high piled hairdo and—

"Oh, she's wearing the hat!" wailed Virginia. "The one she promised me I could have when she was tired of it. Oh, I do hope it doesn't blow away or get damaged by a tree branch!"

"The hat" was indeed beautiful, of wide-brimmed wheat-colored flexible straw with a sweep of lavender plumes. It had been made in the islands and the plumes added in Williamsburg. Virginia had long coveted it.

Carolina ignored her. Where her parents might be going dressed so fashionably was much more intriguing.

The girls followed at a discreet distance. Their father was taking his usual route for a "drive," a route which led along the bay. The carriage had reached the beach now and was running smoothly across the white sand. A stand of trees now obscured the carriage and Carolina reined up before she left their shelter.

"I don't think we'd better follow," she announced—for well she knew her father was quite capable of turning the carriage around, riding his daughters down and telling them the price of their curiosity was to miss the next ball given in Williamsburg!

Virginia, who had been thinking much the same thing, promptly reined in her mount. "But how will we see what they are doing?" she fretted.

"I'll just climb into this tree." Carolina rose in her stirrups, seized a tree branch overhead and swung herself up so that she stood for a moment atop her saddle before she boosted herself to a crotch in the branches. "And now a little higher."

"You'll tear your dress," chided Virginia. To her, clothes were of prime importance. If asked, she would have said with conviction that it was her blue flounced petticoat that had first attracted Hugh!

"Oh, bother my dress!" retorted Carolina impatiently. She maneuvered herself up higher in the tree until she had a clear view of the bay and the drive along the beach.

"Can you see what's happening?" called Virginia.

"Yes, now I can see them. They're still driving along the beach." Her voice changed, grew excited. "Father's turned the carriage. *He's driving straight into the bay!*"

"He's mad!" gasped Virginia.

From her high perch, Carolina was staring, fascinated, out toward the bay. "They've gone farther into the water," she reported. "Both their backs are very straight—I don't think they're talking."

"Oh, of course they're talking!" cried Virginia in an agony of excitement. "*Nobody* would drive straight into the bay without saying anything—not even Father!" And when Carolina was silent for a moment,

61

Virginia shrilled, "Are they drowning?" and then corrected herself in confusion. "No, of course they aren't drowning. Mother would *refuse* to drown!"

"Well, the horse seems to be floundering, he's going under—no, there's his head, he's up! They seem to have come to a halt. The water is lapping around the floorboards of the carriage. Mother's skirts must be getting wet."

"And in her new dress too!" moaned Virginia.

"Oh, I'd give *anything* to hear what they're saying!"

What the senior Lightfoots were saying to each other at that moment was indeed edifying. Letitia had maintained a lofty silence as her frowning and elegantly garbed husband turned the carriage toward the bay and drove the astonished horse across the sand into the water. But as that same water licked up over the floorboards and threatened to inundate her lilac silk skirts she had lifted her winglike eyebrows along with her skirt hem and said, looking straight ahead at the seemingly endless expanse of the bay, "Have you lost your senses, Field? This is not a ford! Where do you think you're taking me?"

"To Hell," was the brisk but savage reply. "Where you'll be much at home, Letty!"

"Indeed? Then do drive on," was his lady's calm rejoinder as she hitched her skirts higher around her lavender silk ankles. "For since it would seem I'm married to the Devil, 'tis only natural you should seek your own domain!"

Fielding's dark head swung toward his wife. He regarded her in amazement. From her treetop perch Carolina reported, "Oh, *now* they're talking. I'll wager Mother is giving him a piece of her mind!"

"Does nothing frighten you, Letty?" he asked wonderingly. "Are you not afraid I'll do it?"

"Nonsense, anywhere *you'd* go I could certainly follow," was his lady's tart rejoinder, delivered with a toss of her smartly coiffed curls. "And as for your 'doing it,' Fielding, that's your favorite horse out there fighting to keep his head above the water. And since you have far more regard for that beast than you have for me, I'm very sure you're not going to drown *him!* And in any case, I've something of such importance to talk to you about that I intend to hold your ears above the water if necessary until you've heard me out!"

The response to this astonishing speech was a look as blank as any she had ever seen on her husband's face. For a moment his gray eyes glinted and his taut mouth worked as if he was trying not to smile. Then his white teeth flashed as he gave himself up to mirth. He threw back his dark head, nearly losing his periwig as he did so, and roared with laughter.

Letitia, still affronted and with a caustic expression, blinked. Then she too saw the humor of their situation, stranded there upon the bright glassy waters of the bay with the white beach serene and deserted behind them and their carriage seeming like a tiny island of civilization adrift in an endless sea. She too threw back her golden head and joined in her husband's mirth. They both shook with uncontrollable laughter while the unfortunate horse floundered about with eyes rolling and the water came over the footboards of the carriage to wet the forgotten hem of Letitia's lilac silk gown and cascade over the toes of Fielding's shiny boots.

"They must have made up," reported Carolina from the tree. "He seems to be hugging her—and now she's hugging him. She's lost her hat," she added laconically for Virginia's benefit.

"Oh, *no!*" wailed Virginia. "Are they trying to get it?" she asked hopefully.

"No, they seem to have forgotten it," replied Carolina with suppressed laughter. "It's floating away, plumes and all."

"Are they still in the water? Are they sinking as they embrace?"

"No," said Carolina critically, squinting her silver eyes at the glittering waters of the bay. "The water seems to be over the floorboards now but they aren't drowning. Now Father's turning the carriage around, they're coming out—I can see the floorboards rising

63

from the water and now the wheels." She choked with mirth. "I'm sure the horse is relieved to be changing directions!"

"But her hat!" cried Virginia, keeping to the main thrust of her interest. "Surely by now they've noticed the hat? Are they trying to rescue it?"

Carolina could hardly trust herself to speak. Their parents might be out there battling, drowning, perhaps even killing each other—for in sudden rage Fielding might have seized his beautiful wife by the throat and it was not beyond imagining that she might at such a moment thrust a long hatpin into his heart—and all Virginia could think about was a hat! When she spoke, her voice was mirth-laden.

"No, they seem not to have noticed the hat. The carriage is on the beach now, the horse is shaking himself off—I don't blame him. They're sitting there and Mother is shaking out her skirts. Now they've turned toward home. They're driving back—"

"Without the hat?"

"Without the hat." Firmly. "It's floating out into the bay—oh, there it goes, I can't see it any more."

Virginia wailed.

"She seems to be leaning on his shoulder," reported Carolina, who had begun to scramble down from her perch. "It's obvious they've made up and we'd best get out of here—fast. We wouldn't want them to know we were spying on them!"

But even as she made her way down she cast one last long look at the sparkle of the bay through the tree limbs.

Oh, God, don't let my life be like that! she thought passionately. *Don't let me be like my mother, too imperious ever to give ground! And if I can't avoid that, at least let me find a man entirely different from my father, not some dark tyrant who will rage at me and never truly love me—not a man that I can never understand!*

"They may have made up, but it won't last," predicted Virginia gloomily. She still felt very cut up about the hat. "And besides, my chances were better while they *weren't* talking. Now that they're back on speaking terms they may come to some awful decision—about Hugh."

Carolina, back in the saddle, gave her sister a sympathetic look. Virginia was probably right.

The blow fell the following morning. Later Carolina realized her parents must have discussed it during that long companionable walk they had taken at sunset, strolling like lovers beneath the magnolias and oaks, stopping to admire the roses, embracing once or twice.

Letitia called to Carolina to wait as the others were leaving the dining room after breakfast. Virginia choked but Carolina turned with a sigh. She guessed that her mother would not mince words when she was told to close the door. She was right.

"I have no intention of letting you wed that penniless miller's son," she told Carolina briskly.

Carolina had already decided on her best line of defense.

"Very well," she agreed cheerfully. "I promise not to marry Hugh. But could he come calling now and then?" she asked wistfully, thinking of Virginia. "It does my heart good to see someone so besotted."

Her mother drew a quick breath. "What a hard-hearted thing to say!" she remonstrated. At her daughter's indifferent shrug, she frowned suspiciously. "He will never be able to support you, I hope you realize that." She paused to let that sink in, and Carolina had time to get a slightly new view of her resplendent mother. Letitia was clad this morning in a rippling amethyst silk dressing gown (she had not bothered to dress today, for she intended to go back to bed after breakfast as she and Fielding always did during these brief "honeymoons" in their turbulent marriage). Her mother, Carolina thought critically, had a kind of glow this morning; her dark blue eyes were velvet soft, her cheeks had a peachy bloom, and her slight gesture toward the mainland when she spoke of Hugh's unsuitability had a kind of silken grace that made Carolina

65

realize suddenly what a splendrous woman she must have been at eighteen—such a woman, she realized, startled, as she might herself one day be.

"I have always realized Hugh could not support me," she told her mother calmly. "Especially not in the style to which I wish to become accustomed," she added on a humorous note.

Her mother gave her a sharp look and her mouth tightened. Her expression showed she didn't believe a thing Carolina had said and her next words proved it.

"Last night your father and I came to a decision. You are too wayward and may come to a bad end here. So we are sending you away—to Mistress Chesterton's school in London."

Mistress Chesterton's school! But that was where Sally Montrose had been sent, and *she* had described it morosely as strict, tiresome, and with never enough food! Granted, Sally was not thin but—

"I don't want to go!" cried Carolina, shocked.

A mocking smile lit up her mother's beautiful face. "That's beside the point," she said. "You are sailing day after tomorrow on the *Bristol Maid*. We will all go in to Williamsburg tomorrow and stay the night with Aunt Pet, and see you off on your voyage the following morning."

"But there may not be room aboard for another passenger!" Frantically Carolina sought for a way out.

"The captain is a friend of your father's. He will find a place for you aboard."

"My clothes! I lost so many in the storm. I will need new clothes if I am to attend a fashionable school."

Her mother frowned. "Yes, I thought of that. We talked it over and Fielding will give you a purse when you board with enough gold to outfit you handsomely in London. Mistress Chesterton can take you to the proper shops and guide you in your selections."

Mistress Chesterton! Carolina was speechless. Sally Montrose had described her as a shapeless crone in her dotage who was still wearing a wheel farthingale! And Mistress Chesterton was to supervise the buying of *her*

66

wardrobe? Indignation welled up in Carolina, for along with her mother's beauty she had inherited that indefinable sense of style that would make her stand out in any crowd.

But there was no use protesting. Plainly her mother's mind was made up. She was to be removed from the scene. She would undoubtedly be watched every minute until she left, a purse of gold would be plumped into her hand along with a goodbye kiss and she would be put aboard the *Bristol Maid* willy-nilly.

Virginia found her a few minutes later seated on a stone bench in the garden. "Is it true?" she gasped. "I was listening outside the door but I couldn't hear very well. Are you really going to school in London?"

Carolina, who had been lost in thought, studying the grass blades beneath her feet, nodded without looking up. "Oh, it's true, all right—I'm going. Mother has made up her mind."

And suddenly she didn't mind at all.

It had just occurred to her that there would be an ocean between her and all the problems of "Bedlam"—no more being bossed by her mother! And whatever the school was like, it would all be new and different. And exciting, for there would be a great city pulsing around her, day and night. A city teeming with men of all shapes and sizes—dukes and merchant princes and country gentlemen, they would all be there!

Thinking about it, she hardly heard Virginia's heartfelt groan. In distant London adventure waited for her, romance waited for her. In distant London there would be a man for her—not a dishwater-dull clerk such as Penny had chosen, not a cheerful bumbling dolt such as Virginia was pining for, and certainly not that unknown faceless fellow with whom her mother would shortly try to plummet her into an arranged marriage—but a man of her own choosing.

In London, she would meet at last The Golden Stranger of her dream! She shivered slightly, imagining what it would be like to hold him, to love him.

"Carol, you aren't listening," complained Virginia.

That little-girl squeak that was so like Aunt Pet's had crept into her voice. "I said I'm so sorry Mother's sending you away—I know you'll hate it."

Carolina lifted her head and her gray eyes held a wicked gleam for she had just thought of a way to ensure that dowdy Mistress Chesterton didn't choose for her a sober-sided wardrobe—and do something for her sister at the same time.

"Virgie." She turned to Virginia with a resolute look. "Do you still want to run away with Hugh?"

"Oh, Carolina, you know I do! But Hugh has no money and neither have I. How would we live until he could find a position?"

"Send word to Hugh," said Carolina ruthlessly. "Tell him you're pleading a toothache and will not accompany the family into Williamsburg to see me off, that you will wait for him here. Tell him to come to the ship to see me off. Tell him to throw his arms around me at the last minute just before I board and kiss me goodbye."

Virginia gaped at her. "But why would Hugh—?"

"And while he is kissing me, I will slip him a purse of gold. This is your chance, Virgie. You can take the gold and run off together to the Marriage Trees!"

PART TWO

The Winning Wench

Reckless she is and always was, reckless she'll always be,
Her silken body will respond to some wild destiny,
And even though she may repent, deep in her heart she'll
    know
That dangerous loves are heaven sent—and shiver that it's
    so!

Chapter 5

Carolina was to think of The Golden Stranger of her dream quite often in the months that followed, but when she met him at last it was quite by chance and she did not recognize him. Not at first.

Her first year at school had been an unhappy one from the beginning, when she had been forced to trudge up to Mistress Chesterton's school from the ship—she had no money to pay for a hackney coach—and forlornly tell the scandalized headmistress that her baggage was still on shipboard waiting to be called for. Never before had Carolina realized how much money counted in this world.

The headmistres had pursed her lips and given Carolina's plain clothing a scathing look, but the baggage had been duly sent for.

The girls were another matter. Led by Vanessa Snipes, they had stared her down scornfully that first night at supper, and all that first week she had heard them giggling over "the rag-tag Colonial" as they chose to call her. Homesick and unused to the fogs of London, Carolina had come down with a deep cold and coughed away all through Christmas. While the city glittered with holly and Yule logs blazed and carolers roamed the streets, those other luckier girls went home for the holidays—home to Christmas goose and parties and presents. Carolina, thin and brooding, had lived for letters from home.

All that first year she had not made a friend. Indeed, the gregarious girl from the Eastern Shore had reacted thornily to her schoolmates' disdain, scorning back where she was scorned and walking a haughty path of her own. She hated London that first year, blaming in part for her unhappiness the big, sprawling, uncaring city with its choking sea-coal soot, so different from the clear air of Virginia. Her entire allowance from home had to go for desperate necessities such as woolen scarves and mittens to wear against the bitter cold, and this prevented her from attending plays and boat trips with the other girls, for Mistress Chesterton cannily insisted that the students pay their own way on all such outings.

Holidays were the worst times, for during holidays the school was deserted save for herself, those teachers who had nowhere else to go, and the few servants who lived in. Even Mistress Chesterton was gone on holidays, visiting "friends," she said vaguely. And Christmas, which the girl from the Eastern Shore loved with all her heart, was the worst time of all.

Carolina's second Christmas in London was almost as lonely as her first, even though by now gifts of money from home had enabled her to buy at least a few items of clothing so that she did not look quite so downtrodden among the elegant company she was forced to keep. Like her first, that second Christmas away from home left scars, and Carolina would never forget looking out the window from an empty school on Christmas morning and seeing a sleighing party, with sleigh bells ringing and girls laughing and merry young men squiring them, glide by in the snowy street below.

She had felt so hopeless, so ground down, that she had almost run away.

But with the spring everything had changed. Vanessa Snipes, who hated her, went back to Lincoln, and a new student had arrived, a wealthy merchant's daughter from Essex, Reba Tarbell.

71

The lonely girl from the Colonies at last had found a friend.

And with that friendship she rediscovered London. In the freshening air of spring the old city—so newly reconstructed since the Great Fire, some twenty years ago, had leveled the quaint medieval town—seemed to open its heart to her. Now she had enough money to accompany the girls on their outings. Her young heart was light as she rode across the cobbles in hackney coaches or prowled the little shops. With the other girls she munched hot roasted chestnuts bought from street hawkers and viewed the city from London Bridge while the White Tower gleamed in the sun. All the pageantry and pomp, the great gray buildings of commerce, the scarlet coats of "Chelsea Pensioners," the colorful processions that wound through the crowded streets or floated down the Thames on barges, seemed to reach out to her so that afterward, she would always hold London in affection. When Big Ben chimed she would look up from some tiresome lesson and smile, and on Sundays, when all the world seemed to peal, she would find herself humming, like any English schoolgirl:

> *"Oranges and lemons,*
> *Say the bells of St. Clement's.*
> *You owe me five farthings,*
> *Say the bells of St. Martin's.*
> *When will you pay me?*
> *Say the bells of Old Bailey.*
> *When I grow rich,*
> *Say the bells of Shoreditch.*
> *When will that be?*
> *Say the bells of Stepney.*
> *I do not know,*
> *Says the great bell of Bow."*

And Carolina, lighthearted and laughing at last as she strolled with the other girls through the green vistas of Hyde Park, watching the rich and the royal ride by on glossy horses beneath ancient trees, did not care if she ever grew rich. With the other girls, she watched the changing of the guard before Whitehall or St. James, and was breathless at the sight of white-plumed helmets and scarlet coats and flashing steel breastplates or blue coats and red plumes, so vivid against a backdrop of silver-gray stone and what seemed to her enchanted archways. She roamed teeming markets, jumped out of the way of gilded coaches, and stared at passing chimney sweeps in their black clothes and tall hats, at masked ladies and soberly dressed bankers with gold chains. Young and far from home, she sprang past aged flower sellers into doorways to escape the sudden drenching of London's ever changeable weather—and was happy.

Summer had sped by and early autumn, with banks of fog rolling in from the Thames.

Now it was late fall. All week the city had been shrouded by fog. At least one wag had muttered that the fogs misting up from the Thames this past week were thick enough to cut with a knife. But that was yesterday. This morning a clean crisp wind from the west had blown the fog away, and all London seemed to be outside, celebrating this welcome change in the weather.

The students of Mistress Chesterton's School for Young Ladies, out for the first time since the fog had closed in the city, were filing two by two behind majestic Mistress Cardiff, one of the school's instructors—and walking eagerly for today, as a great treat, they were to attend a play at Drury Lane.

"I'm told the last headmistress would never have allowed it," whispered Reba Tarbell behind her hand to Carolina. They were roommates and trailing last in the trim line of girls that had just turned a corner into the Strand and found it jammed with hackney coaches, carriages, horsemen and—darting between them at their peril—pedestrians. "We're lucky we weren't here during *her* reign!"

For it was old Mistress Chesterton of whom Sally Montrose from up the James had complained so much. The new headmistress, young Mistress Chesterton, had inherited the school from her aunt. Indeed, had she

73

known what young Mistress Chesterton was like, Carolina rather wondered if she would have thrust the entire purse of gold her father had given her into Hugh's eager bumbling hands that morning when he saw her off aboard the *Bristol Maid* and—to her mother's vexation—broke through the little knot of people around her and threw his arms about her and gave her such a resounding kiss that she was nearly toppled from her high red heels. For young Mistress Chesterton, who had taken possession of the school while Carolina was on the high seas, was a far cry from her farthingale-wearing aunt: for one thing she was slender and fashionable, she did not wear somber black, but peacock blue and scarlet and other vivid colors. For another, she had a lover.

"I wish I'd known about the change," said Carolina wryly, looking down at the rather worn sprigged calico which she had brought from home and which looked considerably less smart than the clothes of the other girls, who were wealthy merchants' daughters.

At that precise moment a roguish wind—one of the capricious winds which had been buffeting the city all morning—whipped down the street and carried Carolina's calico skirts and light chemise up around her thighs.

The sight of those dainty silk-stockinged legs emerging from a froth of delicate ruffles was too much for two hackney drivers who, their minds momentarily not upon the traffic, locked their wheels together and were promptly beset by a third driver who managed to get his reins entangled with a passing carriage whose horse, more used to country lanes than to crowded town thoroughfares, had zigged when he should have zagged.

Overcome with blushes as she frantically fought her flying skirts back down to her ankles, Carolina raised her head and found herself looking directly into the face of a gentleman in a tricorne hat whose hackney driver had been the initial cause of the accident. The gentleman watching her from the hackney window had a handsome face and a florid complexion beneath his sand-colored curls. He was dressed in tawny orange satin. And now he looked her appraisingly up and down and then, to her fury, he winked at her.

What, did he think her some passing trollop or serving girl that he could be so familiar? Carolina's aristocratic head went up and she whirled on her high red heels and refused to look at him. With her cheeks very red she passed on down the street beside a giggling Reba, who was wearing heavy damask skirts and thought the whole incident very funny.

Carolina felt that London had changed her. Actually her changing looks this past year had made a different impact on the world about her. She had blossomed suddenly from a coltish young girl into a young lady of blazing beauty—and the incident in which the sight of her had distracted the hackney drivers for an unwary moment was mute testimony to the effect she had on men.

She was too young yet to know her power or how to wield it, but she knew that the people around her were suddenly different. Her schoolmates sometimes gave her envious glances; young Mistress Chesterton frowned at her thoughtfully; apprentices—of whom there were thousands in London—sometimes stopped in the street to stare; cook's helper dropped his pots and pans and blushed and stammered when she appeared—it was a whole new world that had opened up to her there in the sheltered confines of Mistress Chesterton's fashionable school and she did not know how to deal with it yet.

Now Reba leaned her luxuriant red curls closer and murmured with a throaty chuckle, "*You* were the cause of that accident—you and your legs! Tell me, when you get home will you use them to run for the Marriage Trees?" For Reba knew all about her sisters' elopements.

"I may never go home," said Carolina with a toss of her head.

"I'm surprised they haven't already dragged you back!"

Carolina was surprised too, and at first, hurt that in

75

her rare letters her mother never mentioned her return. But she was adaptable and beginning to feel at home in London.

"I won't go!" she told Reba blithely.

Indeed, the Eastern Shore had faded from her mind as the intrigues of life at Mistress Chesterton's school captured her attention. The girls whispered excitedly about Mistress Chesterton's clandestine affair, Madge Wentworth had invented a lover and some wild tales that had kept them agog for a fortnight, Binnie Chase had come briefly into the limelight when her brother had been accused of murder but that had died down when a suicide note had been found, and Lina Delford was so homesick that she enlisted the aid of all the girls in detailing imagined horrors of the school to her parents in endless letters which were all ignored.

Carolina's closest friend was still red-haired Reba. She had taken one look at Carolina in her worn and none too fashionable clothes and promptly proffered her friendship, which had helped Carolina's status at the school enormously, for Reba's father was a very rich merchant with a handsome estate in Essex.

It had never occurred to Carolina to wonder why stylish Reba, who mostly kept to herself, evading the childish pillow fights and other rowdy behavior of girls still children at heart, should have chosen to bestow her friendship on a Colonial whose wardrobe was easily the worst in the school. It had never occurred to her that Reba, who had inherited her father's keen bargaining sense along with his copper hair, might have a use for her. . . .

But the months had passed by and Reba had been nothing but charming. She had urged Carolina to borrow her clothes, she had shared with her a staggering array of pomades and scents, she had helped Carolina arrange a more fashionable hairstyle. Reba sat beside Carolina at table, making low-voiced comments that kept Carolina gasping with suppressed laughter. When young Mistress Chesterton had responded vaguely to Alice Lapham's question, "Did you spend a pleasant day?" Reba had muttered, "A marvelous day. Entirely spent in Lord Ormsby's arms. Her maid confirms it." When Tessa Grimes had reported innocuously that her sister Clothilde was coming down to London to visit her but would not be staying at the school, Reba had murmured, "One could hardly expect it—she'll be staying with her married lover while his wife's away in Bath!"

Close friend and confidante, Reba had learned all there was to know of Carolina's life back home in Virginia. She even knew that Farview was derisively called Bedlam by the gossips of Williamsburg. Openhearted Carolina knew far less about Reba than Reba knew about her. She knew more about Reba's wardrobe than she did about Reba's innermost thoughts. She suspected there was a lover somewhere that Reba had not told her about—at least someone for whom she yearned. But she would wait for Reba to tell her about him.

The girls had left the Strand now and reached Drury Lane. But in the milling crowd about the theatre entrance massive Mistress Cardiff had discovered an old friend from Sussex. They greeted each other joyously and the line of girls fidgeted as their chaperone enthusiastically discussed old times.

It gave Carolina time to think. So much had changed since she had left the Eastern Shore and Reba's chance remark had brought it all back to her. She had been so homesick at first, and had felt so strange in this large bustling uncaring city. She had missed her sisters and her madcap friend Sally Montrose, whom she had frequently visited at her plantation up the James and from whom she had borrowed so many exciting novels, she had missed vivacious Ramona Valdez with her snapping black eyes and lustrous black hair—Ramona who had been for a while her closest friend, but from whom she never heard after that first letter telling her she was betrothed to the new Governor of Havana. Ramona had drifted away into another life, it seemed, just as she herself had drifted away.

Everything was so changed. . . .

Poor Virginia had indeed fled with her lover toward the Marriage Trees, but it had all ended in disaster. They had made an unfortunate choice of mounts and one had gone lame barely five miles from home. Rather than try to make it riding double, they had returned for fresh horses and the miller's son, always hungry, had decided there was time for lunch. They had looked up from their meal to see the family returning unexpectedly early.

Virginia had lost her chance. Her mother, who did not see the miller's son make his escape before their arrival, brought news that her father had betrothed Virginia to Algernon Vance, only son of Lyle Vance of Clannington Plantation. It was an excellent match for the "homely Lightfoot daughter" and Letitia had been exasperated when Virginia had promptly burst into tears.

The miller's son had heard about the betrothal and, believing his true love had changed her tune, had taken the gold Virginia had entrusted to him and promptly married a farmer's daughter and gone north to live near the Falls of the James. Virginia, bullied by her mother, had capitulated and married Algernon in a driving rain; the groom had caught pneumonia and was dead within the month. Pregnant and heartsick, Virginia was back home again, for Algernon's grieving mother could not bear the sight of her, believing it was "overstraining" on his honeymoon that had run down his resistance. She might have been able to return to Clannington Plantation in triumph had she borne a boy, but she had fallen downstairs and suffered a miscarriage and so— widowed and no better looking—she was now permanently "at home" unless her mother could again arrange a suitable marriage, which grew less likely every day.

Carolina had shuddered when she had learnt Virginia's fate. Nothing like that was ever going to happen to *her!*

But now, of course, there was hope for Virginia. For Fielding's brother Darren, never much of a sailor, had taken a boat alone across the Chesapeake. When a sudden squall came up he had capsized and drowned—without leaving a will.

And so Fielding the Disinherited had come at last into his father's fortune. All of it. And as a result the house on the York was no longer a foundation and a dream but was nearly finished. *"And it is to be the handsomest house in all the Tidewater,"* Virginia had written excitedly. *"And we are soon to move in. I am very glad about it all,"* she had added honestly. *"For Mother is so occupied with fabrics and furniture and paint colors that she has put my problems into a back pocket. I doubt I will be able to bear up under the pressure when we finally do move in and Mother decides to 'launch' me."*

Thinking about it, Carolina's young face grew bleak. If she returned to the Eastern Shore, she too would be "launched" and her mother would attempt to decide her future for her. It was a daunting prospect.

She came back to the present when Reba nudged her.

"Look at that!" she whispered, and Carolina's attention was drawn to a statuesque brunette who was wearing so many bright magenta ruffles that she resembled a large puff. Along with the other girls, she watched in fascination the painted women (who must surely be actresses with all that makeup) and a motley collection of gentlemen surge back and forth in front of the theatre. With her attention thus diverted, she never saw the tricorne gentleman in tawny orange who, having deserted his hackney coach, was just now striding toward them. He had not seen them yet for the crowd still obscured his view but his blond head was swinging as his blue eyes searched the crowd for the girl he had glimpsed on the street corner.

But the handsome attire of the group of schoolgirls and their carelessness with their purses had not gone unremarked. A cutpurse now edged close to the end of the double line of girls. Seeing Carolina's velvet purse dangle unnoticed from her gloved hand, held only by a plaited silken cord, he promptly snatched the purse and ran.

79

Carolina's reflexes were excellent. She had noticed the slight pull as the silken cord parted company with her glove and whirled in time to catch sight of a narrow fellow in brown wool who was even now darting through the crowd back toward the Strand.

With an angry cry, Carolina darted after him. For the purse, while it contained but one gold piece and that a present from her mother sent inside a letter, *did* contain a most entertaining letter from Virginia. Carolina had meant to reread the letter tonight, especially the part that said, *"A friend of Aunt Pet's told her he saw Emmett when he was in Philadelphia last month and that Penny is not with him. When he asked Emmett about her, Emmett grew red in the face and refused to discuss it! He just said he was leaving the city for good and wouldn't say where! Mother is writing to everyone she knows in Philadelphia in an attempt to find Penny's whereabouts, but if Penny doesn't want to be found, I'm sure she won't be!"*

There was more and now this thief was running away with it!

In her wild charge as she tried to follow the twisting individual ahead of her, Carolina tripped over an accomplice's outstretched foot and was catapulted directly into the arms of the gentleman in tawny orange who had stepped forward and now caught her soft form as it plummeted into his. He looked down for a hot moment into the lovely upturned face with its flashing silver eyes looking over his shoulder at the departing thief, noted the soft lips into which her unbelievably white teeth were clenched—and tightened his grip.

Lord Thomas Angevine regarded his struggling catch with delight. A glorious creature this! He thought he had never seen a girl so pretty—although in truth he had thought that before about other girls, for to Lord Thomas new loves always burned the brightest.

"Well, well," he murmured, making no move to release her.

"Let me go!" cried Carolina. "I am chasing a thief who has stolen my purse!"

Lord Thomas's sandy head swung round but he made

no move to release her. "It would appear the fellow is gone now," he said politely. "Did you lose much?"

By now Carolina had recognized him as the gentleman who had winked at her when the wind blew her dress up, and an angry red flush spread over her face. He had followed her here!

"If you do not let me go—" she threatened, but she was never to finish her sentence. Mistress Cardiff had been attracted by the commotion, observed that Carolina was the center of it and now, moving with surprising swiftness for one so large, had caught up with her.

"Carolina!" she said severely. "Come away at once. You are disgracing us!"

"My purse has been stolen!" cried Carolina wrathfully. "And this stupid fellow that I crashed into as I pursued the thief won't let me go!"

Mistress Cardiff's huge bulk stiffened. She gave the "stupid fellow" a daunting glance. With alacrity he released Carolina.

She turned to glare at him as Mistress Cardiff hauled her away by the arm. "You have cost me my purse!" she accused.

"What color was it?" he called after her.

"Dark blue velvet!" She might have said more but that Mistress Cardiff was shushing her.

"I'll look for it," he called.

At that she turned to give him a grateful glance and he swept off his tricorne and made her an elegant bow. As he straightened up, the sun and wind both caught his fair hair and Carolina caught her breath. For a moment he might have been The Golden Stranger of her unforgettable dream. She was jerked from her sudden reverie by Mistress Cardiff, who propelled her forward.

"Into the theatre, girls," she piped, with that voice that was so tiny for one so large.

The play was Wycherley's popular comedy *The Country Wife*, but Carolina never remembered later what it was about. Somehow the actors seemed faded and overwhelmed by that one startling image she had seen outside the theatre of a golden stranger smiling as

81

he doffed his hat to her. And she only nodded absently when, on the way home, a giggling Reba reported how Mistress Cardiff had blushed at the dialogue and even given one shocked involuntary gasp of, *"How* could young Mistress Chesterton recommend such a play to her students?"

Since that time it had been reported excitedly by several of her schoolmates that the tawny orange gentleman had been seen several times passing by the school—he must have followed them home after the play! Always Carolina had been in class or otherwise occupied.

Carolina had been moved to stand frequently by the window and study the street below. Once she thought she saw a figure there but she could not be sure and she quickly turned away lest she seem to be displaying too much interest in who was out there—for she was determined not to pursue, but to be pursued!

And pursued she was, for the following Sunday, with the merry sound of church bells pealing all over London, Carolina's "admirer," as he was called, had shadowed the girls not only to church but to the Sunday morning market in Petticoat Lane.

And on the girls' next outing the jaunty young gentleman with the slightly risqué air was right on hand, matching his stride to theirs—albeit slightly behind and on the other side of the street—and studying Carolina narrowly, much to the interest of the other girls.

Their object today was to explore the new St. Paul's Cathedral which had been built to replace ancient St. Paul's, whose 460-foot spire had dominated the city's skyline until it had burned in the Great Fire some twenty years ago. But while the girls might lack interest in architecture, they were all fascinated by Carolina's "admirer."

"There he is again, that man who's been following us," whispered Geraldine Darvey excitedly. She tapped Carolina, who was walking just ahead with Reba, on the shoulder with her velvet muff. "Oh-h-h, isn't he dreadfully handsome?"

82

"Stop turning to stare, he'll think we're interested!" Reba snatched her new green hat, bought yesterday, to keep the gusty wind from taking it and shivered in her thin fashionable green cloak. For all that they had had several warm days it was still late fall and a chill wind was now blowing from the North Sea.

Carolina, who was wearing a dark blue broadcloth cloak borrowed from Reba, cast a slanted look toward the young gentleman in tawny orange who strolled across the narrow street, pacing them as he whistled a tune. Then her gaze picked out Mistress Blanton, marching at the head of her charges, who—Mistress Cardiff having contracted a cold at that "shocking play" at Drury Lane—was chaperoning the girls today.

It was too bad the headmistress had chosen Mistress Blanton, she thought regretfully. So much better if it had been lively young Mademoiselle Vaupier who was supposed to teach them French but told them naughty French stories instead—Mademoiselle understood about tawny young gentlemen. But Mistress Blanton was old and heavy and severe and very very deaf and she had long since given up the idea of taking a lover—if indeed she had ever considered it.

Not so the young headmistress! For a green and gold coach with the Ormsby coat of arms painted on the door in gilt had been seen in the area, which meant that Lord Ormsby was back in town. Old Mistress Chesterton, rest her soul, had never understood how her young niece made her money stretch so far—to visits to Bath and even the Continent. Bright-eyed Jenny Chesterton, with her full red mouth and her lissome figure, had kept the truth from her, thinking, rightly, that she would have been cut out of her aunt's will—and here she was, a woman of property, in charge of a school of character and reputation! Still she had not quite forsworn her old life, although she thought she had kept her secret well. Jenny would have been appalled to learn that her wealthy charges guessed her every move. When Lord Ormsby was in town, Jenny Chesterton sometimes chose to entertain him at the school (although usually she still visited by stealth a small London flat he had taken long ago for the purpose). On days when Lord Ormsby came calling, the new headmistress bundled up her young charges, willing or no, and sent them, well-chaperoned, out on long jaunts about London. *To improve their cultural appreciation,* she was wont to say.

And to get us out of the way, someone was always bound to whisper.

This was one of those days. Even though it had turned damp and cold, the girls had been hastily put in the charge of old Mistress Blanton, the Latin teacher, with orders to take them sightseeing to St. Paul's, after which they might stroll about and have some sweets—it was all right if they returned late. And tomorrow—here the headmistress had paused and cocked her head—tomorrow they were to be off bright and early to Greenwich. By boat.

Blinking, Mistress Blanton had put on a heavy wrap to keep her rheumatism from flaring up and lumbered off, blissfully unaware that her employer was about to receive a gentleman caller.

"Do you think he'll follow us into St. Paul's?" giggled Geraldine, turning to look at Carolina's admirer.

"Of course," said Reba. "He's come this far, hasn't he?"

Before them, crowning the hill, loomed the mighty bulk of St. Paul's Cathedral, their cultural target for today.

"My Cousin George, who is studying law at Gray's Inn, says old St. Paul's was built on the site of a Roman temple to the goddess Diana," whispered Reba with an irreligious giggle as the girls filed into the vast echoing interior.

Diana, goddess of the hunt. . . . Carolina cast a quick look backward. *She* was the huntress today and the young fellow who had just unobtrusively followed them into the cathedral's dim interior was her quarry! For Carolina was young and glorying in the first blush of a beauty that would become legendary—and she was, like any immature huntress, eager to sharpen her skills.

Above them rose the high inner cupola and it was up there that a puffing Mistress Blanton led her charges. From the Stone Gallery which encircled the base of the dome, they stood clutching their hats in a whistling wind. But at least her clothes were up to snuff today. This was Reba's second-best cloak covering a dress too thin for this weather. Granted the cloak was dark and a bit plain but both cloak and dress had a *very* fashionable cut since Reba would have nothing but the latest fashion. Carolina was unaware that the very plainness of the dark blowing cloak brought out startlingly the flawless complexion and moonlight pale hair which looked like silver gilt in the dim light of the cathedral and caused the young man following to catch his breath at the glowing sight of her there, flickering like a candle in the dimness before him.

The girls caught Mistress Blanton's last words.

". . . designed by Sir Christopher Wren," she was saying, just as Reba nudged Carolina with her elbow and muttered, "He's here. I just saw him."

"Who? Sir Christopher?" laughed Carolina, who was enjoying her new notoriety.

"Oh, you know who I mean! Your admirer. He *did* follow us in."

Carolina shrugged and the girls filed up the stairs to the Golden Gallery at the base of the lantern. On the way up they paused in the Whispering Gallery to view the cathedral's cavernous interior below.

"He's waving," said Reba suddenly. "I think he wants you to—yes, Carolina, lean close to the wall, he's going to speak to you."

"But he's clear across the gallery," objected Carolina, sure that a voice that could boom across that great space would attract even Mistress Blanton's deaf-eared attention.

"No, this is the Whispering Gallery," insisted Reba. "If he whispers something at the wall over there, you can hear it over here—if you lean against the wall."

Instantly Carolina inclined her ear to the wall, entirely ignoring Mistress Blanton's trembling treble that informed them the top of the cross rose 365 feet.

"Mistress Carolina Lightfoot," said the wall. And Carolina turned with an involuntary start to view the stranger in the dim distance across the cupola.

"How do you know my name?" she whispered.

"I inquired of a friendly chambermaid at the school," was the cool rejoinder.

"Who are you?"

"I am Lord Thomas Angevine," came the answering voice. "And I have for you a dark blue velvet purse to replace the one you lost when I blocked your way on Drury Lane."

Carolina caught her breath. "It was *I* who ran into you," she protested.

"Not so," insisted her admirer sturdily. "But it is cursed hard to gain access to that school of yours. I have tried three times without success."

Carolina felt a twinge that she had not been told. "We are not allowed gentlemen callers," she explained in a breathless voice.

"Then how may I reach you?"

"We go by boat to Greenwich tomorrow," she said recklessly.

"I will see you there," came the disembodied masculine voice.

Beside Carolina, Reba was agog. "Oh, he's going now," she said regretfully, her words cut into by Mistress Blanton's high falsetto "—and the cathedral was built at a cost of millions."

"Raised by a tax on sea coal," spoke up Geraldine Darvey loudly. "*My* father thought it was a scandalous waste of money!"

Mistress Blanton heard that and frowned at this sacrilege. Huffily she led her charges down the stairs. As they clattered down on their fashionable high heels, word spread among them like wildfire that Carolina had arranged a "meeting" tomorrow with the tawny stranger.

Chapter 6

Lord Thomas Angevine's pursuit was always single-minded. True as an arrow he would home in on his target, doing his best never to be out of sight of his current objective's tossing skirts.

It was no different in this case.

When the girls' barge slipped by the red brick walls of Lambeth Palace, the splendid seat of the Archbishops of Canterbury since the thirteenth century, Reba, seated next to Carolina, muttered, "There he is!"

And Carolina turned to look into a sunny face dominated by a pair of wicked blue eyes and to see Lord Thomas bowing to her from a boat that had miraculously appeared alongside. Fortunately their chaperone, Mistress Cardiff, pressed into service despite her slight cold when Mistress Blanton's rheumatism acted up after her damp windy walk to St. Paul's, did not notice, among the busy river traffic, that they had acquired an admirer. The girls did and giggled and turned to stare.

Carolina felt acutely uncomfortable.

Thomas did not. He enjoyed causing a stir among young females.

"Have you noticed how he keeps staring at you?" whispered Reba.

Carolina had noticed. It was impossible not to notice the openly admiring gaze of the man in the next boat.

"When my brother Bertie called last evening, I asked him if he knew anything about a Lord Thomas Angevine," little Polly Moffatt had piped this morning just before they left for Greenwich. "And *he* said"—Polly's voice had fallen to a scandalized whisper—"that Lord Thomas was the wildest rake London had ever seen and that I was *not* to get mixed up with him. When I assured him that I *wasn't* mixed up with him, he said that he was quite relieved, that Lord Thomas had more bastards than could be counted and had ruined three young ladies that he knew of last season alone!"

"I am surprised the father of one of them did not force him to marry her," had been Reba's yawning comment.

"Oh, I asked him *that* and he said that none of the young ladies in question had any real *force* behind them, no fierce fathers or swordsmen brothers or powerful friends. He said they had simply melted away into wherever one goes at a time like that."

"Back home," said Carolina, frowning. "That is where they went." *Or out upon the streets!* No, that was too awful to contemplate. "They went home, of course," she said more confidently.

Now, looking across at Lord Thomas, being rowed so nearly alongside, it was hard to imagine that he had deserted anyone. He had such an open-hearted face, such a winning smile. And perhaps it was all lies anyway. Polly Moffatt's brother could have been repeating vicious gossip circulated by Lord Thomas's enemies. And besides—her gray eyes grew dreamy, a shaded silver—a rake could *change!* With the right woman beside him, of course. . . . Her spirits soared.

The barge continued its stately way downriver toward the sea. Now they had reached that part of the river dominated by the massive bulk of St. Paul's. Here the river writhed in great sweeping curves that made the towering skyline seem to turn about and regroup. It was a dramatic view but Carolina was covertly watching Lord Thomas instead.

From the front of the barge Mistress Cardiff beckoned toward a group of buildings and gardens on shore. "Look, girls, we are just passing the Temple—see that ancient round church? It belonged to the Knights Templars in the twelfth century!"

"It's the Inns of Court we're passing," said Reba, more practically. "I have a cousin studying law there at Gray's Inn."

The adjoining boat was now dangerously close, and its passenger heard Reba's comment. "It was in those gardens that the Red Rose of Lancaster and the White Rose of York were first plucked," he commented, smiling at them. "And so began the Wars of the Roses."

Mistress Cardiff luckily did not hear his comment, and the boatman pulled smartly away to avoid some passing river traffic, but Carolina could not pull her gaze away from the young gentleman who had made the romantic comment. He was still studying her raptly. She blushed and looked away.

King's Reach, Blackfriars, Southwark, even London Bridge lined with houses that peered down at the water, passed Carolina in a kind of bright blur. She seemed to hear inner singing and it was a siren song, endlessly sweet, that lulled her senses.

Could it be that she had found The Golden Stranger . . . at last?

Her enchanted mood continued as their barge rounded the loop of the Isle of Dogs and they all disembarked at Greenwich and stared up at the white expanse of the palace with its lines of pillars on either side, double-curved stairs, and wide sweep of stone balusters.

Exclaiming about the view they would have from the top of the hill, Mistress Cardiff beckoned her charges to follow her and led them upward, trudging through groves of handsome Spanish chestnut trees toward the top, where they could observe the sparkling river winding back through the Old City. There were several other strollers out for the view on this bright day, and among them sauntered Lord Thomas. He did not bother to ascend to the top, but lingered just below, and when Mistress Cardiff, quite winded from her climb, led her charges down, he stepped forward as if to pass them.

At that exact moment Mistress Cardiff, who had turned to speak to one of the girls, tripped (Reba ever after insisted she had seen Lord Thomas stick his foot out) and Lord Thomas adroitly caught her in his arms.

With great formality he set the surprised older lady back on her feet.

" 'Tis unsteady walking here," he volunteered.

"Indeed it is," gasped Mistress Cardiff. "And I thank you, sir, for catching me. I must have caught my foot in the turf!"

"Allow me to offer my arm to assist your journey down to your barge," he said gravely.

It had been a very long time since any young man had offered to assist Mistress Cardiff anywhere—especially one so handsome as Lord Thomas. All the girls held their breath—and expelled it slowly when she bridled with pleasure and accepted the proffered arm.

They were all silent, listening to his easy banter as they went down the hill. And it was no surprise to anyone that Mistress Cardiff, on learning that his boat had mysteriously departed, offered him a place in their barge for the return journey.

"I shall find a seat back here among your charges," Lord Thomas said easily. "It will advance my education to hear you describe the sights we pass."

Mistress Cardiff pursed her lips in disappointment but he was already moving to the rear when he paused beside Carolina.

"I have been to a deal of trouble to get here," he murmured with a smile at Reba. Reba, taking the hint, rose and said vaguely, "I must speak to Binnie about my notes for Latin class."

Lord Thomas sank into the empty seat beside Carolina.

She learned a vast deal about him on the journey back up the Thames. He was unmarried, twenty-seven years old, had been educated (slightly) at Cambridge, and had traveled (for two whole years) in Europe. His father had died last year and he, an only son, had succeeded to the title and the family estates in Northampton, where his mother and sisters still resided. He had a small town house in London and an excellent income which he did not have to work for. He was in short vastly eligible, and he was telling her so.

What he did *not* tell her would have interested her even more. He had never been faithful to one woman for more than a few weeks—and usually far less. Of late he had become an even more restless lover, using tactics of "search and destroy" as he mercilessly centered his dangerous attentions on various unlucky maidens. He had been in numerous scrapes and had fought at least two duels, out of which he had come, luckily, unscathed, his opponents being even less proficient with the blade than he was. And last winter a girl he had loved and left—the impoverished daughter of an ancient house—had hurled herself into the Thames and drowned on his account.

He did not tell her any of *that*—and perhaps with reason. He could easily have assumed that gossips would tell her soon enough.

Carolina, flattered by his attentions and impressed by his travels, listened eagerly and answered all his questions.

No, she was not betrothed. "I may never marry," she told him with a slanted look through her long dark lashes.

"Ah," said Lord Thomas. He smiled that sunny smile at her and the sunlight struck his hair in a way that made her heart skip a beat. "One can only hope that you will change your mind else some poor devil be left languishing." He thought about it. "Have you considered the alternative?"

"Oh, yes," she said lightly. "I have in mind to become an interpreter. I speak Spanish fluently and know Latin—and a little French."

"Latin is a dead language," he pointed out, amused.

"I will become a translator as well," countered Carolina.

He laughed. It was a very pleasant sound. "I know only boudoir French," he admitted ruefully. "And boudoir Italian. Of Spanish I am completely ignorant."

She gave him a look. Boudoir French indeed!

"But I will be glad to trade you my boudoir Italian for your boudoir Spanish," he added outrageously.

Carolina could see this conversation was getting out of hand. It occurred to her suddenly that Sandy Randolph talked in this manner and that it always made her mother laugh. Sandy Randolph, the man everyone agreed her mother *ought* to have married. . . .

"Are you staying in London long?" she asked.

"As long as you are here," he said instantly, and she felt her heart give a peculiar thump and then surge on strongly as he murmured, "Tell me, how does one gain access to that school of yours?"

"One doesn't unless one is related to one of the inmates," she admitted with a sigh.

"Perhaps I will find a way," he said genially.

The next day he did.

Carolina was told by a smirking chambermaid that a gentleman had recovered the purse she had lost in Drury Lane and wished to return it to her personally. She tripped downstairs to discover Lord Thomas standing in the drawing room waiting for her. He was debonair as usual, and wearing an elegant suit of ivory satin trimmed in gold that seemed to light up his own sandy mane. She thought breathlessly that he looked like a golden-maned lion as he made her a sweeping bow and rose to fix his smiling blue eyes upon her.

"I really can't accept this, you know," she laughed, as he held out a dark blue velvet purse of a distinctly different shape from the one she had lost.

"Consider it not a purse, but an excuse," he declared

urbanely. "A foot in the door, a chance to get you alone."

"Not alone for long," she warned him, looking through the drawing room doorway into the empty hall. "For Mistress Chesterton, our headmistress, is expected back momentarily and she will come directly into this room when she arrives."

"Mistress Chesterton?" He thought a moment, then he snapped his fingers. "Jenny Chesterton! Yes, I think I know her. Have I not met her in Lord Ormsby's company? But"—he looked startled—"you say that she is a schoolmistress?"

Carolina choked back a laugh. "If you have met her in Lord Ormsby's company, you had best not say so! She wants none of us to know that she is his mistress!"

"Tell me," he said abruptly, "the names of your schoolmates. I realize that I was presented at the barge but I was looking at you and their names escaped me."

Surprised, Carolina reeled off their names and he nodded with satisfaction.

"But why do you want to know—?" She fell silent as Jenny Chesterton entered the room and stopped dead in the act of removing her gloves.

"Do I know this gentleman?" she asked in a frosty voice.

"Lord Thomas Angevine." Lord Thomas came to his feet and made her an even more elegant bow than he had made Carolina. "A friend of this young lady's family," he added hastily.

"This young lady is from the Colonies. She has no family friends here." She studied him. "You will no doubt be the man who helped Mistress Cardiff down the hill at Greenwich yesterday and about whom she babbled all through dinner. Carolina, you may leave us."

Reluctantly, Carolina went.

Left alone, worldly wise Jenny Chesterton gave Lord Thomas a sunny smile that matched his own. She had not accepted his breezy "friend of the family" routine. Indeed she had gazed at him from her depth of experience and known him at once for what he was: a London rake up to no good with one of her charges. Still . . . he was most attractive. There was no great hurry to close the door in his face.

"Friend of the family or no, I would like to call upon Mistress Lightfoot," said Lord Thomas bluntly.

The headmistress gave a leisurely pat to her chestnut curls.

"I am afraid that will be impossible," she said indifferently.

His smile grew even more genial. The embroidered *fleur de lis* flashed from his satin cuffs. "It is entirely possible that I am a friend of the family of more than one of your students," he remarked. "I believe I know Jane Blackwell's parents in Surrey. I am quite certain I know the little Ross girl's aunt in Kent. Come to think of it, I believe you and I have a mutual friend—Lord Ormsby."

Mistress Chesterton's smile grew somewhat stiff as he went on and her gloved fingers tapped her violet skirts. "Perhaps I could get Lord Ormsby to vouch for me. I could even ask his help in contacting the parents of your other young ladies in an attempt to verify my eligibility."

Across from him the woman in violet tensed. She knew she was being blackmailed. But she also knew that she had had a tiff with Lord Ormsby yesterday and if he withdrew his support she would be entirely dependent on this school for her income—and she could not afford to lose it. And her mirror had told her there were delicate crow's-feet lines about her eyes and the beginning of a slight droop to her chin. Lord Ormsby, if he decided to graze in other pastures, would be hard to replace. She was in no position to refuse the smiling confident man who watched her cat-a-mouse.

Her hazel eyes hardened. "Very well," she said briskly. "Since you come so—so well recommended." Her voice shook a little. "I will reconsider. You may call upon Carolina."

"And take her out walking?"

She nodded, frowning.

94

"Unchaperoned," he added lightly. "Since I am such a close friend of the family."

Mistress Chesterton looked astonished. Such a request was surely unthinkable. Even he——! She looked into his glittering blue eyes and saw there a hardness that matched her own. If she did not yield he would not hesitate to bring her house down about her ears.

"Yes," she choked. "But if you get her into trouble—!"

"Why, then I must be prepared to deal with it," he said silkily. "As indeed I will. Shall we say that I will call tomorrow afternoon and take Mistress Carolina for a stroll?"

Jenny Chesterton nodded silently. She had been vanquished. After Lord Thomas had gone she sat for a long time with her head in her hands and then rose to peel off her gloves and go back to her room. She felt old today and—worse—she was beginning to look old. *And what happened to roses after they lost their bloom?*

When Carolina, curious to see if Lord Thomas was still there, found an excuse to come downstairs and passed her in the hall, the headmistress gave her a rather wistful look.

The girl is lost, she was thinking. *But*—she realized cynically—*she will no doubt enjoy the road to her downfall!* Certainly she herself had enjoyed it when Lord Ormsby had discovered her, thrown from her horse and limping, on a country road, and forthwith had taken her into his carriage and not long after into his bed. . . . Her expression changed to envy as she watched Carolina's lighthearted walk and swinging skirts. *Oh, to be that young again!*

"However did you manage it?" Carolina asked breathlessly, when she found herself the next afternoon, strolling unchaperoned down Drury Lane with Lord Thomas.

"I persuaded your headmistress that I was indeed a friend of your family," he told her. "And on the basis of that, she agreed that I could take you out whenever I liked."

Carolina gave him an uncertain look. She did not

know how he had gotten around Mistress Chesterton, but she did not think the sophisticated headmistress had bought *that* story!

"This is the first time I have seen you wear a mask," he said, smiling down at her as he guided her past an orange vendor. The mask was black. He approved of it—it gave her an enchantingly clandestine look.

"It is the first time I have worn one," admitted Carolina ingenuously. " 'Twas Mistress Chesterton's idea. She met me as I was going out and told me that I should have a care for my complexion, that London's soot would leave its mark if I did not—and she gave me this mask. I think that was very nice of her," she added.

Lord Thomas laughed. Jenny Chesterton was afraid her young charge would be recognized, perhaps by the mother of one of the girls, and the school would fall into disrepute. "Very thoughtful of her," he agreed dryly.

Carolina gave him another puzzled look. *That* explanation had not yet occurred to her, for back in Virginia her mother—when she noticed Carolina at all—had usually been chiding her for not wearing a hat in the sun.

But whatever magic Lord Thomas had used to persuade the headmistress to give Carolina so much freedom did not seem to matter. In the crisp late fall weather Carolina found herself whisked away to plays, she walked beside Lord Thomas in the gardens of the Inns of Court and leant down to bury her hot face in the last late-blooming roses that haunted sunny spots, while Lord Thomas paid her extravagant compliments.

He was forever inviting her to visit his town house and she was forever declining. For in the street he could be passed off as a distant cousin escorting her home, but if she were to venture across his threshold unchaperoned she felt she would become an object of gossip and she was wary enough to want to avoid that. For twice they had run across old flames of his—girls whose cheeks had flamed at sight of him, who had stared indignantly at Carolina and then cut him dead. And

Lord Thomas's colorful past was beginning to shape up before her eyes.

There was an even more exciting day when a coach nearly ran them down on Picadilly. Lord Thomas jerked her out of the way at the very moment that a dark-haired woman in a plumed hat leaned out of the coach and focused a pair of black accusing eyes upon Lord Thomas. "Murderer!" she hissed as the coach clattered by on the cobbles.

"Who was that?" gasped Carolina.

"An unimportant woman on some no doubt unimportant errand," ground out Lord Thomas. His ivory suit had been splattered with mud by the coach. He bent down, trying to brush it off the *fleur de lis* embroidered on his orange cuffs.

"But she called you a murderer!"

"Her younger sister drowned last winter in the Thames," he explained without looking up. "I was not even in the city at the time."

But she believes it was your fault. . . . Carolina looked down on that bent fair head. "It was an accident?"

"No, she threw herself off London Bridge." Lord Thomas straightened up and looked squarely into her eyes. His tone was crisp. "Surely it was not my fault that I could not love her!"

Carolina looked quickly away. It was a shock and yet somehow it added glamour to the handsome rake beside her. Young women threw themselves off bridges out of unrequited love for him! Another thought occurred to her—a disturbing one.

"She was—your mistress?" she asked him hesitantly.

"No, of course not," he lied. He gave her a steady look. "She was very young and she kept following me around in a most disconcerting way. When she followed me to my house in the night and I promptly sent her home in my coach, she became so upset that she leaped out of the coach and threw herself off the bridge before my coachman could stop her."

Hanging on his words, believing him, Carolina did not notice the contradiction in his story—not then.

It was only one of many stories that kept cropping up about Lord Thomas, and Lord Thomas denied them all.

Carolina, young and desperately in love, chose to believe him.

"He isn't *bad*," she told Reba defensively. "Despite what they say of him. He is a victim of circumstance in every case."

"Unlucky," echoed Reba in a disbelieving tone. She gave her friend a cynical look. "Has he asked you to marry him yet?"

"No-o-o," admitted Carolina. "But"—she laughed—"he's asked me to do everything else!"

"You could do worse than marry him, you know."

"Yes." Carolina blushed. "I have been thinking on it."

And she had. She had imagined herself strolling beside Lord Thomas beneath the elms of his country estate, arranging hunt balls, riding to hounds, coming down to London to her town house, which would have to be redecorated, of course. Lord Thomas had told her it was very shabby and his latest ploy to lure her there had been to ask her advice as to how it should be redone.

"I'm completely ignorant of these things," he had argued. "I'm in need of your good taste and advice, Carolina."

That had been in late November. They had been good-naturedly sparring about the matter ever since.

Lord Thomas, used to easy conquests, had been surprised at the difficulty he was having bringing this tantalizing American beauty to his bed. True, she would kiss him in the shadows of old overhanging trees, and once or twice in darkened doorways—always, then, he was surprised at the passion of her response—but she would not cross his threshold, she would not go upstairs in inns, insisting she preferred the common room to the private rooms upstairs.

A most obstinate female—but endlessly desirable. Sometimes when he touched her hand he could feel his whole body heat up just at that casual contact.

He redoubled his efforts.

On Monday he told her he loved her. He had said that before but this time his voice had the deep timbre that came of long practice.

Carolina was enchanted.

On Tuesday he took her to a very risqué play at Drury Lane and they ate little China oranges. Carolina, who was wearing a brilliant scarlet dress she had borrowed from Reba for the occasion, was sure several young gentlemen nearby considered her a prostitute, for prostitutes, she had just learned from their over-heard conversation, usually wore masks when they attended plays. Instantly she jerked the mask from her flushed face and sat the whole time with it in her lap. Lord Thomas, who did not follow this reasoning, viewed her quizzically. That afternoon she refused to kiss him in the shadows of a nearby alley, but she found herself thinking longingly of his "shabby" town house whose interior she had never seen.

On Wednesday he took her (scandalously) to a music hall. There she was glad of her mask as Lord Thomas bowed to friends and whisked her on by—except for one sturdy young gentleman with merry hazel eyes and a dark wig slightly askew who stepped straight out in front of them, barring their way.

"Well, Thomas," he cried jovially. "This, I take it, would be the lady you've kept so well hidden from us all? Come, come, don't be shy—introduce me!"

Lord Thomas's lips compressed.

"Mistress Lightfoot," he sighed. "This bumbling oaf is my good friend, Lord Reginald Fanshawe of Ipswich, Suffolk."

"Your servant, Mistress Lightfoot." Lord Reginald made Carolina an exaggerated bow that nearly cost him his wig.

Lord Thomas frowned. "And now, Reggie, you've had your introduction and you'll oblige me by getting out of my way, for I'm in no mood to introduce Carolina to that hungry pack that's just converging on us!"

Lord Reggie looked about him, gave his wig a slap

and saw several gentlemen lounging their way. "Oh—I do see what you mean, Thomas. Yes, be off by all means and take your lustrous lady with you!"

"Come along, Carolina," said Lord Thomas grimly, and led her on a zigzag course that neatly circumvented his bright-eyed friends from intercepting their departure. He was, Carolina felt with quivering joy, trying to safeguard her reputation for it really would not do for an unchaperoned young lady to be seen about music halls! She lifted her chin proudly. She was certain now that Thomas loved her. And yet . . . and yet he had never asked her to marry him, to share his life. . . .

And then on Thursday, Lord Thomas proposed.

Chapter 7

On Friday she lost her virginity.

It all happened so simply, so naturally, that it was long after before she would ascribe it to anything but chance.

On Thursday Lord Thomas had called for her as usual and suggested a jaunt in the brisk December air. Even though Christmas was just around the corner and all the girls were making plans for the holidays, the weather had continued fair. A playful wind blew across London and sang about the chimneys. It reddened Carolina's peachbloom cheeks and made her silver eyes seem to sparkle the brighter.

Lord Thomas had called for her by coach and had taken her to the north of London and now they were strolling about on Highgate Hill. Lord Thomas, who believed all young girls to be of a fanciful turn of mind, was at his most engaging. He was telling her the lovely legend of Dick Whittington, the young apprentice who thought he heard Bow bells call his name while he rested here on Highgate Hill. He returned to discover that the cat he had lent to his master as ship's cat for a voyage had been bought by a foreign prince as mouser for his palace. Made rich by the fabulous price the cat had brought, Dick married well and became thrice Lord Mayor of London.

"The cat was Dick Whittington's good luck charm," he finished whimsically, and then, very grave, "Will you be my good luck charm, Carolina? Will you marry me and grace my days?"

The sky above them was very blue, the noise of the city seemed to have stilled. Carolina stood dizzily beneath this endless blue vault and considered the sandy-haired man before her.

Thoughts flooded into her mind of her own bickering parents back in Virginia, of their jealousy, of how gossip said they sometimes strayed to other arms. And there were those stories about Lord Thomas's wicked past—stories she had not believed, of course. Still . . . there had been other women, and perhaps Thomas had loved them too.

"Would you be—faithful to me, Thomas?" she heard herself ask in a soft troubled voice.

"That I would." His voice was deep-timbred. Convincing.

And as he said it, Lord Thomas meant every ringing word. Caught up by her beauty, by his desire for her, he could not at the moment imagine ever leaving her side. At that moment he would have stormed a castle for her, or leaped off London Bridge. He would lie by her side, she would stay wrapped in his arms forever.

Carolina felt a shiver of intensity go through her. *Thomas had promised to be faithful.* And his voice had had the ring of truth.

It was a moment when Jenny Chesterton could have come to her aid, had she been there. She could have outlined the future:

Lord Thomas was always faithful. Until he was out of sight. Mothers of eligible daughters had wailed that it was his only failing. He had looks, charm, wealth and a fine old name. He would make *such* a desirable son-in-law—but always he escaped the net. Thomas fell madly, passionately in love—over and over again. And

102

somehow managed each time to skip away from marriage. To him every new met young beauty was a challenge, a citadel to be stormed, a love he was always instantly sure was the love of his life.

Just as he was sure this time.

Carolina was so right for him. The One Woman who could fulfill his dreams. He would never want to leave her.

She felt the deep intensity of his feelings for her in Thomas's rapt gaze, in the catch of his breath that was just audible, in the quick involuntary ripple of his muscles as he touched her.

And her young body and her young heart responded to that intensity—just as had so many other (and long since wiser) girls. Looking into his blue eyes at that moment, she was entranced.

"Then I will marry you, Thomas," she said in a soft vibrant voice, and all the love and loyalty that was in her shone at him from her luminous silver eyes.

His arms went round her like a benediction. It was a long and heady kiss there beneath the blue skies over Highgate Hill.

He let her go with a sigh. "Then there is now no reason why you should not come to my house and decide how you will redecorate it," he told her happily. "For God knows it needs a woman's touch!"

Carolina gave him her lovely confident smile—and tried to hold onto her swaying senses, for she was as shaken by that kiss as was he. "There is every reason, Thomas," she chided him. "For now that I am to become your wife, I must be more circumspect. You would not want me to become a scandal. Suppose your mother were to hear that I had visited you alone in your house?"

"She is in Northampton and she never hears anything," he said bitterly, for he had not expected this turn of events.

On Friday, Lord Thomas decided to give fate a helping hand.

It was raining and Mistress Chesterton in her violet skirts met him at the door when he called for Carolina.

She looked a trifle wan for Lord Ormsby had not called all week.

"Surely you are not going to take Carolina out in this weather?" she remonstrated. "Indeed you see her too often. All the girls are buzzing now—you will manage to ruin me if you insist on being so obvious!"

"The devil take your 'buzzing' girls," said Lord Thomas unpleasantly. "I thought we understood each other."

Before his cold gaze she wilted. "Very well," she said unhappily. "But do not keep her out too late."

Lord Thomas ignored that. He would keep the girl out as late as he liked!

Carolina was surprised that in this downpour Lord Thomas had not called for her in his coach, or at least a hackney. But she accepted without question his explanation that his coach had thrown a wheel and that all the hackneys were already taken due to the rain. But there was a new play at Drury Lane and they would be late if they did not hurry.

Carolina had thoroughly enjoyed the last play. She picked up her skirts, ducked her head, and hurried along the drowned cobbles beside Lord Thomas.

They were about to cross the Strand when it happened.

A wagon was lumbering by, sloshing water from its wheels, and as they started to cross the street a horseman, thinking to cut round the wagon, shot by, dangerously close. Lord Thomas jerked Carolina back —but somehow not so deftly as was his wont and she went down into the muddy cobbles of the gutter.

"Oh, Lord, are you hurt?" He was bending over her, all solicitation, awkwardly stepping upon the hem of her skirt with his muddy boot. He jumped off with alacrity but in moving aside he managed to push more of her skirt down into the muddy water.

"No, I'm not hurt." Carolina looked down ruefully at her water-logged skirts as he helped her up. "But my clothes are ruined!"

Lord Thomas contemplated the truth of that in apparent alarm.

"You cannot attend the play soaking wet—but I hate to take you back to the school in this condition," he worried.

Carolina winced. There would indeed be need of explanations if she arrived soaked and muddied! "My hood fell off, it's down there in that muddy water," she said unhappily. "Would you please rescue it?"

Lord Thomas retrieved the hood, turned it about so the water would pour off. Silently he handed it to her.

"I could take you to a dressmaker's shop," he said uncertainly. "To fit you for a new dress—but that would take some time."

Yes, and what explanation would she make at the school, for having left in one gown and returned in another? The headmistress might decide she had become Lord Thomas's doxy and forbid him to call on her! For Carolina had no idea that Lord Thomas had blackmailed Jenny Chesterton into letting him squire her about London—she had put it down instead to his very real and compelling charm.

"I would far rather find some place to dry off," she sighed.

"Well, there's my house," he said wistfully. "But it's rather far and besides you've expressed a marked dislike for going there. But we're very near the Star and Garter—it's an inn where I sometimes spend an evening gaming in the common room. The innkeeper knows me and he's discreet. We can take a room for you and dry your clothes there."

Carolina, dabbing at her muddy skirts and entirely preoccupied with how disreputable she must look, nodded in agreement and went directly along to the Star and Garter.

There she was whisked upstairs past an innkeeper who, after a moment's conversation with Lord Thomas, turned his attention to other things. "We'll need a bath sent up," Lord Thomas called over his shoulder as he escorted her up the wooden stair. Carolina might have protested but she felt so filthy after falling into the gutter that a bath sounded endlessly desirable. She let Lord Thomas usher her into a commodious room with a very conspicuous bed in one corner. The bed had a plumped up mattress and a spotless blue quilt and looked most inviting. Quickly she averted her eyes from the bed and turned to look nervously at Lord Thomas.

"The room will be warm soon." He noted Carolina's shiver in her damp clothing as he watched the chambermaid kneel to light the fire which had been laid upon the hearth. "I'll wait for you downstairs in the common room."

He was gone and the chambermaid came up off her knees to flash a smile at Carolina. "A hot bath will cheer you up," she told Carolina blithely and went out, closing the door.

Carolina, standing before the fire, began to feel warmer. She had taken off her cloak when the chambermaid returned with a metal tub and hot water and soap. She helped Carolina undress, tch-tching at the state of her clothing.

"I don't see any towels."

"Oh, Lor', I forgot the sponge and towels! Well, no matter, I'll just whisk all these clothes downstairs to get the mud spots off and dry them before the kitchen hearth—"

"Oh, no," protested Carolina, as her chemise came off. "I'd rather—"

"It'll take them forever to dry up here," warned the chambermaid as she scooped up Carolina's stockings along with her other clothes. "Room's too damp. Landlord's too penny-pinching to light a fire till a room's taken. But there's a roaring fire down in the kitchen!"

"Oh—well, all right." Carolina snatched up the bed quilt and gathered it around her as the girl reached the door.

"You just hop into your bath before you catch cold," said the chambermaid cheerfully, departing with her arms full of Carolina's wet things. "I'll be right back with a sponge and towels."

Carolina nodded. Stripped naked now and finding that the quilt felt damp and cold in spite of the newly

106

made fire on the hearth, she tossed it aside and slipped down into the warm coziness of the tub and let the water lap over her legs and hips. It was very relaxing. Indeed the room was fast being warmed by the fire and Carolina, who had not been sleeping well of late—indeed her sleep had been interrupted by wild dreams in which she ran away with Lord Thomas to the Marriage Trees while her father shot at them—felt drowsiness steal over her as she waited for the sponge. Outside the cold rain pattered against the window panes, lulling her with its sounds that covered up other noises in the inn.

Behind her—for the chambermaid had positioned the metal tub before the hearth so that Carolina sat with her back to the door—she heard the door open and lifted up her hand for the sponge. It was promptly given to her—and a soft masculine voice behind her murmured, "Anything else I could do for you?"

She gasped and sprang up, whirling about and almost overturning the tub. She was holding the sponge inadequately in front of her and her whole body pinked at the open admiration mirrored on the face of the smiling man who stood there holding his coat folded over one arm and some towels in the other.

"Thomas!" she cried accusingly.

"The chambermaid was bringing up your towels," he told her with a grin. "I relieved her of her burden!"

"Well, put them down and go!" she told him in a suffocated voice.

"You're so beautiful," he sighed, letting his lingering gaze rove over her. "Wet or dry—beautiful." He dropped what he was holding and took the short step needed to close the distance between them.

Carolina tried to back away and almost keeled over backward as the calf of her leg collided with the edge of the metal tub. Thomas caught her wet body in his arms and she slipped downward from his grasp, splashing back into the tub. But his strong hands slid under her armpits and grasped her to him. He lifted her effortlessly. She felt his clothing slide over her naked skin as she was pulled upward against him, felt her stomach

107

glide up across his trousers, felt the slight rasp of his white cambric shirt against her tingling nipples as he dragged her slight form up along his own. The touch of him throbbed through her. It was exciting, it was nerve tingling, it gave her a wild sense of panic—she fought to free herself. Thomas's shirtfront was soaked by now from the struggle but he obviously did not care. He was holding her close, close. And then his sandy head bent down and she felt his chin, his lips wander down over her wet breasts even as his warm hands kneaded the soft flesh of her back.

"Thomas, we can't—no. *No*, Thomas!" Even as she struggled she was crying out softly, trying not to arouse the inn, not to make a great scandal. For after all, weren't they to be married soon? And then a moment like this one could be an everyday occurrence. . . . "Thomas!" Her protests sounded weak even to her own ears, for as he held her, fondled her, she was being swept away by her own senses. Her heart beat unevenly, there was a flutter as of the whir of wings in her ears, she desired him—*oh, God, how she desired him!* And he was here. And the moment she had longed for was upon her.

"Thomas—no." She made a last half-hearted attempt to push him from her. It seemed to drain her of her strength. Still imprisoned within the circle of his arms, she looked up at him, saw the fiery glow in his blue eyes, felt the possessive stance of him.

"Why not?" he demanded hoarsely. "Are you not my woman? Are we not betrothed? Who is to stand in our way?"

Standing naked in the tub, pressed against his hard masculine body with the rain beating down outside and shutting out the world, she found it a very potent argument. And the girl from the Eastern Shore, who had believed herself so sophisticated, so well acquainted with the ways of men, found his words breaking through the chinks of her resistance, overwhelming her with their warm flow.

"Oh, Thomas. . . ." She spoke his name on a great inward sigh, and the patter of the rain melted into the beating of her own heart as Thomas toweled her dry. Slowly, luxuriously—and with especial impudent attention to those quivering parts that responded most readily to his masculine assault.

Her eyelids drifted closed, the damp lashes resting upon her cheeks. She could feel him lifting her, she knew he was carrying her to the big bed, that bed that had looked so inviting. . . . She felt her naked back sink into the softness of the feather mattress.

She knew she should have waited. Every feminine instinct had warned her that with a man like Thomas, one should wait until the wedding bells had pealed and the band of gold was safely around one's finger. But the lure of the rainy afternoon, the built-up tensions that she had fought so oft of late, the startlement at finding him invading her privacy, the very real love she felt for him—all had combined to veil her eyes to what might happen.

Her future was now—here in his arms. She would take the consequences. They would be worth it.

She heard, rather than saw, for her eyes were closed, the careless ripping off of his clothing. Curiosity made her dark lashes lift a bit and she saw a blurred vision of a handsome naked male with strong clean loins and a sunny cloud of hair, turned amber by the firelight.

And then he was lowering himself into the big bed above her, blocking out the light, blocking out the world. His naked body was grazing lightly over her own and she felt a quick involuntary response ripple through her senses. A sweet wild madness swept over her. His heartbeat had become her heartbeat, his lips her lips. All of her body yearned for him, strained toward him.

Exultantly he felt her swift surrender. She heard a soft pleased sound in his throat, unintelligible, satisfied. She melted toward him and let his clever fingers work their will with her.

Lord Thomas was an experienced lover—and he had waited long to snare this elusive beauty. He meant to make the most of it. Long did he dally, toying with a breast here, nipping a shoulder there, planting a sudden unexpected kiss on a tingling nipple that trembled to hardness beneath this sweet assault.

She was his now—and he knew it.

When the moment of penetration came she was ready—and even though she bit back a scream as a sudden sharp pain tore through her loins, even as she sagged, half fainting in his arms, the moment did not last.

Lord Thomas, who had hesitated lest the pain be more than she could well bear, felt the surge of passion sweep back to her, and cradled her the more confidently in his arms.

"The worst is over," he whispered. "From now on, 'tis down current all the way."

And down current it was. Caught up by his fanciful allusion, she felt herself picked up and swirled along some mighty river. The pulsing current of her own desires swept her along. There were dips and eddies when life seemed suspended, unreal, moments out of time when the world seemed far away and eternity near and real and wonderful. The touch of his strong thighs was fire, the touch of his fingers flint to kindling, the soft encouragement of his voice a goad unneeded as she rode with him through the wild rapids, on an ever ascending scale of passion. And went over the roaring falls at last as passion peaked, to drift down softly, endlessly, in a bridal veil of foam to a warm sweet-flowing river that received them gently on its breast.

"I never imagined that it could be—like this," she whispered, with her face pressed against his chest.

"Oh, yes," he murmured, resting. His hands moved over her body skillfully, feeling every naked part of her, making her heart flutter again and again, arousing those strange new feelings that would not be denied.

Until at last he entered her again and they made love again and shared all the delights and intimacies that lovers know.

It was a long lovely afternoon and it left her spent and feeling somehow wise and changed.

And she *was* changed, for after all she was no longer a girl—she had become a woman.

His woman. And soon to be his bride.

She reveled in the thought of that, lying there lulled by the sound of the rain, listening to Lord Thomas's steady breathing. For after the exertions of the afternoon, he had drifted off to sleep and now lay relaxed beside her, his battle won.

Abruptly the world came back to her. She must return to the school and at once—she had a reputation to protect! Had her mother not said wryly that reputation was a woman's dearest possession and most easily lost? There were some who would have snickered that her mother had not practiced what she preached, but Carolina was not one of them. She had listened and she had taken the words to heart.

The play would be long since ended. She must get back to the school!

Hiding behind the door, she stuck her head out and saw the chambermaid at the end of the hall. She beckoned and the girl came toward her and at Carolina's whispered, "Are my clothes dry yet?" she nodded and hurried away to get them.

Very quietly, Carolina began slipping into her clothes. When she had smoothed her chemise down around her hips she paused for a moment before stepping into her petticoat to look tenderly at Lord Thomas's form lying spent upon the bed.

He looked very young lying there, with a carefree innocence about his face, so given to wicked laughter. She would always remember him like this, she told herself, on this, her true wedding night. For whatever words were spoken over them later, whatever public vows exchanged, *this* was the moment she had plighted her troth and chosen her mate. The rain coming down in sheets outside the inn window was her bridal veil, this white chemise her wedding gown, this commodious room whose fire had long since died down and that was now growing cold, her bridal chamber.

She turned and looked once more about her. She wanted to remember every detail of this room, to memorize all the furniture, so that she could remember every bit of it years from today when her children were

111

hanging onto her skirts in some drawing room she had yet to view and Lord Thomas, their father, was impatiently urging his horse homeward from overseeing his proud estates.

She knew a wonderful burst of pure inward joy as she imagined their life together. A world without cobwebs and a lover to whom she had given herself without regret.

She was very young. . . .

As if at a signal, there was a discreet knock on the door and the chambermaid, with a knowing grin, held out her stockings.

"Forgot your stockings, I did," she muttered, and tried to peer inside.

Cheeks flaming, Carolina snatched the stockings, choked a "Thank you," and closed the door in the curious girl's face. Everything was too new, too tender for public view. Even the hot emotions of the last several hours were too fresh and raw to be spoken of.

Those muttered words, that quick closing of the door brought Lord Thomas awake.

"Have I slept long?" He passed a hand over his eyes and then stared at her. "But you're dressed!" He sounded almost accusing for he had thought to have one last romp with her before he returned her to that brood of females at the school.

"No, not long. And of course I'm dressed." She was tugging on her stockings as she spoke, blushing as he admired her legs. "I must get back—do you want me to become a scandal?"

He sighed, lying there looking at her in the last glow of the fire. She was the most fabulously constructed female it had ever been his good fortune to meet. Her skin was satin, and her slender body seemed to have no bones. She was wonderful.

"Come here," he said in a rich, yearning voice.

"No." She gave him a wary look. She was putting on her cloak. "I must hurry else I will be late for supper and have to account for my absence."

He sighed again. Wonderful she was, desirable she was, but she had certain irritating qualities. Among

112

them was this unfortunate passion for doing the correct thing.

But there was always tomorrow.

Lord Thomas gained his feet in a single bound, stretched—noting in amusement that she hastily averted her eyes from his supremely masculine figure— and silently began to dress. Halfway done, he began to circle the room toward her but she backed away from him.

"No," she said. And again more firmly, "No, Thomas. You must take me back to the school."

With a sigh of regret, he capitulated.

That Saturday she let Lord Thomas take her to his town house, for was she not his already? And the servants would hardly dare to whisper against someone who was soon to be mistress of the house!

The house was smaller than she had expected and although the original furniture had been handsome, the draperies rich, both were now very worn and shabby. Obviously it had not been redecorated for at least a generation.

"You see?" he said ruefully. "I told you it needed renovation."

She drifted from room to room, murmuring phrases like, "Green would be best here, I think," and "That orange is awful," and "A few touches of red would do wonders for the library," and "I wonder how the arm of that chair got that deep gouge?"

Lord Thomas could have told her. It was on this spot that his one-time French mistress, Paulette, had tried to stab him—and stabbed the chair arm as he dodged. Lord Thomas was awfully grateful to that chair. But he doubted Carolina would approve of the story. So he followed her, smiling and silent—and stopped her in the last bedroom.

"I think I feel the need of a nap," he said huskily.

She laughed and—more sure of herself than she had ever been—let him close the door and lead her to yet another big bed, this one a handsome fourposter with a threadbare monogrammed silk coverlet.

And another afternoon flew by in an ecstasy of

touching and laughing and yearning and feeling emotions surge into her very soul.

"Doesn't your mother ever come to London?" she wondered, as they were dressing, her body still aglow with the wonder of it all.

"No, she isn't well and prefers to stay in Northampton."

Carolina digested that. "Do we journey to Northampton then?" she asked at last. "So that I can meet her?"

Lord Thomas looked up from pulling on his boots, which he had worn against the inclement weather which had persisted until today. "No, I'll be going home for the Christmas season," he said lightly. " 'Tis best I see her alone, Carolina, for her heart is very weak. Any surprising news might send her into an attack. I must break it to her very very gently." His voice had grown pleasantly vague.

"But after Christmas?" she insisted.

"After Twelfth Night I'll be returning to London, and then we'll see." He grinned, and nipped at her ear.

Carolina eluded him. She was frowning. "Will I see you tomorrow?" she demanded.

His sandy brows shot up. "Of course! Do I not always follow you to church and skulk along behind you, watching your hips sway as you walk?"

She laughed in spite of herself. "Yes, you always do, Thomas," she admitted.

"And so I will tomorrow," he declared.

But the next day, after a long wicked afternoon spent in his arms in the big bedroom of his town house, he told her that a friend of his was getting married down in Kent and he was to be a member of the wedding party.

" 'Tis not something I can avoid," he told her almost pleadingly. "Faith, I'd rather be here with you. But Roger will think me daft if I fail him at the last minute. Could you come along?"

She knew she could not go. The headmistress might countenance her spending her afternoons with Lord Thomas but would never allow her to go away with him to Kent.

"How long will you be gone?"

"A week," he said casually and her face fell.

"Thomas." She looked down very fixedly at her shoes. "If you are to be gone a week, that will bring us very close to the Christmas holidays. Will I see you before you go home?"

"Of course!" He sounded astonished. "Does the sun light my days? I'll see you on my return—honor bright!"

But something unforeseen happened that week in Kent—which turned out after all to be only five days. Young Mistress Chesterton, who was a distant cousin of the bride's and thus had been invited, chose to attend the ceremony on the off chance of seeing Lord Ormsby, who had vanished from her life as abruptly as he had entered it.

He was not there and when she realized he was not there, her face, so bravely made up, looked very haggard.

It was at that precise moment that she looked up and saw Lord Thomas Angevine, one foot on the hearth rail, drinking a stirrup cup, for he had just come in from riding. She drifted toward him and managed a moment alone with him.

"You're looking very well, Mistress Chesterton," he greeted her coolly, for he did not like the malevolent expression in her eyes.

"Let us have no discussion of how *I* look," she said waspishly. "It is Carolina who has stars in her eyes these days, and a certain disheveled look to her hair that I well recognize!"

"So?" He stared down at her chestnut head coldly, determined to brazen it out.

"I will have you know, if you have been so foolish as to ruin the girl, that this is no little lightskirt from a music hall that you have deflowered. Her family may be a long way off but they have excellent connections in London. I would advise you to have a care, my lad, else they will bring you to heel—and to the altar as well!"

"The bridegroom is beckoning to me," said Lord

Thomas hastily. "We will have to resume this conversation later."

He strode away and her resentful gaze followed him. She knew the truth now: Lord Ormsby was infatuated with a younger woman; she had heard it muttered behind a fan only moments ago. Which meant she was now without a protector. And in a city where women outnumbered men several times over, that was a gloomy prospect. She was no longer in the first flush of her youth, she had been reckless with the money and gifts Lord Ormsby had so freely showered upon her. All she really had, save for some remarkably handsome clothes, was the school.

And on the school she must depend to make her living—a situation that could change to disaster if a breath of scandal were to reach the ears of the wealthy merchants and their wives who sent their daughters to her to be given the finishing touches before making excellent arranged marriages.

Lord Thomas could topple her, if he had been fool enough to ruin the girl from the Colonies!

The thought made her heart beat rather too fast and caused her to consume enough wine to make her very tipsy. It didn't help.

Lord Thomas meanwhile kept his distance. He knew when he was treading on thin ice.

And while he was avoiding Jenny Chesterton, he collided with another guest and instinctively caught her by the shoulders to set her straight.

She was small and dark and her figure was very very lush. Her ripe red mouth was pouting and her lids drooped heavily over extremely bright black eyes.

"*You* are Lord Thomas Angevine!" she cried merrily. "I know you from a description I have had of you from my cousins who are down from London. Come, they are anxious to see you!"

And Lord Thomas, glad to be borne away from Jenny Chesterton, was drawn into another group.

Shortly he was dancing with the small dark girl, whose name was Catherine Amberley, and who, it was easy to discern, was the belle of this part of Kent.

116

Shortly after that he was kissing her. Shortly after that he was asking her if she could not come up to London. He would be leaving for the holidays but there'd be several days before that. Her stay in London would be vastly entertaining—his wicked grin was promise of that!

Catherine Amberley, who was a dedicated flirt, twinkled at him from behind her fan. She *might* come, she said. *If* she could manage it. *If* her betrothed continued to have that miserable cold which had kept him from the wedding. *If* her aunt could receive her so that she would have a place to stay in London.

Lord Thomas knew when he was being baited. But her face and her figure were enchanting. He leant down and tweaked one of her curls.

"You'll come to London," he predicted in a low-timbred voice.

Catherine Amberley laughed and flirted her fan. For all that it was winter, fans were fashionable. She was of the opinion that she'd come to London too—and that she might even bed handsome Lord Thomas. After all, she was being married in three weeks' time, she did not have to be so careful—and there was always the excuse of needing some things for her trousseau to send her coachward to London.

In Lord Thomas's defense, he had not *intended* matters to turn out this way. He never did. It was just that out-of-sight was out-of-mind with Lord Thomas. His was a nature that could heat to boiling in a moment—and cool just as fast.

He had not *forgotten* the girl from the Eastern Shore, he had just temporarily pushed her to the back of his mind. For now there was a new skirt to chase—Catherine Amberlcy of the black hair and black eyes and beckoning wanton smile.

Carolina, moping about restively at the school, missing him, never guessed the truth. She thought he was spending restless nights dreaming about her, just as she was dreaming about him.

She was living in a fool's paradise. But she did not yet know it.

117

Chapter 8

Mistress Chesterton returned from Kent with her mouth in a thin straight line. She surveyed the school bitterly as she alighted from her hackney coach. Those plain straight walls were her future. Lord Ormsby was dancing attendance on someone else.

The first person to greet her eyes as she came into the front hall was Carolina Lightfoot and sight of the girl brought her grievances against Lord Thomas Angevine to a head.

"Carolina," she said as she tore off a fur tippet that seemed to be choking her, "I ran across Lord Thomas while I was in Kent."

Carolina, who had just placed her foot on the bottom stair tread preparatory to ascending, turned and swept her headmistress a very correct curtsy. "Yes, Lord Thomas told me he was to be a member of the wedding party," she murmured.

"I think you should arrange to see less of him." The headmistress's next words were delivered petulantly. "Family friend or no!"

"But—why?" gasped Carolina. *Oh, she has found us out!* she was thinking in panic.

"Because he—" Jenny Chesterton had been about to say "he womanizes" but looking into that startled face she was sure in her heart that if she said anything like that, Carolina would go storming to Lord Thomas and then what would Lord Thomas do? He would make good his threat! "He—gambles," she muttered, wishing she dared tell Carolina the truth. "I thought you should know it."

To her irritation, Carolina's face lit up. So *this* was the real basis for all the gossip about him! He *gambled!* It explained so much: the shabby condition of his town house, the fact that his mother and sisters never came to London, his reluctance to present her in Northampton when his mother was probably hoping he would bring home an heiress of the first water to set his affairs in order!

"I—I know he gambles," she told the headmistress diffidently. "But it is truly his one bad fault," she added earnestly. "I only came back to look for my Latin book. Class is about to start."

With a sense of outrage the headmistress watched her go. *You came downstairs because you heard coach wheels stop and you thought it might be Lord Thomas come calling for you*, she told Carolina's departing figure silently. But she dared not warn her; she was too frightened about her own uncertain future.

Skipping up the stairs, Carolina was jubilant. Mistress Chesterton was back from Kent, which meant Lord Thomas would be coming back too—indeed at any minute his coach might be pulling up at the front door and Lord Thomas's athletic form would leap to the cobbles and stride up to bang the big iron door knocker. And now she knew his darkest secret—and it was something she could help him with, she was sure. There was so much else to do in life besides gamble—not that there wasn't plenty of it in Virginia. She had been one of a group of interested watchers one night at the Raleigh when an entire plantation had changed hands over the dice.

And even if he did not choose to abandon gaming, even if he ruined himself, she would love him still. She

119

was thinking dreamily of a descent into a kind of roving romantic poverty as she walked down the hall and opened the door to the room she shared with Reba.

Reba, looking bored with life, was seated on the edge of the feather bed. It had sunk with her weight and ballooned up around her striking crimson dress for Reba was partial to red. Now she looked up from buffing her nails with a piece of chamois.

"Well, was it Lord Thomas?" she demanded.

"No, only Mistress Chesterton. She was pulling off her furs as if they strangled her and she told me Lord Thomas gambles."

"All men gamble," said Reba calmly. She held up her left hand and studied her nails. "Except my father. *He* schemes. And Mother won't allow cards in the house even though they're the fashion."

Carolina looked surprised. From an easygoing aristocratic background herself, she was always surprised when the remnants of Puritanism turned up in Reba's. She had visions of Reba's mother as a dour upright woman who wore subdued colors and starched aprons abrim with lace. A woman of vast housewifely virtues and sadly lacking in charm.

"Well, at any rate we can expect Lord Thomas soon," said Reba cheerfully, tossing away the chamois as they prepared to go to Latin class.

But the day passed, and the next—it snowed, it rained, and the mixture turned to ice—and still Lord Thomas had not arrived. Carolina felt crushed. He must have gone away to Northampton for the holidays —and surely he had passed through London on the way, and yet he had not tried to see her, had left no message. He had gone away without telling her goodbye!

Mistress Chesterton looked upon Carolina with fleeting sympathy and secret satisfaction. Perhaps the affair was over? Lord Thomas had certainly shown a marked interest in the Amberley girl in Kent.

"Perhaps he stayed over in Kent," she suggested at dinner when Carolina asked her diffidently if by chance

Lord Thomas's coach had passed her on the way back to London.

"Yes, perhaps he did," murmured Carolina. But she did not believe it. Nor did Reba, who greeted the suggestion with a thoughtful frown as she spooned up her inevitable small custard dessert. For Mistress Chesterton kept a lean table, her excuse being that the girls must not be allowed to grow fat and unmarriageable while they were in her charge.

"You might go looking for him," Reba suggested after dinner when she and Carolina were again alone in the big front bedroom they shared.

Carolina, who was standing by the window watching the snow come down through the soft blue dusk, shook her head. She felt hurt that Lord Thomas had not come dashing back from Kent to claim her but—she told herself there could be good reasons, of course.

"I—can't do that," she said in a voice muffled by pride.

Reba's father was not the only member of his family who schemed. Reba's auburn head was cocked on one side as she thought. "Well, you could prowl the town without his knowing it, couldn't you?"

Carolina turned to give her a gloomy look. "No. Lord Thomas would recognize me even if I wore a mask. And anyway he's seen most of my wardrobe—and yours too!"

"I have something else in mind," said Reba. "Do you remember the box I received for my Cousin George and did not bother to open? It is from his tailor and was delivered to me because George gave up his rooms when he went home to Hampshire and means to take new rooms when he returns next term to the Inns of Court."

Carolina knew that George was studying law at Gray's Inn, one of the romantic stone buildings she had smiled up at when Lord Thomas took her walking in the gardens of the old Inns of Court. Like the law, they had been there since time immemorial, she had thought, although she had never been inside any of

121

them or met Reba's Cousin George, who had always been too much the young man about town to bother calling upon schoolgirls.

"You aren't suggesting that I dress up in your Cousin George's clothes and roam the streets looking for Thomas, are you?" she gasped.

Reba laughed. "Something like that. Although I had thought you might do it in, say, a chair? Or a hackney coach? At any rate, you could alight when you chose and have a look about without fear of Lord Thomas or any of his friends recognizing you." Reba had never believed Carolina's story about Lord Thomas "protecting" her from her friends to save her reputation; she was sure in her heart that all his closest cronies knew Carolina well by sight even if they did turn their heads away when she was near.

"Oh, no—I couldn't." Carolina brushed the idea aside. "Besides," she added with more conviction, "I am sure he has gone to Northampton."

"Are you?" asked Reba, amused.

"Yes." But she did not turn to face Reba lest Reba see the doubt mirrored upon her countenance. Instead she stared out at the falling snow.

She was holding fast to something Lord Thomas had said. She had been sitting on the corner of his bed in the town house trying to pull on her stockings—no easy task for Lord Thomas kept tickling her and pulling her back into the bed.

"I hardly dare stop by London on my way to Northampton for the holidays," he had said, half seriously, as he played with her hair. "For if I see you again, I'll never get me home in time for Christmas!"

"You can ride harder," Carolina had flung mercilessly over her shoulder.

He had laughed in delight at her retort and hugged her to him, pulling her over on her back and easing the chemise she had just struggled into down off her shoulders again and over her breasts and leaning down to kiss both trembling pink nipples. " 'Tis a hard ride this time of year in any event," he told her in a rueful tone, "with the roads either slippery with ice or clogged with mud. No, I'm afraid to stop by to see you, wench—you'll take my mind off home and family!"

She had thought he was teasing at the time, but now she told herself bleakly that he had been serious. He had *chosen* not to see her on his way north and what construction could she put on that? That he no longer cared for her? No, she could not believe that—his eyes, his lips, his whole body had all told her otherwise such a short time ago.

But then, why—?

Gaming! He was a gamester! He had lost at cards. Heavily. And needed time to recoup, to raise new money. Nothing to do with her. So she lulled her sense of anxiety as she watched the snow fall upon London.

The next day brought a piece of news that turned her face pale with shock, a humiliating piece of news for it was delivered to her in public before all the girls. Little Clemency Dane, whose brother had stopped by the school in London on his way down from Cambridge to Surrey for the holidays, had taken his little sister to the theatre in Drury Lane. Clemency was the youngest of the girls, quite immature, and given to blurting out things before she thought.

"Guess who we saw at the theatre?" she cried, as she came running through the door in the lavish furs her wealthy family provided and ran into the girls coming down the stairs to supper. "And squiring the dashing Mistress Bellamy no less?"

All the girls paused to hear who was squiring Mistress Bellamy for Mistress Bellamy was a beautiful actress, notorious for her affairs. Indeed she was credited with wrecking three noble homes, and by her excessive gambling ruining half a dozen wealthy men. Her doings were the gossip of London.

Clemency, delighted to be the center of attention of the older girls, turned to Carolina, who was just reaching the bottom of the stairs. "It was *your* Lord Thomas Angevine!" she reported excitedly.

Carolina almost missed the bottom step. "Oh, it

couldn't have been," she protested, aware that all eyes were focused on her. "You must have been mistaken, Clemmie."

"No, I wasn't!" Stubbornly Clemency held her ground. "I wanted to run and speak to him and ask him why he hasn't been to see you lately but my brother said it wasn't seemly and dragged me away."

"And well he should," muttered Reba, glowering at Clemency. "Anyway," she added loudly, "how could you be sure who anyone was in all that crush? Did you actually see his face?"

"Well, no," admitted Clemency, crestfallen. "But I certainly couldn't mistake his clothes! That odd orange-colored suit and all that elegant gold braid and *especially* the *fleur de lis* on his cuffs—I saw those very clearly before John dragged me away."

The fleur de lis on his wide cuffs! That staggered Carolina. She had never seen cuffs quite like those and when she had commented on them, Lord Thomas had said they were of his own design. He always had a *fleur de lis* embroidered on his cuffs, he told her. A little habit he had picked up on the Continent—a kind of signature. And that odd shade of orange of his favorite suit. . . .

Clemency Dane had seen Lord Thomas all right. And squiring the notorious Mistress Bellamy! Carolina felt sick for a moment, as if she might faint.

"Come along," urged Reba beside her. "She's making it all up!"

Clemency heard that and stamped her small booted foot. "I am *not* making it up!" she shrilled.

All the girls were agog at dinner. Clemency sat sullen and pouting, wolfing down her food. But the rest of them whispered, sometimes casting a covert look at Carolina.

Mistress Chesterton noticed the little knot of heads leaning toward each other, the buzz of voices unintelligible from the head of the table. She rapped her knife upon her trencher and spoke sharply.

"Do not whisper, girls. Most impolite. What were you saying, Geraldine?"

124

Geraldine Darvey, who had just wondered aloud if either of Mistress Bellamy's two reputed children could be credited to Lord Thomas, jumped. "I was saying how I would miss London and all my friends here when my schooldays are over," she said hastily.

"A commendable sentiment." Jenny Chesterton bobbed her chestnut curls and tried to conceal her boredom. She was trying to learn to speak in clichés and to maintain a wise expression, but it went against the grain in one who had played Blind Man's Buff in her chemise in a room full of hearty half-drunk young bucks. Lord Ormsby had enjoyed rowdy games. . . . So, come to think of it, had she. She gave an inward sigh. *That* life was behind her, she supposed. And ahead lay years of what she considered martyrdom as a headmistress. In *that* her carefully cultivated autocratic manner would stand her in good stead; even though she was young it had seemed to keep the students somewhat in awe of her. All but a few. There was Carolina Lightfoot for instance, who looked directly at you and seemed to judge you for what you were inside and not for your stance of authority—doubtless the Colonies bred that kind of insolence. She wondered briefly if Lord Thomas really had dropped the girl, and how she would take it if he had. Hysterics probably—but that could be dealt with by a good slap and smelling salts.

Her gaze passed scathingly over Carolina and softened as it fell upon Alice Lapham. A lovely girl, Alice. So docile, so sweet. She was completely unaware that under the table sweet Alice had just kicked Polly Moffatt, to make her lower her voice as Polly stage-whispered, "But does Mistress Bellamy know about *Carolina?*"

Reba heard and frowned. Seated beside Carolina, she stabbed at her pigeon pie and kept up a vivacious nonstop conversation about fashion dolls, and how her London dressmaker had received a new shipment of them from Paris. But Carolina showed little interest in fashion dolls. She sat silent beside Reba, answering only in monosyllables, staring down at her plate. She felt her life had ended.

Thomas was false to her. He had come back from Kent—but only to squire a famous actress about the town. A woman more experienced, more scintillating, and doubtless—from a man's point of view—more desirable. He had forgotten her. . . . The pain of it pierced clear to her heart. She felt like weeping, like gnashing her teeth and rending her clothes, the way women did in plays. And now it came back to her stabbingly—something Thomas had said when that woman had called him a murderer. He had said, "Her younger sister drowned last winter in the Thames. I was not even in the city at the time." And *then* he had said, "When she followed me to my house in the night and I promptly sent her home in my coach, she became so upset that she leaped out of the coach and threw herself off the bridge before my coachman could stop her." He had been lying to her even then! And she—fool that she was—had been too blind to do more than bob her head at everything he said. *She had believed him!* Her face grew hot as she thought about it.

It didn't help that as they all trooped upstairs after supper, little Clemency Dane, still smarting from Carolina's disbelief and Reba's disdain, flounced up to deliver a parting shot.

"If you'd let me finish before," she said with a toss of her childish curls, "I could have told you that I asked my brother if that wasn't Lord Thomas Angevine. And he said he didn't know but that he'd seen the same fellow last night at the Star and Garter with her, and since Mistress Bellamy is so beautiful he inquired who she was and was told that it was a famous actress from Drury Lane which this gentleman in orange had brought to the Star and Garter these past several nights, and he'd understood he brought her here because she loved to gamble and there was usually a dice game going on in the common room. And my brother heard several gentlemen chuckling about it, and *they* said that she was reduced to gambling at inns ever since she had overturned a table full of money in a fit of rage at one of the gaming houses when she lost. Afterward she was barred from all the gaming houses who used to

126

let her in and *that* was why the gentleman in orange brought her to the Star and Garter!"

Head high and with enormous dignity, Clemency picked up her expensive bronze skirts and swished past Carolina and Reba up the stairs.

"I've a mind to box her ears!" said Reba, glaring after her.

But Carolina had no mind to box anyone's ears. Her desolate gaze followed Clemency, who probably didn't know what havoc she had created. It was true then, for she had no reason to doubt indignant little Clemmie. With an aching sense of loss, she plodded on up the stairs. It was a relief to reach her room and throw herself down upon the bed.

"Don't grieve for him, Carolina," Reba advised pityingly. "He isn't worth it."

Carolina turned sideways on the bed and looked at her. Her cheeks were tear-stained. "The awful thing is that I really don't know," she said huskily. "I know Clemmie *thought* she saw him, but did she? *Did she really?"*

"There's one way to find out," said Reba steadily, eyeing her.

"Yes." Carolina sat up with decision. If Lord Thomas was still in London and squiring an actress about, she wanted to know it! "There's one way to find out. Where is that suit of your Cousin George's?"

The tailor's box, when Reba opened it, surprised them both. Carolina's gray eyes widened as Reba drew out an ice green satin suit heavily decorated with silver braid.

"But it's *gorgeous!*" she gasped. "I wonder your Cousin didn't stay in London to collect it!"

"Oh, I knew it would be," laughed Reba. "George is a true peacock!"

"Of course," added Carolina, for sight of the beautiful suit had made her spirits rise inexplicably, "I realize that when I do find Thomas there will be some perfectly good explanation of the whole thing. He will have accompanied that woman only because his coach broke down as he was leaving Kent and she took him into

127

hers, or one of his horses slipped in the mud on the way here and was injured and he stayed out of concern for it and finally let her pick him up in her coach—" Her voice dwindled away. She didn't really believe what she was saying.

Reba gave her friend a cynical look. Carolina might make all the excuses for Lord Thomas she liked but *she* was of the firm belief that no coach breakdown would have kept Lord Thomas from London. If his horse had been injured he would simply have had the poor beast shot, for his impatience was famous. As for his striking up a chance acquaintance with the actress, *that* was perfectly possible, but where had it now led?

"At least now you'll know," she told Carolina bluntly.

"Yes." Carolina didn't meet Reba's eyes. "Now I'll know."

"We can bribe Angie the scullery maid to let you out and then back in again. Geraldine Darvey says she's done it for others, that it's all in the way you ask her. I'll just get Geraldine!"

When she came back with tall reed-slender Geraldine in tow, Carolina was holding up the ice green suit, surveying it with measuring eyes. Geraldine was in animated conversation with Reba as they came through the door.

"I'll go down and ask Angie for you, if you like," Geraldine told Carolina. "She won't mind. I remember before you came"—Geraldine had been a student at Mistress Chesterton's longer than anybody else—"she used to let Eleanor Wattle out and in. Night after night. Of course that was before Eleanor Wattle ran away with her lover."

Carolina looked up sharply. She hadn't heard about Eleanor Wattle. "What happened to her?" she asked.

"To Angie? Nothing. Cook never found out Angie was staying up to unlatch the door."

"No—to Eleanor who ran away?"

"Eleanor? Oh, nobody knows. All we heard was that her lover left her in Dover and her parents turned her out." She hesitated. "I thought I saw her on the street

128

the last time we went to Drury Lane. She was thinner, of course, so I couldn't be sure. She was wearing a face mask but her mouth is so distinctive, the way her lips curl up at the corners."

And prostitutes wore masks to Drury Lane. . . .

"Did you speak to her?" asked Carolina.

"No. I was about to but some man swaggered up just then and spoke to her. Somehow I didn't think she knew him. But she took his arm and away she went—away from the theatre."

"I hope it wasn't Eleanor," said Carolina soberly.

"Yes. So do I."

For a moment the three girls were silent, each thinking her separate thoughts. Life, which had seemed to Carolina only yesterday like a smooth and sunny plain, was suddenly spiked and rocky. How many girls, she wondered, ended up like Eleanor, abandoned by their lovers, cast out by their families, turning away from old friends as they roamed the streets, making a shaky living from men from day to day? What happened to them when their fresh young looks turned shopworn? When they grew old or got sick? Carolina gave an inward shudder at young Eleanor's fate.

It never occurred to her to think that she was just as reckless, that she had indeed contemplated running away with Lord Thomas—that she was even now, in the back of her mind, contemplating it.

Or to think of what might happen to her if she did.

Chapter 9

Geraldine had gone to find Angie, and in the spacious front bedroom Carolina was down to her chemise and studying the satin suit which Reba had now laid out on the bed.

"You won't have any smallclothes," Reba pointed out.

"I'll do without," said Carolina grimly. If she was going to roam the London streets dressed as a man, who would know she wasn't wearing underwear?

"But we don't have a man's cloak for you, you'll freeze out there in the snow!"

Carolina shrugged. She might get awfully cold, true, but at the moment she had her anger at Lord Thomas to keep her warm. For her emotions swung like a pendulum, back and forth: *He had turned to another woman, he deserved nothing but scorn! He had not, there was some terrible mistake, he loved her!* Back and forth!

"Do you know, I really believe this will fit." Trying to control her own tumultuous emotions, Carolina held the gleaming new ice green coat with its wide cuffs against her own figure. She sighed and put it down.

Common sense was coming back to her. "Your Cousin George will kill me if I wear this suit, Reba. Suppose I tear it or spill wine on it?"

"No matter. I can placate George." Reba picked up the new suit and held the fabric close to Carolina's flushed face. "And the color suits you admirably." She laughed. "George couldn't have done better if he'd had you in mind!"

"How? How can you placate him?" Carolina demanded bluntly.

The russet eyes that were suddenly turned on her were as unyielding as oak. Reba wore the same expression her father's creditors had so often met. "Because if he complains," she told Carolina in a hard voice, "I shall remind Cousin George that I have only to tell his mother about his affair with that chambermaid he's so enamored of, and his mother will remove him from his studies at the Inns of Court and bring him home to Hampshire where he will never see her again."

"Oh, you wouldn't really do that, would you?" Carolina was shocked, for she had always felt that life was quite unfair to lovers.

"Well—at least I could make George believe I would," laughed Reba, who had long ago realized that Carolina's standards and hers were worlds apart. She had no wish to appear hard or unyielding in her young friend's view. "So you are not to worry, Carolina, you may treat these clothes as your own—and if you wreck them, I'll make it up to George by covering up his affair. For I've no doubt George will move the wench in with him again when he returns!"

"Oh, Reba, you *are* a good friend!" Carolina gave the merchant's daughter an impulsive hug.

Reba stepped back and considered Carolina's figure. "Of course you'll have to bind your breasts down else you will not look flat enough for a boy," she said critically. "But never mind, I have yards and yards of this stuff." She pulled out a length of gauze. "And it should do the trick."

Carolina gave the gauze a look of distaste. She would

have preferred to breathe during this venture but plainly it was not to be. She submitted to Reba's nearly crushing her ribs in her efforts to flatten out a pair of firm upthrust young breasts.

"Enough, Reba!" she finally panted. "I'm certainly flat enough now, but what will I do for a shirt?"

Neither girl had thought of that and they looked at each other in alarm.

"Maybe Angie can—" began Reba when Geraldine came tearing back with disastrous news.

"You can't go!" she cried dramatically. "Cook says Angie went home with a stomach ache, she won't be back till morning. And I dare not ask Cook to do it—she'd run straight to the headmistress!"

"Nevertheless, I *am* going." Carolina was struggling into the satin trousers as she spoke. At least she had a pair of green silk stockings and green garters that would do nicely! She looked up at Geraldine. "But I *will* need a man's shirt or at least something that resembles a shirt."

"But you can't go!" wailed Geraldine. "All the doors will be locked."

But having finally made up her mind, nothing could stop Carolina now. She felt carried forward irresistibly, as if she were in the first wave of a cavalry charge. Her future with Lord Thomas hung in the balance. Tomorrow might be too late!

"I'll go out the window," she said dispassionately.

"From the *second floor?* With these high ceilings?"

"Yes. There's a coil of heavy rope in one of the pantries. I saw it when I was searching for one of the maids to press my petticoat the other day."

"Well, I don't mind fetching it," said Geraldine doubtfully. "For you certainly can't go downstairs dressed like *that*." She eyed the green satin trousers dubiously. "But I still think you'll be killed."

"No, I won't. I'm used to climbing trees. 'Tis not so long a drop."

Rolling her eyes, Geraldine left the room again. When she returned she had not only the rope secreted under one of the brocade panniers that decorated her hips, but a man's shirt as well.

"It must belong to Cook's nephew," she told Carolina excitedly. "I filched it from a pile of clean laundry that hasn't been sorted yet—Cook must let him send his laundry here to be done—I'll wager Mistress Chesterton doesn't know about it! It should fit you." She held up a flowing shirt of coarse white cotton. "Too bad it's so plain; it could use a ruffle or two."

"And it shall have ruffles!" cried Reba, seized by inspiration. "I'll rip the lace ruffles from one of my chemises."

"We haven't time to sew it all on properly," objected Carolina, who was no hand with a needle.

Reba shrugged. "Then I'll baste it on with big stitches. And you'll have a spill of white lace at your wrists and a whole cascade of white lace at your throat—you can pin it in place with my emerald pin."

Carolina gave her a grateful look and struggled into the wide-cuffed, skirted coat, trying it on. She turned about before the handsome cheval glass Reba had brought with her from home. What she saw was a handsome stripling with a girl's flushed face and a thick cloud of unruly silver-gold hair. Her boots—the inclement weather made boots almost a necessity this time of year—were quite correct for a young man since there was little difference between men's and ladies' boots anyway. The trousers fitted her sleek hips admirably. "Do you think it needs a little padding in the shoulders?" she asked Reba anxiously.

"No, you're fine." Reba, who had sacrificed a chemise to the project, looked up from her hasty stitching. "I think the tailor made a mistake on the shoulders anyway. George will never be able to get into that coat. At least it fits *you!*" She laughed as she expertly bit the thread in two. "Indeed I think you're a better man than George in that suit."

"My hair worries me," muttered Carolina. "I don't see how I can—"

"Make it look like a man's periwig? Well, maybe *you*

133

can't do it and I can't do it, but Madge Wentworth down the hall could have made her way dressing wigs if her father hadn't happened to be such a successful wool merchant!"

"Madge doesn't like me," demurred Carolina with an uneasy look at Geraldine, for Geraldine was Madge's roommate and best friend. "When her betrothed called on her two months ago, she thought he paid too much attention to me and not enough to her."

"Nonsense," said Reba airily. "Madge owes me a favor. Didn't I lend her my best fur-trimmed cloak to go out walking with him? Even though I hadn't worn it yet myself!" She waved her needle peremptorily at Geraldine. "Bring Madge!"

A natural follower, Geraldine ran from the room and returned dragging her roommate, who seemed to have forgotten all animosity in the excitement of the venture.

Madge had brought with her a comb and a curling iron and she swiftly proved Reba's assessment of her prowess. She heated the curling iron in the candle flame and promptly set to work on Carolina's hair. Carolina choked back an involuntary screech as the hot curling iron seared the flesh of her neck.

"It's a small burn and it's where it won't show," Madge assured her contentedly. "And butter will ease the pain. Geraldine, do you think you could bring us some?"

Seated at Reba's dressing table, Carolina looked up at Madge in some alarm. She was almost sure Madge had let the curling iron slip deliberately for in the mirror she could see that Madge's movements were very deft and sure. Could it be that Madge was getting her revenge?

She was never to know, for after that one small burn Madge plunged into her endeavor with effortless ease. Before the hour was out she had transformed Carolina's neat feminine hairstyle into a reasonable facsimile of the great periwigs that had come into fashion when Charles II was restored to the throne and had grown in popularity ever since—a mass of fat curls that crowned the head and framed the face, hung down the back and cascaded over the shoulders.

"We *could* powder it," suggested Madge, standing back critically to view her work.

"Oh, bother powdering it," said Carolina, who was so impressed with Madge's work she had forgotten all about the burn. "What you've done is wonderful, Madge. I can't thank you enough. Indeed I wouldn't know myself!"

"And now the shirt!" Reba bit off the last thread, stood up and proffered a man's shirt so changed that they all exclaimed over it.

"Reba, you're a sempstress at heart!" laughed Madge. "Just as at heart I'm a hairdresser!"

Reba gave them a knowing smile. She'd have been a sempstress *in fact* if her father hadn't succeeded beyond anyone's expectation. As a small child Aunt Bella had actually been training her, drilling her in each stitch, for "You'll have to make your living with your needle one day, Reba, make up your mind to it!" And now her father had set up Aunt Bella (his favorite sister) in style down in Hampshire and she was sending her oldest son George to study law at Gray's Inn at the celebrated Inns of Court while Reba herself, who might have ended up a sempstress, now had London's dressmakers, with endless sempstresses, at her beck and call. How things changed! With money, anything was possible! But she didn't tell the girls that. She only smiled graciously and accepted their compliments.

Completely suited at last, Carolina studied her reflection in the mirror, turning about critically to view herself from different angles. She made, she decided, a very good lad. A trifle too pretty perhaps, too downy-faced, too delicately built, but that could seem to be extreme youth.

Reba's emerald pin flashed in the waterfall of chemise lace at her throat and wrists, Cousin George's cut-too-narrow ice green satin shoulders gleamed. And Madge's magic with her hair—which now looked for all the world like an expensive silver-gilt periwig—had completed the transformation of a winsome girl into an elegant lad. The glittering silver braid which decorated the coat made her entire front—even the wide fashionable cuffs—resemble a greensward in first frost. She moved about, studying herself in the mirror, trying to move in a less feminine and more boyish fashion.

Ready at last!

But finding a secure place to tie the rope proved an insurmountable obstacle. It would not be long enough if they tied it to the door. Not a nail in the room would support it. The big oaken wardrobe would doubtless tip over with a crash that would wake the house.

"There's nothing for it but to get some of the other girls," said Reba sensibly. "For I doubt the three of us can hold you."

By now Carolina was so eager to start her venture that she didn't care who knew about it. And noise was not a problem, as it would have been under the last headmistress. Cook slept like the dead, Angie—who wasn't here tonight anyway—didn't care, Mistress Blanton was stone deaf, Jenny Chesterton drank herself insensible each night and passed out before the moon was high—and everybody else, instructors and servants alike, slept elsewhere and came in by day. Swiftly the dramatic word was spread by Geraldine that Carolina was going out the window, Carolina was going out on the town dressed as a man—and she needed to be let down to the street below on a rope!

Whispering and giggling, they gathered in the room shared by Carolina and Reba. Everybody had a suggestion as to how to do it. They had just decided that all the girls would hold onto the rope as if engaged in a tug of war when Lina Delford, a latecomer, danced into the room and held up a small vial. "Look what my brother has sent me from Europe," she cried (thereby reminding everybody that *her* brother was enjoying the Grand Tour just like the sons of tenth-generation aristocrats). "'Tis called 'Bavarian red' and he swears in his letter that 'tis better than either Spanish paper or Spanish wool to color the cheeks to a fair blush. Would you like some, Carol?"

"Carol's cheeks are red enough," snapped Reba. "She's trying to look like a man, not like a prostitute!" And Lina subsided.

Nearby, Alice Lapham, who had trailed in with a book on cosmetics called *The Queen's Closet Opened,* which all the girls revered, lifted her head from its pages with a glad cry. "It says here that May-dew and Oyl of Tartar when mixed will remove spots on the face!" she cried happily. "Oh, indeed I must get some!"

Madge Wentworth tossed aside her comb and gave that sunny freckled face an impatient look. "Oh, *do* leave your freckles alone, Alice," she cried. "They don't look bad at all and look what happened to Jane's cousin in Surrey—*she* tried to remove a wart with boiled stone lyme and barrel soap—and she burned her face."

"Yes, she said it was agony. She should have used salted radishes in a pewter dish," murmured Jane Blackwell, letting the rope go slack in her hands as she spoke for she had just been gesturing as to how the descent should be made. Now her naturally animated face grew perfectly expressionless for she had just remembered that to change expressions was to invite premature wrinkles—her own mother had said so!

"Oh, I *dare not* ignore my freckles!" cried Alice. "For my mother says that I am so plain that I must at least have a skin like milk if I am to attract a proper suitor. *She* had a great aunt whose doctor cured *her* spots by hanging her until her face turned quite blue and then he cut a vein to let out the blood! And mother threatens to have the same thing done to *me* if I have not lost my freckles after a year in London!"

All the girls were big-eyed and silent at this drastic remedy. Tessa Grimes, who slumped and was therefore forced at home to walk about with books on her head to straighten her posture, shuddered and considered herself lucky. Even sophisticated Jane had changed her expression for a moment to horror before she recollected herself and went back to her masklike stare.

Carolina sighed. It was like this whenever they all got

137

together. Complete confusion, no organization. She took the rope and handed it firmly to Reba. "Hang onto it," she warned, "or you'll drop me into the street for there's not even ivy to cling to on that smooth brick front." And that would be a drop of over twenty feet, for the English basement accounted for six feet, the ceilings of the first floor were twelve feet high and the window out of which Carolina was about to climb was more than two feet above the floor.

"Oh, you're not really going to *do* it?" cried Clemency Dane, who was over her sulks and now felt guilty that her gossip might be the cause of Carolina's death.

"We should all be allowed to decide our own manner of suicide," quipped Madge, who was eager to learn if her contrived "periwig" passed the inspection of the town.

Carolina shrugged. She had never been afraid of heights. She was more afraid the girls would bungle it and drop her.

"At least it's stopped snowing," said Geraldine nervously. "I'm going to brush off the sill so Carol won't get her clothes wet going over it."

"Oh, don't open the window ahead of time," groaned Madge, who hated the outdoors, especially in winter. "You'll freeze us!"

Reba gave Madge a derisive look. "Don't *you* talk about freezing," she said blithely. "Carol's going out without a cloak and with no underwear!"

"Go ahead," directed Carolina. "I'm ready."

For a moment there was awed silence as Geraldine opened the window, brushed away the snow from the sill with her hands and turned with a hissed demand for a kerchief to dry it off.

The room had already turned cold and Madge had begun to shiver when Carolina swung a satin trouser leg over the sill and looked down at the icy street below. Suddenly this venture seemed very different from climbing some familiar tree where she could always stop if the ascent seemed too perilous. There was hard ice and harder cobbles below her, and a fall from this height could very well break her neck.

138

"I knew she'd be afraid to do it," giggled Clemency as Carolina hesitated.

Those words were a goad to Carolina. She caught hold of the length of rope which all the girls were now holding as if in a tug of war and began to ease herself gingerly down the brick face of the building to the icy cobbles below.

There was a brief terrible moment when she went over the sill when the rope gave suddenly and she heard a concerted gasp from the girls above her. But they quickly adjusted to her weight. Madge and Reba at least had strong hands and two of the other girls stood plump as little pillars which helped balance Carolina's weight as she was lowered down the face of the building.

Her hands felt damp and the cold struck her almost like a blow through the thin satin, but her grip on the rope was desperate. The tight binding across her breasts bothered her and interfered somewhat with her breathing, but she clung to the rope and concentrated on keeping the rough bricks from snagging or tearing her clothes during her descent.

There was a street light directly outside Mistress Chesterton's front door and that light made Carolina's descent glaringly apparent. But she had looked both ways before starting and had seen no one.

When she was halfway down, an elderly gentleman wearing a stocking cap came out of a house across the street and saw her—although Carolina did not, in her single-minded concentration on winning her way down to the cobbles alive, see him. The old gentleman paused in indignation. Young men boldly climbing in and out of the front windows of a girls' school—what was the world coming to? Despite the hour, he was half of a mind to cross the street and wake up young Mistress Chesterton and tell her what he thought of her laxness! But even as he took a step forward a slide of snow from the roof above caught him and almost buried him in an avalanche of white. When he managed to brush off the snow and get his breath, the figure was gone, the rope had been hauled up and the window across the street was being hastily—and quietly—shut.

Half frozen and nearly wetted through by the fallen snow, the old gentleman shook the snow from his stocking cap, pulled it back down over his ears, and trudged forward shaking his head. The lad was gone, the virgin doubtless left deflowered, and when he happened to run across her would be time enough to tell Mistress Chesterton what he thought of the slipshod way she ran her elite establishment.

He trudged on down the icy street while around the corner a "young gentleman" in an ice green suit of most fashionable cut shivered along the shortest path to finding a hackney or a chair.

And now that she was out on the dark cold street alone, Carolina realized the folly of her endeavor. Around her the houses were dark and shuttered against the cold. Icicles hung glittering from the dark eaves. A pale moon was staring down at the city, uncaring what it saw. She'd be lucky if footpads did not leap upon her at this hour, and she'd be no match for them! "You really should have a small dress sword," Reba had murmured, seeing her suited up like a fashionable young buck. Carolina had replied with perfect truth, "I would not know how to use one if I did!" But right now, despite her greenness with weapons, a small sword banging against her thigh would have given her comfort.

But she was in luck. Not two blocks from the school she found a hackney coach to take her to Lord Thomas's town house—for despite anything little Clemmie might have said about Lord Thomas being a recent visitor at the Star and Garter, she meant to confront him where he lived!

A servant she remembered all too well sleepily answered the insistent bang at the door knocker, and stuck his head out, peering into the night.

Carolina counted on the indifferent light and her disguise to keep her identity secret. She struck a masculine pose. "I am a friend of Lord Thomas's," she

said, speaking in as deep a voice as she could muster.
"Is he about?"

"No, sir. He's off to Northampton."

"What? At this hour?" The exclamation was drawn
from her, even though her heart sank. Lord Thomas
had most likely been in London, then, since he had left
Kent. . . .

The servant sighed. "If ye're a friend of his lordship," he said, shaking his gray head, "then ye know he
starts out when it pleases him, whether it be night or
day. Ye've missed him by perhaps half an hour."

Carolina felt suffocated when she asked the next
question. The binding around her breasts was too tight,
it stopped her breathing. "Do you think he might be
stopping by the Star and Garter on his way there?" she
managed to inquire most casually.

The old man grinned at her. "I see ye know his
lordship's ways. Aye, I think he might. I do think
though"—he leaned forward conspiratorially—"that he
may be stopping by to say goodbye to a lady before he
leaves."

A lady! Why, Lord Thomas could well be coming to
see *her,* to throw a pebble at her window in the
moonlight and wave her a goodbye on his way to
Northampton!

"Do you know who the lady might be?" she heard
herself ask.

The servant shook his gray head again. "His lordship
does not tell me these things. They come, they go."

His shrug was expressive and Carolina felt her face
coloring.

"But you're of the opinion he may end up at the Star
and Garter later for a throw of the dice?"

At so much knowledge of his lordship's habits, the
servant grew more confidential. "For a bit of play—
yes." His head lifted. "I think his lordship might be
going by way of Mayberry Street," he added vaguely.
"But he said he'd be breakfasting elsewhere and he'd
not return here till after the holidays."

Mayberry Street! That was some distance away. It

should give her time to reach the Star and Garter ahead of Lord Thomas. She could confront him there. No . . . she would melt into the crowd and observe him at the dice.

If she had known who waited for Lord Thomas at Mayberry Street, Carolina would have burned with indignation. For Lord Thomas had had instant success with Catherine Amberley and they had enjoyed three reckless nights together while her aunt was down with a cold. It was his actual intention to lure Catherine to the Star and Garter if possible and leave for Northampton from there—preferably rising from a warm bed occupied by an even warmer wench, to breakfast cozily, naked beneath the sheets, alongside her, and then begin his journey.

But the lush brunette had other plans. Even as Carolina directed her hackney driver to the Star and Garter, Catherine was ushering Lord Thomas—with a finger to her lips to command silence—into the front hall of the house on Mayberry Street. "My aunt is still suffering from her cold and the doctor has given her laudanum," she whispered blithely. "She'll be asleep soon and the servants will all be abed—we'll have the house to ourselves till morning, Thomas!"

In the face of this delightful prospect, Lord Thomas promptly changed his plans. He sent his horse back to his own stable with his groom and directions to return to Mayberry Street and wait for him outside just before dawn. He would spend the night with luscious Catherine, breakfast at the Star and Garter, and *then* leave for Northampton.

But Carolina could not know she was on a hopeless quest. It was with excitement seething in her blood that she listened, shivering, to the clip-clop of the hooves of the hackney coach horses on the way to the Star and Garter. She was on her way to Thomas!

Outside the Star and Garter she alighted, paid the driver and took a deep shaky breath.

Before her lay the acid test: the inspection of the gentlemen wreathed in pipe smoke who would be lounging about the inn's common room. But if she was going to learn the truth about Lord Thomas there was no point in hesitating. She swung the door wide and went in.

Inside the low-ceilinged common room Carolina paused and looked about her. The Star and Garter was crowded tonight, filled with smoke from long clay pipes, noisy from raucous discussion. The advent of one more young gentleman to swell the throng occasioned no notice.

Encouraged by that, for the masculine clothing she wore made her feel conspicuous and the tight gauze binding made her overconscious of her ripe young breasts, Carolina eased her way through the crowd. A quick glance around told her that Lord Thomas was not among the company and a dash of disappointment went through her. But she buoyed her spirits by telling herself that he was still saying goodbye to his friend in Mayberry Street (as indeed he was, between the sheets, and would be saying goodbye in his own fashion all night!). She was sure he would soon be coming through the doors. And, she hoped, alone! She tried to position herself so that she could view the door but all the seats seemed taken.

Then at a far corner of the room she saw a table set up for dicing and clustered around it a group of men. Her eyes gleamed. That table would be a sure lure for Lord Thomas, he would certainly stroll over to observe the play even if he arrived late intending to ride on and breakfast at some inn along the way. She would have a good view of the door from there too, for if Lord Thomas arrived with a woman she wanted to see *him* before he saw her. It would give her the edge on deciding what course to take—and with every moment that passed she grew more unhappily certain that Lord Thomas was indeed with a woman, that it had been a woman he was going to say goodbye to in Mayberry Street, and that he might well show up with that same woman dangling on his arm. And that woman would probably be the famous actress, Mistress Bellamy.

So, half right and half wrong in her speculations, but with alarm making her eyes bright and her step wary,

Carolina drifted toward the table in the back where a little knot of men observed the players. Halfway there she had to jump back to avoid a fast-stepping, blue-aproned serving maid who sidled by laughing, carrying a large tray above her head. That jump backward nearly cost Carolina, for the loud talk of a pair of half-drunk young bucks in travel-stained clothes just behind her erupted suddenly into fury as both leaped up with their hands on their sword hilts. To Carolina's intense relief—for she had stumbled almost between the warring parties—their friends promptly pulled them back down upon the wooden benches amid ribald remonstrances and calls for more ale.

The gaming corner was brightly lighted by comparison with the rest of the dim low-ceilinged room where smoke drifted blue among the rough hewn beams, for the wagers were large and the players intent on their game. Only two men among those crowded around that wooden table, set up for dicing, could be said to be truly sober. The rest were all in various stages of inebriation, ranging from drunkenly merry to completely sodden, for the holiday spirit had already pervaded London.

One of those two, a tall man in gray, had ridden hard to reach this inn and this table tonight. He had not even stopped to dine, but had tossed aside his snow-covered cloak, shaken the snow from his dark gray tricorne hat, and joined the players. Now the intentness of his expression was shadowed by the brim of that same hat, worn indoors as was the fashion. Its brim cast his lean face in shadow, allowing the candlelight from the wall sconces to play along a clean-shaven jawline of exceeding firmness. His thick dark hair, somewhat carelessly cut, was a bit too short for fashion in a day when men vied with each other in the size of periwigs that sat upon them like pagodas and streamed down over their shoulders and backs. Had he been asked, he would have said wryly that the only thing that justified such a hairy monstrosity was a cold winter. *His* dark hair was very obviously his own and it fell thick and gleaming to

144

a formidable pair of shoulders encased in dark gray broadcloth. Even the casual observer would have noted how his deep-chested frame tapered athletically to the waist, how narrow was his hip line and how long and muscular were the strong legs encased in dark gray broadcloth breeches, how light his step in his polished black jack boots. His cold gaze had briefly surveyed the company, flicked over the players with the sharpness of a sword cut, found his man, imprinted that face forever on his memory—and then he had joined in the play with all the fervor of a dedicated gambler, which he was not. For some minutes now his hard gray eyes had never left the dice—or the hands that threw them out to spin upon the table.

The other sober fellow at that table was shifty-eyed and clad in that particularly obnoxious shade of red known as puce. His name was Twist. He was by trade a gambler and he had drifted across Europe, fleecing inebriated young gentlemen where he found them—and leaving for the next town when his welcome was worn out. He spoke a polyglot of half a dozen languages but England was his home and he had drifted back mainly because of a foolish young gamester he had fleeced in Naples. Ruined, with no prospects, the lad had committed suicide and his uncles, guessing that Twist had won the lad's fortune by means other than fair, had set a hired swordsman on his trail. Their paths had crossed in an alley on the Naples waterfront and it was only by luck—and a slippery mud puddle from a recent hard rain—that Twist had escaped with his life. He had run all the way to England, for surely an Englishman born and bred could hide easier there than in some European town where he would immediately attract comment as a "foreigner." And he was back at his old ways, fleecing the unwary. Indeed he was riding high right now on what he had won only last week from a rash young gentleman from Colchester—an aspiring gamester who considered his "luck" invincible. Twist ate that kind for breakfast. Now he had a pocket full of gold and a strongbox upstairs half full of gold—mostly from that same young gentleman. Such a good haul it had been that Twist was thinking of moving on after tonight.

But tonight there was gold on the table, a crowd full of ale, and two reckless young bucks up from Hampshire for the holidays. One of them he had already broken, the other was losing steadily. Yes, after tonight he would move on. . . .

Carolina noted all of the players at a glance—and it was a pity someone knowledgeable at her elbow could not have briefed her about those two, Twist and the tall man with gray eyes, for between them they were to change her life.

THE STAR AND GARTER
LONDON, ENGLAND

December 1687

Chapter 10

With her radiant beauty, had she been dressed seductively in skirts, Carolina would have commanded everybody's attention as she joined the group around the gaming table. But dressed as a youth, regardless of the elegance of her garb, the players were impatient at having her crowd in between them, and the man on her right—a heavyset individual wearing a gravy-stained pink coat—promptly shouldered her away.

"Give me room, lad, if ye're not going to bet," he grumbled and swept his elbow around so that it nearly grazed her tightly bound breast. Not used to such rude treatment, Carolina stepped nimbly back a pace. It put her out of position to view the door—that all important portal through which Lord Thomas might soon be striding. And to regain her place she fumbled with the coins in her pocket. Thank heaven her parents had sent her money for Christmas with instructions to "buy herself something pretty in London." Her mother had suggested a ballgown, for "there will be plenty of balls, I promise you, when at last the house on the York is finished and we can move in!" Well, the money would go for something else now—perhaps she would even win! The idea exhilarated her. It would be very pleasant to have Lord Thomas arrive and see her scooping up a double handful of gold pieces from the table!

She wondered what she would say to him if he did come. It would be so obvious that *she* was now the pursuer—really, it would be very embarrassing. She almost wished she hadn't come. Let him have the dashing Mistress Bellamy if he wanted her! Much *she* cared!

But in her heart she knew that she *did* care, and she felt that if she lost him she would weep forever. And besides, she could not be left dangling throughout the holidays—she must *know*.

So—what better way to appear dashing in Lord Thomas's eyes than to be out on the town dressed as a young buck and winning at dice?

And all the while she was inwardly scolding herself. For it was inconceivable that Lord Thomas would pursue her so resolutely and then forget her in less than a fortnight!

Which only went to prove how little she knew Lord Thomas.

Fired by a desire to win, Carolina fingered her coins and began to watch the play critically. One man in particular seemed to be winning all the money. The others called him Twist. He was very thin and wearing a suit of puce broadcloth loaded with black braid. She did not like his sly pointed face or the flat rather shifty look of his pale eyes as they rested on first one player and then another, but she watched with fascination the flash of the ruby ring on his finger as he threw out the dice.

Watching, she became almost certain there was something wrong with the dice. Old Crump, who had long worked for her father, had in his younger days been something of a gamester and he had told her how dice could be drilled and weighted with lead so they would roll over the way you wanted them to. As she watched she became more and more certain she was in the presence of a professional gambler—and a dishonest one at that.

And if that were true, and *she* bet as he did, then surely she could not lose! She would startle Thomas!

She began to bet cautiously along with Twist, following his lead, play for play. And she was winning. Twist noticed what she was doing and gave her one of his blank looks, assessing her.

At first she had been afraid to bet very much, but now she grew bolder, spilling several coins upon the table. From the end of the table the other completely sober player, the tall dark-haired gentleman in the tricorne, raked her with his keen gray gaze.

She had hardly noticed him in her concentration first upon the door and then upon the dice and Twist's agile fingers. Indeed the gentleman in gray had been bent over slightly, studying the play. But now as he straightened up she was aware of a commanding figure with a hawklike face. As she met his hard narrowed gaze she blushed, suddenly uncomfortable in her boy's clothing, and looked away. But she had observed enough in that one swift glance to remember what he looked like, and the thought passed idly through her mind that although he was not nearly so fancily garbed as, say, the red-bearded gentleman in scarlet who was betting recklessly at the opposite end, he was by far the more arresting figure even in his inconspicuous grays. She looked up and caught the gaze of the dark-haired gentleman again; he was regarding her more quizzically now and she could not fathom the look he gave her. Once again she looked down, suddenly flustered, and found it hard to remember what she had bet.

She had been winning steadily, following the play of the puce-clad professional, and now, with her mind oddly disturbed by the tall gentleman in the tricorne, she decided suddenly on a reckless move. Thomas would surely be arriving at any moment—it would be wonderful if he could see a pile of gold before her! She would gamble all the money she had brought with her and all she had won on the next throw of the dice. In her excitement she did not notice that the gambler whose play she was shadowing had made but a trivial bet this time.

The dice spun out. An eight. Carolina watched with confidence. Those dice would not throw a seven!

The dice rolled over: A four—and a three. Seven.

She had lost!

Carolina looked up, stricken, and her eyes met Twist's. And although there seemed not a flicker of expression on his pointed face, she saw for a moment something grinning at her from deep in his pale eyes. Triumph, that was it—triumph that he had tricked her.

She stiffened.

"Break the dice!" she cried.

All eyes swung to her and the murmur of voices at the table was suddenly stilled. Even as Twist's puce-clad arm reached out and he scooped up the dice, she was leaning forward, snatching at his cuff to prevent him from "sleeving" them or whatever it was men did who played with crooked dice and switched them.

"Break the dice!" she cried desperately. "This man is cheating us all!"

A torrent of oaths broke from the puce-clad man before her and he shook her hand from his cuff as if it had been a feather. In a single bound he had cleared the table, almost knocking her down as his boots landed on the floor beside her, and seized her roughly by the shoulder.

"Ye'll not call *me* a cheat and live to tell of it!"

Carolina glared into Twist's contorted face. "You *are* a cheat!" she screamed, trying to wriggle free and wondering if that hard hand clamped on her shoulder was going to tear her arm from its socket.

Suddenly there was a third entrant in the fray.

From the head of the table the tall gentleman in gray had shouldered his way swiftly through the excited group and his hand closed now over the gambler's arm with a force that caused Twist's head to swing about to face him.

"Easy there, Twist," said a deep attractive voice. "Can't you see it's a wench you're holding?"

150

Twist turned back to give her a bewildered look. It would be one thing to maim or even to kill a young man who had accused him publicly of cheating, but quite another to injure a girl in men's clothing. Now his gaze took in again the quality of those ice green garments that he had already remarked and he saw what in his greed he had missed before—the peachbloom smoothness of her fair skin and flushed cheeks. It was brought home to him that the shoulder he was clenching was too soft for a boy's shoulder. His hand dropped away abruptly. "Ye'd best watch your mouth, wench," he said in surly warning and Carolina, released, took a wary step away from him.

"Go back to your game," the tall gentleman in gray advised Twist. "I'll attend to the wench and join you in a moment."

Grumbling, Twist went back to the table and the play began again—only this time there was a new hand on Carolina's arm and it held her as firmly as Twist's grip upon her shoulder had held her a few moments before —only not so painfully.

"That man cheated me!" she cried wrathfully. "I've lost all my money—and it was a Christmas present from my family."

"Be quiet," was the imperturbable advice of the man who had hold of her. As he spoke he was dragging her ruthlessly along beside him through the crowded common room. People parted to let them pass; many turned to stare over their tankards.

"Innkeeper." The man in gray now spoke peremptorily to the worried-looking individual who had heard the commotion and hurried in from the kitchen. "Can ye give me a private room to lock up this wench until she can be dealt with later? She'll make trouble if she's left near the table. She cannot be turned loose upon the town at this hour for footpads would make short work of her, and I've no mind to leave the game while I'm losing."

Carolina remembered the innkeeper, but he was looking at her now without recognition. She opened her mouth to tell him who she was and closed it again.

151

After all, how would it sound to blurt out, *You must remember me—Lord Thomas Angevine brought me here recently half-soaked with muddy water from the gutter and ordered up a bath for me!* Oh, she could not do it! She closed her mouth again.

The innkeeper looked as if he might protest such summary disposal of the girl in boy's clothing, but a sudden lowering look from the tall gentleman decided him. "There's a private dining room upstairs that's not occupied at the moment," he admitted. He moved forward, hurrying to a trot, for the tall gentleman's long stride was threatening to run over him. Carolina too found herself half running to keep from losing her footing as she was propelled along.

"Toss me the key," said the tall gentleman when they reached the door of the private dining room. He pushed Carolina inside.

Her eyes flashed silver.

"If you lock me in, I'll scream the house down!" she warned him.

"If you do," said her tormentor, and there was a wolfish gleam of white teeth as he spoke, "I'll return and bind and gag you and leave you here till morning when I can let you walk home alone in safety!"

Rage nearly overcame her. She was sputtering as the door was slammed in her face and locked.

The innkeeper made a helpless gesture as the tall gentleman stuffed the key in his pocket and clattered downstairs. Then he threw up his hands. None could say *he* ran a bawdy house—a jail would be more like it! He hurried back downstairs, hoping the raucous clamor of the common room would drown out the pounding tattoo of the wench's fists upon the heavy door.

Meantime the tall gentleman who had locked Carolina in returned to his play as if nothing had happened. His daunting gray gaze with its glitter of steel defied anyone to comment on his summary handling of the wench.

The play continued. The tall man in gray bet only minimally. Twist continued to win. Time dragged on. By now a group of roisterers at the far end of the

152

common room were clinking their tankards and bellowing out one drinking song after another to the accompa-
niment of merry laughter around the room. All that
noise effectively drowned any outraged sounds that
might be coming from the private dining room upstairs.

By now Twist had won most of the money on the
table and all but two of the players had left, disgusted.

One of those, the red-bearded fellow in scarlet,
drained his tankard, bet the last coin he had on him,
lost it, and took himself elsewhere.

That left only Twist and the man in gray—whose
hands had seemed surprisingly skillful for one who
looked more like a soldier than a gambler—as well as a
few yawning watchers.

Smirking, Twist made a large bet. He would test the
lingerer's mettle!

It was promptly covered.

"And raise you a thousand guineas," came the cool
rejoinder from the man in gray as he spilled a number
of gold pieces on the table.

Twist's eyes widened. "I have not so much money on
me."

"Oh, surely you have," drawled his adversary. "I'm
even willing to wait while you go to your room to find
it—provided these gentlemen watch the table and the
innkeeper and I accompany you to make sure you don't
have a sudden change of heart and leave by the back
door."

At this insult Twist's face turned ugly and he fingered
his small sword.

"I wouldn't," advised the tall gentleman. His own
hand had dropped and now hovered above the steel
basket hilt of a very long and serviceable blade that
hung inconspicuously at his side, partly covered by his
coat.

Twist growled, but something steady in the gray-eyed
man's countenance persuaded him not to bring matters
to a head. After all, he had his skillful fingers to count
on and he had no doubt that he could bring about an
even more satisfactory conclusion—and gain himself
another thousand guineas!

He nodded agreement and the three of them went upstairs. There the money was forthcoming—from a leathern box that Twist pulled out from under his mattress.

"Ye should keep that money with the goldsmiths, Twist," said the landlord gruffly, frowning at the sight of so much gold being stored beneath a mattress.

"I will when I've won me a thousand to match it," said Twist airily. "For my run of luck's not over yet!"

The man in gray gave him a sardonic smile.

They went back downstairs and play was resumed.

By now everybody in the common room was gathered around watching.

Amazingly, Twist lost.

He looked bewildered and his glance shot upward in alarm at his adversary. *The dice must have been switched!* he was thinking. *These couldn't be his own— he'd have won! The man in gray had switched the dice!*

Now the man in gray was drawing from his finger an enormous pigeon's blood ruby ring—Twist's mouth had watered for it ever since he had first seen it. It was worth a fortune! He smiled into Twist's avid eyes.

"This ring against the contents of your purse and pockets, Twist," he said. "And that leathern money box we saw upstairs. All your valuables."

For a moment Twist's gaze faltered. Then his mouth grew slack with avarice for the ring. His own was a fake, but this one was real! He was almost drooling as he studied it. And now he buoyed himself up by remembering contemptuously how many fine gentlemen had tried some trick to match him—and always ended up losing fat sums.

"Aye," he said, and wiped his hand across his mouth. "If *I* throw the dice."

There was a grim smile opposite him and the tall man nodded. "Agreed," he said. "With new dice."

Twist's point was a nine. The landlord had furnished these and they were honest dice.

Twist knew he could not be sure of his skill in matching that throw. He needed his own dice. He was sweating now and it gave him the excuse to pull out a dirty handkerchief and mop his brow. As he did so he palmed a pair of dice from the kerchief—a pair that could be counted on not to throw a seven. He had no mind to lose!

"Play," said the man across from him evenly.

With alacrity now, Twist picked up the dice from the table. He had big hands and he needed big hands because he now had four dice held in one of them—two he was maneuvering between his skillful fingers and two—the honest pair—were held rigidly in his palm.

He was about to throw them out when the tall man moved with a speed that none of the company later deemed credible. At one moment he was standing still across the table, then before anyone could blink, he had pounced on Twist. His hard left hand had slammed down on Twist's right wrist and he was now inexorably turning Twist's hand around so that the palm came up and four dice were exposed to view.

There were gasps and murmurs of anger from the company.

"We now know how you've been winning, Twist," said the man in gray dispassionately. "All here have seen your method." His voice rang out. "Can anyone here think of a reason why I should not kill this man?"

There were growls of assent and murmurs of "Good riddance!" The landlord blanched. A killing at his inn? He'd be accused of running a gaming house! But he dared not take Twist's part, nor did he have any sympathy for the man. Had he known Twist was using crooked dice he'd have denied him access to the table!

Twist knew he was trapped. As the tall gentleman let go of his wrist to pick up the coins he staggered back and clawed at his small sword.

He never got it from its scabbard.

In another lightning gesture the man in gray had his long sword out and its point at Twist's throat.

Now he looked down that long clean blade into Twist's terrified face and to Twist those steely eyes held the fires of hell. He yearned to kill Twist but there were reasons, good reasons, why he should not. Twist felt this urge to kill and blanched.

155

"I give you your life, Twist," said the tall man softly. "Although God knows it goes against the grain to do so. And I warn you to leave London by the shortest route for if ever you should cross my path again, I promise you no such reprieve." He laughed. "I will not even give you warning."

The sword was drawn away.

Twist swallowed. It had been a near thing. Almost holding his breath, he watched the point of that blade retreat and his left hand came up to stroke gingerly the place on his throat where the blade had almost but not quite broken the skin. Yet even in his terror his right hand was creeping to the table's edge. That sword was about to be sheathed. If he could but upend this heavy table and throw its weight against the sword's owner, it would give him time to duck past the landlord, who was no force at all, and make it up the stairs. He could grab his gold from beneath the mattress, shinny over the roof and be gone while everybody was still scrambling over everybody else in drunken confusion.

Twist tensed. The moment was now!

But even as his grip on the table whitened his knuckles, his adversary made one more lightning gesture—and this was one that would be talked about by the company for years to come.

So fast that nobody really saw the movement, he brought the hilt of his sword down with crushing force on the hand that was even now raising the table.

Twist let go of the table with a howl. The "ruby" in his ring was shattered, broken into bits of red glass. He staggered back moaning, holding his aching hand to his mouth.

The tall gentleman, who had already become a legend among those present, sighed, sheathed his sword with an easy gesture and stepped back. He observed Twist's pain without compassion. "Shall we upend him, lads, and make him pay his wager?"

There was a bellow of approval and Twist went down as rough hands tore at his clothes. They made a good job of it. They found not only his purse, but the money in his belt and in his shoes. They rushed him upstairs, where Twist's money box was turned over to the winner, the man in gray, who poured the gold into a couple of leathern purses.

"The rascal has done well these past weeks," growled one bystander who felt Twist deserved worse than he had got.

"Aye," was the grim rejoinder from the winner. "And he got most of this gold from my brother—by the same method he used tonight."

Clutched by so many ungentle hands, Twist was nearly sobbing in pain and fear and fury.

"Here, here, you can't take *all* his gold," cried the innkeeper, waking up to his own position in this thing. "He owes me for his lodgings, he does!"

A pair of bleak gray eyes were turned on him. "He'll not be paying you with *this* gold, for he's already gambled it away. I suggest you sell his clothes. His boots should bring something."

"You can't!" screamed Twist, turned pale at this new menace. "You can't turn me out on a night like this without my clothes! I'd freeze to death!"

"Why, so you might," said his adversary genially. "And rid us of you for all time." He turned and clapped the disgruntled innkeeper on the shoulder. "Take heart," he said, pouring some gold into the man's hand. "This will buy drinks for the company."

It was more than a generous amount and a general cheer went up from the group.

The tall gentleman held up his hand for silence and the cheers died down. "I make but one condition as you drink my health," he said, smiling. "And that is that this devil be gone from the inn by the time I come back down these stairs!"

There was a roar of approval and Twist was seized anew and dragged back downstairs to be divested of all but his smallclothes. To Twist it was a terrible experience. A graduate of the city's slums, he had lived his entire life by deceit, by stripping gullible fools of their money. And now he was to be turned into the street with an injured hand and without even proper clothes on his back!

157

"I'll get even with him!" he was sobbing as they pushed him out the door. "I'll get even with that gray-eyed devil if it's the last thing I do!"

The tall gentleman in gray never heard the threat. He had turned his attention to something more to his liking—the locked private dining room and the little wench who waited for him there.

He wondered what she'd have to say to him when he poured into her dainty hands all the gold she'd lost— and all her winnings too!

His hawklike face wore a wide smile as he unlocked the door—and then he hesitated, and knocked before he opened it. For his brief encounter with the silvery-haired wench had told him she was a lady born, and something deep inside him wished her to recognize in him a gentleman born and bred.

He couldn't have defined it, but the feeling was deep and compelling. And so his hand fell away from the tempestuous entry he would have made had she been a tavern wench, and he rapped twice on the door.

"Are you awake?" he called, with a trace of humor in his deep pleasant voice. "For I've come to let you out."

When there was no answer, his impatience overcame him. Asleep with her head on the table, or awake and about to brain him with an uplifted chair, he would still confront her.

He swung the door wide.

An empty room greeted him. The window was open. The bird had flown.

And the tall gentleman in gray knew a stabbing disappointment such as he had not felt in years.

She was gone, the little silver wench who had so intrigued him.

Chapter 11

Left alone in the locked private dining room upstairs in the Star and Garter, and sure after drumming on the door until her knuckles were bruised that no one was going to come to her aid, Carolina had begun to pace the floor as restlessly as any caged animal.

How *dare* he lock her in? she thought indignantly. Oh, that insufferable—! If he was going to be on her side, why hadn't he insisted that the dice be broken once she had demanded it?

It had completely escaped her—but not the tall gentleman in gray—that Twist had managed a bit of sleight of hand with the dice just before he had vaulted the table to seize Carolina. The first dice they would have found on his person, had they searched him, might even—when broken—have proved to be honest dice. Or so the tall gentleman had speculated.

Besides, Carolina was not to know that the tall gentleman had made this trip to London especially to seek out Twist and wrest from him the money Twist had won from his brother. Carolina's move had been premature; the tall gentleman had had other plans—and the tall gentleman rarely let anyone or anything stand in the way of carrying out his plans.

Knowing none of this, Carolina had little charity in her heart for the tall gentleman's actions. She yearned for nothing so much as to slap his altogether too attractive face.

And in her heart was a wail: *Lord Thomas could be coming through the inn door right now and she would not be there to greet him!*

Tired—indeed worn out from the excitement of the evening and from pounding on the door and pacing the room—she sank down upon a chair and disconsolately let her head fall onto her arms at the table. Downstairs the clamor of voices that penetrated even the thick door ebbed and flowed. She thought she caught herself falling asleep and lifted her head quickly—she was unaware that she had been sleeping the better part of two hours while below her the game went on.

But that bit of sleep had refreshed her and she began to consider her situation from a new angle. If she waited here quietly until the tall gentleman let her loose in the morning (or worse yet, he might insist on escorting her back to the school!) she would become a scandal. Indeed she might be sent home forthwith, and then she might never see Lord Thomas again.

Such a possibility was not to be borne!

She must make her escape from here.

She studied the heavy door, considered trying to crash through the panels with one of the chairs. But she decided against it. Even if she did manage to break through one of the panels—which wasn't likely—the noise of rending wood would probably be heard downstairs and excite attention. No doubt the tall gentleman would be standing with crossed arms at the foot of the stairs even as she started down from the top!

The window seemed a better possibility—but this time she had no rope, no group of friends eager to lower her down from the second floor. She went to the window and pulled aside the curtains.

And saw what would have made her eyes sparkle if

she had looked out before: a low sloping roof that slanted down from the window. If she slid down that roof (which was now covered with snow), she might be able to cling to the edge and so avoid much of a drop. Certainly it was a chance!

A chance she must take.

There was a disturbance down below, some kind of shouting and uproar, but she ignored it—she could not know that Twist had just had his hand slammed down upon the table by the man in gray who had locked her in. And as she hesitated by the window there was the thunder of feet on the stairs as the company from the common room crowded upward, dragging Twist along to make him pay off his lost wager.

She heard the commotion as if in a dream. She was concentrating on the slant of the roof, on her chances of breaking an ankle if she could not hold on at the end and fell off awkwardly.

The clamor outside her door mounted. Whatever was happening there she did not wish to be involved in it. Any scandal might see her expelled from school and sent home in disgrace.

No longer hesitant, she sat upon the sill, threw her legs over onto the roof, and pushed off. She slid downward through the snow, trying to slow her descent, but beneath her the icy surface was too slick, the incline too steep. Carried irresistibly forward, she skidded down the roof to go zooming over the edge and made a wild but silent landing into a deep pile of snow that had been shoveled up to allow patrons and their coaches and horses to have free access to the inn.

It was that heaped up snow that saved her from injury, for she might well have suffered broken bones if she had landed awkwardly upon the icy cobbles. But as she came up out of the white mound, gasping and brushing the snow away from her eyes, she saw something she had missed in her swift descent.

A man and a woman were just hurrying toward a waiting coach whose driver was muffled to the ears and whose snow-laden hat was pulled down over his eyes. The horses were stamping and tossing their manes, their breath making white clouds in the cold night air. The couple had obviously just come from the inn. Indeed, they had left the inn hurriedly for the same reason that had propelled Carolina to make her instant decision to descend via the roof—the commotion. Downstairs it had appeared that murder might be done at the dice table and neither the lady nor the gentleman hurrying toward the coach relished being caught up in yet another scandal.

Carolina saw that the woman had a very feline walk and an enormous amount of golden orange hair from which her fur-trimmed hood had fallen back, allowing the moonlight to burnish it. Her clothes were very elegant. She was wearing a fox-trimmed dark blue velvet cape. And the man beside her had a wealth of sandy hair and was wearing a velvet suit laced in gold of the same unusual shade of orange that Thomas—!

Carolina's breath caught painfully in her throat. Just then the woman gave a high tinkling laugh and said something in a mocking voice. The man flung out his arm in an expansive gesture and Carolina tensed as she saw the distinctive *fleur de lis* embroidered on his wide orange velvet cuff gleam suddenly gold in the moonlight.

That was Thomas striding toward the coach, and clinging to his other orange-clad arm was the famous Mistress Bellamy. She recognized that back, that feline walk—she had seen Mistress Bellamy once in a play.

They were *leaving* the inn, not arriving! It was even possible they had been here before she arrived, making love in some comfortable upstairs room!

"Thomas!" she choked.

The fellow in orange turned and she was startled to see that it was not Thomas's face that looked back at her. Just a man who, from the back, looked like Thomas.

"I'm—sorry," she stammered. "I thought you were—"

"Lord Thomas Angevine?" The strange gentleman in orange gave her an engaging grin. "No, I'm Lord Frederick Bates. I don't wonder you thought it was

162

Thomas for 'tis Thomas's suit I'm sporting. Won it from him over a game of whist." He chuckled and turned to the sparkling lady beside him. "You were a witness to that game, weren't you?"

There was laughing agreement from the lady, who said, "But your friend is covered with snow, Freddie. Why don't we take him with us? He's but a lad and you have a coach waiting and how is he to find a hackney coach or a chair at this time of night?"

Lord Freddie frowned and peered at Carolina. "Do I know you?" he wondered.

Carolina hesitated. "Not exactly," she admitted. "But Thomas swished me past you very fast once at a music hall—and once at Drury Lane." For now she remembered him very well as one of the friends Lord Thomas had been anxious to avoid. "Where is Thomas?"

"Gone to Northampton, I suppose. At least he was headed there." Lord Freddie squinted his eyes to give her a closer look. Suddenly he slapped his thigh. "You're not a lad! You're Carolina Lightfoot! You're Thomas's schoolgirl! I remember you now. You were at that music hall but Thomas waved me away. He was determined not to introduce me—afraid I'd try to cut him out, I suppose. But what are you doing here dressed like that?"

Carolina explained reticently that she was there on a ridiculous wager—that the girls had bet her a small fortune she wouldn't dare go out on the town alone disguised as a man. They seemed to believe her, which cheered her, for she wouldn't want Thomas to hear that she'd been out scouring the town for him! And the actress, whom Carolina took an instant liking to, found it all a wonderful joke.

"I wonder," she asked wistfully, "could you take me by the school? It *is* rather late and—"

"Late?" said Lord Freddie in surprise. "Egad, it's almost morning!"

"Of course we'll take you to the school!" By now they were in the coach and Mistress Bellamy pulled aside her velvet skirts to make room for Carolina's satin-breeched legs. "But not, I take it, to the front door?" she twinkled. "I presume you'd rather we stopped the coach a few doors away?"

"Yes, I would," Carolina said, smiling. "The headmistress is not to know I'm out and I'll thank you not to noise it around!"

Her heart felt very light. Clemmie was wrong! Thomas had been true to her, he had gone to Northampton after all! It was his friend Freddie, wearing clothes he had won from Lord Thomas, who was escorting Mistress Bellamy about the town!

Seeing that Mistress Bellamy had taken a fancy to Carolina, Lord Freddie not only directed his coachman to drive directly to the proximity of the school, he insisted on walking Carolina back there himself and making sure she got in all right.

Carolina would have preferred to make this last leg of the journey without him and was about to say so when—Lord Freddie having already sprung down from the coach—Mistress Bellamy leant forward and touched Carolina's arm.

"Never trust a man," she murmured.

Carolina gave a slight start. Did Mistress Bellamy mean Freddie or—?

"Not even Lord Thomas?" she asked in a level voice.

"Oh, especially not Lord Thomas!" Mistress Bellamy went off into peals of laughter.

Feeling slightly nettled, Carolina let Lord Freddie help her down from the coach, and shushed him all the way to the school for he was very noisy and bent on carrying on a merry conversation.

"All the girls will be asleep but if I go around to the back, I can tap on the kitchen window and if Angie is back, she'll let me in," she told him, noting uneasily that by now the sky was pinkening with dawn.

They went around back.

"You can't reach the window, it's too high for you," said Lord Freddie masterfully. Like his actress friend, he was thoroughly enjoying Carolina's escapade. "Let me do the tapping."

They were in luck. Angie, afraid of losing her job, had just got back and roused Cook, who had sent her into the kitchen to build up the fires and then gone back to bed for a few more winks.

At first Angie didn't recognize Carolina and wasn't going to let her in, but when she heard Carolina's voice she hastened to unlatch the back door. Lord Freddie promptly rewarded her with a gold coin, gave Carolina a graceful bow and went away whistling. He was relishing what a story he'd have to tell Lord Thomas—how the sweet innocent little schoolgirl he'd been keeping away from wild parties and shielding from rakes like Lord Freddie, had gone out on the town on a wager, somehow got herself locked into an upstairs room at the Star and Garter, and slid off the roof almost on top of his and Mistress Bellamy's heads! It was likely to top any tale Lord Thomas brought back with him from Northampton!

And even as Carolina made her way softly up the back stairs to let herself quietly into the room she shared with a now sleeping Reba, the tall gentleman in gray, who had bounded down the Star and Garter's front stairs with even more speed than he had gone up them, was searching London for her. He had secured a hackney coach. Fanning out in ever widening circles, his keen gray eyes that missed nothing combed the icy streets for a slight shivering figure in ice green satin. He leaped out of the coach and peered down every alley. He saw Twist, shivering and dancing up and down on stockinged feet on the icy street, being drawn into a doorway by a woman. The man in gray snorted. It seemed to him that men of Twist's stripe never suffered the fate of ordinary mortals. Luck had been with Twist; he had been taken in by a woman, probably some kindly prostitute. He turned away and continued his search. It was slow going, lurching along the dark icy streets. He discovered an amazing variety of drunks lurching home in the wee hours; he was set upon once by footpads and twice by dogs and subdued them all.

At last—and with a nagging sense of loss—he made

his way back to the Star and Garter, took a room there and left word that he was not to be disturbed till noon. Yet tired as he was, sleep eluded him. And when he did sleep it was restlessly, with troubled dreams of a silver-haired witch who came and went on a shaft of starlight, a witch with mocking silver eyes who seemed to beckon and then as he approached, to disappear.

He awoke, sweating, and wondered uneasily if she was all right, the little wench. And then laughed at himself for a fool to be so stirred by a chance meeting.

Still, he determined that tomorrow he would go looking for her again—just to make sure she had made it safely, of course. Sternly chiding himself now for acting like a fool, he forced himself to turn over and go at last to sleep. The sun was high by then, but he managed to sleep till noon.

When he woke, the memory of the girl still troubled him, and after a hasty breakfast he found himself once again roaming the city streets, staring up at the windows, combing the alleys. He tried to tell himself that, having been so long away, he was more interested in seeing London than finding the girl but at last, chuckling ruefully to himself, he admitted that was not the case. He was lured by the memory of an impudent wench who would have turned up her dainty nose at the sight of him!

Once he was very close, for his hackney coach passed by the school, but all the girls were in class at the back of the building and Carolina knew nothing of his passing.

Even though staying in London could well be dangerous to him for his face was too well known in certain quarters, the man in gray determined to stay one more night. If he had not found her by then, he would ride north, back to the home he had seen so little these recent years.

But the evening passed and another cold night went by and still he did not find her. The great uncaring city, glistening in the snow and already ringing with bells and Christmas carols in advance of the season, seemed to have swallowed her up.

The following day the tall gentleman, still wearing inconspicuous gray, rode north.

Carolina, sitting in class along with the other girls, being lectured on the importance of keeping household accounts precise and legible, had no idea her former "jailer," as she was now inclined to call the man in gray, was riding by, staring out the window of a hackney coach and studying the windows as he passed.

She *was* aware, however, that something had happened to Reba ever since she had received a letter early this morning. Reba had read it, crumpled it, smoothed it out, read it again, and finally thrown it into the fire and burned it. Indeed the delivery of the letter had waked them up when a sleepy-eyed chambermaid had knocked on their door and told Reba the letter had come from Essex by coach.

Reba had jumped up and snatched it. When finally she had thrown it into the almost dead embers of last night's fire on the hearth, she had kicked the still smoldering lumps of sea coal over the paper until it flared up and burned to a crisp.

Carolina, only half awake, had watched this performance in silence from her bed. She was amazed that Reba did not turn from the fire to ask her what had happened last night and how she had got back, for plain evidence of her escapade lay in full view: the ice green suit, still wet from contact with the snowy roof of the Star and Garter and the mound of snow into which she had plummeted, was spread out to dry over a chair, and the rope with which the girls had let her down the building wall to the street reposed in a corner.

She raised herself up on one arm, fully awake now. "I found out what happened to Thomas," she told Reba. "He went to Northampton."

"Did he?" said Reba absently.

"Clemmie saw someone else wearing his suit."

"That's nice."

Carolina stared at her friend. Could this be Reba, who had taken so much interest in helping her find Lord Thomas, who had even furnished the suit and sewed on the shirt ruffles to make it all possible? What on earth had been in the letter?

"I'm afraid I've ruined your Cousin George's suit," she told Reba apologetically as she jumped up to dress for breakfast. "And I've no money to make it good for I lost every cent gambling."

Reba gave her an unseeing look. "It doesn't matter," she said.

Carolina was burning to ask what was in the letter, but she forebore. Reba was a Long Planner. She would tell her in her own good time. But finally Carolina could bear it no longer. There were sounds of life about the school, the girls were rising. Soon somebody would be dashing in to ask what happened last night.

"Reba," she asked. "Was it bad news?"

Reba looked up, her expression still veiled. "In the letter? Oh—no. I'm going home."

There was a finality in Reba's voice that prompted Carolina to ask, "You mean, for the holidays?" Because everybody was going home for the holidays—all but herself of course, and Reba had asked her to spend the holidays with her. The family coach would call for them tomorrow.

"Not just for the holidays," Reba said, sighing. "For good. The letter was from my mother telling me to pack all my things, that I wouldn't be coming back to the school."

Carolina blinked at her. "Why? Has something happened?"

Reba gave her a sardonic look. Her answer was roundabout. "My oldest sister was married last spring to a wool merchant in Bristol where we used to live," she told Carolina. "And you remember I told you that early this fall my other sister, who's two years older than I am, married a shipowner's son in Plymouth."

"Yes," said Carolina, adding frankly, "I was surprised you didn't attend the wedding."

Reba gave a short laugh. "My mother *wouldn't let me* attend. The wedding was held at the groom's home in Plymouth. The reason given that it couldn't be held at our home was my mother's ill health, but there was no truth to that. It was because it would look strange if I didn't attend a wedding held nearby in Essex but plenty of excuses could be given why I didn't go all the way across England to attend! The truth is I haven't been allowed home since the day I was caught behind the hedge with one of the footmen."

Carolina's eyes widened. She had known that there was something mysterious about Reba's relationship with her family, but she hadn't known what it was. And Reba, for all that she talked a lot, rarely said anything about her personal life away from the school.

"Were you in love with him?" she asked. "The footman?"

Reba gave her an astonished look. "Good heavens, no! I was just terribly bored! We live out in the country now, you know—not like Bristol where there were lots of people and things to do. I was just *amusing* myself!"

Seeing the startled look on Carolina's face, Reba laughed. "Oh, nothing really *happened,*" she said. "I was just—experimenting. You know." She sighed. "But my dress was half off and—well, the upshot was that now my mother considers me 'unreliable' where men are concerned. She decided she was too busy trying to get the house in Essex in shape and trying to make her way with the neighbors to 'watch me as she should' so she stuck me down in Hampshire with Aunt Bella—George's mother."

"I'm surprised she didn't send you to her own people."

Reba gave her a droll look. "Oh, she doesn't have anything to do with them. They're all poor as church mice and live around Bristol. Mamma's family didn't want her to marry Papa because he didn't have a steady job"—actually Jonathan Tarbell had started life as a tinker but Reba chose not to add that enlightening tidbit!—"and Mamma swore if he ever made a success she'd dress up in silks and hire a coach and six and ride around in front of their houses and cut all of them dead!"

Carolina stared. This was certainly a new view of Reba's mother. "And did she?"

"She did," said Reba grimly. "And now we own the coach and six. There's only one of her blood relations Mamma speaks to. I think that's the real reason she egged Papa on to leave Bristol and buy himself 'a proper house' somewhere else. So we moved to Essex."

And promptly consorted with footmen under hedges. . . .

"Why aren't you still in Hampshire since your mother sent you there?" wondered Carolina.

Reba laughed. "Because after Aunt Bella packed George off to London to study law, Willie—her other son—came down with the pip! Willie's the apple of Aunt Bella's eye and nothing would do but that she must take him all the way to Bath where he could 'take the waters'—and she didn't want to be bothered 'watching' me along the way. So she'd heard about this very strict school in London—remember, it had the reputation of being the strictest school in London during old Mistress Chesterton's reign." Carolina well remembered hearing Sally Montrose wail about it— lights out at dark, walk with your head down, speak when spoken to, the list went on and on. "So Aunt Bella got in touch with Mamma, and Mamma said fine, and Aunt Bella brought me up to London herself and put me in school here. Of course"—her laughter bubbled up—"she didn't know that the school had changed hands and that the new headmistress wasn't quite what the old one had been! George got wind of it but I promised him I'd kill him if he told her!"

"Your Aunt Bella sounds dreadful," said Carolina with feeling. "I'm surprised you went to visit her last spring."

Reba shrugged. "I didn't. I was right here in London all the time. With a man."

"But—but her coach called for you!"

"Not *her* coach—*his* coach. I said it was Aunt Bella's coach—and Jenny Chesterton was too wrapped up in her own affairs to notice the difference! We spent two whole weeks together at rooms he took. We never went out at all!"

170

Carolina's head was whirling. Reba had never told her a thing about it! She had returned looking somehow —different, Carolina now remembered. More worldly perhaps. But then Reba had *always* looked worldly! Carolina hadn't given it a thought.

"But you—haven't seen him since, I take it?"

"No. He went away," said Reba shortly. "I've waited all this time and now, before he can come back, Mother's dragging me back to Essex. For good!" She brought her fist down on her ink stand with such violence that the black India ink spattered her lace-trimmed nightdress.

"You've ruined it!" cried Carolina, staring at the handsome gown.

"I couldn't care less," said Reba ruthlessly.

She might have said more but at that moment a bevy of giggling girls burst into the room, demanding to know from Carolina what had happened last night. They examined the water-stained suit, they listened raptly while Carolina explained why Clemency Dane was so certain she had seen Lord Thomas, and they all agreed that it was marvelous that Carolina had gone and that her escapade had ended with her meeting the scandalous actress, Mistress Bellamy, and *particularly* in the company of young Lord Freddie Bates, who everybody knew had a teenage wife in Denham who wasn't allowed to come to London lest she learn of Lord Freddie's excesses! Their excited voices chimed into a chorus.

But Carolina noticed that Reba didn't join in. She felt sympathy for her friend and a kind of bewilderment. Reba knew all about *her* affair with Lord Thomas but she had never confided in Carolina about a lover who was important enough to make her smash her ink stand—indeed Carolina still did not know his name!

She was excused from classes to help Reba pack, for the messenger who had brought Reba's letter had also brought a short note to Mistress Chesterton explaining that Reba was leaving the school and no refund for the remainder of the term would be expected. This had cheered Jenny Chesterton considerably for the school was full and she had just heard from an aunt of little Clemency Dane who desired to send her daughter there "directly after the holidays." The school could now admit the girl and Mistress Chesterton would be paid for two places while feeding and housing only one for the rest of the term.

After her first outspoken burst, Reba had fallen remarkably silent, but she kept glancing thoughtfully at Carolina as if she might be about to speak. Carolina kept on folding chemises and nightrails and bodices and kirtles into trunks while Reba tossed fans and gloves and pomades and kerchiefs and pinners—all the plunder a wealthy schoolgirl might collect—into assorted boxes.

"I will wear my plain brown worsted," announced Carolina without looking up. "And my dark blue woolen cloak. For 'tis bound to be cold in the coach."

About to toss an embroidered silk shawl in on top of her fans, Reba paused to rescue a gold pin set with an amethyst. "*And* you shall liven up the effect with my red fox tippet and fox hood and muff," she announced cheerfully.

Carolina lifted her head from the packing and gave Reba a grateful look. Reba had been so generous in letting her wear items from her wardrobe ever since Carolina's first day at the school, when she and her new roommate had dressed for dinner and Reba had studied Carolina's plain worn dress and petticoat. Casually Reba had suggested, "Do you know, my plum velvet petticoat would look much better with that lavender gown? I've never worn it so nobody will know it's mine. Why don't *you* wear it?" And Carolina had joyously accepted the petticoat and gone down to dinner with gold embroidery glittering from the handsomest petticoat she had ever worn in her life. And after dinner Reba had said lightly, "That petticoat looks *much* better on you than it does on me, and do you know, it doesn't match a thing I own? That's because *I* think plum clashes with my auburn hair." And she pressed the petticoat onto Carolina as a gift.

And gradually, encouraged by Reba, she had slipped

172

into almost regarding Reba's wardrobe as her own. But for this trip to the bosom of Reba's family, she knew she would feel awkward wearing Reba's clothes.

"Wouldn't your mother think it distinctly strange if I arrived wearing your clothes?" she asked Reba dryly.

"Oh, not a bit of it," laughed Reba. "Indeed she'd never know. Mamma buys things and forgets them! And Papa pays the bills from my London dressmaker—Mamma really doesn't know what I buy and doesn't care so long as it's handsome. You see, she was so poor when she married my father, and their first years were hard, and then suddenly they had money, always more and more of it. Mother revels in spending. She orders everything by the dozen and doesn't care what happens to it once it arrives. I assure you, she won't know you're wearing my tippet!"

Carolina's view of Reba's mother spun round again. She now envisioned a giddy female, delicate and shallow, lilting through life as she tried to match—with vast expenditures on trivial things—the elegance of the aristocrats she had so long admired.

She joined in Reba's laughter, but she shook her head. "Nevertheless," she said stubbornly. "I'm going to arrive wearing my own clothes!"

But she cast a thoughtful look at Reba. She was glad that Reba was in a good mood again but she wondered what had transformed her gloom.

She would have been astonished to know that it had been the beauty of her own face as she had looked up at Reba's remark and the brilliant sunlight off the snow outside had caught her silver-gold hair, giving her face a glorious halo.

Breathtaking, Reba had thought. *Any man would want her!* And she laughed inwardly.

She had a feeling she was about to ask Carolina to do her a favor: a favor which had to do with her absent lover and being sent home. A favor which at the moment scheming Reba considered to be the most important thing in her life. A favor that she felt—of all the girls at school—only Carolina, with her lustrous beauty, could accomplish.

PART THREE

The Betrayal

---

*Although she lures him with her smile, she knows that with
   the dawn
She'll hurry back to other arms and he will find her gone.
She knows she plays a devious part, and worries that it's
   so. . . .
Should one betray a lover? How far should friendship go?*

December 1687

Chapter 12

Beneath sunny skies the Tarbell family coach that had come south to collect Reba and Carolina from the school skidded over the slippery melting ice of London's streets. But once they had left the old city behind them and were rolling through the countryside the weather changed abruptly. The sky turned overcast as they headed northeast, driving arrow straight up the Great Essex Road—that road the invading Romans had built some sixteen centuries ago to connect London with their mighty fortress on the River Colne, Colchester.

It was snowing when they lumbered into Chelmsford, where Reba pointed out the market that had been there "since the beginning of time" and where her father sent his livestock to be sold.

"I thought he was a merchant," demurred Carolina, as they went by the square-towered parish church and drew up before an inn.

"He *is* a merchant," Reba told her blithely as they alighted. "He has ships going in and out of London all the time. His profits are fantastic—that's because he's been so lucky. Usually, oh, maybe two out of three ships get through on long voyages—maybe less. But Father's ships have always skimmed right along home!"

She gave Carolina a speculative look as they sat down in a corner of the inn's common room near a group of pipe-smoking men. "Maybe you'll be sailing home in one of his merchantmen."

But she wasn't going home. She was going to stay right here in England and marry Lord Thomas. She wasn't going home ever. Well, maybe for a brief visit but that was all. She was about to tell Reba that but Reba was busy asking an aproned serving girl what was on the bill of fare today.

"Oysters and pigeon pie," answered the serving girl politely. She gazed wistfully at Reba's furs. Reba was wearing an emerald green velvet cloak and hood trimmed richly in fox which seemed to light up her auburn hair. Carolina thought she looked wonderful.

"Good, we'll have that," said Reba dismissively. She leaned toward Carolina and nodded her head slightly toward the group of smokers. "I think one of that rough lot over there is about to come speak to us. I can see them nudging each other, egging somebody on. Quick, cast your eyes down—the coachman will be in here in a minute and he'll ward them off!"

Carolina snapped a quick glance at the roughly dressed men. They had honest faces, she thought, and would have looked right at home in buckskins. But to Reba clothes and money were everything. "I think you'd better cast your eyes *up*," she countered. "Look out the window, Reba. It's snowing harder. We may have to stay here!"

"Oh, we'll make it," declared Reba confidently. "We Tarbells have the devil's own luck—everyone says so. Remember what I told you about Papa's ships? They *always* get through!"

Carolina wondered if fate, which had so long smiled on Jonathan Tarbell, might not suddenly withdraw her favor and sink his whole fleet during one of the wild storms in the Atlantic, but she forbore saying so. The "rough lot," being ignored, took their attention elsewhere, and steaming platters of oysters and thick-crusted pigeon pie were served to the girls, along with hot spiced cider.

The weather did not improve and both girls bent over and kept their hoods half obscuring their faces in an effort to keep off the fast falling snow when they once again scurried on tall pattens to the waiting coach.

"Tell me about your lover," Carolina said, when they had been handed inside the cold coach. "What does he look like?"

Reba bent to adjust the big fur lap robe over her emerald velvet lap as she answered. "Quite tall and dark," she said. "And very dashing—in a conservative sort of way. He is much given to wearing black and gray."

She could be describing the man in gray at the Star and Garter, Carolina thought, amused. As Reba spoke, Carolina was just taking a last look outside before firmly fastening the leathern flap that kept the snow out of the coach's window on her side. She saw that a rider was just dismounting at the inn. He was paying no attention at all to the departing coach; his full attention was directed toward his horse and the stableboy to whom he was just in the act of tossing a coin.

Carolina caught her breath and forgot what she had been about to say.

The man she was staring at through the fast-falling snow—tall and with his broad shoulders supporting a gray cloak on which the snow was quickly piling up—was surely the same man who had dragged her upstairs at the Star and Garter and locked her into a private dining room to await his pleasure.

"What is it?" asked Reba curiously as the coach lurched away. "You're sitting there like a statue! What do you see out there that's so fascinating?"

Carolina had managed one more startled glimpse before the tall man disappeared into the inn. She had seen the snow crested upon a low-crowned tricorne hat, its broad brim cocked rakishly above a dark saturnine profile, which confirmed her memory. Her last view of the tall figure was as he turned with a swirl of his dark gray cloak to go into the inn.

"It *is* the same man!" she cried—and for a moment

she felt a twinge of panic, as if the stranger could return and claim her from the coach. "It's the man I told you about, Reba, the one who rescued me at the Star and Garter—and then tried to hold me prisoner!"

"Really? Where?" Excitedly Reba reached over and tore open the leathern curtain on her side and stuck her head out. At the same time they heard the whip crack above the horses' heads and the coach started forward over the icy ruts with a lurch that nearly jolted them from their seats.

"He's gone now," gasped Carolina. "He went into the inn." She was searching the floor as she spoke for the velvet muff that had skidded from her woolen lap as the coach careened forward. She turned to Reba with a sudden frown. "You don't think he could be headed the same way we are, do you?"

"Oh, I doubt it," shrugged Reba. "Most of the traffic from London goes on up the Great Essex Road to Colchester, but *we* turn off here toward Cambridge."

"But couldn't he be going to Cambridge?" Carolina really didn't know why she should feel disappointed.

"No, if he was going to Cambridge, he'd have gone straight north through Bishop's Stortford, instead of going out of his way to Chelmsford, I would think."

"I wonder what he's doing here?"

"Perhaps you should have stayed locked in and found out what his intentions were—getting you drunk and seducing you, most likely!" laughed Reba. "'Tis fairly obvious what he had in mind since you said he saw through your disguise so easily."

"Yes, he did that," agreed Carolina, pondering. "But somehow, I don't quite think he meant to get me drunk and seduce me."

"Whyever not?" asked her friend carelessly.

How could she explain it? Reba would laugh her to scorn if she said there had been something chivalrous about the man in gray, something reassuringly protective, despite the effrontery of that massive sweep upstairs that had carried her irresistibly out of harm's way. "I just don't think so," she said sulkily.

179

Reba quirked an amused eyebrow at her and Carolina returned her friend a haughty look. *"I* think he intended to take me home, just as he said."

"Which would have gotten you expelled, of course."

"Yes, but *he* didn't know that!"

Why was she defending the fellow? she asked herself wildly. She tossed her head and told herself it didn't matter. Suddenly what Reba had said came back to her. Reba's lover had been tall and dark and given to wearing gray.

The gentleman she had just seen on the road had been tall and dark and he was dressed—just as he had been at the Star and Garter—entirely in gray. A terrible suspicion crossed her mind, but she put it immediately aside. Half the gentlemen in England must be wearing solid gray! But she knew that was not the case. Men's fashions were quite colorful. She was distracted from her thoughts when Reba suddenly remarked, "You should count yourself lucky, Carol, that you are far from home and *your* lover cannot be snatched from you so quickly."

So Reba's lover had been snatched away. Carolina put aside her suspicions about the man in gray as she suggested softly, "Why don't you tell me about it?"

Reba began obliquely. "My mother sometimes despaired of making good matches for my sisters, despite Papa's money."

"Why?"

Reba gave her a jaded look. "Both my sisters resemble my father. And my father has a face that, all agree"—she shrugged and her furs rippled slightly—"resembles his horse."

Carolina blinked at this harsh pronouncement. She waited while Reba plucked delicately at her velvet cloak, brushing away the flakes of snow that had blown in through the open flap. "Because I'm the best looking of the three"—Reba's white teeth flashed in a fleeting smile—"my mother, who has force but no imagination, has overlooked the fact that I have inherited my father's wit."

That wit which had made him one of the leading

merchants of England, was doubtless Reba's point.
Plainly Reba was trying to tell her something. Carolina
waited.

"My mother," said Reba, with a frown, "would have
been overjoyed to marry her eldest daughter to a
widowed knight of ninety merely for the sake of
hearing her called Lady Jane, but none turned up so she
had to accept the next best thing, an untitled old
widower with money, a friend of Papa's who cares
nothing for Jane—he wed her for the trading advantage
it would give him with my father." She twiddled her fur
muff. "Nell is not so homely as Jane, and Mamma
entertained wild ideas of marrying her to the younger
son of a baronet—I heard her talking to Papa about
it—but none appeared."

"Perhaps she was too impatient," murmured Carolina. It seemed to her that there were always younger
sons eager to wed fortunes no matter *what* the bride
looked like.

"Perhaps," Reba shrugged. "I'll grant you she was in
a hurry. She *yearns* to dance with earls."

So Reba's mother wanted to climb the social ladder
via her daughters' marriages. Certainly it was not
unheard of!

"When none came instantly to hand, she fobbed Nell
off on what Papa called 'a good catch'—the nephew of a
wealthy shipowner in Plymouth. Nell's dowry bought
him a ship! And when his uncle dies, with what Nell will
inherit, they could well have the largest merchant fleet
in all the south of England, according to Papa."

Carolina thought, perplexed, of the wild times her
father and mother had had. There had been jealousy,
rage, revenge even—but none of it with commercial
intent. Still she had to admit that even her own mother
had demanded "good" marriages for her daughters and
they—having more spunk than Jane and Nell or perhaps just more prospects—had resorted to the Marriage Trees.

"Now I am to be Mamma's last throw of the dice,"
said Reba, "and she has kept me hidden away like the
crown jewels. And I know she will try to marry me off

181

to some younger son as well, just to hear me called Lady Reba. But I am better than that, better than my sisters who have no looks, better than my mother who has no brains—I have a sense of style and my father's wits and I will do better than any of them!"

Carolina's breath was expelled on a long slow sigh. "So whatever your mother decides, you intend to choose for yourself?"

Reba gave her friend a sidelong secret smile. "I have already chosen," she murmured.

"The man you went away with in the spring—when everybody thought you were in Hampshire?"

Reba nodded.

"And nobody knows about him?" It all sounded very romantic to Carolina.

"Well, George knows for he saw us together by chance, going into our lodgings—but I warned him that if he told anyone, I would swear he had helped me and he blanched. George is afraid of me," she added lightly.

And perhaps with reason! "You will run away with your lover?" said Carolina raptly. The Marriage Trees had come irresistibly into her mind.

"He is not here to run away with," frowned Reba. "And Mamma will be in a hurry to see me wed 'before the bloom of my youth fades away' as she is so fond of saying."

At seventeen it seemed unlikely that Reba's youthful bloom would soon take flight, but Carolina was moved to remark, "If that is how she feels, I am surprised that she has not betrothed you long before this."

"She has an orderly mind, has my mother. She intended—and it is working out that way—that her daughters shall be married in the same order as they arrived in this world—first Jane, then Nell, and now me."

"But will he not be back soon?" Carolina asked, returning to the fascinating subject of Reba's absent lover.

"That is the problem," sighed Reba. "We must wait until his wife dies."

Carolina opened her mouth and closed it again. The coach took a lurch that gave her an excuse for starting as if she'd been stuck with a pin. Stunned, she stared at Reba.

"He is the Marquess of Saltenham and he has been married for four abominable years to a wife who languishes at the point of death and never quite goes on to her reward!" Reba burst out. "On her doctors' advice he has taken her to Italy for her health and there they remain. Oh, it is very vexing!"

The snowy countryside fled by as Carolina found her voice. "Does he write to you?"

"No." Reba sighed. "He told me he would not—it is too dangerous. He says we cannot afford a scandal, for while he has the title, the money is all hers."

"Does your mother know about him?"

"No, of course not. Had she known she would have married me off at once to the first halfway acceptable suitor to cross our threshold. Oh, I know what she would say—she would say my marquess is a married man and that he is toying with me!" She sounded aggrieved.

Carolina had the feeling that perhaps Reba's mother was right.

"But surely she must see that it would be a great match," she said slowly, trying to be on the side of her friend. "If you told her in just the right way?"

"Indeed she would not, for she is pig-headed and listens to no one!" Alarm filled Reba's features. "And you must not tell her—or anyone else! I have entrusted you with my very deepest secret and you must swear you will not reveal it! Oh, do close that flap, Carol—the snow is coming in."

"Of course I won't tell her," said Carolina, hastily closing the flap. She had wanted to see the countryside but now she was glad to be back in semidarkness for she was certain she must be showing the shock of Reba's startling revelation. Certainly Reba had given no inkling of a clandestine liaison of such proportions when they were in school! "But"—she could not help bringing up the main point—"suppose it doesn't work out?

183

Suppose a sojourn in Italy cures the marchioness? What then?"

"Oh, of course it will work out," said Reba pettishly. "She can't hang on forever—all I need is a little time!"

But how could Reba be certain that absence would not make the marquess's heart grow fonder—perhaps of some doe-eyed Italian contessa?

"Did he ask you to marry him when—when he is free?" Carolina asked reluctantly.

"Well, as good as." Reba tossed her auburn head. "He said *if only he wasn't married,* and sighed, and then—well, I won't tell you what he did next!" She laughed and gave Carolina an arch look in the dusky coach. "But he made it quite clear he'd marry me in a minute if only she were gone! Am I shocking you?"

She was, but not for worlds would Carolina, lurching about as the coach skittered over icy ruts, have admitted it.

In truth the marquess had only heaved a great sigh as he ruffled Reba's thick auburn hair and murmured, burying his face in its musky expensive perfume, "If only I weren't married . . ." before he carried her off to bed, but Reba chose to remember it in such a way as to suit herself. "I told him to come back single and court me! That I'd wait!" she confided blithely. And she had been picking up her chemise from the floor as she spoke and so had not seen the look, almost of consternation, that had passed over his dark face when she said that, or noted how swiftly he had pulled the bell rope and ordered his coach to take Reba back to the school "because we cannot afford a scandal." Just before she left he had given her a melancholy smile and presented a ruby pin to remember him by. Reba exhibited it, pinned inside her muff.

"How will you explain it?" asked Carolina, troubled. If *she* were to bring home a ruby pin, explanations would be demanded!

Reba shrugged. "Mamma will never see it. I'll keep it pinned inside my muff—or my underthings."

Carolina, studying the pin by opening the flap for a moment—which let in a shower of snow—thought the marquess had held Reba rather cheap, at least if this rather insignificant pin was any indication!

"How did you meet him?" she wondered. For merchants—even successful ones from Bristol—did not usually take tea with marquesses and marchionesses.

Reba seemed glad to tell someone about it. Her russet eyes sparkled in the gathering dusk. "Aunt Bella was bringing me up from Hampshire to install me in Mistress Chesterton's school. She was going to stop by to see George and give him his marching orders and then scurry back to Hampshire to scoop up Willie and carry him away to Bath to take the waters. Well, it was sunny when we started—then it started to rain. It rained and rained and Aunt Bella refused to stop. She said she couldn't afford the time, with poor Willie waiting for her back there with the pip! She said I was an ungrateful girl to suggest it! And as it happened, Robin Tyrell—the Marquess of Saltenham—was on his way out of London to visit his estates near Basingstoke. The roads were a sea of mud, Aunt Bella kept sticking her head out, screaming at the coachman to hurry—and every time she opened the flap buckets of water came pouring in. Robin was in a hurry too. Our coaches chanced to meet at a narrow bend of the road and in the confusion as the drivers tried to rein in their horses, *our* coach overturned. I was thrown clear and so was Aunt Bella—but *she* landed on her head in the road and was knocked quite silly, to say nothing of her hat being ruined. I wasn't at all hurt. I had landed on a great clump of soft clean wet grass and I was just sitting up when I saw this tall handsome man in dove gray satin leap out of the other coach and run toward me. His coat had gunmetal velvet cuffs and it was trimmed in yards and yards of silver braid and the skirt of it was stiffened so that it stuck out and he was wearing a burst of silver lace at his throat and cuffs and a huge black periwig and shiny gray leather boots—oh, you should have seen him, Carol, he was *magnificent!*"

Carolina could see him indeed. A fop of the first order. She put aside all thought that the man in gray who had dragged her upstairs at the inn might be the

Marquess of Saltenham—and somehow she found that comforting. She told herself that was because it would be terrible for Reba to be mixed up with such a domineering creature.

"So of course I didn't want him to know I was *all right,*" said Reba. "For then he'd have turned all his attention to Aunt Bella! So I promptly sank back with a groan and pretended to be in a dead faint and let him carry me to his coach."

"And your aunt?"

"Oh, Aunt Bella's wits seemed quite knocked endways and she moaned and gibbered and held her head, and the marquess was very alarmed. He said he would take us to the nearest inn and summon a doctor and he did. The doctor put Aunt Bella to bed and said that was where I should be too, but after he left I pouted and insisted that dinner and some wine would quite restore me and we had *that* in a private dining room."

"I am surprised your aunt would let you do it!"

"Oh, she was in no condition to protest! The doctor had filled her with laudanum and she was dead to the world. I can't remember what Robin and I ate, but it was all *very* romantic."

Carolina could well imagine. A schoolgirl and a handsome marquess, candlelight and wine. . . .

"He told me all about his wife," said Reba frankly. "About how the doctors had tried to help her, and none had, and he was taking her to Italy in a few weeks' time in an effort to restore her to health, but that he really had very little hope. And I was *very* sympathetic and said how tragic it all was, and when finally I got up to go and he pulled my chair back I pretended to be dizzy and I swayed and he caught me in his arms." Her wicked chuckle seemed to fill the coach. "And I leaned against him all the way back to the room he'd taken for Aunt Bella and me. He'd taken a room for himself too for he said he felt most responsible for the accident. And there was a terrible spring thunderstorm that night, the most *awful* thunder and lightning, and I got up out of my bed and ran to his room and pounded on the door in fright—I am sure I *sounded* frightened at

186

least—and I told him that with my aunt lying there like the dead and all that wild thunder and lightning bolts I was afraid to stay there alone."

"And of course he took you in?" Carolina could hardly keep the irony out of her voice.

"Of course," said Reba blithely. "Sometimes, Carol, things must be *contrived*. He poured us some wine and we sat on the edge of his bed and drank it, and the blue lightning would light up the room in bright flashes like day. And of course my trunks were still back on the road lashed to the coach, so I had dashed down the hall in my chemise, which was very sheer indeed!" She giggled. "And one thing led to another and I ended up spending the night with him."

"You mean—!" Carolina sat straight up and the rocking of the coach almost pitched her against Reba. *"Just like that?"*

"Of course," said Reba airily. "I wanted to make an indelible impression, didn't I? And going to bed with him certainly accomplished *that!*"

Chapter **13**

Silent and white, the snow outside continued to fall upon the sweeping Essex countryside, the straining horses made clouds with every breath, and the coachman tugged his snow-covered hat down farther over his eyes and cursed beneath his breath as the coach lurched into yet another icy rut unseen beneath the drifting snow.

But inside the cold, dim coach, a bolt upright Carolina was staring at the elegant fox and velvet-clad figure huddled beside her beneath a fur robe as if she'd never seen her before.

"Oh, Reba, you'd only just met him and you *knew* he was married! How *could* you go to bed with him?"

"Well, he was my first marquess," said Reba reasonably. "And I may not soon meet another, and I don't wish to be parceled out to some 'younger son' of low rank—or anyone else my mother may have in mind! It seemed a wonderful opportunity—the accident, the storm—and so of course I took it. He was astonished that I was a virgin. He said I seemed so—'experienced,' I think was the word he used."

Carolina's level of sophistication left her not quite prepared for this. She struggled to understand Reba's reasoning for she wanted desperately to be on her friend's side—and gave up. "What now?" she asked. "You do not know where he is or even if he has returned to England!"

"Oh, I hear reports of him occasionally for he is well known, and his wife was a great heiress—which is undoubtedly why he married her. But he spends money very fast, does Robin. I estimate that his wife and her money should be gone at about the same time. He will," she added contentedly, "need another great heiress, and my mother would be so overcome if a marquess sued for my hand that she would demand my father beggar himself to give me a suitable dowry. She'd *make* Papa buy him for me! And then"—Carolina could not see the wickedly knowing smile that played over Reba's face—"I'd end up with everything, wouldn't I?"

The interior of the coach was suddenly very quiet—and not just because outside they were running over soft snow. Carolina found herself speechless at such foresight, but Reba, now that her secret was out at last, could not talk enough about it. As the darkness of the snowy world outside deepened, she described the marquess's estates in elaborate detail—for she had insisted he tell her all about them—"to show a proper interest in things, you know, Carol." She described what she would wear when, as a marchioness, she was presented at Court. "Or perhaps Robin will arrange for me to be presented even before that—during our betrothal period."

"Don't press your luck," said Carolina hollowly, for she was wondering how—if Reba's present unlikely plans did not work out—Reba would ever explain to some outraged bridegroom about not being a virgin? "Marry him out of hand if you get the chance and let all else go!"

"Yes, I'll probably do that," agreed Reba. "I—" She ended with a screech as she was flung forward, the coach having given a violent lurch and then skidded crazily to a halt. The girls tumbled together in a corner.

Carolina realized that she had landed on Reba. "Are you hurt?" she cried.

From beneath her came Reba's sputtered "No"—for she had brought her hand up to brace herself and her muff was half stuffed into her mouth. She could hardly speak for the fur.

Assured that Reba wasn't injured, Carolina fought her way clear of Reba's body and clawed open the leathern flap only to confront the crestfallen face of the coachman, vague in the white darkness of the snowy world outside. He made sure they were all right and told them glumly that they had lost a wheel.

Reba had struggled up now, and she interrupted Carolina's bewildered, "Where are we?" with a relieved, "Oh, thank heaven, we're at the gates—I can just see them over there. Untie the coach horses, Giles, and boost us up—we'll ride in. Our trunks and boxes can follow later."

So it was by this novel method of travel, riding bareback and astride on coach horses unused to riders, that the girls reached the great house at Broadleigh via a long winding driveway. Snow kept falling on them in small avalanches from the branches as they rode beneath the overarching trees and they looked more like snowmen than young ladies as they came out of the driveway suddenly to be confronted by a long Jacobean timbered facade. They dismounted through sheets of now blinding snow. The coachman leaped off his mount to bang the huge iron knocker. And then they were going through the big oaken door, and a chambermaid appeared from somewhere to scurry forward and take their wet cloaks and hoods and cluck over the condition of their wet skirts.

From the outside Carolina had not had time to appreciate the size of the house, but once she was stamping her pattens in the great hall to rid them of the snow and letting a servant take her cloak, she was startled to realize that she was standing in a room large enough to encompass the whole of Farview back home on the Eastern Shore. She looked with awe at the ancient yawning fireplace, the echoing stone floors, the dark beams lost somewhere above the glow of candle-light, the rich medieval look of everything.

"You didn't tell me your home was anything like this," she murmured as they brushed snow off each other's hair.

"Well, it isn't exactly an ancestral seat," laughed Reba. "Papa bought it."

Carolina's mouth opened—and shut again. Back in Virginia she had been told of the wealth of England's new merchant princes, but somehow to be confronted with it was staggering. Perhaps Reba was right and she could aspire to a marquess after all, she thought, studying the echoing vastness of the hall and the roaring fire in a fireplace which would easily accommodate the tallest man standing erect.

"Oh, here comes Drewsie," cried Reba. "*She* always sees through me!"

A stoutish woman with a homely pleasant face was hurrying toward them. She wore a spotless white linen apron over her serviceable dark wool dress, and a white cap just barely held back the strands of gray hair that kept escaping.

"Reba, child, ye're back!" she crowed and threw her arms around Reba and hugged her. "'Tis good to have ye home for the holidays!"

At Reba's laughing, "No, I'm home for good, Drewsie," the older woman stood back, held Reba at arm's length and fixed her with a severe expression. "That fancy school threw ye out?" she hazarded a guess.

Reba gave Carolina a droll look out of the corner of her eye. "Of course not, Drewsie! I left in good standing. Didn't Mamma tell you? She sent for me. I'm home to stay."

"Lor' no! She didn't tell me!" Drewsie hugged Reba again. "That's the best news I've had!" she declared warmly.

Reba extricated herself from the older woman's embrace. "Where's Papa?"

"Your papa's gone to London and he'll be away all through the holidays," declared Drewsie importantly. "He's tied up in some business deal or other. I heard your ma talking about it with him but I couldn't make hide nor hair of it. Something about some young Lord in London gambling away his fortune and needing money and being willing to put up his country estate as collateral."

Reba sighed. "Papa's always away chasing after some business deal. Carol, this is Drewsie, our housekeeper. She's had a time of it, trying to keep me out of trouble! This is Carolina Lightfoot, Drewsie, my friend from school. She's from the Colonies—Virginia."

The stoutish woman regarded Carolina with immediate interest. "You're a pretty girl, Carolina," she said approvingly. "From the Virginia Colony, you say? But you wasn't born there surely?"

"Indeed I was," said Carolina, amazed not only by the question but by a servant's casual use of her first name and comment on her appearance. Plainly Reba did not remark any strangeness.

"But I thought they was all red Indians over there!" insisted Drewsie. "Excepting for them as just went over!"

Carolina laughed but the older woman's words brought home to her again just how alien a Colonist could feel in the Mother Country. The girls at school had made her feel that way too—at first, before she became wealthy Reba's roommate and therefore acceptable. "I should have brought along my moccasins," she muttered to Reba as the housekeeper disappeared and they turned toward the wide stairway.

"Oh, indeed you should have," agreed Reba. "You'd have created a sensation padding around in them—and they do make wonderful bedroom slippers!"

But of course Reba wore satin mules for bedroom slippers. Carolina decided to drop the subject of moccasins. "Drewsie must be a very old retainer, I take it?" she asked.

"Oh, she's much more than that. Drewsie's a second cousin of Mamma's—you remember I told you Mamma

192

only speaks to one of her blood relations? Well, Drewsie's the one! There were sixteen children in Drewsie's family, mostly daughters, and they simply couldn't get them all married off. Drewsie was one of the leftovers and she came to live with us before I was born. But Mamma says she's not well spoken and will never be 'accepted' by the county gentry and she mustn't appear to be related to us, so she's to have the post of housekeeper now that we've 'moved up in the world'—and Drewsie says she doesn't mind." She laughed. "You mustn't let on to Mamma that I told you Drewsie is related to us."

But of course Drewsie would mind! How it must hurt her to be treated as an upper servant when actually she was a member of the family! Carolina's head whirled. In Virginia, you might cast off your blood relations as unacceptable, cut them out of your will, turn your head away from them at social gatherings or cut them dead on the street—but they were still your blood relations and she couldn't imagine a situation in which a cousin of her mother's would live in the house with them and not be acknowledged as a relative.

She began to understand how Reba could speak so casually of waiting for her lover's wife to die. She was her mother's daughter!

The maidservant who had helped them out of their wet cloaks was back with a candle to light their way up the broad Jacobean stairway they must climb to greet Reba's mother who, Drewsie had told them, was feeling "indisposed."

"Never you mind, Rumsey," said Reba, taking the candle. "We'll light our own way up." She turned to Carolina. "I'll show you something of the house as we go." She picked up her emerald green velvet skirts and prepared to ascend.

Carolina, all too aware of her sensible brown worsted traveling dress and worn shoes, gave her splendidly garbed friend a fleetingly wistful look. It would be much more fun right now to be padding around in a pair of Reba's high-heeled satin slippers—even though those Reba found too tight were a little too large on her—and wearing one of Reba's beautifully sewn creations, always in the latest style from Paris. Even the gentleman's suit she had borrowed from Reba for that night at the Star and Garter was more becoming than her own dowdy things!

She sighed. Not much chance she would get to do anything like that again!

From what she'd seen and heard so far, Reba's family was nothing like she'd expected. These were the "upstarts" she had once overheard Mistress Chesterton complain of at the school, for Jenny made up in lineage what she lacked in morals and it annoyed her to be running a school for the daughters of merchants and wealthy tradesmen rather than the "true aristocracy."

Carolina followed Reba up the stairs and stopped when Reba paused and raised her candle to highlight a large but rather stiff portrait of a willowy overdressed woman with hard russet eyes and a face hauntingly like Reba's.

"That's my mother," said Reba.

Carolina paused before the portrait and wondered at the hardness of those eyes.

"But it doesn't look a thing like her," scoffed Reba and Carolina felt relieved. There was something she didn't like in those eyes, something harsh and cold. "She told the portraitist to make her look younger. And prettier. And thinner. And he did because he wanted to be paid for his work!"

At the head of the stairs stretched a long balustrade with pillars. Ordinarily this would have made a wonderful balcony from which to look down and observe what was going on in the great hall but it had been hung with a number of large tapestries depicting chivalrous scenes. The effect was to obscure the view for tapestry after tapestry, hanging like a solid wall, rendered the corridor behind dark and gloomy.

"Those were there when we came and Mamma's going to take them all down come spring." Reba nodded casually toward the handsome tapestries. "But meanwhile she says they make the upstairs halls less drafty."

"What does your father say about it?" wondered Carolina. She was thinking that Reba's father rather got lost in the shuffle as Reba spoke of "Mamma says this" and "Mamma does that."

"Oh, he couldn't care less," laughed Reba, lighting their way down a long corridor. "He's interested only in making money. And perhaps," she added, "getting his daughters all married off to men who can support them!"

Carolina sighed. That seemed to be the preoccupation of all the parents she ran across—interfering in their offspring's matrimonial plans. She decided that what England needed was Marriage Trees, at least one group at the border of every county!

When they reached her mother's door, Reba turned to Carolina, suddenly nervous. "Don't say much," she cautioned. "Just go along with anything I say. You have to be careful with Mamma. She wrote me that she hasn't been well," she added as she gently knocked on the door.

"Come in," said a sharp voice.

They went inside.

The furnishings of the spacious bedroom did not jibe with the force and drive Carolina had sensed in the woman she had seen in the portrait. Pale rose satin draperies obscured the tall windows and matched a coverlet trimmed in ecru lace. A big delicate canopied bed with fluted posts and carved gilded angels was set like a wedding cake in a shower of French gilt furniture that looked out of place in this big square English bedroom with its dark heavy Tudor paneling and lofty beamed ceiling. But the square-faced heavyset woman in the elegant rose satin robe, who turned about from the ministrations of a maidservant who was combing her tight orange curls before the mirror of the delicate gilt dressing table, certainly matched the architectural surroundings by strength alone. In fact she seemed to overpower the whole room.

"So you got through the snow?" Mistress Tarbell greeted her daughter.

"Yes, Mamma," said Reba meekly.

Mistress Tarbell pushed aside the hovering comb. "From the look of things outside, I thought you might be staying over in London until the weather was better."

"No, Mamma."

No embraces, thought Carolina. *No warmth.* She was glad this wasn't *her* mother. For whatever Letitia Lightfoot's other failings might be, she always greeted people as if she was glad to see them!

Now those flashing russet eyes—her best feature in that square dogmatic-looking face, and even more like Reba's than they had looked in the portrait—narrowed as she surveyed Carol. "And who's this?" she asked bluntly. "If you've hired yourself an abigail, you can send her right back to London—I do my own hiring!"

Reba winced visibly at this crude assessment of her friend and Carolina's cheeks were burning as her young body stiffened. She knew that her heavy worsted dress was plain and unfashionable but it was the warmest thing she owned for a coach ride in weather like this—and she certainly did not think she looked like a lady's maid! Taut with indignation, she lifted her chin haughtily and glared back at her formidable hostess.

"Mamma, this is my best friend from school—Carolina Lightfoot," Reba said nervously. "I've brought her home with me for the holidays."

So Reba hadn't written to tell her mother she was coming! Carolina could feel her face turn crimson.

The stocky figure in satin sat straighter, and a pair of thick heavy brows elevated in amazement. Carolina could almost feel what the woman was thinking: *This is one of your friends from that elegant school I sent you to? Lor', she looks more like one of the chambermaids!* Mistress Tarbell pushed away the hovering maidservant and came to her feet. She was not very tall but she had a commanding presence. Behind her the maidservant's covert grin completed Carolina's humiliation.

Carolina made perhaps the most elegant and exaggerated curtsy of her career. "I must apologize for my condition," she told Reba's mother in a frosty voice. "The snow. . . ." Her little deprecating shrug fairly

196

dripped hauteur—for was she not her mother's daughter? She gave her wet woolen skirts a slight illustrative shake that deposited tiny droplets all over the rich green Aubusson carpet. "I do hope I have not come at an inconvenient time, Mistress Tarbell," she added distantly. "Reba led me to believe that although you have but recently moved in, the house was in condition to receive guests." Her gaze passed disdainfully over the delicate gilt furnishings that seemed so out of place against the stout dark paneled walls. "But of course if it is not, I will betake me to an inn."

The moment Carolina spoke, it was plain to all in the room that this was no servant girl speaking but a daughter of the aristocracy. She knew she had overdone it a bit but she had been goaded by that awful woman in rose satin whose square form faced her. Behind Mistress Tarbell the maidservant's smirk disappeared and she regarded Carolina in some alarm.

Her hostess looked a bit dazed but she recollected herself immediately. "Oh, 'tis a most convenient time," she insisted with a reproving glance at her daughter. "Reba should have told me she was bringing home a friend. *Shouldn't you, Reba?*" Her russet gaze was so fierce that Reba took a step backward as if she expected her ears to be boxed. "But indeed you're most welcome —Carolina, is it?"

"We call her Carol at school, Mamma," said Reba.

"And where is your home, Carol?"

"Virginia," said Carolina firmly. "The Eastern Shore."

"The *Colonies?*" Mistress Tarbell could not keep the incredulous note from her voice.

"Oh, Carol's father has a magnificent estate over there," cried Reba, seeing her mother's expression. "Doesn't he, Carol?"

He might not now, but according to Virgie's letter they soon would have one. Carolina gave her hostess a grim smile.

"Thousands and thousands of acres," babbled Reba. "And he's building a fine new house with a stairway broader than ours!"

"We are not all savages in Virginia, Mistress Tarbell," said Carolina softly. She tried to make her tone light but the words came out sounding like a challenge.

"No—no, of course not." Again Mistress Tarbell's view of things was knocked askew. "I will put you in the green room," she decided.

"Oh, Mamma, couldn't Carol have the room next to mine?" cried Reba, almost childishly. Carolina was amazed how much younger Reba seemed here with her mother. Plainly the presence of her formidable parent reduced her to quivering jelly!

Her mother frowned. The green room was by far their handsomest guest bedchamber and had just been given elegant new draperies and French wallpaper over the plastered walls. But Carolina was looking as if she might join in Reba's request. "I suppose so," she said reluctantly. "But the draper hasn't got to that one yet."

"Then I'll take her there right now," cried Reba in relief. "And she can join me in my room while the chambermaid makes up her room. And Mamma, we're starving, we haven't had supper. Could we have something sent up?"

Mistress Tarbell calculated quickly in her head. Which would impress her daughter's aristocratic friend most—a forest of silver in the cold dining room or an elaborate tray such as could hardly be carried? She decided on *two* elaborate trays—the forest of silver in the dining room could wait till tomorrow. And tomorrow morning she would corner her daughter and learn all about this cool-eyed ill-dressed young beauty she had brought home with her. Her manner suggested aristocratic lineage—and younger sons of great houses went out to the Colonies all the time. It was too bad Jonathan wasn't home—he was a miracle at finding out things about people.

"I'll see to it. Take Carol along with you." She made a dismissive gesture and watched Reba bear her friend away.

The room Carolina had been assigned was delightful, she found. Soft shades of orange and russet blended in the heavy damask hangings and cast a warm glow by

198

candlelight upon the buff walls and the gold of the faded carpet.

"Mamma hasn't had at this room yet," Reba told her cheerfully. "Papa bought the house furnished, but Mamma had almost everything sent up to the attics. This room she's left alone until she could get to it. She's planning puce draperies and coverlet and a red Turkey carpet to brighten it up."

Carolina gave the mellow colors a regretful look. "I like it the way it is," she said wistfully.

"Oh, but these things aren't *new*," laughed Reba. "Everything must be new and expensive if we are to take what Mamma calls 'our place in society.'"

Carolina blinked. Reba had not talked this way at school. There she had been the sleek young sophisticate leading the way. Here at home she was something else. And then Carolina chided herself. Reba was her best friend here in England and she had been endlessly kind. But in the easygoing plantation aristocracy of the Tidewater and the Eastern Shore such a remark as Reba's would have been considered vastly peculiar. People knew exactly who they were and where they fit and so did everybody else. It seemed to be different here at Broadleigh.

"Mother expected you to be wearing velvet and furs," confided Reba.

"I would *love* to be wearing velvet and furs," said Carolina crossly. "Could I but afford it!"

Reba could have pointed out that she had invited Carolina to wear hers, but instead she laughed. "Well, that's what marriage is all about, isn't it? I mean, that's undoubtedly why your mother sent you overseas to school—so you could marry a fortune in London!"

Carolina grimaced. "My mother sent me overseas to school because she was afraid I would run away to the Marriage Trees with a miller's son," she said frankly. "And as to finding a fortune in London, she was careful to send me to a place where I'd be chaperoned to death!"

"Yes, I wonder how they expect us to do it?" puzzled Reba. A frown creased her smooth forehead. "I mean,

199

we walk about in groups, always watched, always being hovered over. Do our mammas expect us to break away suddenly and hurl ourselves into some passing coach that has a coat of arms emblazoned on the side, appropriate the occupant and straightaway marry an earl?"

That brought a smile to Carolina's mouth—it was more like the old jaunty Reba. "Some magic like that, probably," she agreed.

"I get the distinct impression that Mamma is terribly disappointed in me that I didn't return with a baron under my arm," murmured Reba.

Or at least a baron's sister!

"Well, perhaps you can furnish her with a marquess," suggested Carolina dryly.

"If only I'm given enough time," Reba sighed. "Mamma is a very *sudden* sort of person. At any moment, now that I am home, she may march in a candidate for matrimony and demand that I accept him!"

Both girls looked momentarily gloomy.

"*Arranged* marriages without our consent ought to be illegal," declared Carolina with sudden vehemence.

"Agreed!" laughed Reba, her mood suddenly lightened. For a pair of simpering maidservants had appeared at the door with two enormous silver chargers piled high with all manner of good things, and were depositing the big trays on a table. "Food at last!" she sighed—for Reba was fond of eating and would one day be as stout as her square-built mother even though for now she was lithe as a reed. But after the maidservants had left she turned impulsively to Carolina. "Oh, you *will* help me if Mamma decrees I am to marry some choice of hers while you are here, won't you?"

Carolina envisioned aiding a runaway—as she had aided her older sisters back home in Virginia. Reba's request appealed to her reckless nature.

"Of course I will," she declared warmly.

Reba went back to munching bullace cheese spread on little cakes. But the sidewise look she cast upon her friend was entirely satisfied and more than a little triumphant. She had planned her campaign well and Carolina was moving exactly in the direction she had schemed for while she was at school. Her bright gaze played over Carolina for a moment. Even in her plain dark brown woolen dress she was as lovely as a delicate piece of porcelain. So beautiful with that wealth of shining fair hair, silver in one light, gold in another. And those luminous silver eyes with their fringe of dark lashes. And that smile that would melt stone.

Oh, yes, she had chosen well. Mamma was definitely on the brink of springing something on her—she had sensed it from the suddenly intent look on her face when she had turned and seen her standing there—and she would be ready for that something when it came. All these months she had planned to be ready for it—with Carolina.

And now she was.

If Mamma chose to spring her trap, it would be Carolina and not Reba who was caught by it.

THE TWELVE DAYS OF CHRISTMAS
BROADLEIGH, ESSEX

1687

Chapter 14

Christmas Eve and Christmas Day both passed at Broadleigh with surprisingly little merriment. Carolina tried to put it down to the head of the household being gone and to Reba's mother being indisposed—but gave it up. Indeed she had begun to suspect that her hostess's "indisposition" was no more than drink, for she consumed more port than Carolina had ever seen a woman drink. Although she did not appear actually tipsy, she became belligerent and red-faced over supper every night, and once Reba muttered apologetically, "Mamma's in her cups again!" as they scurried upstairs to bed. Mistress Tarbell always vanished right after supper and Carolina wondered if she did not drink herself insensible in her bedchamber, which could certainly account for her bad temper at breakfast every morning.

Carolina found it a strange Christmas. Nobody called. The snow that fell steadily became an excuse not to go to church, the girls prowled the halls restlessly—and even Reba admitted that it would have been more fun to have remained in London and listened to the sleighbells and the carolers and the bell ringers on the streets.

Carolina thought with a homesick pang what Christmas would have been like at Aunt Pet's in Williamsburg where Letty and Fielding, at Aunt Pet's insistence, always brought their little brood for Christmas.

Aunt Pet's pink brick, green-shuttered house would be transformed for the holiday season. The front door would sport an enormous wreath of holly and bayberry tied with a wide red velvet bow. Mistletoe would hang from the brass hall chandelier and over the front doorway—for Aunt Pet thought Christmas kissing quite appropriate. All the downstairs fireplaces would be ablaze with fragrant hickory logs, the tall brass candlesticks would be ringed with holly. Ropes of fluffy green pine needles and holly berries would adorn the stairs—Carolina and her sisters had usually made those.

And in the dining room holly and red satin bows would have been tied to the shining brass wall sconces, the long dining table would groan beneath a huge roasted wild turkey stuffed with oysters and fresh ground cornmeal and walnuts and spices. Seated at that table, the family would face each other across an elaborate centerpiece of pine cones and red apples and golden oranges set upon a bed of boxwood and holly. Soup would be ladled out from a big steaming tureen, there would be a rich plum pudding to end the meal, and on the heavy polished sideboard, centered among the mincemeat pies and spicy gingerbread and crabapple jelly and fruitcake and plum tarts, on a bed of dark green waxy magnolia leaves, a cornucopia basket would spill out oranges and lemons, red holly berries and juniper.

And after dinner they would all merrily toast each other's health—the adults in Aunt Pet's best Madeira and the younger children in hot fruit punch.

Carolers would come singing to the door, their breath making little steamy clouds as they lilted *"God rest ye, merrie gentlemen . . ."* and then stamped snow off their shoes as they were invited in to drink tankards of hot chocolate or hot rum punch.

Guests would call—and be invited in joyously. And kissed amid gales of laughter under the mistletoe. And they would sally forth to go calling themselves, taking with them baskets containing white linen-wrapped Christmas fruitcake and little cakes and fruit and nuts. And there would be dances and frolics and sleighrides in the snow—a joyous season, full of memories.

Christmas at Broadleigh was nothing like that.

They exchanged gifts. Carolina apologized to Reba for having to give things she already possessed, "for as you know, I lost all my money in that dice game and had none left to shop with in London," but Reba did not seem to care. The whole idea of Christmas bored her. Costly gifts were exchanged between Reba and her mother—but without kisses and without hugs. And without laughter.

There was plenty of dark green shiny-leaved holly in Essex, rich with red berries—indeed Carolina could see it from the windows of the house! But not so much as a sprig of holly or a spray of mistletoe did she see about the place, and there was more cheer in the servants' dining hall, where everybody was getting drunk on Christmas ale and roaring out bawdy songs, than there was at the master's board!

Christmas dinner at Broadleigh was elaborate and meant to impress—as indeed were all the dinners there—but it varied from the other dinners served only in that it featured a Christmas goose. And Carolina found the sugar plums and marzipan and candied orange peel and exotic fruits and nuts small substitute for all the homely goodies that enriched Aunt Pet's holiday season. There was not even a Yule Log to burn its way through the season in that cavernous fireplace! And she had expected one, at a country house in England! Instead a perfectly ordinary fire blazed upon the hearth in the great hall.

By comparison with this subdued Christmas in Essex, Christmas in the Colonies—at least in Williamsburg—seemed a mad social whirl.

When Carolina wondered if the neighbors might not come calling, Reba shook her head.

"You see, we haven't really been accepted by the gentry here," Reba told her in an offhand way. "Oh, Papa bought the hall and all that, but it takes more than that to be *accepted*." And at Carolina's puzzled frown she added briefly, "No one who counts has called since we've been here."

Steeped in friendly Virginia ways, where hospitality was offered to all, Carolina tried to take that in.

"No one?" she asked, shocked.

"Well, only one," amended Reba. "Sir Kyle Williston from Williston House—that's the estate next to ours—did pay Papa a brief call to talk about a broken enclosure and some cattle that had got out, but his wife didn't come. Lady Williston was 'indisposed' when Mamma returned the call; she didn't come down herself, just sent word. And that was after she'd been seen riding all about Essex in a carriage!"

That would indeed have been a social slap! "Perhaps Sir Kyle will come again," Carolina suggested. *And you will get another chance at him—and perhaps win him over, so he will send his wife calling!* "But there must be other people," she added desperately. She had been about to say "other merchants and their wives" but she thought better of it.

Reba had guessed what she meant.

"Oh, there are," she said dryly. "All *dying* to be invited to Broadleigh now that Papa has bought it. But Mamma doesn't want to see *them*. She nagged at Papa to buy a place where she could run with the gentry—and this was supposed to be it. Only so far it hasn't happened that way."

Reba's mother was just the type to drop all her old friends, thought Carolina wryly. *It served her right that she hadn't been able to make new ones!*

The snow stopped falling late on Christmas Eve, and Christmas Day dawned bright and clear with a chill in the air carried in from the North Sea. Carolina was delighted to wake and learn that while she and Reba were still asleep an invitation had come for Jonathan

Tarbell's family to attend a ball that night at neighboring Williston House and "weather or no," they were going.

"Mamma feels it will be 'Getting a Foot in the Door' to attend a ball at Williston House," Reba informed her friend excitedly. "Of course Sir Kyle isn't rich but she says he Carries Weight with the local gentry!"

Carolina would have been glad to hear it put less baldly but she was sure it must be true. The invitation made her feel a little less homesick for Virginia. She wondered what Lord Thomas, in Northampton for Christmas, was doing now—and if he was missing her as she missed him.

That evening, when they were all dressing for the ball, she learned her real mission here at Broadleigh. Which was to be something more, it seemed, than just a friend. She was here to Save the Day, as Reba dramatically put it.

This was to be Carolina's first ball in England, for as a schoolgirl she had been allowed nothing of the sort at Mistress Chesterton's and Thomas had "sheltered" her from his friends. She felt very excited about it and wandered into Reba's room to find out what Reba was going to wear.

She found her friend in a dressing gown seated before the beveled French mirror of her ornate ormolu dressing table, nervously dabbing crushed alabaster powder on her face.

"Wouldn't you know, Carolina?" she cried with a groan. "On the *very day* I learn that my marquess is coming home to England, Mamma must ruin it all?" She lifted another puff of powder to her face and dabbed it on so energetically she nearly choked on the cloud of white powder dust.

"Oh, do stop," cried Carolina. "You're already chalk white—people will think you're ill!"

"Yes, I suppose you're right." Reba stared despondently at her ghostly reflection in the mirror. "But I'll remind you that I haven't got your flawless complexion, Carol—mine needs some *help!*" She began to rub the powder off as energetically as she had applied it.

"How do you know your marquess is coming home?"

"I overheard Papa's farm manager tell Mamma that Papa was hoping to sell some horses to the Marquess of Saltenham now that he was coming home. Robin's a famous horse fancier, you know."

"Did he say anything about the marchioness?"

"No, and since I was eavesdropping I could hardly break in and ask. But she *must* be gone by now," said Reba impatiently. "After all, Robin described her as practically dying then. But now that he's actually on his way, something dreadful has happened—just as I knew it would." She leaned forward and began to dab at her cheeks with Spanish paper, rouging them. "You should try this, Carol—no"—she looked at Carolina's pink cheeks regretfully—"I suppose you don't need rouge any more than you need powder!"

"But *what* awful thing has happened?" asked Carolina, surprised that Reba was making her drag the story out of her.

Reba tossed away the Spanish paper, picked up her silver hairbrush and threw it down again. She took a deep breath and whirled to face Carolina.

"Mamma told me I am to meet Lord Gayle's third son at the Willistons' ball, that Papa has spoken to him about me and they hope to reach an understanding as soon as he has met me."

"And what is Lord Gayle's third son like?" cried Carolina, thoroughly absorbed.

"Oh, I've never seen him." Reba shrugged with complete disinterest. "Although once in Colchester the fourth son was pointed out to me—a spindly sort of fellow. He had his head in a book as he walked and his clothes were downright shabby—oh, I couldn't *bear* to be married to a man like that!"

Carolina could well imagine that Reba, with her earthy interest in life's pleasures, would find it galling to be cooped up with a bookworm!

"But anyway, what does it matter what he looks like?" Reba surprised her by adding. "He's the *third* son, mind you, not even the second. No chance of a title in that. I'd *never* be Lady Gayle—*both* his older brothers would have to die first!"

Carolina wished unhappily that Reba hadn't said that. A romantic herself, she preferred to imagine that Reba had tender feelings as well, that her interest in her marquess was strictly a misguided affair of the heart rather than misplaced ambition. She might have spoken at that point but Reba raced on.

"The worst of it, Carol, is that Mamma has given me to believe that it is all virtually settled except that he wants to meet me first. Doubtless Papa has told him what a huge dowry I will have as a lure and he will want to assure himself that I don't have two heads as well. And once he's established *that,* my parents are sure to *betroth* me to him," Reba rushed on tragically, "because Lord Gayle is a viscount from a terribly old family, which impresses Mamma, and their family seat is near Colchester instead of clear across England somewhere, and Papa will say that counts in his favor because they can 'see something of me after we are wed'—indeed I can hear him saying it now! And Mamma with her usual energy will force me right into wedlock just as she did my sisters, and the ceremony will already have been held before my marquess can get back home a widower to claim me! Oh, Carol!" Reba's voice held a pulsing entreaty. "You *will* help me?"

Carolina saw her vision of her first ball in England flying out the window. Reba obviously wanted to run away and she wouldn't want to do it alone. Two girls would be much safer than one. She'd want to go somewhere and wait until her marquess "returned to claim her." She stifled her regret.

"Of course I'll help you, Reba," she said staunchly. "Where do you want to go?"

Reba gave her an uncertain look. "I don't want to go anywhere," she said, puzzled. "I want to stay right here. I want your help with Lord Gayle's third son at the ball tonight."

At the ball tonight? Carolina peered at her friend. "What do you want me to do to him?" she asked in some alarm.

208

"I want you to *lure him away!*" cried Reba passionately. "Just for now, just for a fortnight or so—until my marquess can come to claim me!"

Carolina drew back in alarm. "But I've no great fortune," she protested. "Indeed my clothes proclaim it." She looked down at the simple blue ballgown with its modest edging of lace that was the best she owned. "If, as you say, he is interested in a dowry—"

"Oh, Carol, you can make him forget the dowry if only you will try! You must dazzle him. You may have your choice of my clothes to wear the whole time and my jewelry too—and I will persuade my mother's own maid to arrange your hair in the very *latest* mode!"

"But she'll be too busy helping you and your mother with your hair," protested Carolina—although the chance to wear the loveliest ballgown in Reba's wardrobe was very tempting for she had often yearned over it at school.

"Oh, no," said Reba in a jaded voice. "She'll *make* time for it! And when I remind her that I saw her slip the gold mourning ring Mamma got at Uncle Micaw's funeral into her pocket—later she declared the ring to be lost—she'll be afraid *not* to do it."

Carolina stared back at her, speechless.

"Well, don't just stand there—you can't wear *that!*" Reba gave the blue gown a look of vast distaste. "Here, I'll help you choose."

Minutes later Carolina found herself wearing sheer gray silk stockings with embroidered clocks that seemed to flash silver ("because you have good legs and you must make sure you show them as you climb out of the coach or whirl about the dance floor") and a new and delicate chemise frothing with lace. ("Because the lace will spill out at your elbows and it *must* be beautiful if it is to attract attention to how good your arms are"—adding carelessly, "You can keep the chemise, Carol. I have two more just like it.") Her dancing slippers were a pair of Reba's that were two years old. ("My feet were smaller then so they'll fit you perfectly, and although these aren't new, at least they *are* gray satin and have high red heels!") Her petticoat with its small train was a marvel of gleaming gunmetal satin heavily embossed with a lattice of silver embroidery. ("It's my best petticoat and it's new—mind that you lift it high as you get out of the coach. I wouldn't want it to get wet or splashed!") And her gown was Carolina's favorite of all the gowns Reba owned, so lovely she had yearned to wear it. It was daringly cut of thin rippling dove gray velvet with a burst of brilliants at each shoulder. It had a breathtakingly low décolletage that showed to advantage the flawless expanse of Carolina's white bosom, the pearly tops of her breasts. Its tight pointed bodice molded her round breasts and clasped her tiny hand-span waist and then burst forth into a great full skirt with an impressive train. Reba gathered that skirt—which was split down the middle for the purpose—into wide panniers at each hip to show off that miraculous silver-encrusted petticoat. "And you need not worry about Mamma knowing the gown is mine because she has never seen it. I bought all my own clothes in London—and Papa pays for them."

Marveling at the elegance of her own reflection, Carolina practiced before the mirror, turning and kicking aside that train so that it would not trip her—and looked back to admire it following her with rippling grace across Reba's red Turkey carpet as she walked.

"A fan—you'll need a fan," cried Reba, absorbed into making Carolina over into a fashion doll.

"But I already have a fan," protested Carolina, meaning the small ivory one she had been given three years ago for her birthday.

"You must have a better one." Reba rummaged, then turned triumphantly to place in Carolina's hand a sculptured ivory fan trimmed in silver lace and set with brilliants. "There," she said contentedly. "That will look well with the silver lace at your elbows."

Carolina gave the fan an expert wave (for at least she had practiced wafting a fan gracefully back home in Virginia) and the deep frilled cuffs at her elbows seemed to melt into the edging of the fan.

"Now these gray kidskin gloves—don't worry if you ruin them, they're too small for me anyway, I was going

210

to throw them away. And with your hair piled up as only Mamma's maid can do it," said Reba contentedly, "you'll look quite nice."

Nice was certainly an understatement when all this had been accomplished. Carolina's silver-gold hair was piled high and gleaming and there were fetching little curls dancing at her ears from which dangled a pair of perfectly matched teardrop pearl earrings. Other curls rested lightly against her white neck or seemed to float, feather light, over her gleaming shoulders. Her face was flushed with excitement, her high winglike brows arched over luminous silver eyes, and to crown it all Reba had placed a tiny bit of black court plaster near the corner of her mouth "like a dimple—it will show how fair your complexion is and how perfect!"

"Now, take a look at yourself," Reba told her.

Carolina stepped to the mirror and looked in wonder at this new silver vision of herself.

"How am I to know him?" she asked, conscious of her mission.

"Oh, we'll be introduced at the outset, I would imagine—unless he's late. In which case Mamma will be furious, because she's eager to get on with it." Reba laughed.

"Suppose he doesn't like blondes?" worried Carolina. "Suppose he prefers brunettes? Or worse yet, redheads like you?" She gave her friend's auburn tresses an uneasy look. "Suppose he has an aversion for Colonists and prefers English girls, born and bred?" Her gaze came back again to Reba's thick gleaming locks, her brassy-bright russet eyes, the faintly insolent air of challenge—not quite nice but very sexy—that she exuded. "Worst of all"—her voice dropped to a nervous whisper—"suppose he likes *you?* Suppose he takes one look and says, 'I have to have her!'"

"He won't." Reba shrugged all that away. "Not the way you look in that dress!" Her critical russet gaze scanned the blinding loveliness that was Carolina's own, the charming regular features, the cloud of fair hair light as the wind, those wide luminous silver eyes with their tarnished setting of darker lashes and above

211

them the delicate high riding wings of her brows. She took a step forward and seized Carolina by the arms.

"*Make* him fall in love with you!" she entreated in a voice pulsing with intensity. "Oh, *do* this for me, Carol—remember I would do the same for you."

Carolina stopped waving her fan and fixed her friend with a gaze as steady as any that ever looked over the battlements of an English castle. "I will try," she promised earnestly, remembering all that Reba had done for her. "I will somehow divert his attention so that at least he cannot ask for your hand *tonight*— indeed I will do my very best to win him."

Although what she would do with him once he was won was a matter to which she had so far given no thought. . . .

Chapter 15

It was with a feeling of intense relief that Carolina —muffled to the ears in Reba's French gray velvet cloak trimmed with fluffy black fox—arrived at Williston House in the company of Reba and her overdressed mother, and learnt that Lord Gayle's third son had not yet arrived. Indeed, they were told, he probably could not be expected to attend "in this uncertain weather, with the roads in such an icy condition that it has kept half our guests home!" Well, now that that had been established, she could set herself to enjoying her first ball on English soil!

Williston House was a fairly typical Jacobean manor house, of blackened timber and wattle construction, with high-ceilinged drafty rooms and great banks of brick chimneys and tall casement windows. The dancing was held in its great hall, smaller and cozier than the great hall at Broadleigh, which had been transformed from its normal gloom into brilliance by a forest of candles.

Sir Kyle, their host, was a florid smiling gentleman of middle size and middle age. He greeted them warmly in an out-of-date plum coat with worn gray velvet cuffs. One knee of his velvet breeches also showed a trace of wear. But he had a Yule Log burning merrily on his hearth, Carolina noted, his wine flowed as freely as his easy conversation, and his house was ablaze with holly and mistletoe. With his warm courtly manner, he could have been a Virginia gentleman. She felt at home in his company.

Lady Williston was something else altogether. She was tall and cool and her face had always been too angular for beauty, but it had weathered well and she had achieved in age what she had never had in youth— distinction. Her clothes too were old and somewhat yellowed about the hem, but the simple cut of her mauve brocade gown with its touches of gray lace provided a perfect setting for the handsome antique jewelry she wore—all family pieces, Carolina guessed. She greeted the Tarbells with cool civility although a vestige of surprise passed over her face when she looked at Carolina—and was quickly gone when Mistress Tarbell explained that Carolina was not her daughter but her daughter's friend from school. By contrast Lady Williston's very plainness made Reba's effusive mother in her amber and green cut velvet with its overlying layers of bronze lace ruffles and endless brooches and bangles seem expensively frumpish.

As if to make up for his wife's coldness, Sir Kyle showed them great attention. Carolina guessed that he felt he should notice his neighbors, no matter what his wife's feelings in the matter. He showed great interest in the Colonies and for that Carolina was grateful. It was a refreshing change to have somebody ask intelligent questions.

Carolina's advent into the room created quite a sensation among the young bucks (more men had made it over the icy roads than women) and she was shortly surrounded by such a crowd of them that her hostess looked scandalized and Reba's mother frowned darkly that her own marriageable daughter should be so eclipsed.

Carolina found the attention a heady wine. She danced with first one and then another as a succession of young men vied for her favor. None of them stood out very clearly because all the time she was thinking,

214

If only Thomas could be here, if only I could be dancing with him. . . .

She looked over the latest masculine shoulder at Reba, handsomely garbed in auburn velvet that exactly matched her auburn hair which had been dressed with spangled ribands. Reba was dancing with Sir Kyle himself and very obviously flirting with him. Carolina's gaze sought out Lady Williston and saw that she was watching Reba too and that her thin lips had tightened.

"Mamma vows she will not let me wear this gown again," Reba whispered when the two girls made a brief escape from the dancers and went upstairs to resurrect the damage so much skipping across the floor had done to their coiffures. "She swears you eclipse me! Indeed she drew me aside a few minutes ago and asked me severely why you'd been wearing plain brown woolen when you had gowns like this one. I told her it was the custom in the Colonies to arrive simply gowned and to step up the elegance as the visit wore on! And do you know, I think she believed me?" Reba shook her head.

Carolina guessed that Reba enjoyed outwitting a mother who kept such a heavy hand on the reins. Under the circumstances she could hardly blame her!

"'Tis as well she does not know this is your dress I'm wearing," laughed Carolina. "She might demand we exchange gowns here and now!"

"Yes, had I known Lord Gayle's son wouldn't be coming"—Reba peered into her hostess's dressing table mirror and artfully dabbed Spanish paper across her cheeks to give herself more color—"I'd have worn the dress myself!"

But you wouldn't have looked as good in it as I do, thought Carolina with amusement, for these are *my* colors! In the tall pier glass they had passed in the hall she had observed with satisfaction how the gray and silver of her gown somehow brought out the freshness of her complexion and the silver-gold gleam of her hair and made her gray eyes seem to flash the brighter in the dark tarnished frame of her long thick lashes.

"Have you learnt anything more about your mar-

215

quess?" she asked as she patted a stray strand of blonde hair back into place.

Reba turned an excited face toward her. "Yes!" she cried. "He is—" She stopped as a bevy of ladies surged into the room to renew their makeup and tuck hairpins into stray locks that had come loose in the dancing. "I'll tell you later," she said hastily. "And by then I may have learned more about it." She jumped up. "I hear the music striking up again and this next dance is promised to someone who may know. I'm going on downstairs, Carol." She dashed away through the oncoming ladies, leaving Carolina with her comb still poised.

Left alone, Carolina could not help but notice the cool envious looks the other women gave her, or how they pointedly chose not to include her in their conversations. Obviously her popularity with the gentlemen had not endeared her to the female contingent!

Carolina told herself she did not care. This whole Christmastide stay in Essex was but an interlude, after which she would go back to London and Lord Thomas. And fortunately Lord Thomas's family seat was not in Essex but in Northampton. She gave an already perfect coiffure a minute finishing touch, rose with an airy smile at the assembled ladies—who either averted their eyes or gave her baleful looks—and took herself back downstairs.

She made her way at a leisurely pace down the wide Jacobean staircase with its ornate carved balusters. The coolness of the ladies upstairs—to most of whom she had after all been introduced by her host—had brought out the devil in her. She had given her low-cut neckline a downward yank when she reached the head of the stairs and on the top step she took a deep breath that strained her velvet bodice to the utmost. Then she trailed gracefully down the stairs and halfway down paused to look over the assembled dancers, turning her head about to survey the room. She was wickedly aware that the brilliants at her shoulders were catching the light, and that same gleam of candlelight was showing to advantage the pearly luster of her breasts and haloing her pale hair.

Yet she looked out over the dancers without really seeing them individually, but more as a colorful moving mosaic of rainbow-hued silks and satins, swirling in time to the music. Again she was wishing that Thomas was here to swing her out upon the floor.

Still irritated, she gave a coquettish flirt to her light curls and moved on leisurely down the stairs.

When she reached the bottom step the vision of Lord Thomas vanished.

A gentleman who had been watching her descent with interest now stepped forward. A tall gentleman clad more soberly than most of the guests in a charcoal velvet coat, wide-cuffed and edged with silver braid, his long muscular legs encased in gunmetal satin breeches. Frosty point lace spilled from his cuffs and throat as he made a deep bow before her and when he rose from that bow she saw with shock that she was looking into the sardonic face of the man who had locked her into an upstairs room of the Star and Garter!

Before Carolina could more than gasp, he had murmured, "May I have the honor?" then seized her hand and led her, unresisting, out upon the floor.

Her senses whirled. This man could create a scandal if he told what he knew about her. Reba's mother might be so upset that she would send Carolina back to London to drag through the holidays at an empty school.

She could think of nothing appropriate to say.

The tall gentleman however seemed completely in command of the situation. A little smile played about his mouth.

"So I find you again," he murmured. "And in rather better case! At least no one is about to shoot you down or run you through with a sword. Tell me, is that sort of adventure usual to you?"

That comment brought a fiery response from his dancing partner.

"Of course it is not! I did it for—for—" She sought

for a reason other than sheer wildness that would bring her dressed as a man to a London inn by night. "For a wager," she finished, using the same story she had told Lord Freddie, for she had no intention of telling this arrogant stranger that she had been skulking around London trying to find her lover!

"For a wager?" He considered her with interest. "Faith, I'm surprised your brothers did not put a quencher on that!"

"I have no brothers!"

"Your parents then. One must presume you have parents?"

"My parents are in the Colonies," she snapped. "Virginia."

"Ah," he said. "So you are far from home. . . . A schoolgirl, one would surmise."

Her chin came up at this implication that she was not far removed from the nursery. "That's right, I do attend Mistress Chesterton's school in London."

"So that is how I missed you," he murmured. "You found your way back to the school. Faith, you must have run all the way!"

"I was taken into a friend's coach after I slid off the roof," she said resentfully, making an intricate turn that billowed her skirts. "And I might have broken my neck when I went over the edge—and it would have been *your fault* for locking me in like that!"

"Oh, I'm well aware of how you departed." His genial smile rested upon her and she could not help but notice how white his teeth were, against his dark face, or how intent his gaze. "The marks were plain in the snow. What I'm wondering is *why?* What was so pressing that you could not wait to be taken home in comfort in a hackney coach?"

Her cheeks were reddening uncomfortably as he spoke.

"Ah, I see," he said softly. "You had decided that, having dragged you upstairs and locked you into a dining room, I would be back to ply you with strong liquor and seduce you?"

She gave him an indignant look.

"You thought worse of me than that?" he mocked, swinging her expertly about. "You expected me to tear off your clothes perhaps and rape you?"

This conversation had gone far enough! There was something steady and reliable in those gray eyes that were studying her so intently that told her he would never have done any of those things. But his insolence drove her to fury.

"I thought you would game away the night and most probably return me in the morning to the school and that I would be promptly expelled!" she told him in a suffocated voice.

"And you did not wish to be sent home to Virginia in disgrace?" he murmured. "Well, that at least is understandable and somewhat lightens the dark opinion I felt you must hold of me." His dark head bent toward her and the music was suddenly very loud in her ears. She felt herself being swept away by it.

"I hold no opinion of you at all!" she cried, missing a step in her confusion. "I don't even know your name! And it is most improper of you to ask me to dance before we have been introduced!"

"Indeed?" He considered that, and a shadow of amusement passed across his sardonic face. She was more beautiful than he remembered and entirely feminine, he thought, with those luminous eyes and sooty lashes. She reminded him of a gray kitten he had found as a lad. Long-haired and fluffy and big-eyed and lost, the kitten had spat at him every time he tried to pick her up to remove her from the ruined cellar into which she had fallen. He had chased her around the cellar. She had watched him with big light baleful eyes—dark-fringed like the eyes of the girl before him—and dashed away hissing every time he tried to approach her. She had struck at him and bitten him when at last he pounced upon her. And when he had picked her up she had wailed and set her claws into his shirt, digging like tiny needles into his flesh. But he had carried her out triumphantly. Stroking her outraged fluffed-out fur, he had taken her home—and she had glared at him balefully all the way and made ferocious sounds. Once

219

home and lapping up milk, she had still considered him warily over the edge of the bowl, and then his little sister had come toddling in. She had promptly appropriated the kitten, naming her "Pussy Willow" for the silver gray catkin color of her fur. But "Willow," as she came to be called, had somehow considered herself *his* cat, ever since she had come out from behind the chair where she had retreated when first he set her down upon arrival. His sister had fed her and carried her about, had even slept with the cat around her neck. But ever after, the kitten—at first so wary of Rye—would stroll indolently toward him when he came into a room and rub her soft whiskers against his boots and purr and wave her long fluffy tail. Rye would stoop and gently rub her silky ears. They had come to an understanding, he and that cat. He wondered if he would ever come to an understanding with young Mistress Lightfoot, who—as outraged and fluffy as Willow had been—was just now rebuking him about the proprieties. Indeed he wondered if he would even reach a truce!

"I had thought our night together at the inn might have served as an introduction," he sighed on a note of amusement and Carolina gave him a look of vast alarm. For one of the young bucks who had been pursuing her so ardently had just danced his partner by very close and there was a good chance he might have overheard that remark and misconstrued it.

"I would hardly describe it as 'our night together,'" she said bitterly as he swung her away from the young buck who was now staring at her in amazement as if questioning his own ears. "And you are making me a scandal, for you were overheard in your last remark!"

"By whom?" His dark head swung round. "Ah— that lad in buff who just danced by?"

"Yes, the one who is giving me such an accusing look! It will be all over the countryside by morning that I am given to visiting inns with strange men!"

Rye frowned. "Rest easy, Mistress Lightfoot," he said and she noted that his voice had deepened and become extremely resolute. "I will see that the record is set straight. Your admirer will learn that I had never laid eyes on you before this evening. And if he chooses not to accept my word, he will find himself in need of a long convalescence!"

She gave him an uncertain look. Almost, he had sounded like her protector.

"It seems I have spent too much time away from England—I have forgot some of the niceties." The music had stopped now and he bowed again before her. "Permit me to introduce myself. Rye Evistock, at your service."

"I am Carolina Lightfoot," she said nervously. From a distance she could see several of the young bucks with whom she'd been dancing converging on her. "And I do hope you won't tell anyone that you saw me at the Star and Garter," she added quickly. "I mean—"

"Mistress Lightfoot," said that deep voice on a rather humorous note. "I am the soul of discretion. You may depend upon it, I will keep your dark secret to my grave."

Carolina flushed again. He was mocking her, indeed looking down upon her from his great height with amused delight. Oh, he was impossible! She lifted her chin and turned away from the tall figure in gray and immediately accepted the offer to dance of the first young buck to reach her side. From that dance she was promptly claimed by another. And then another. But over a variety of satin shoulders, she was constantly aware of Rye Evistock's dark head, as he conversed first, at length, with his host—with whom he seemed to be on most familiar terms for his host ended up laughing and slapping him on the back—and then with a variety of other people. He seemed, she thought in some chagrin, quite popular here—which she was not. Pursued, yes, but not popular.

She was not really afraid Rye Evistock would fail to keep her secret. There was indeed something very solid and reassuring about him for all that he had amused gray eyes and a wickedly wolfish grin. She really could not have said what it was about him that so disturbed

her. Reba danced by deep in conversation with someone, and then Rye Evistock was dancing with her
again.

"I have learnt considerably more about you, Mistress
Lightfoot," he told her softly. "I have learnt that you
are a guest of the new people who have bought
Broadleigh. And are to remain there for at least a
fortnight."

"I am to spend the Twelve Days of Christmas with
them," admitted Carolina warily, noting how easy it
was to follow Rye's lead in the dance. He had an easy
grace and there was a feeling of sureness in his step and
of great strength in the way he moved. He was lean, she
realized, as a fencer is lean, with long arms and long
legs and a muscular spring to his gait. But she still could
not forgive him for his arrogant treatment of her at the
inn.

"Good," he said. "I will hope to call upon you
there."

His confident expectation that he would be joyfully
received by her at Broadleigh nettled Carolina. She
decided to take him down a peg. "There will probably
be a round of outings," she said vaguely. "I may not be
at home to be called upon."

His dark face came alert at her offhand tone. "Surely, Mistress Lightfoot," he remonstrated, "you cannot
hold it against me that I saved your life the other
night?"

Put like that, it did seem churlish of her not to allow
him to call. She let him whirl her around several times
before she answered.

"It was the *manner* of your saving," she declared
heatedly. "I am not used to being dragged about and
treated as if I were some—"

"Young lad who needed strong measures?" he said
coolly. "But you were dressed as a lad, I'll remind
you!"

"Yes, but you knew I was not. You knew—"

"I wonder how I knew?" he murmured. "Could it
have been the way you blushed and looked away when

222

you met my eyes? Could it have been your feminine gestures?"

Carolina felt stung. "My gestures were *not* feminine! I practiced them before the mirror!"

"Did you now?" He chuckled. "Well, they seemed feminine to me. And no lad ever had skin like yours!" He looked down meaningfully at the lovely line of her outthrust young breasts. "I do recall you were much flatter then. I'll warrant it was painful, binding those pretty things down so tightly."

"How dare you talk to me like that?" she flared. "No gentleman would say such a thing! Indeed I'll not dance with you, sir!"

"Ah, but perhaps I am not a gentleman," he laughed. "Perhaps I have forgot how to be one!"

That was his affair! She tried to fling away from him but he kept a steely grip on her hand and managed to whirl her about so that her violent motion away from him seemed to be merely part of the dance. "But if you choose to dash suddenly away from me on the dance floor, I may be called upon to explain it." His smile was remarkably sunny. "And what then could I say but the truth?"

He meant he would tell about that night at the inn!

"Oh, but you promised!" cried Carolina, shocked. "And a gentleman would never go back on his promise!"

"Ah, so I am back to being a gentleman again?" There was laughter behind his gray eyes. "Then am I to understand that your aversion to me is not so great as to leave me stranded alone upon the floor?"

"I did not say that either!"

She gave him a smoldering look as the music stopped and his boots came to rest beside her sinuous gray velvet skirts.

"I will bid you good evening," she told him crisply.

"Ah, not so fast!" He had kept his hold on her and now that the music had started again, he swept her unwilling form out again upon the dance floor before any of the disappointed young bucks who had been heading in their direction could reach her. "I am but a visitor to these shores," he told her. "My time is short and I must make the most of it."

He whirled her into an anteroom off the great hall, a curtained alcove momentarily deserted, where tall many-paned Tudor windows pierced the building wall. The draperies over the windows had not been drawn and they seemed alone in a snowy landscape. Outside the gnarled old trees bent beneath their glistening burden of white, the ancient boxwoods bore crowns of snow and the sweeping lawn was a white glitter. It was a breathtaking view.

He had stopped dancing by the window and paused to let her admire the view—but he kept his hold on her, as he once had kept his hold on a cornered kitten.

"It is lovely—Essex," he said softly. "But not for me. No longer for me."

Curiosity overcame her antagonism. "Why not?"

He smiled down at her. "Would you care?"

A white moon rode the dark sky above the glittering branches. In the crisp clear air the stars were myriad and bright as flung diamonds against the velvet dark. The moonlight had softened his hard features, given depth to his eyes. Suddenly she *did* care for there had been an undertone of sadness in his voice. After all, he had not done anything so terrible to her—it was not his fault that she had slipped and fallen off the roof. And there had been some justification for his actions that night at the inn. He *had* saved her, perhaps from death, and he could have dragged her upstairs merely to keep her from getting into more trouble. Something steady in his gaze had told her that.

"Yes." It was barely a whisper. "I think I *would* care."

He looked surprised—and suddenly vulnerable. So had a kitten won him once—by purring at just the right moment.

"Tell me," she said softly, "why Essex is no longer for you?"

He looked past her, out past the snowy landscape to far distances, somewhere beyond this pleasant land.

224

"We all take steps in our youth," he murmured. "And some of them are irrevocable."

Such a step as she had taken with Lord Thomas. . . . Somehow the elusive Lord Thomas seemed far away tonight. And Rye Evistock was very close. She felt with him a communion of the spirit—his troubles, her troubles. . . .

"Perhaps not so irrevocable," she declared.

"You think not?" he said quickly.

"Of course not." She tossed her head. "A man may change." *Or a maid.* . . .

"Yes," he murmured. "A man *could* change . . . with the right woman."

It all happened very quickly. His long arms went round her and she went into them with a quick involuntary yearning. His dark head inclined, his mouth was upon her trembling one, and he brought her slight velvet-clad body close against his own. Magically she seemed to fit there as if the gods had designed the two of them as a set. In that dreamy moment Carolina did not ask herself the rightness or wrongness of what she did. She melted against Rye and her lips were soft and pliant beneath his.

He felt the gentle yielding of her, the—almost—submission. And gave back gentleness in return. There beneath a cold moon he cradled her head in his hand and stroked her hair and let his questing lips rove lightly over her flushed face, brushing her long dark lashes, her high winged brows, her smooth forehead, the pale gleaming curls that lay so lightly, silvered by the moonlight over Essex. He took no liberties—although he sensed he might and not be repulsed—but showed her, as he felt was her due from a gentleman of Essex born and bred, all the respect owed an aristocratic maiden from a suitor.

But Carolina was shaken by the contact and pushed away from him, trembling.

"Mr. Evistock—" she began.

"Oh, I think you might call me Rye at this point, don't you?" His voice was ever so lightly mocking.

She stiffened. *"Rye* then. If we are to be friends, you

225

must not pounce upon me like this whenever we chance to be alone."

So a kitten had once said to him—only not being able to say it in plain English, she had said it with her sharp little teeth and tiny claws and spitting hisses. But he had persevered and the kitten had come round to purring, and this girl with her willow-gray eyes, shining in the moonlight like silver catkins, would come around too. His heart burst with the sudden knowledge of it and all the harsh years were swept away.

"Mistress Lightfoot," he said earnestly. *"Carolina,* if I may—if you will but smile upon me, I will promise not to pounce."

She smiled, showing a row of even white teeth. "I would I could believe you, sir," she said archly.

"Well, there is one amendment," he told her in an easy voice. "I promise not to pounce *unless invited.*"

The implication was clear—and delightful. For the moment, in the tumult of her emotions, she had forgotten Thomas, forgotten Reba, forgotten the man she was supposed to charm should he appear. Rye Evistock, she thought dreamily, would be an easy man to love. A woman could feel *safe* with him. Protected. And his lips had been intoxicating. She had not dared let herself succumb to her feelings.

It was a very promising moment.

"Then I may call upon you tomorrow?"

"Oh, yes," she said happily.

He sensed that happiness and stood the straighter. He who had taken so many women so lightly—who had had only one love and she was gone—now found it easy to step into the role of suitor. He would make her charming speeches, he would dance attendance, he would be all that young Mistress Lightfoot desired—at least for a season. Come Twelfth Night he would have to make a decision and it would be a hard one. He would put it off. For here was a maiden worthy of being chased, a kitten worth the taming. . . .

Carolina liked his courtliness, for she sensed that it was out of respect for her. She liked that respect, for she sensed behind it wildness and audacity. And that he was holding himself in check meant—*it meant that he held her in higher regard than Thomas had, who had pounced upon her unawares while she was naked in the tub!* The memory of *that* brought color flooding to her face and Rye, looking down, thought that it was his kiss that had brought it on and felt a warm sense of triumph suffuse him.

"Perhaps you will be staying in England then?" she asked quickly, conscious of his regard.

"Perhaps," he agreed. For who would not risk danger for such a maid?

"We should get back—we will be missed," she said hurriedly, for she sensed that he was about to kiss her again, and she felt that with one more kiss she would be lost.

Without comment, Rye took her away from the alcove, back to an inconspicuous corner of the great hall where she would be shielded from view by the clustered backs of a group of gentlemen, deep in discussion. He smiled down fondly upon her. "Wait for me here and I will bring you a glass of wine and we will toast the good fortune of our meeting," he said and strode away through the dancers.

Reba, coming up just then, caught her arm almost as Rye departed. "I've just learnt that the Marquess of Saltenham has landed at Dover and will spend the holidays at his estate in Hampshire!" she whispered.

"And his wife?"

"Died in Italy." There was triumph in her voice.

So Reba had been right, the poor woman's health had indeed been frail!

"Robin will need to observe a suitable period of mourning and then of course he will come for me," she declared confidently. "Oh, Carol, I can't thank you enough. But you must not weaken," she cautioned. "If only I can get through these next weeks!"

"Well, I hope you can, but I don't understand why you're thanking me—I certainly haven't done anything to merit thanks!"

"But of course you have," said Reba, squeezing her hand. "You've been distracting him."

"Distracting who?"

Reba was fast losing patience. All this adulation, all these young bucks who had been clustering around Carolina all evening, must, she decided, have gone to her friend's head. "The man you've just been dancing with, of course, who's just gone to bring you a glass of wine."

"But that's not—he told me his name is Rye Evistock."

"And so it is. Rye Evistock is Lord Gayle's third son."

Carolina felt her breath leave her. *Rye Evistock* was the aristocratic fortune hunter who'd been arranging a betrothal with wealthy Reba? *Rye?* She could hardly credit it.

But a further shock was in store for Reba gave her an amused look. "Don't look so thunderstruck, Carol," she said in a voice gone just slightly malicious. "It isn't just your beautiful body he's after."

"What—what do you mean?"

Reba couldn't resist crowing over her own cleverness. "While I was dancing with Sir Kyle early in the evening, I made a point of telling him all about your father's great wealth. His country seat at Farview on the Eastern Shore, his forty thousand acres on the James—or was it the York? His vast income from ships and trading posts. The elegant house he's building that will beggar anything Essex has to offer!" Her glinting russet eyes said better than any words that it had gone against the grain to have Carolina getting all the attention—and in *her* clothes.

"Oh, Reba, you didn't?" cried Carolina.

"I did indeed," laughed Reba. "I told him your father was *far* wealthier than mine, that you were his only child. I talked about your fashion dolls from Paris and your London dressmaker—"

"*Your* London dressmaker," corrected Carolina bitterly.

"And then we talked about Lord Gayle's third son, and it turns out Sir Kyle's very thick with Rye Evistock

—known him since he was a lad, he said, and thinks highly of him. So of course Sir Kyle must have told him what a great fortune you possess, for here he is, plying you with wine!"

Carolina recalled that Rye had let her go rather lightly when first they had been dancing. And then he had had a long back-slapping talk with his host and when he had come back he had said—what had he said? *I have learnt considerably more about you, Mistress Lightfoot!* Indeed he had—and most of it lies. At the moment she wasn't sure at whom she was the more indignant—Rye or Reba. Reba for getting her into this mess, Rye for neatly changing the target of his pursuit. For had not Reba said, *I told him your father was far wealthier than mine . . . ?*

She felt—hurt. For Reba's words had blasted to bits her view of Rye Evistock, whom she had been comparing so favorably to Thomas. To think that she had begun to like him, despite his effrontery at the inn! And now it seemed to her that he was as bad as Reba, edging this way and that for advantage. If some other girl came through that door and Sir Kyle told him she had more money that either Reba or Carolina, would Rye instantly turn coat and pay court to *her?*

And she had let him kiss her—she who was betrothed to Thomas! It proved, she told herself bleakly, that she was something she had never admired—what they called in Virginia "a hot wench," else how could such a slight contact with his lean body have sent her blood racing? Resentment flamed up in her and she yearned to strike back at him. If he could be false in this, he could be false in something else as well. For all that she thought she had sensed in him a kind of honor, she could well be wrong. He could protest all he liked, but who could say what he might have done had she been such a fool as to wait for him there, locked in that private dining room at the inn?

Her wild thoughts were interrupted by Rye's arrival, carrying aloft two glasses of wine.

"Ah, I see I have found not one but two ladies."

From his great height Rye smiled down upon them. "And fortunately I have a glass for each." He proffered one to Reba.

"Why, we thank you, sir!" Carolina's silver eyes gleamed and she swept him a mocking curtsy, as befitted the shameless fortune hunter that he was.

But when she rose again her face was angelic as she took the proffered wine.

Oh, she would make Rye Evistock fall in love with her, all right—but not to please Reba! She would do it for the pure joy of first enchanting and then rejecting him—*she would do it for revenge!*

Chapter 16

They had barely risen from the breakfast table at Broadleigh the next morning when Rye Evistock was announced.

Reba's mother looked startled, but pleased. It had not occurred to her that perhaps Rye had not come to see Reba. "I don't care for that dress," she muttered, surveying Reba's plainer than usual tawny rose silk. "You must have known he was coming—you should have worn your ruby velvet."

Reba, whose mind was currently on her marquess and not on her gown, gave both her mother and Carolina a blithe look. In point of fact she had not known Rye Evistock was coming, but she did not want her mother to know that. She went forward to greet her guest and made him a deep curtsy.

But even as he made an elegant leg to Reba, Rye's gray gaze was searching out Carolina, who was wearing a gown she had carefully chosen from Reba's wardrobe —a tailored sky blue velvet trimmed in bands of silver braid. Rye Evistock caught his breath at sight of her.

Reba's mother found she had duties which demanded her elsewhere. At the door she paused and gave Carolina a look that clearly said she too should leave Reba alone with her new suitor. Carolina pretended not to notice. Once her mother had gone, Reba tactfully excused herself and left Carolina alone with Rye.

"You are good friends, I take it?" Rye's gaze was on the door through which Reba had departed as he seated himself on a plum damask settee.

"The best," said Carolina staunchly. Not for worlds would she have admitted to this despicable fortune hunter that she found Reba's mother unacceptable or Reba's conduct sadly wanting. It occurred to her suddenly that he might merely want to learn more about his second choice—in case he should decide against the first! She found the thought deflating and there was a trace of resentment in her voice as she began to extoll Reba's virtues, from her sense of style to her sagacity.

"I would judge *you* to be amply endowed with all those things," observed her companion easily. "And with loyalty besides," he added thoughtfully, for he shared the county's general opinion of these upstarts who had bought Broadleigh.

Carolina flushed for she could not help but wonder what Lord Thomas would be thinking of her loyalty now if he could but see her smiling seductively at Rye Evistock!

"I hope so," she said in a suffocated voice.

"Tell me, do you miss Virginia?" he asked, studying her keenly.

Now he wants to hear about my wealth, my vast mansion! thought Carolina angrily. She had thought she could bear it, but suddenly she could not. With a recklessness that would have become her mother, she threw back her head and set her jaw.

"Whatever Sir Kyle has told you about me is false and you may as well know it now!" she burst out.

He was gazing at her imperturbably. "And what is it you think he told me?"

"That I am a great heiress, that my father has forty thousand acres!"

"I knew that was false," he said.

232

"Nor do I have a London dressmaker or—what did you say?"

"I said I knew you were not a great heiress. Sir Kyle told me that Reba is spreading such a story but he knew it to be untrue."

"How? How did he know?"

"Sir Kyle is well acquainted with a certain Captain Mercer of the *Bristol Maid*."

But that was the ship that had carried her across the Atlantic! Captain Mercer was a friend of her father.

"And he had told Sir Kyle about his friends in Virginia. Naturally Sir Kyle told me."

So Rye had known all along that she was not an heiress!

"He told you—about Bedlam?" she asked uneasily, guessing that Captain Mercer would have regaled Sir Kyle with some good stories about the turbulent Lightfoots.

Rye hesitated. Then, "Yes, he did," he said.

Carolina gave him a bitter look. "My family's fame follows me to England, I see."

"Better a colorful family than a dull one," he told her evenly. "Bear in mind that they are dull sticks who have never done anything worth remarking!"

She gave him a grateful look. "I once heard Sandy Randolph say something very like that," she murmured, and forthwith launched into a description of life on the Eastern Shore. "And what of you?" she finished. "Here I am doing all the talking and I know nothing about you."

"I am a younger son," he shrugged. "Which in a way speaks for itself. The family estate will come down by primogeniture to my eldest brother and there will be little to divide by inheritance once my father is gone. So I took myself away early and made my way elsewhere. I went out to Barbados and became a planter."

"So you are a Colonist like myself," she laughed. "I am afraid I will never be accepted here," she confided. "All the ladies at last night's ball seemed to be looking down their noses at me!"

"Accepted? Oh, I should think you could manage it easily." He gave her an inscrutable look.

Something in that look made her blush and quickly drop her gaze. She wondered suddenly how far she should go with this farce. It was a dishonorable thing she was doing. How had she allowed herself to be dragged into it?

Restless under his scrutiny, she was delighted when he suggested they take a stroll through the grounds. He knelt at her feet to assist her into her tall pattens, and swept the fur-trimmed cloak she had borrowed from Reba around her shoulders with some determination.

"It is good to be outside," he told her once they had cleared the door and were strolling down the driveway, along the edges of which snow was melting in the morning sunlight. "I remember too well the family who lived here before the Tarbells. Hal was a close friend of mine and I keep expecting him to come through the drawing room door and clap me upon the shoulder."

"Where did they go, the last people?" she asked him.

"Hal's father went under," he told her. "Couldn't meet his debts and eventually sold the place. Trying to keep it up had broken his health and he took his family down to the Scilly Isles where the climate is milder. All but Hal, who'd left home some time before." He sounded sad.

"And Hal?"

"He died last winter."

There was something bleak in his voice as he spoke and she guessed that it was hard for him to come back to Broadleigh remembering the friends of his youth and find these new people bringing in new furniture and new draperies but somehow losing the atmosphere that he had known and loved. A sense of gentility had come with Carolina's people when they settled in Virginia and it stood her in good stead now. She understood what made him want to leave the overfurnished drawing room at Broadleigh to walk about the familiar grounds in the brisk cold air.

"I am sorry," she said softly. "It is terrible to lose a friend."

"I have lost many friends," he said, sighing. "It gets no easier."

They strolled about, dodging the snow that would fall suddenly from the heavy laden branches, and she felt a rapport with him that surprised her. It was a deeper rapport than she had ever felt with Thomas, who was the very essence of town. Rye could have been a Virginia gentleman, she thought. Like Sandy Randolph. . . .

She felt depressed when he left, promising to return upon the morrow. She felt herself a deceiver.

Reba's mother regarded her as a deceiver too but for quite another reason. She was just descending the stairs when Carolina bade her caller goodbye at the front door and she stood solidly at the foot after Carolina had shut the door upon her departing guest.

"Where is Reba?" she asked coldly.

"I'm here, Mamma." Reba popped in from the library. "It was nice of you, Carol, to show Rye about the grounds."

"And where were *you?*" demanded her mother. "Why were you not showing him the grounds yourself?"

"Well, I—" Reba gazed about her with a hunted look. "Mamma, Rye really came to see Carol. He told her last night that he would call." She looked at her friend for confirmation and Carolina nodded.

"But you knew," burst out her mother. "You *knew* what your father had planned! Oh, it is a good thing he is not here to see this!"

"Yes, I knew, Mamma," said Reba swiftly. "But Rye was so taken with Carol last night—I am not to blame for that, really I'm not!"

"But he would *not* have fancied her had you stayed beside him and got rid of your friend!" stormed her mother and Carolina felt her cheeks flaming with embarrassment.

Reba's mother gave her a sour look. She was still harping on it at lunch and Carolina would not have been too surprised had she been bundled into the family coach and promptly returned to London. But

235

by now her hostess's indignation had taken another turn:

"Why, I've half a mind to deny Rye Evistock the house!" was her angry comment as she stabbed at her dessert. "After practically *settling* things with your father, he arrives and *ignores* you and takes up with your houseguest!"

"Mamma, it doesn't *matter!*" protested Reba. "I don't care at all, and I'm sure Carol doesn't. And anyway," she finished, "we have all of the holidays before us and even though he noticed Carol first, I heard Eleanor Wannsdale say last night that although Rye had squired a lot of girls he had never remained long with any one of them, so maybe he's just following his usual pattern. Ask yourself, would you want a philanderer in the family?"

Carolina thought that very unfair and wondered what Eleanor Wannsdale really knew. For herself she thought that Rye Evistock had a very steady gaze and a face you could trust. It was her opinion that if he once chose a woman he'd stick to her—regardless of Eleanor Wannsdale's opinion.

Reba's mother subsided, muttering.

That afternoon brought several more callers—young bucks with smiling faces who asked for Mistress Lightfoot. But they were fashionable and of the gentry and Reba's mother welcomed them all. Indeed she suddenly looked on Carolina with more favor—this bright star with the silver blonde hair was bringing the social life of Essex to her: Such a girl could not be all bad! She concentrated her ire on Rye Evistock.

The next day the three of them had just walked into the great hall after breakfast when Rye was again announced. Mistress Tarbell surged forward with a frown to meet him.

"Oh, dear, Mamma's on the warpath," muttered Reba.

Rye Evistock must have caught the warlike gleam in his hostess's eye for he was instantly equal to the occasion. He swept Mistress Tarbell a low bow and

236

before she could voice the cutting comment that had come to her lips, he was speaking suavely.

"My apologies for arriving so early to call upon Mistress Carolina," he told his hostess gravely. "But I come not only as a caller but as a messenger. On my way here I happened to meet Lord Hollistead, who asked me to convey his felicitations and hoped that you and your daughter, and of course your houseguest"— his smiling gaze played over Carolina, waiting uneasily in the background—"will honor him by your presence at the castle tomorrow night. He is giving a small dinner party and has invited a few friends you might enjoy meeting."

Mistress Tarbell's frown washed away so quickly it left her face ludicrously blank. This was good news indeed! She had been hoping for an invitation from Lady Hollistead ever since they had bought Broadleigh but so far she had been ignored by the people in the castle. And to be invited to a *small* dinner party! She beamed graciously upon Rye.

"You *knew*," Carolina told him delightedly when they were alone. "You *knew* exactly what would mollify her!"

"That was not precisely my intention," he admitted. "I happened to meet Lord Hollistead upon the road. I'd not seen him for years and we stopped to talk. When I told him a young lady in whom I had an interest was visiting at Broadleigh, he clapped me upon the shoulder and said, 'Bring her over to dinner tonight— bring the whole crew over!' I took him at his word."

Carolina's smile twinkled; they shared a perfect understanding. They both knew Reba's mother for what she was—a social climber. And Rye was but exploiting her hostess's weakness.

Carolina had seen the Tower of London, she had seen Greenwich and St. James—but always from the exterior. That evening at Lord Hollistead's ancestral home would always be counted as her "first castle." She approached the battlements with excitement, stared up with awe from the coach at the tall crenellated towers that had withstood siege in the Middle Ages, and thrilled as she crossed the moat on an ancient drawbridge that she was later to learn was never raised.

As they went inside, Mistress Tarbell was muttering instructions to Reba to "Be nice to Lord Hollistead's younger sons—I'm told neither of them is married," but Carolina hardly heard. She gazed enraptured at the ancient standards that hung from the lofty beams of the castle's great hall, larger by far than Broadleigh's, at the battle shields and other weaponry that lined the walls. An enormous Yule Log crackled in a massive stone fireplace taller than a man's head, and Lady Hollistead, a frail ethereal beauty from Kent now gone gray and fragile with age, met them like a faded swaying rose and bade them welcome.

But if the Tarbells were welcomed by reason of Lord Hollistead's longstanding friendship with Rye Evistock, Carolina of the Colonies was not so warmly received by the ladies of the party, most of whom had been at the ball at Williston House and had watched her sweep all before her. And that faint dislike of the interloper was nowhere so apparant as at dinner which was elegantly served in the echoing Great Hall.

"What a wild coast you must live upon, Mistress Lightfoot." From across the table Dolly de Lacey, a pretty brunette of about Carolina's age, fixed Carolina with her innocent blue gaze.

"It is none so wild," said Carolina, conscious that Dolly's comment had been rather loud and that conversation at the table had died down as everyone sought to hear her reply—and the party was none so small after all; some twenty-four people sat around Lord Hollistead's long board, facing each other over a magnificent display of gleaming silver.

"Really?" Dolly's laugh tinkled. "Curtis Webber visited Philadelphia and he described the *entire coast* to the south as infested with red Indians, freebooters, adventurers and pirates!"

"Indeed, Mistress Dolly, pirates too have their uses," interposed one of Lord Hollistead's sons, a pale-eyed lad of twelve who sat on Dolly's right. Mistress Tarbell had been discomfited to learn the other unmarried lad was even younger! "My tutor told me it was some fellow named Fleming—and a pirate at that—who first alerted the English forces to the arrival of the Spanish Armada in the English Channel."

"Ah, but I do not mean the sea dogs of Queen Elizabeth's time," laughed Dolly. "For I am told that pirates from the Caribbean boldly sail their ships right up to the American coast. Tell us, Mistress Lightfoot, have you met any?"

Carolina flushed with annoyance, for Dolly had used a bantering tone, and there was a subtle inference in her challenging gaze that Carolina might somehow have entered English society by the back door and might have a father who trafficked with pirates. She was about to return a stiff answer when Rye, seated beside her, suddenly interrupted.

"I think you do not mean pirates when you speak of the sea rovers of the Caribbean, Mistress Dolly, for those men are buccaneers—and many carry privateers' commissions."

"Yes," interrupted their host with a frown. "And did ye know as much about history, Mistress Dolly, as ye do about curling your pretty locks, ye would know that Commissions of Reprisal have been granted to English merchantmen since the thirteenth century to redress what is stolen from them on the high seas!"

"Do you not realize," Rye added, looking at Dolly de Lacey, "that the Spanish would have taken Jamaica and broken the power of England in the Caribbean had it not been for the buccaneer Henry Morgan, who discouraged them by sacking Panama?"

"A noble venture," agreed his host, nodding solemnly. "And well justified."

"And one without which Mistress Lightfoot here would scarce have been able to make so safe a journey over the sea to England," commented Rye, his gray eyes contemplating Carolina without expression.

Carolina disdained this fine distinction between buccaneers and pirates. She was still smarting under Dolly's barb. "I for one have never met a pirate," she said airily. "And never choose to meet one!"

"Pray God you do not," said Rye under his breath.

His comment was covered up by the general laughter that greeted Carolina's blithe remark. Lady Hollistead rose and led the ladies to the withdrawing room while the gentlemen were left comfortably to smoke their pipes and drink their after dinner brandy.

"Rye Evistock certainly sprang quickly to your defense," laughed Reba, when they were back home and Carolina was undressing for bed. Reba had followed her into her bedchamber.

"Why should he not?" retorted Carolina. "For have I not flung myself quite shamelessly at his head?"

There was such a note of bitterness in her young voice that Reba looked for a moment fearful. "Carolina," she pleaded. "My whole future hinges on your being able to keep him dangling. It's only for a little while."

Carolina had now donned her nightrail and was seated before her dressing table, combing out her long fair hair. "What makes you so certain that if I drop Rye he will turn to you?" she demanded challengingly.

"Why—the arrangements that he was making with Papa, of course, before you came."

"He may have changed his tune."

"About money?" Reba laughed. "No, I think that men are always seeking rich wives—even if they do waver now and then when a pretty face passes by!" She studied Carolina. "Maybe you should marry Rye."

"How can you say that?" cried Carolina, throwing down her comb, "when you *know* I am promised to Thomas?"

"Oh, well, I realize that Thomas has money and a title—of course he's the better catch. It's just that Rye seems so very taken with you and—the way you look at him sometimes. . . ."

Carolina gave her friend a scathing look. Rye Evistock was very attractive—sometimes almost overpoweringly so. But Thomas was her lover. She'd promised to marry him—and along with that promise went being

240

true to him. And she intended to *be* true to Thomas even if for the moment she'd let herself be caught up in this charade on Reba's behalf. She had begun to feel very ashamed of herself for her part in this whole affair but certainly Thomas didn't deserve treachery such as Reba suggested!

She glared at her friend. Her opinion of Reba was sinking lower every day!

The next morning brought its own turmoil in the form of two letters that arrived by special coach. One was from little Clemency Dane to Reba—the other, which carried more weight, was from Clemency's mother to Reba's mother.

Both letters had much the same thing to report.

"Oh, it is deliciously scandalous!*"* burbled Clemency's letter, which was being read avidly by Carolina and Reba at the same time. *"Mistress Chesterton has been* found out! *It all happened like this: Binnie Chase's mother came to London for some last-minute shopping before Christmas and took it into her head to pay Mistress Chesterton a call, to ask her how Binnie could come home with a cold when she had* specifically *told her how delicate Binnie's health was and that she should have a bedwarmer every night. She noticed a coach outside the school but she paid no attention. She must actually have pushed past Angie, who tried to close the door in her face. Anyway she burst in on a wild game of Blind Man's Buff with Lord Ormsby and some of his friends. Lord Ormsby was in his smallclothes and Mistress Chesterton was in her chemise and it seems they came careening down the stairs and almost ran over Binnie Chase's mother. Well, the word is* out *now. Mistress Chase is writing to every parent who has a daughter in the school and* no one *will return to Mistress Chesterton's after the holidays! Isn't it smashing? I am hoping to be allowed to remain in Surrey, but Mamma may well find me another school. I am sure we may never see each other again but I thought you would like to know."*

There was more but both girls paused to gaze into each other's eyes in horror at that point. Jenny Chesterton's dark secret, so well kept by the girls, was public knowledge now. She would no longer be able to operate the school, for all doors would be closed to her.

But for Carolina a whole new world had opened up: a world where Lord Thomas could come calling every day, a world where Mistress Chesterton would hardly refuse to let her go away with him if she chose, a world in which she could be married whether her parents back in Virginia sent their blessing or not—for it would take time for a letter to cross the ocean.

"*I* will be going back to the school," she told Reba firmly.

"*If* Mamma will let you," murmured Reba. "I don't doubt she'll insist you linger on as our guest until your parents can be heard from. And oh, Carol, won't you do it? You'll be able to keep Rye Evistock at bay for me! Oh, *please* do!"

Carolina gave her friend a strange look. She would be able to keep Rye Evistock at bay for Reba, no doubt. But would she be able to keep him at bay from herself?

"I don't know," she said in an uneven voice. "I don't know how long I can go on like this."

It galled Reba to have to be constantly begging Carolina to keep up her flirtation with Rye, and there was a light edge of malice in her voice when she told her the next afternoon about the gossip she'd heard from one of the young bucks who now wore a path down Broadleigh's smooth drive to see Carolina.

"There's a story going around about you and Rye," she told Carolina. "That you spent the night together at an inn somewhere. That Rye himself said so! I suppose that partially explains your enormous popularity!" She gave Carolina a bland look. "Are you *sure* you told me all that happened that night at the inn when he locked you in?"

Carolina flushed to her ears. The young fellow in buff, whose name, she now recalled, was Farnham, must not have been impressed by Rye's protestations that he had only just met Carolina that night at

Williston House! "Of course I'm sure!" she snapped. She was tempted to add, *I'm not like you, falling into bed on first acquaintance!* But she thought better of it. Reba, for all that she had lain in the hedge "experimenting" with a footman, really seemed to be in love with the marquess. In her fashion, of course.

But when she told Rye the story, his lean face hardened.

They were strolling alone together across the snowy lawns of Broadleigh, their boots crunching companionably over the crust. The air was crystal clear and the sunlight sparkled on the snow, making all of Essex seem a white wonderland.

"It seems I must have a word with Farnham," Rye said softly.

Spoken like Sandy Randolph! she thought ruefully. For he too was given to quick denouements. She hoped Rye's "word" with Farnham would not lead to bloodshed!

She suddenly imagined Rye in Yorktown, calling on her at Aunt Pet's. He seemed to fit very well there in her mind.

"Do you like to ride?" she asked, for it was horsey country, there along the James.

"Hell for leather," was his calm rejoinder.

"No, I mean—do you ride for pleasure? Race for pleasure?"

His dark face split into a wide grin. "I seldom have the time for either. But I will race you to the gates now—my horse against any nag you may find in the stables! And the loser pays a forfeit."

"I have no riding habit here," she protested.

He gave her a wistful smile. "One can ride in anything. Perhaps you fear the forfeit?"

His tone taunted her with its clear assumption that he would best her. Letitia Lightfoot would never have let such a remark stand unchallenged—nor would her daughter!

"You're on!" cried Carolina, giving her silver-gold curls such a reckless toss that the hood of Reba's cloak tumbled down upon her shoulders. Chuckling, Rye followed her to the stables where she selected a bay the groom promised her was "a fast mare."

The driveway of Broadleigh was icy, the going was dangerous, but Carolina, who—like most Virginia-born aristocrats—had ridden almost from babyhood, set a fast pace down the tree-lined avenue. Rye's big horse was the faster but somewhat tired from his ride over and Rye eased down and let Carolina dash on ahead of him down the long drive. He smiled to watch her slender back, arrow straight in the saddle—indeed he *wanted* her to win; there would be no joy in besting her.

She was laughing as she looked back at him with her pale hair flying in the wind, for they were nearing the gates now—and she was ahead. But suddenly he saw what she did not—a high-sided farm cart just lumbering onto the drive from behind a wall of snowy foliage with a load of firewood for the hall. If she did not rein up, she would collide with it!

"Carolina!" he cried, urging his mount ahead. "Look out!"

At his warning, Carolina's head swung back to see the big farm cart appear from nowhere just ahead of her. She tried to swerve her unfamiliar mount—and the mare slipped. Rye, who had thundered up and had just cut around her at a breakneck pace, reached out and swept her from the saddle even as the mare went down into the snow, sliding past the farm cart on the underlying ice and almost gliding through the gates. With the strong hand of the expert horseman, he brought his horse to a skidding halt. It had all happened so fast, his swift move to save her had been so instinctive, she could not believe she was pressed against him, legs dangling, while her slim waist was caught securely in the grip of one strong arm—when she should have been plunged headfirst into the snow!

Ahead of them the mare, who had been frightened by her narrow escape with disaster, scrambled to her feet, shook herself off and stood with her sleek bay flanks trembling, giving all and sundry a baleful look.

The driver of the farm cart, rolling his eyes, clucked at his big plough horses and passed by, muttering.

But Carolina, her heart pounding, found herself suddenly swept up and seated sideways, her skirts all tumbled, on the saddle before Rye. He was looking down at her with grim intensity for in his mind he had seen her fall off, seen her lying in the snow—still and hurt.

"I think perhaps I should not propose such dangerous games," he said ruefully.

But this was the most dangerous game of all, this close proximity to his strong masculine body, to this warmth of his that seemed to radiate right through her. She knew she should leap off but she could not seem to move. She sat staring up into his dark intent face with her eyes large and luminous, pinned like a collector's butterfly.

"I believe I have won," he murmured. "Shall I name your forfeit?"

She glanced toward her mare, standing trembling in the center of the gates. "Indeed that could be disputed," she said with an attempt at a laugh that caught nervously in her throat. "For my mount has finished the course even though her rider was swept off—and you have not!"

"I agree, you are the winner," he said instantly. "Name your forfeit, Carolina. *Have of me what you will!*"

The intensity of his gaze, the strong winning timbre of his voice were almost overwhelming. And suddenly she wanted never to forget these days with him in Essex, she wanted to remember them always—just as she would always remember the dark intense man in the curve of whose strong arm she now rested.

"I—will have a lock of your hair as a forfeit," she heard herself say on the ghost of a sigh. "To remember you by."

She was vaguely shocked at herself for having said it. But then this was a magical moment—and at such moments foolish words are often spoken. Her face flamed as she realized how her request must have

245

sounded, but there was satisfaction in the dark visage so close to her own. Satisfaction—and desire.

"And you shall have it," he said, his lips almost brushing her cheek as he spoke. "In a locket."

But the word "locket" went unheard by her, for his mouth was already pressing against the velvet of her cheek, moving downward toward her soft half-opened lips. Somewhere in the distance through the trees, sleighbells tinkled and the wind moaned a melody through the snowy branches. Involuntarily her arms crept round his neck and for long pulsing moments she was his—the world forgot.

A sigh soft as a fall of snow from the heavy-laden branches escaped her lips as he let her go. For those brief treacherous moments when she had clung to him, tasted his lips, felt his warmth, wanted to stay—for those long heartbeats she had been his and they both knew it. Swept away. Gone.

But that had been some other Carolina—not the wary breathless wench who now leant back upon the horse's neck to put at least a little distance between herself and her fiery lover. "I think—we had best go back, Rye," she said unevenly. "Before we do something we will both regret."

His smile was tender, his voice a caress. "I would never regret anything you gave me, Carolina."

But she could not give him herself—and that was what he wanted. It was written plain in his eyes.

"I"—she was struggling free of him even as she spoke—"I think my mare is too nervous to be ridden just now. And your horse is too tired to carry us both back to the house."

He made no move to release her. He was smiling but his dark brows had shot up. "Faith, he'll have to carry me all the way back to Williston House! And you think he cannot make the driveway now?"

She was red with embarrassment at how ridiculous she must have sounded. "I mean we should not tire the poor beast further," she explained as loftily as she could. "Oh, do let me dismount, Rye—we can walk back."

Responding to the appeal in her voice, he slid down from his mount, reached up and lifted her off. Holding her only a moment too long, he let her slide caressingly down his body to stand upon her own two feet. Once on the solid ground again, Carolina took a couple of wary steps away from him. Any contact with his lean masculine body was dangerous with her heart in this precarious condition! He took the reins of both mounts and with courtly formality offered her his arm.

There was nothing for it but to take that proffered arm and to feel the pressure of that arm through her velvet cloak sighing against her breast like a whispered word of love, causing a tumult within her that he could not know of.

What am I thinking of? she asked herself wildly, as she forced her reluctant feet to accompany him back down the snowy driveway. For her feet—like the rest of her—wanted to stay and never leave him, wanted to go racing through the gates and ride away with him forever!

Now he shortened his stride to match hers as his boots crunched along beside her. Somewhere nearby a little screech owl loosed a plaintive call . . . to its mate, perhaps, hidden somewhere in the branches of those old, old trees.

They were silent as they walked along together, man and maid, caught up by the magic of a magical country. This was Essex, she told herself dreamily. And Essex was far from London—just as her heart at this moment was far from London.

She was being swept along as if by a fast coach—and she did not know where the coach was bound.

Reba met them, bright-eyed, at the door. She watched Rye toss the reins of Carolina's horse to a groom who came running. "You have been riding then?" she asked, fascinated. "Wherever to?"

"A short ride to nowhere," Rye smiled at her. "I challenged Mistress Carolina to race me to the gates—and she won and claimed her forfeit. A locket. And now I must be taking my leave. Ladies." He swept them both a low bow.

Carolina, startled, gasped. "I said nothing about a locket, Rye. I said—"

"A locket," he corrected her. "A forfeit is a forfeit and must be paid. I will bring it with me tomorrow. Meantime," he added, "I will have a word with Farnham."

He mounted up and departed.

Carolina felt depressed as she watched his tall erect form disappear around a curve of the drive. Once more she felt the weight of her deception.

"Well!" Reba's knowing smile played over her. "What did you *really* ask for as a forfeit? A diamond necklace?" She laughed.

That laugh stung Carolina. A diamond necklace was just the sort of thing Reba might demand as a forfeit, if she thought she could get away with it. "Of course not!" she cried, outraged. "I only asked for a lock of his hair!" She stopped and bit her lip at the admission.

Reba's russet eyes widened and she burst into wild laughter. "You're *falling in love with him,* Carol!" she gasped.

"Don't be silly, of course I'm not!" Carolina ran past her and up the stairs, as if by her flying feet she would outdistance this wild craving of the heart that Rye excited, this yearning to be someone else, someone who was free to love him.

The locket, when he brought it round the next day, was a great disappointment to Reba—and it was presented in no clandestine manner. Indeed it was before Reba herself in the long drawing room of Broadleigh that Rye clasped the dainty gold chain with the plain little locket around Carolina's slender neck. Carolina gave him a grateful look for it was the kind of gift that a young lady of quality might accept as payment of a forfeit without feeling the world would scorn her as an adventuress. *He was so very thoughtful of her,* she realized with a pang. *Thoughtful as Lord Thomas, always hot in pursuit of his own pleasures, had never been.* . . . And swiftly she caught herself up short, for this was dangerous ground she trod upon.

"Did you have a word with Farnham?" she asked.

"Oh, yes." He shrugged. "You may consider the matter forgot."

Later in the week she learned that his "word" with Farnham had ended up in a duel, that the young buck in buff had—in terror at realizing how easily he was being overpowered—suddenly turned and fled, and Rye had nicked him painfully in the buttock with the tip of his blade so that he could not now sit down without discomfort.

Reba told her about it, convulsed with laughter. "Of course it is bad enough that Farnham turned out to be such a coward—but to bear such a wound!" She went off into peals of mirth.

With a slight glint in her eye, Carolina brought up the subject with Rye as they strolled late that afternoon through the snowy gardens of Broadleigh. The sun was low and there was a mist in the air for the afternoon had been warm.

"Ah, you have heard about that?" he murmured, and a grin broke over his face. "I thought the lad no force to reckon with but I hardly imagined that he would break and run! I was of no mind to let him off without some souvenir of our meeting so I lunged after him as he fled and lightly pinked the part nearest." He studied her. "You do not approve?"

"Oh, yes, I do approve." Carolina's lips quivered from trying to hold back her own mirth. "For you have done him no great hurt. But I imagine the stories about me will be even wilder now!"

"Oh, I doubt it," he said easily. "Those who saw me work out with the blade will have told *that* story around as well, and there will be few who would care to offend the lady of my choice."

The lady of his choice. . . . The phrase rang clear upon the evening air and for Carolina the words suddenly stilled the sighing of the wind through the snowy branches.

For there was a growingly possessive look in Rye's eyes and a warmth in his voice when he spoke to her, a warmth that she felt could mean only one thing: He was going to ask for her hand in marriage.

He was going to ask, and in spite of all she had said to herself about loyalty to Thomas, in spite of all her protestations to Reba and her noble resolves, it was going to be a wrench to say no to him. . . .

Chapter 17

The remainder of the Twelve Days of Christmas in Essex were a time of trial for Carolina. She felt torn, battered.

Rye Evistock remained a guest at Williston House, where he had been staying since the ball. From there he rode over every day. Rye kept a stern grip on himself, believing Carolina to be virginal and untried and not yet ready, even though he could not but sense the interest gleaming behind those shadowed lashes. But although he yearned for her, he bore in mind that he had promised not to pounce "unless invited." And Carolina was careful not to invite him for she did not trust that inner Carolina who had been too deeply stirred by their first kiss. So she was careful to keep people around them—or at least to stay within sight where she would have the quick excuse, "Oh, no— people will see," in case he got too close. And every day she strolled with him, or rode with him, or sat opposite him in the long drawing room of Broadleigh and wondered how long she could keep up this sham that she was a free woman, free to choose—instead of a woman betrothed.

Whenever she weakened, there was Reba, tugging at her arm, giving her little digs with her elbow, almost wringing her hands when they were alone: "Oh, please, Carol, just a little longer—I will be *eternally* in your debt!"

And indeed she found it exhilarating to walk beside that tall commanding figure in gray, noting the power in his light booted stride. It was exciting to know that the sword that swung at his side was feared throughout the county, to smile into that dark, dangerous-looking countenance and imagine for a treacherous moment that she was once again in his arms. . . .

Oh, Thomas was getting short shrift these days—it was Rye who occupied Carolina's thoughts.

He had become her champion—and indeed she needed one, for as Reba ruefully put it, her outspoken Colonial tongue was constantly getting her into hot water—as witness when she again crossed swords with Dolly de Lacey, this time in the Beaumont ballroom just before Twelfth Night where the young people, who had just concluded an energetic game of Blind Man's Buff, now returned to join their assembled elders for dancing and refreshments.

Mistress Dolly's blue eyes narrowed as she saw Carolina stroll back into the room surrounded by eager young bucks. She felt it diminished her position as belle of the county to have all this uproar over a mere Colonial who was visiting the upstarts at Broadleigh. Carolina had reached the center of the big room with its rows of pier glasses marching down the sides and reflecting the assembled company—everybody in the county who "counted"—when Dolly spoke. She gave Carolina, fresh and lovely in her blue and silver gown, a look of pure malice and her piercing voice carried across the room.

"My father says that Colonials are so much trouble," she said in a baiting tone. "Always desperate for more credit. . . ."

Carolina's eyes flashed at this aspersion on the hard-pressed Virginia planters. When her voice rang out, it was in defense not only of Fielding Lightfoot, but of all the rest. *"My* father says the laws are wrong else he would not have to ship his tobacco to England so *English merchants"*—she emphasized the words, staring straight at Dolly, whose father, she'd just been told, was not only a younger son of an old Essex family but a London merchant who reshipped Colonial goods at great profit all over Europe—"can trig out their wives and daughters in"—her gaze dropped insolently to Dolly's ermine-trimmed velvet gown—"velvet and ermine."

Dolly, who had not expected such a hot rejoinder, bridled, and a red spot appeared in each of her cheeks. "That is treason!" she said sharply.

"That is *truth,"* snapped Carolina. "And 'tis high time you heard it!"

Her clear voice had carried to Rye, who was watching them sardonically. Now he grinned and sauntered over as the music struck up.

"Allow me to claim our combustible Colonial visitor for a dance," he said, sweeping her a low bow.

Carolina took to the floor with her color high, so much so that with her flushed face, her blue and silver gown and her cloud of gleaming white-metal hair, Lord Hollistead, watching, was moved to remark to Sir Kyle, "Our little Colonial wench is red, white and blue—like a flag, is she not?" and Sir Kyle beside him murmured, "Aye, she is—and Rye Evistock carries her like a banner flung on high."

The two approving older men were not the only ones whose eyes followed the vivid couple whirling about the floor. A few paces away a vengeful Dolly stood tapping her gold-chased fan across her kid-gloved hand and watched as well.

"You're a hot-headed wench," Rye told Carolina, amused.

"Dolly got no better than she deserved!" she protested. "My father and all his friends are constantly in debt and 'tis all because by law they're not allowed to sell their tobacco for the best price, but must needs send it over to England so the English merchants can reap the profits! Indeed they do not even know what price their crop will bring or whether they will have a profit at all until they hear from their London agents!"

"Life is deucedly unfair," agreed Rye urbanely. "And what would you have us do?"

"Change it!" declared Carolina promptly. "Be fair to the American Colonies! Go to the King—"

"Who is busy with other matters," murmured Rye.

"His mistresses, no doubt!"

"Ah, a firebrand indeed." But some of the humor went out of his gray eyes. "But I'd lighten up on that tack. This King has a vengeful nature and you'll wear out your welcome with the Tarbells if you speak out against him too harshly. As a London merchant, Jonathan Tarbell well knows on which side his bread is buttered."

"Thank you for your warning, Rye," said Carolina bitterly. "But 'tis time 'this King' came to view his American Colonies and witnessed their plight."

"Ye'd do well to heed my advice," he warned her.

"I never listen to advice," she told him coldly, taking an intricate step that swung out her blue velvet skirts. "I follow my own judgment!"

"Spoken like a foolish wench," he observed as those pliant skirts rippled back to flutter between his legs as he took a long graceful step and swung her around again. "But if you continue in this line—gossip being what it is—there'll be speculation that back in Virginia you deal with smugglers' ships. Remember, you live on the coast."

"On the Chesapeake." She tossed her head, careless if her silver-gold hair lost a few pins.

He grinned. "A lovely bay for smugglers. But once gossip starts, hot words are like to become fact in everybody's mind. You could do your father a disservice if you cause him to be thought disloyal!"

Carolina gasped. "Why, no more loyal man ever

lived!" she protested, and it was true, in spite of the fact that Fielding Lightfoot had sometimes been driven to desperation by the Crown's disregard of Colonial problems.

"Just so," he said dryly.

Carolina subsided, smoldering. She must watch her tongue here! And that would be hard when there were wenches like Dolly about!

She was still thinking about that when her host begged her for a dance and in a pun about her name told her that she "had indeed a light foot—the lightest foot in England!" Carolina smiled perfunctorily—she had heard that line before. She was about to make some light rejoinder when the music stopped and a surprised voice behind her said, "Why, 'tis Carolina Lightfoot, I'll be bound!"

She turned to see the only one of Lord Thomas's friends to whom he had ever introduced her, Lord Reginald Fanshawe, dressed in mauve velvet and with his ever elusive dark wig, which seemed to have difficulty staying on his head, inclining slightly to the right. His hazel eyes were alight with interest as he impetuously claimed her from their smiling host and whirled her out upon the floor.

"Is Thomas about?" he asked.

"No, gone to Northampton," said Carolina.

"Ah, that's where he said he was going," sighed Lord Reggie. "A pity. I'd hoped he'd be around to liven things up!"

"I didn't know you lived in Essex. I thought Thomas said—"

"Oh, I don't," Lord Reggie hastened to inform her. "I live at Little Grange near Ipswich, Suffolk, just as Thomas told you. But I've an uncle here in Essex and I'm making the rounds of my relatives before I'm off to Somerset to be married in February." He sounded a bit rueful and she guessed that he hated to leave the excitement of London for the quiet countryside.

"I'm surprised Thomas let you from his sight," he said frankly, looking at her admiringly for she was indeed a blue and silver wonder in Reba's expensive ballgown. "Indeed I've never seen Thomas more taken with anyone!"

Carolina felt her face flush beneath that admiring gaze.

"When did you see Thomas last?" she asked.

"Just before I left London. He was going the other way at the time." He didn't enlighten her with the fact that Thomas had been headed for the wedding in Kent at the time he had begun to "make the rounds" of his blood relations. "Come to think of it, Thomas gave me a letter for you. I was to drop it by the school on my way out of London but I forgot all about it when my horse took it into his head to buck me off right atop a fruit vendor's cart and the fellow wanted reparations for his apples. It quite rattled me when I remembered I'd just spent my last guinea and I had to gallop off as if the constable was after me!"

"A letter?" Carolina asked quickly. Thomas had sent her a letter! "Oh, I hope you didn't take it by the school after all?"

"No, I've got it on me someplace—in my boot, I think. I'll dig it out for you later. But why shouldn't I have taken it by the school?"

Carolina recounted what Clemency Dane had written them and Lord Reggie gave a silent whistle.

"Well, I'd heard of Jenny Chesterton of course, knew she ran with Lord Ormsby and that crowd, but somehow I never connected her with Mistress Chesterton's school! Suppose nobody did—different kettle of fish altogether!"

Carolina agreed and, impatient for her letter, went with him to a curtained alcove where he bent down and fished about in his boot, and finally found a somewhat crumpled letter which he thrust into her hand.

"There," he said, giving the wig he had nearly lost in his search a slap that sent it tipping precariously over his left ear. "And that's my last errand of the Christmas season before I'm off to Somerset!"

Nervously Carolina broke the seal. Her own guilt at

how she was enjoying her stay in Essex—indeed, how she was enjoying Rye Evistock's attentions—gave her the uneasy feeling that there would be some dreadful retribution inside; perhaps the letter would be filled with reproaches. But there were none. Indeed it was a lover's letter, fond and vibrant.

"My heart's darling," Lord Thomas wrote (and he had written it with some passion for he had yet to meet dark enchanting Catherine Amberley when he had penned it just before departing for the wedding in Kent). *"I can hardly tear myself away from London, knowing I leave you here—indeed I am half of a mind not to go. I fear to see you lest my resolve weaken and so am penning this note which Reggie will leave for you at the school as he leaves London. Rest assured that not a day, not an hour will pass but that I will think of you and miss you, every night without you will find me tossing in my bed unable to sleep for thinking of you. I pray you be faithful to me for you are the one woman, the only woman, who will ever have my love. I will come round to call upon you as soon as I return, never fear I shall forget—despite another letter I have received yesterday's eve from Northampton importuning me to hurry home for my sister is taken ill and they fear she may worsen. Should that happen, they intend to send me a message to hasten—but do not worry your pretty head, dearest, for my sister Millicent was ever a sturdy lass and will shortly recover from her distemper."* And he signed it, *"Ever your own Thomas."*

Carolina put the letter down with a pounding heart. *Now* she knew why Thomas had left London without coming to see her—he had received a message that his sister had worsened and he had dashed away, not sparing his horses! And she had thought him faithless!

"What does he say?" demanded Lord Reggie irrepressibly.

"He says"—she blushed—"he says he will hasten to call on me the moment he returns to London."

"I don't doubt it," grinned Reggie. "For as I told you, I've never seen a man so taken with anyone as

257

Thomas is with you. Lord, he could speak of little else! Well, I had thought not to be able to deliver the letter—"

"Why?" she interrupted. "Are you not going back to London at all?" For she had been hoping to send Lord Thomas a message by way of his friend.

Lord Reggie slapped his thigh. "D'you know, you've given me an idea? Indeed I just might! If I rode away tonight, making my excuses to everybody, I'd have time to sweep through London and have me a game or two and say goodbye to old friends before making the long cold trek to Somerset! Damme, I'll do it!" He jumped to his feet, throwing back the damask hangings, eager to be gone.

Carolina had been about to say, "Will you carry a note to Lord Thomas?" But before she could voice her request, Lord Reggie was saying energetically, "I'll just turn you over to"—he cast quickly about him—"this gentleman here!" And she saw that Rye Evistock had magically appeared outside the alcove. "And I'll be off!" cried Reggie merrily as Rye stepped forward to claim her.

Gone was the chance to write to Thomas, gone was the chance to send him a message. Confused as to how she felt, Carolina let Rye lead her out onto the floor.

"Who was that fellow?" he asked as they moved into the graceful pattern of the dance.

"Lord Reggie Fanshawe."

"Oh, I know his name," he said impatiently. "Who *is* he?"

You mean, *What is he to me?* she thought, and was guiltily aware of the letter from Lord Thomas which she had just stuck into one of her big side panniers, which billowed out the better to reveal her handsome petticoat.

"He is a London acquaintance," she said with perfect truth—and stopped with a vexed little cry as the letter from Lord Thomas fell from her pannier to the floor at their feet.

In a single smooth gesture Rye's long gray velvet arm

swooped down and he retrieved the letter without missing so much as a step of the dance.

"And he came, I take it, to bring you this?" he shot at her. "Delivered in private, in an alcove?"

Her face was flaming. She had the ridiculous feeling of being found out. "No, of course not! It was just that he had the letter for me in his boot and he needed to sit down to get it out! I am sure," she added with an attempt at humor to divert him, "that if Lord Reggie had removed it while standing he would have lost his wig entirely—for it seems to sit ill upon his head!"

That steady gray gaze was on her, very direct and level. Over Rye's shoulder she could see Lord Reggie, very jaunty with his wig now sitting askew over his right ear, bidding his host and hostess goodbye, and taking his leave. She could now lie outrageously for Lord Reggie would not be here for Rye to question and trip her up!

"Lord Reggie did bring me upsetting news," she told Rye in a suddenly confiding voice. "The letter is from one of my schoolmates, who is a cousin of his— Clemency Dane."

"I was not aware that the Fanshawes and the Danes were related," he murmured.

Oh, God, she thought. *I had forgot that the Fanshawes are from the next county and Rye knows their connections! Aunt Pet always told me that liars trap themselves!* But she was committed to her course and plunged on. "Clemency Dane has written me bad news about the school." She told him of Jenny Chesterton's mishaps, ending with, "I intend to go back but I am sure my mother will retrieve me as soon as she hears what has happened!"

A smile quirked the corners of his lips and she felt a wave of relief go through her—he had accepted her story completely; it was evident in the sudden relaxation of his manner. "Perhaps you will choose not to remain in London," he suggested, "but will go even farther afield."

To Barbados, he was suggesting. . . . She thought of

Lord Thomas's impassioned, *"I pray you be faithful to me for you are the one woman, the only woman, who will ever have my love."* And of Lord Reggie's admiring, *"I've never seen Thomas more taken with anyone."*

In the tumult of her clashing thoughts she missed a step and Rye smiled down at her confusion, for he thought he knew the reason for it.

He was wrong, of course.

"It is to Virginia I will go if my mother has anything to say about it!" Carolina admitted truthfully.

He laughed, a low rich laugh. "But perhaps your mother will not rule your heart?"

No, she thought, suffocated by this double-dealing role she was playing. *Lord Thomas will rule my heart. But of course you do not know that. Lord Reggie could have told you—but he is gone, and Reba will make very sure that I do not tell you, she will plead and storm and I will give in.* She felt very ashamed of the role she was playing—and even more ashamed of the fact that her pulse quickened whenever Rye touched her, even with the light touch of the dance, and that her heart beat unsteadily whenever he came near.

I am like my mother, she thought miserably. *Knowing what is wrong, but unable to keep a straight course.* And again she felt that pull of emotions as he turned her about lightly in the dance and his sleeve chanced to brush her breast.

Her color flamed again and she turned her face quickly away from him, hoping to hide the way she felt—and heard, in agitation, his low laugh.

She was deeply glad when one of the young bucks who pursued her—and whose name in her confusion she suddenly could not remember—claimed her for the next dance. For even being near Rye had become a tumultuous experience that made her heart thunder and her knees grow weak and her senses sway. *He is sweeping me off my feet, this gentleman of Essex,* she thought in a dazed breathless way—and felt, like a stab, the sharp corner of Thomas's letter graze her hip through her billowing pannier. *And what kind of a woman does that make me?*

Shortly after, Reba pulled her aside. "I know you've had another brush with Dolly," she told Carolina. "But you must watch out for her. I'm told she carries tales."

"What tales?" asked Carolina absently, for her mind was on her own mixed feelings.

Reba gave an expressive shrug. "Anything she can get her hands on. I've been pumping one of the chambermaids and *she* says that everybody knows Dolly is to blame for Robin Prestwood's breaking off his romance with Elvira Carr. It seems that Dolly carried a tale about what Elvira had said about Robin's drinking—and it was only *half* true and anyway Elvira was laughing when she said it; but Robin took it to heart and now he has married somebody else!"

Somehow that story of Reba's sobered Carolina more than Rye's earlier warning had. It told her on what gossamer threads was gossip built.

"I have more important news," she told Reba. "I have just had a letter from Thomas! Lord Reggie brought it."

Reba's expression went suddenly wary and her figure in rosewine taffeta seemed to stiffen. "What does he say?"

"Oh—only that he misses me and will call upon me at the school the moment he returns to London. He said he had received word that his sister was ill in Northampton—I am sure her condition worsened and that was why he left without telling me goodbye." She shivered, all too aware of her divided heart. "Oh, I wish—I wish I were going back to London right away, Reba. Tonight! I wish I had asked Lord Reggie to take me along!"

"Lord Reggie would promptly have taken a room at the inn in Chelmsford on grounds that the weather was too cold for the horses, and you'd have found yourself in bed with him!" laughed Reba. "For I took pains to find out about his reputation after you told me you'd met him. He's near as wild a blade as Thomas!"

"Thomas is none so wild!" Carolina gave her friend a reproachful look.

"Oh, I know he's changed!" Reba said instantly.

"Oh, don't desert me now, Carol—for I can see it on your face that you've half a mind to! If you do, Mamma may make one of her sudden moves—and *you* will be to blame for my downfall!"

I will be to blame for everything, apparently, no matter how things turn out, thought Carolina with resignation. *For Thomas, for Reba, for Rye—oh, what a mess I have gotten myself into! And the terrible thing is—I don't seem to want to get out!*

"Look out," warned Reba. "Dolly and two of her friends are converging on you—and I see she's waving her fan at a great rate despite its being so cold in here! She means to make you say something before witnesses that she can quote to your disadvantage!"

Plainly Rye Evistock was of the same opinion for he appeared just then, cutting out two young bucks who were fast approaching, and swept Carolina out onto the floor right under Dolly's disappointed nose.

"I think I have just saved you from saying something that could land you in jail!" he grinned. "For I overheard Mistress Dolly brag that she was going to bait you on the subject of tobacco planters."

Carolina's silver eyes glinted. "I would have given her as good as she sent!"

"I feared as much," he laughed. "Better you not meet!"

Flawlessly, Carolina executed an intricate dance step. "I thank you for saving me, sir!" she mocked. But there was no mockery in her heart—or in her glowing eyes. *Oh, Rye,* she thought yearningly. *How alike we truly are! I feel I know what you are thinking even when you do not open your mouth. And even before I need you, you intercede for me!*

For Rye had become her protector here in Essex. Of that there could no longer be any doubt. And—Carolina was guiltily aware that that was the way she wanted it to be.

THE TWELFTH NIGHT BALL
BROADLEIGH, ESSEX

January 6, 1688

Chapter 18

It had snowed again and the Essex countryside was an icy fairyland on the evening of the Twelfth Night Ball. It was being held at Broadleigh, for Mistress Tarbell was letting no grass grow under Broadleigh's newfound popularity. She was astute enough to realize —galling though it might be—that their newfound popularity came to them via her daughter's beautiful school friend, that any lady Ryc Evistock squired was bound to be accepted by the community and, along with her, the family of "upstarts" Rye's current lady was visiting. So, craftily, she was giving the ball in Carolina's honor, knowing that Rye would personally take offense at any refusal to attend such a ball. For Nan Tarbell was a woman of no illusions. She knew that improving her grammar and changing her name to "Nanette" and sending her daughter off to a fashionable school had made no dent at all in the local gentry.

The ball tonight, she promised herself, would.

Outside, the grounds were a shimmer of snow and ice, and the boughs of the old trees were encrusted with a fresh fall of snow; the very twigs glistened. The air was cold and clear and carried with it the distant tinkle of sleigh bells as all the nearby county gentry streamed toward the Twelfth Night Ball at Broadleigh—just as Nan had dreamed.

Inside, Broadleigh had a glitter of its own. The Yuletide season had come late to Broadleigh, but it had come at last. As decorations for the upcoming ball, boughs of cedar and branches of holly had been placed everywhere, and a long garland of holly wound its way up the balusters of the wide Jacobean staircase. Mistletoe cascaded from the chandeliers, and wine ("enough to float away London," one guest would be heard to murmur) sparkled from expensive goblets. The serving staff had been increased threefold for the occasion and unfamiliar servants were tripping over each other and getting lost in the maze of corridors. Had Nan had time, she would have refurbished the entire house for this gala occasion, but as it was she had trotted out all the silver she owned, all the best linens, and raided all of the goodies from the capacious cellars.

The musicians had been brought up from London and had already consumed too much ale. By the time the guests arrived they were studying their instruments with bloodshot eyes and muttering tipsily to each other that it was a good thing they were to play from yon minstrels' gallery—that is, if they could make it up the narrow stair that led to it—for otherwise they might fall hiccuping among the dancers' feet.

Upstairs Carolina and Reba were watching the finishing touches being put to their hair by a brand new hairdresser brought up from London along with the musicians, for all the regular help had been pressed into supervision of the new servants.

"'Tis wonderful of you to lend me this new gown, Reba." Carolina studied her reflection in the long mirror; it gave her back a glory of crystal-encrusted pale ice green velvet, swirling skirts and an elegant figure-hugging bodice that outlined deliciously her soft breasts. At the sides those supple velvet skirts were drawn up into puffed panniers above a rippling ice green satin petticoat that matched the ice green satin ribands that fell in a shower of brilliants from her piled up silver blonde hair. "Indeed," she murmured, "I have let you do far too much for me." *And if I had not accepted so much, I would not now be wondering what to say to Rye Evistock when I trail downstairs in this lovely gown. . . .*

Reba caught that troubled note in her friend's voice. "But just think what you are saving me from!" she cried instantly.

Carolina turned to study Reba, who looked strikingly handsome in an attention-grabbing gown of champagne taffeta worn with a black velvet petticoat and trimmed in acres of trailing black lace. Her contemplative gaze took in the big garnets set into bangles in Reba's auburn hair and the garnet and feather fan she was wafting experimentally as her long russet eyes narrowly considered her reflection in the mirror.

How could anyone wish to be "saved" from Rye Evistock? she asked herself silently. *Reba's marquess must indeed be charming! Why, if she had not already promised herself to Thomas—!* She let the thought die aborning, for it was a dangerous thought—one of many dangerous thoughts that had crept into her mind lately. She told herself briskly that she must get herself back to London—that would set her back on an even keel! And all would be as it had been before between Thomas and herself. . . . A sense of desperation seized her. She would use some pretext if necessary, she told herself restlessly. Perhaps she would tell her hostess she had left valuable possessions at the school which must be personally collected. . . .

Meantime, she was flirting shamelessly with Rye Evistock, holding him off but leading him on, leading him to expect—!

Nan Tarbell, hoping to bring her own daughter into prominence, had told Carolina that she need not be on hand to receive the guests but could come down later. Carolina understood and took the hint. But her troubled thoughts were still with her when she drifted like an ice green vision down the great stairway into a sparkling sea of guests and found Rye waiting for her.

He cut a handsome figure indeed, she thought with a sudden pang, for all that he was tall and dark—and she had always mistrusted tall dark men as being too much like her father! For all that his clothes were not flashy and memorable like Lord Thomas's, that French gray velvet coat rode his broad shoulders masterfully. And the strong hand that emerged from a froth of white lace below a wide velvet cuff to sweep the tricorne from his dark head as he made a leg to her was a fine hand, strong and chiseled like the features of the sardonic face that looked down on her, smiling. Then once again—as fashion dictated—he donned the tricorne and offered her his arm.

"I had thought to be greeted by you at the door," he told her.

"Mistress Tarbell said my presence would not be required," she said, wishing her voice would not always go so breathless at the sight of him.

"But the ball is in your honor," he protested.

She gave him a mocking look from her silver eyes. "Not from Mistress Tarbell's point of view. She only said that because she assumed people would come lest *you* be offended."

He shrugged. "I am not so much feared as all that."

"Are you not?" She took his arm and melted with him into the crowd. She could not help noticing, as always, how many people spoke to him warmly, how many friends he seemed to have although he claimed he had hardly seen his home for years. He was a man who enjoyed the company of his fellows and it was hard to imagine him supervising a plantation every day, living a life of isolation. Easier to imagine him traveling, seeing new places, new faces.

"You don't really stay in Barbados, do you, Rye?" she shot at him. "I mean—all the time?"

Something wary came into his eyes. "Not all the time—I'm here, for instance."

"You know what I mean!"

266

"Well, *someone* must manage the plantation."

"Then you really *are* a planter—like my father," she mused. "I can hardly credit it!"

"Not quite like your father perhaps." He was laughing now. "I would imagine *his* lands are better managed!"

"Well, I didn't mean *just* like my father," she amended. "I meant like all the planters, Sandy Randolph and all the rest."

"Perhaps more like Sandy Randolph," he said thoughtfully.

"You know Sandy Randolph?" she asked in surprise, for when she had mentioned the name before he had not remarked it.

"No," he said. "I do not know him—but I have heard of him."

Of course, she thought. *Captain Mercer!* The garrulous gentleman who had told Sir Kyle about the goings on at "Bedlam" would have regaled him with wild tales about Sandy Randolph too! About his gambling—losing Tower Oaks and winning it back in a single evening at the Raleigh; about his being one of the leaders of the Tobacco Rebellion, though never caught; about the time he had leaped from the roof after saving his mad wife from that dreadful fire that she had set—endless stories could be told about him.

But Rye's rueful tone when he spoke of his plantation had surprised her. Somehow she had imagined a man who seemed so competent to be competent in all things. She thought of her mother, so efficient in managing the plantation when her father was gone. "Perhaps you need a wife," she mused, "to share in the responsibility." And she was instantly sorry she had said that, for his gray eyes flamed.

"Perhaps I do," he said softly as the music struck up. "Perhaps I do." He saw several young bucks bearing down on them and promptly led her out upon the floor. "But tell me, had you the choosing, would you prefer life in England to life in the West Indies?"

He was asking her—oh, no, she had hoped to push off this moment which she had felt coming all along.

267

She had hoped never to have to give him her answer, to be away, back in London, before ever he could propose —and now he was on the brink of asking her!

"I think—oh, I do not know what I prefer!" she cried. "At the moment all I wish is to dance the night away!"

He looked down at her tenderly, this girl that he was swinging about in the dance. How fragile she was, with her shimmering hair and luminous eyes, how ultimately feminine. He felt that if he were to handle her at all roughly that she would crumple in his arms, a broken doll. Seeing her now in her floating ice green gown sparkling with brilliants—that same color she had worn when first he had laid eyes on her—he marveled that he had had the temerity to drag her summarily up the stairs at the Star and Garter, to thrust her in to wait for his return! Only one woman before her had he held in such reverence as this—and she was dead. She had been a dark vision and her memory had kept him solitary, faithful to an old dream.

But now that dream was fading and another was taking its place: Carolina. Carolina, in all her youth and—as he imagined—innocence. Carolina, a bright new goddess to fill his empty heart and send his soul winging.

Caught up in love for her, he had found himself thinking all manner of wild thoughts: to improve his life, to cease his wild ways, to be *worthy* of her.

Like a candle flame, she wavered tantalizingly before him.

He *would* win her, *he must!*

And did she not care for him even now? Could he mistake those shadowed glances, that winsome smile that bade him welcome? Had she not responded tremulously to his kiss? Did she not willingly turn away from other suitors?

All that must mean *something* surely!

But did she care for him enough? Was he but a young girl's fancy? For still he imagined her virginal, untried. Riding home day after day from Broadleigh, remembering how she seemed to be warming to him, he had told himself with a surge of confidence that he would be the first to stir her from misty unformed dreams, the first to hold her, the first to love her. . . . And that she would respond to him he had no doubt—respond wildly, for he felt in her something reckless and head-long that he knew all too well in himself. And perhaps —something lost as well. . . . And it was that lost kitten quality that he sensed in her, that made him hesitate lest by moving too fast he might frighten her away. Life's bitter blows had taught him patience. All things in their own good time. . . .

Meantime the Twelve Days of Christmas had sped by on golden wings. And now it was Twelfth Night and the time for decision was upon him. For safe passage back to the Indies aboard the *Windward Lass* awaited him in London if he chose to take it. But she would sail no later than tomorrow night. He must make his decision now. Tonight.

And that decision—and all that it would mean to him, for it well might cost him his life if he decided to stay—depended entirely on this wisp of a girl in his arms who for some reason refused to meet his eyes. He put that down to maidenly confusion at being so nearly asked to wed.

"Is there some young planter back in Virginia per-haps?" He asked the question reluctantly, knowing there must be *someone* somewhere for such a golden girl. "Someone who claims you?"

"No, there is no one back in Virginia," she told him in a suffocated voice. *But there is certainly someone who claims me and will be back in London looking for me, perhaps tomorrow!*

"Good," he said softly. "I had hoped that would be the case."

She noted with alarm that he was holding her even more confidently now!

Suddenly she saw a way out. Rye, scion of a thread-bare aristocracy, was a planter. And like the tobacco planters of Virginia who were always skirting ruin, he must be in desperate need of money for had he not been dickering with wealthy Jonathan Tarbell for a

269

daughter he had never seen? To gain her dowry! The only alternative was a wife who would be a financial asset, who could run a plantation.

"I—I am not what you think, Rye," she declared.

"Indeed?" He measured her with a penetrating glance and whirled her around once before he said more. "In what way, may I ask?"

He half expected her to blurt out about some childish love affair gone astray on the other side of the Atlantic, but what she said amazed him.

"I am not really suited to plantation life," she told him earnestly. "A planter's wife needs to be able to do all manner of things. She needs to—to conserve fruit and salt fish and unravel stockings to gain thread to weave new fabrics. Unless of course she is wealthy. And I am not. I will have no dowry—my mother is extravagant and my father is always in debt. It is true he has received an inheritance but he will spend all of that and more on the new house he is building. I do not care for isolation—I am not at all what you think me to be."

He considered her in amusement. Did the little wench imagine he was pursuing her for her dowry? Or that he needed a plantation manager in skirts? Was she trying to warn him then?

"I had thought you would tell me you were an inveterate gambler," he said in a bantering tone. "Indeed that you had diced away the family fortune!"

She colored. "I am trying to say," she told him desperately, "that the very clothes on my back are borrowed. Every gown in which you have seen me belongs to Reba, who wished me to"—she could not say "to attract you," which would have been the truth, so she finished lamely, "to appear well before her friends in Essex."

Since it was already obvious to Rye that Reba had no friends in Essex, the amusement on his face deepened. "You are telling me," he asked more thoughtfully, "that you are not in favor with your family and therefore they sent you away to school unsuitably clothed?"

"Oh, no!" Instantly she rose to the defense of her

parents. "They gave me enough gold to buy a whole new wardrobe but I"—she blushed again—"I gave it all to my sister, who wished to run away to the Marriage Trees with a man my parents did not approve of."

"And did they reach these Marriage Trees?" he asked, fascinated.

"No, somehow they bungled it," she admitted.

"Possibly because you were not there to show them how to put on disguises or shinny over roofs," he grinned.

At least she had diverted him from talk of marriage! They quarreled amiably as they danced, over the merits of her "disguise" in London, and so relieved was she to be off the subject of marriage that she found herself laughing and lighthearted—even though she had but a few minutes before been wishing herself away!

She thought she might escape him for the dance was about to end and other young bucks would crowd up, clamoring to dance with her. Rye apparently thought that might happen too because he was suddenly whirling her across the floor.

"If I take a wife," he told her, chuckling, "it will not be to unravel my stockings! And I can salt my own fish if the need arises!"

"I think you do not understand how important a woman is in *plantation* life," she began unhappily.

"I think you do not understand how important a woman could be in *my* life," he said, smiling.

In her perturbation Carolina had not noticed where he was heading. Abruptly she found herself danced into a small antechamber off the great hall, a tiny room that was hardly more than a curtained alcove whose one huge window was framed in ancient velvet draperies that Nan Tarbell had not yet bothered to replace. The tiny room was dim by contrast with the hundreds of candles twinkling down from the chandeliers in the great hall, and hushed by the heavy old rose hangings that seemed to reflect the white moonlight sparkling on the snow and ice from outside rather than the golden candlelight of the interior. She felt herself drawn toward the wide velvet cushioned windowseat and

271

knew that although music and laughter floated in from the great hall, in this curtained alcove they were effectively alone.

Rye smiled down at her and let one hand slip almost negligently to her waist to draw her pliant body toward him. With the other hand he cradled her head and her pale blonde curls cascaded over his fingers.

She felt her heart begin to beat very fast.

"Carolina," he said softly. "I have something to say to you."

Her heartbeat was by now not only fast but wildly uneven. *Oh, God,* she thought, *Rye is going to declare himself! And then I will have to tell him that I have been but leading him on, that I am already promised, that I can never—* No! her inner self almost shouted. *I have waited long enough—too long. I will not let him declare himself, I will tell him the truth now!*

"Rye," she burst out. "I have something to say to you too. I"—She broke off as the music stopped and a dancing couple came to rest just on the other side of the draperies that curtained off their alcove and stood there laughing and talking. She could not tell Rye what she had to say where other people could hear! "I have lost too many hairpins as I danced," she substituted rapidly for what she had been about to say. "I must go upstairs and pin my hair up else it will fall down about my shoulders!"

With a fluttering gesture toward her fashionable coiffure she broke away from him, ignoring his murmured, "That would be none so bad a sight!" and darted back into the great hall. She skirted the dancers, for the music had begun again, and made her way upstairs. For all that there were ladies swishing their ballgowns up and down the hall, her own room at least was unoccupied and she made her way there and sat for some minutes before her dressing table with her head in her hands.

It had come to her with force that it was a very shabby role she was playing. And when she hurt Rye, she was going to hurt herself.

The door opened and she jumped up. "Oh—it's you,

Reba!" She stopped abruptly at her friend's expression. Reba looked wild. She looked as if she might kill someone.

Reba came to a violent halt in the middle of the floor. She ignored the haggard look on Carolina's face. "I have just learnt that the Marquess of Saltenham has departed for the Continent again for a 'change of scene'—and all without a single word to me!" She lunged forward and snatched up a book from a nearby small table and sent it hurtling at the wall with such force that it struck with the sound of a small explosion. "Oh, I could kill him!" she cried through her clenched teeth.

"They'll hear you downstairs!" gasped Carolina, looking at the fallen leather-bound volume.

"Devil I care!" wailed Reba. "Oh, it is too treacherous of him—*and after I waited!*" She was almost sobbing now. "He promised to marry me, Carol!"

Carolina strongly doubted that the actual words had ever been said, but Reba plainly had been seduced and abandoned. Her own anguished heart went out to her friend. "Then you must dance and laugh and be very lively indeed," she told Reba with decision. "For there are those who may know about your affair—even though unknown to you—and they will gain no satisfaction if they think you are not hurt by it."

"Not hurt by it?" cried Reba passionately. "I had planned to become a marchioness! How could I not be hurt by it?"

But it is only your head that is affected—never your heart, thought Carolina, watching her friend helplessly. *You are sorry to have lost the title, but I do not hear you wail about the man!*

"You are right!" cried Reba in a sudden about-face. "I will not let anyone think I feel deceived or upset!" She seized a piece of Spanish paper and dabbed her flushed cheeks even redder. "There! We will go down the stairs laughing, Carol, and we will linger upon the landing so that everyone may see us and view how unconcerned I am by anything Robin has done!"

Carolina felt herself propelled down the hall, while

273

Reba went off into meaningless peals of laughter when they passed several ladies who had come upstairs to freshen up.

Concentrating on each other as if they were actors in a play and the dancers below their audience, the two girls tripped lightly down the stairs and paused upon the empty landing. Behind and above them stretched the elegant old tapestries that "kept out the draft" and by so doing hid the upper hall from view. The long tapestries did not quite come together in their downward sweep and Carolina had come to rest beside one of the long vertical slits where one tapestry almost, but not quite, met its neighbor.

"You are not the only one with problems," she told Reba bleakly. "Oh, Reba, I cannot face what I have done!"

And up above, behind the tapestries, those words carried to ears for which they were not intended. Rye Evistock, who had strolled upstairs to view the great hall from above—and partly to escape the attentions of an overeager matron avid to marry him off to one of her daughters, had seen the girls come laughing down the hall. He had stepped into the shadows, not wishing to seem to be pursuing them down the stairs, and so had heard Carolina's words as they floated up to him where he stood behind the tapestries.

"Well, I hope you will not tell Rye that you led him on only so that I would not be forced to marry him," said Reba unpleasantly. "For if Mamma hears, she will kill me!"

"But Rye is on the point of asking me to marry him!" Carolina cried wildly. Her voice quivered with pain because in truth she did not want to relinquish him—and that was what hurt most. "How will he feel when he learns that I never intended to marry him? That I have been betrothed to Thomas all along?"

274

Chapter 19

Rye Evistock's long frame stiffened and the blood surged so violently to his head that he scarcely heard Reba's petulant, "Come, Carol, we have stood here long enough. To talk longer will make us seem to be perhaps worried about something, and I for one wish to appear *completely unruffled* this night!"

Carolina's answer, if any, was lost in a sudden discordant blare of music from the drunken musicians, and the guests below began again to dance.

But Rye Evistock, who had been fingering in his pocket a gold ring set with an amethyst that had been his mother's, and which he had intended to offer Carolina as a betrothal ring, was as impervious to the sudden blast of music as he was to the back-slapping greeting of two tipsy gentlemen who brushed by him on their way back downstairs.

This plain and stunning proof from her own lips that Carolina did not care for him, that she belonged to another man—indeed was betrothed to the fellow, that she had tolerated his advances only to accommodate a friend, had hit Rye squarely between the eyes, staggering him. He had long prided himself that he was a man who met all circumstances with equanimity, that he would rise above any problem, any loss. But now he felt as if the world had been cut away suddenly from beneath his feet.

For long moments he stood stock-still and stared blankly at the tapestry from behind which had come this enormously enlightening conversation.

Playing him for a fool, was she? That lying wench with her big clear luminous eyes! Well, she'd play him for a fool no more! Rye's knuckles clenched white and he yearned to send them crashing into yonder wall.

When he rejoined the ladies he had got control of himself. The sardonic mask he usually wore had slid down once again over his dark face and he viewed the world with shuttered eyes. For a moment he wondered if he detected a shade of regret in the troubled gaze Carolina turned up to him as he led her out upon the dance floor—a dash of pity perhaps? No, she was without pity!

But it was Twelfth Night and he had one more gift to give her.

In truth Carolina's conflicting emotions which had driven her almost to frenzy upstairs had by now melted into numbness. She was struck dumb by her unhappiness and by her very real sense of guilt that she should have done this thing. And she shrank from telling Rye. To see him stiffen, to read the hurt in his eyes—no, she could not bear it.

And besides—when he knew the truth at last, he would go away and she would never see him again.

As he led her out onto the floor, she thought she detected a subtle change in his manner toward her but she was so miserable she could not be sure she was not imagining it.

They danced silently, their feet moving expertly—and she could not bring herself to look at him.

"There's snow on your boots," she said in surprise.

"I stepped outside while you were upstairs."

She nodded, her curiosity dulled by grief.

"This room is too crowded," he said restlessly. "Come outside, I have something for you."

She nodded and he led her out a side door she had not even known was there. She had forgotten how well he knew this house. The cold met her as she went out that door, it struck the bare skin of her neck and bosom—warm from the dancing—like a blow, but she was too numb to care. It had stopped snowing. Ice and soft snow glittered from the branches.

Her thin slippers mushed down into the snow. At any other time she would have refused to go farther, but she felt so bad about the shabby role she had played toward this man that she would have let him lead her anywhere.

She accompanied him into the frozen garden where the tree branches glistened and the distant music from the house was hushed. Above them in the clear air a cold moon looked down and cold stars glimmered. It was better this way, she thought, to hear the cold truth beneath the cold stars alone—not in an antechamber of a crowded ballroom where at any moment lovers might break in, or some half-tipsy friend might appear who would promptly slap Rye on the back and expect him to joke and be merry.

She had been shivering along beside Rye in her pale green velvet gown, for he had given her no chance to go upstairs and collect her cloak. He had led her past snow-covered boxwood, past mounds of white that come spring would be roses, and into the entrance to the snow-covered maze. She was holding up her skirts but now as the clipped green walls of the boxwood maze rose up about them, she began to protest.

"I'll ruin my slippers, Rye—and they're Reba's. You should have let me stop to put on my pattens."

"No need for pattens—'tis privacy I have in mind."

Privacy? But what could be more private than this place where they stood? Carolina began to feel alarmed here in this cold lost world where the music from the house seemed endlessly far away. She looked up, saw him staring down at her like a stranger—and her gaze fell away.

"On down this path." He stepped behind her. "It's too narrow to go two abreast." With a hand beneath her elbow he was guiding her along the maze, ruthlessly propelling her toward the center.

Ah, there it was at last, the round open place in the center of the maze with its snow-covered sun dial.

Here was where it would happen, she told herself fatalistically. Here was where she would break his heart.

He was silent now, staring down at her. She wished he would speak. She did not lift her eyes above his broad shoulders. Nervously she brushed away the snow from the sun dial and its pale shadow in the white moonlight gave them the time.

"Moon time, . . ." she said in a soft lost voice. And then, looking up with a sigh, "The moon has shining hours too."

"When not obscured by snow," he said, feeling almost physical pain at sight of the glorious halo the white moonlight made of her hair.

She looked down again for her eyes were blurred by unshed tears. She was thinking, *This is the last time I will ever walk out with him—the very last time!*

Oh, it was unthinkable! She would not, *could not* lose him!

Her heart was bursting. She opened her mouth to tell him that she was betrothed to Thomas, but her throat was dry and the words would not come. No, she would wait instead to hear what he had to say. *And then, when he asked her to marry him, she would close her eyes and follow her heart!*

But she knew that she would burst into tears if at this point he were to go down on one knee in the snow and gravely ask for her hand in marriage.

He did no such thing.

"I am sure you thought me a blackguard that night at the Star and Garter," he said grimly.

She gave him a bewildered look. He had brought her outside on this freezing night to talk about *that?*

"For not breaking the dice and thus restoring to you your winnings," he continued sardonically.

Indeed she had!

"You admit then that the dice were crooked?" She was amazed, for this was the first time they had discussed it. Indeed it was a subject she had been careful to avoid!

"Oh, yes, I knew it all along, but by the time I reached you, Twist had had time to secrete the crooked dice in his clothing. So we would have found only honest dice and nothing would have been gained."

She had not thought of that. It cast a new light on things.

"And so you stayed to—"

"To trap him," he finished for her grimly. "Twist had won a great sum of money from my brother, who cannot control his thirst for gambling. I had come down to London to find Twist and wrest the entire sum back from him."

"And did you do it?" She was awed.

"Aye, I did. And yours as well. Hold out your hands." He held up a small leathern purse, untied it, and gravely poured the contents into her cupped hands. "I had meant to return this to you in the upstairs dining room at the Star and Garter," he said sternly. "But when I unlocked the door, intending to take you home, I found you gone. I spent most of the night searching for you, fearing you would come to some harm upon the London streets."

Although they did not know it, from an upstairs window they were being observed. As she hurried simpering toward Lord Hollistead, Nan Tarbell had strayed too near the dancers—and forgotten to lift her train (after all, Nan had come to wearing trains late in life; she had worn only plain kirtles and practical aprons when she was Reba's age) and a tottering old gentleman had stepped upon it. He had been full of apologies for the long tear in the fabric, but that had not mended the situation. Nan, cornering one of the maidservants, had gone upstairs to have her train mended. A restless woman, she had refused to take the dress off but instead had stood by the window staring down into the wintry garden, wondering what it would be like next summer. Would it be filled with strolling guests as the house was filled with dancing guests tonight?

She knew that Rye Evistock had gained them entry into all these great houses during Christmastide. But Rye was only here for the holidays—he lived in Barbados or some such place. And who was to know whether he would drop the Colonial minx or not, once he got what he wanted? For to Nan Tarbell's earthy turn of mind, men were interested in only one thing and once they got *that,* they would like as not cast you aside. And if he *did* cast the girl aside and went back to wherever he came from, come summer would the Tarbells be as popular with the county gentry as they had been at Christmastide? Would they still be invited everywhere to everything? Or would they be included only in those large crushes where people hardly knew one another?

Pondering that, Nan had been surprised to see Rye and Carolina leave the house and go into the maze. Her window looked straight down upon the maze—indeed it was a window from which the former master of the house had often chuckled at his bewildered guests' efforts to find their way out of this clever labyrinth of boxwood. She watched them go into the center of the maze and stand conversing a moment—the girl would catch her death out in the snow without a cloak! And then in shock she saw Rye open a purse and pour glittering gold into Carolina's hands.

Money—he was *paying* the wench! For services rendered? Nan reeled with the shock of it. All week long she had watched with fury as Carolina flirted with Rye. They seemed to be constantly disappearing, leaving Reba somewhere else. She had more than half expected a betrothal announcement. *And now he was giving her gold!*

She tried to regain her composure as behind her the maidservant trying to mend her torn train said anxiously, "If you could hold still but a moment—when you jerked away from me just now, you tore my needle from my hand and now I must search for it."

Had she been looking up, the maidservant would

have been appalled by the expression on her mistress's face—but she did not; her busy fingers were searching for the needle in the thick green Aubusson carpet.

Carolina felt shame scorch her face as the golden coins cascaded down into her cupped palms. "I am sorry for what I thought of you," she whispered, and he nearly melted at her tone.

Then he reminded himself that she was but toying with him, that she was another man's woman, had been all along, that—most galling thought of all—it was not even his personal charm that had enticed her to do this. She was casually making a mockery of him to accommodate a friend.

"And this," he said—and he could not keep the raw emotion out of his voice, "was the toll I intended to take of you for saving your life and restoring to you your winnings."

He swooped down and pressed his lips upon her upturned mouth. He had intended it to be a savage kiss but her mouth was so soft and warm and tremulous that his own lips moved caressingly, turned sideways, and involuntarily his arms went round her, cradled her.

Carolina, who all week long with maidenly modesty had avoided kissing him—it was bad enough to be lying with her eyes and her voice, she had felt, without adding the lie of caresses—now felt a flame of feeling consuming her. Like the crackle of a fire on the hearth it seemed to heat her skin and ripple along her feminine torso—and melt her resolve. The strength of his sinewy body was real and reassuring, the grip of his long arms warm and comforting and his roving mouth promised endless delights.

Her slender form was pressed close against his, her soft breasts in the thin velvet bodice tingling against his velvet coat. Beneath that coat she could feel the strong rhythmic beating of his heart.

She felt seared by large emotions—and dizzy, as if her senses were melting. The world was slipping away. There was only Rye—and he was everything. Her fingers released the gold, and the jingling coins fell in a shining shower to the icy trampled path. Her soft arms

281

stole around his neck, pulling his head down further. And now she was kissing him back, kissing him with all the fiery fervor that was in her.

His arms tightened and he bent her backward, deliberately probing past her lips with his tongue, exploring her mouth thoroughly and impudently—and feeling the hot breath gasp in her throat as she quivered. And at the same time his hand had found its way inside her bodice, his fingers were working their way inside her lacy chemise and now he was stroking her tingling naked breast.

She had forgot the world. She moaned softly in his arms. Her body sagged against him in surrender. She would not, *could not* lose him. All through the Christmas season she had been dreading this moment, fighting it, and now that it had burst upon her she was wrapped in splendor.

She would tell him she loved him, she would *show him* she loved him, she would make him understand—about Thomas, about everything, she would go with him to Barbados or the moon, she was his!

She was gasping, unable to speak for the searing emotions that had held her in thrall, when Rye lifted his head. He kept her face pressed against his chest so that she would not see how shaken he was, how haggard his expression. "God, ye're a hot wench," he muttered, and there was in his yearning voice the same storm of desire that she herself felt at that moment.

She opened her mouth to tell him then, to admit that she loved him, to tell him how wrong she had been.

"Close your eyes," he instructed as he pushed her from him. "For I've one more gift to give you."

Carolina did as she was bid. She closed her eyes—and she put her gloved hands over her face to hide the sudden scarlet that she knew was staining her cheeks. For her body in that close embrace had sent him a message—and the message was clear.

"This will take a little time," he said. "And you will not open your eyes until I tell you to open them. No, lift your head."

She thought he was going to slip some trinket around her neck, something she could treasure. Or perhaps a miniature that she could lift up and smile upon. But what did she care for gifts? The only gift she wanted was the gift of his love and that, she knew triumphantly, was hers already. Oh, she could not wait to tell him how she felt—how, she now realized, she must always have felt—about him. Her heart sang.

Yet she would play his game to please him, of course she would. She held up her head as instructed. He seemed to be moving around in the snow and she wished he would come back, but her thoughts were so tumultuous, the blood pounded so loudly in her ears that she could not focus on whatever he was doing. She knew only that that deep chest and those warm arms—arms that had been forbidden but that now would enfold her forever—had been withdrawn.

When Rye spoke again his voice seemed to come from some distance away, on the other side of the hedge.

"Open your eyes, Carolina," he commanded harshly. "Did you really think I'd marry you? You're a hot wench but not a true one. I've had dozens of hot wenches and can have dozens more—they come cheap."

Her gray eyes snapped open, first in confusion—then in shock. Then they sparkled an indignant silver in the cold moonlight at his tone.

"How can you say that?" she gasped, turning about to confront him. She had been about to add raggedly, "Don't you know I love you?" But he was not there. She was standing alone in the center of the snowy maze. Tall walls of snow-encrusted boxwood rose up around her, high above her head. The moon shone pitilessly down, sparkling off the gold coins that had fallen upon the trampled snow. "Rye!" She looked about her in panic. "Don't leave me here!"

His voice sounded a little farther off. It was hard—hard enough to shod hooves. "Find your own way out," drifted back to her.

Carolina picked up her shirts, and ran in the direction of the sound. "Rye!"

She thought she could hear the crunch of his boots ahead, striking against an icy portion of the path, and she stopped to listen. "Rye!" But there was no sound except a sudden sighing of the wind through the branches and a sudden fall of snow from one of them that bent the boxwood up ahead.

She kept going—and suddenly she came up against a dead end where the towering boxwood enclosed her on three sides. No way out here.

"Rye!" She was almost sobbing.

Common sense came back to her. The snow! It would be easy to find her way out, she had only to follow the tracks they had made coming in. She ran along where the snow was beaten down until she came to a place where the paths crossed—and her heart plummeted. The tracks went both ways. And now she remembered the snowy boots. Rye had been out here ahead of her, making tracks in the snow, preparing the maze so she would not easily find her way out.

He had found out about her deception somehow and he was getting his revenge!

She turned and stumbled back the way she had come, found herself once again standing by the sun dial in the center of the maze. He would come back to show her the way out, she told herself. He would!

Below her in the snow lay the forgotten golden coins. It was all the money she had in the world and the sum had doubled and redoubled and doubled again now that it included her winnings at the Star and Garter. She would wait for him here, she told herself resignedly. When his temper had cooled, he would return. And to that end, she bent and picked up one by one, with freezing fingers, all the gold coins that had slipped from them while he kissed her. She slipped some of the coins into her gloves and some into her shoes. Then she tore a lace ruffle from her chemise and wrapped the rest in it and tucked the makeshift purse into one of the panniers at her side.

From the window above Reba's mother watched with fascination.

"Rye!" Carolina called again. And again, hopelessly, "Rye!"

From a distance, standing outside the maze entrance beside one of the giant oak trees, Rye heard her and his grim mouth took on an even grimmer line. She had led him down a path—and now he had led *her* down one! Let the lying wench find her own way out!

From that upstairs window Reba's mother too heard her call—although it was lost to the merrymakers downstairs for there the sound was obscured by the music and laughter and clinking glasses. And hearing it, Nan Tarbell's mouth formed as grim a line as Rye's.

Down in the center of the maze, turning round and round as she called to him, Carolina realized that—for whatever reason—Rye wasn't coming back. She must find her own way out or be found frozen here in the snow tomorrow morning. For who was to miss her? Reba was wrapped up in her own affairs and would tumble into bed without coming in to say good night. The servants were new and disorganized. Mistress Tarbell wouldn't care if she *did* freeze. And neither . . . apparently . . . did Rye.

The pain of that knowledge cut through her, but her situation was desperate and she tried to put it from her mind.

Grim and intent and silent now that her life hung on her next moves, she tried to find her way out of the maze. It would take time. She broke sprigs from the boxwood and laid them down across the path to block off every path she had explored that led to a dead end. It was slow work, but she was making progress.

Outside the maze, standing in the shadow of the big oak, Rye had begun to worry. He had expected her to come out long before this, because he himself knew every turning of that maze so well. He had intended to frighten her, to make her suffer some small part of what he was himself suffering—but he had never intended to let her freeze to death, forgotten in the maze. He was

285

already striding forward to rescue her when he saw her stumble, shivering, from the maze and run toward the house.

The instant he saw her, he stepped back into the shadows. Gasping in the cold, her teeth chattering, Carolina did not see him. For his resolve, it was just as well. At that moment, had she turned toward him with a woebegone face, he might have melted.

As it was, he watched her run into the house and his heart froze up again. With never a backward look, he found his horse and rode back to Williston House where he bade his host, who was still up with an attack of the gout, a warm goodbye. Asked whether he would be back soon, he evaded the question, saying vaguely that he had received word from home that must take him back to Colchester this very night. And Sir Kyle had only to look into Rye's set face to surmise that there had been a lovers' quarrel at Broadleigh's Twelfth Night Ball and, wisely, to refrain from inquiring too much into the cause of his guest's sudden leave taking.

"Ye're always welcome here, Rye," he was told heartily as Sir Kyle—guessing he might not see Rye soon again—wrung his hand.

Those were the last words he heard in this part of Essex as he headed his horse through the cold night toward Colchester.

By the time Rye Evistock had reached Colchester, the bright anger that had driven him had become a dull ache. Life, which had long ago dealt him a strange hand of cards, had taken yet another swipe at him. And this time, he supposed, he deserved it for believing in miracles. Like some lovestruck boy, he had believed for a fortnight that his world could change, that he could be lucky at last in love. Worse, he had believed that Carolina Lightfoot could love him.

He would not be such a fool again, he told himself as he prepared to say his goodbyes to his family. There was a finality as he made those farewells, for in his heart he did not expect to see any of them ever again.

He had come back to England intending to change

his reckless life, to marry an heiress and settle down, become the country gentleman his father had always been—assume the role that was his natural heritage.

Instead he had met a wayward wench and fallen head over heels in love with her—only to find that she was playing him for a fool.

Now he straightened his broad shoulders and reminded himself that there had been another girl once. A warm beautiful girl whom he had intended to marry. And while she lived she had been true to him.

Oddly, he found little comfort in that.

Before the sun was high he was aboard a fresh horse, saddle bags packed and on his way to London. He would reach the *Windward Lass* before she sailed. He would leave England behind him. Forever.

Meantime in London, Lord Thomas Angevine, who had found Northampton boring and had returned to London after a mere three days there, was just turning over in a warm bed when he encountered his latest mistress's naked thigh.

"'Tis time I got up, Polly," he muttered without much conviction. "Your sister may be coming home."

"Oh, Thomas," she said, pouting from her pillow. "You don't love me or you wouldn't even *think* of rising!"

"I *do* love you," he maintained sturdily. And he did, for he had known her but four days and his ardor had not yet had time to cool.

"But"—she gave him a slanted look in the pale dawn and reached over to slide a caressing hand along his stomach and groin—"I thought there was that schoolgirl . . ."

"What schoolgirl?" asked Lord Thomas thickly. "No schoolgirl is of any importance to me!" Quick to respond to her seductive impudence, he rolled toward her, buried his face in her cloud of dark hair, found her ruby lips. "Let me assure you, Polly, if ye've any doubts at all, that for me there is but *one* woman and that woman is yourself. I have never loved *anyone* as I love you at this moment!"

287

"Oh, Thomas," she giggled. "You say that to all the girls!"

"Never," he said devoutly. "Never!"

Lord Thomas was back in London—and back at his old tricks.

And at Broadleigh, in Essex, the house was settling down after the Twelfth Night Ball—but there was one guest at Broadleigh who would not sleep that night. Carolina had burst in through the side door and raced up to her room in sodden slippers to wrap her freezing body in a blanket and throw herself face down into the big feather bed. Tears streamed down her face.

She was still shivering uncontrollably, but long after the shivering had stopped her slight figure was wracked with hard dry sobs that would not seem to stop.

She had lost something precious to her and she knew in her heart that the loss was irrevocable. Rye had left her to die there in the maze. He would never come back.

And by his going he had left a hole in her life that nothing would ever quite fill.

In the morning she got up tiredly and took off the wrinkled ice green ballgown. She stared at it as if it were somehow to blame and then she hung it in the big press along with those other gowns of Reba's that she had been wearing as if they were her own. But she wondered as she pushed last night's velvet ballgown in among the others if she could ever bear to wear ice green again—for she had worn ice green when she met him and ice green when he went away. . . .

Wearily, as she dressed to meet the new day, Carolina told herself it was over with Rye—and as she thought about it, she decided she had gotten but what she deserved. Rye must have somehow overheard her brief conversation with Reba last night on the stairs—and what a shock it must have been to him! She felt deeply ashamed of her part in the whole affair. And the worst of it was that she had fallen in love with him—and that was treachery to Thomas, who deserved better!

It was Thomas she must think of now, for Thomas

288

was her future—and not some dark, too attractive stranger, who had snatched her from a gaming table debacle and made her holidays bright. A stranger who was gone with Twelfth Night just as the holiday season was gone, but who unlike the holidays would not be back come another year.

As she wandered disconsolately down to breakfast she told herself that she must fight to overcome this ache in her heart, this dull sense of loss that seemed to overshadow everything. She must forget him. And perhaps . . . someday . . . she would.

She would try to forget him in London.

But her hostess, she learnt when she came downstairs, had other ideas.

Nan Tarbell had risen early for she had much on her mind. She swept in as the girls were eating breakfast.

"Both of you, wait for me in the library after breakfast," she told them tersely.

Carolina, who had been pensively regarding her food with downcast eyes, barely heard her. But Reba, who was almost as gloomy as Carolina, although for a different reason, looked up in alarm.

"*Now* we're in for it," she muttered to Carolina as they went to the library.

"In for what?" asked Carolina listlessly. It seemed to her that nothing that happened at Broadleigh now could make any real difference.

"I don't know." Reba sounded uneasy. "But I do know Mamma was very angry with the way Rye Evistock left here last night—taking himself off without a word. And you disappearing too. People were wondering if you had eloped! I heard her muttering about it."

"Oh," Carolina said, sighing. "'Tis obvious—he must have overheard us talking on the stairs."

"Yes, but *she* doesn't know that," said Reba impatiently. "Something's in the wind."

And indeed something was.

The girls were allowed to cool their heels in the richly appointed—indeed somewhat overdone—library for about ten minutes before Nan Tarbell came in and closed the door. She marched to the center of the room and what she had to say shocked Carolina out of her heartbroken lethargy.

She began by addressing her daughter.

"I can hardly blame you, Reba," her mother began. "You are young and therefore easy to hoodwink. You could not possibly know what kind of a viper you were nourishing in your bosom." Here her gaze rested with such distaste on Carolina that Carolina flushed, and her gray eyes flashed silver as her hostess continued. "Not only has your young guest spent her entire time here luring your intended away from you, but—she has done it for *money*."

Carolina felt her breath leave her and Reba's jaw dropped, but before either girl could collect herself sufficiently to speak, Mistress Tarbell continued in her overbearing way:

"I saw him from the window *pay in gold* for her favors before he departed so abruptly during the ball last night! And I have no doubt he left her stranded in the maze for a very good reason—he felt she might pursue him and shower him with abuse that he chose not to continue the relationship."

Carolina, who had been listening to this tirade in mounting horror, found her voice. "It wasn't like that at all!" she cried. "Rye had—"

But her hostess's strident voice overrode her. "Be quiet!" she said so sharply that Carolina blinked at her and subsided. "I realize also that because of Mistress Chesterton's scandalous behavior, I cannot send you back to the school." She was addressing Carolina now. "Nor can I keep you here."

"Rye but paid me back the money I had lost gaming!" cried Carolina. "It was while I was at the school—"

Again her hostess interrupted, this time with a lowering frown. "So we must add gaming to your other transgressions," she ground out.

"No! I mean, it was just the one time when I borrowed a suit and went out in men's clothing to find Lord Thomas!" This was getting her nowhere. She was getting mired in deeper and deeper. "Reba." She appealed to her friend. "Explain to your mother how it all happened. She won't believe *me.*"

"You are right in that," said her hostess grimly. "*I* would not believe you under oath!"

Carolina's gaze was fixed on Reba, who dropped her eyes. "I don't know what you're talking about," she mumbled.

Reba was ducking it! Carolina felt outraged. "Just explain how I borrowed your Cousin George's new suit and went out to look for Lord Thomas," she said crisply. "And then your mother will understand how I came to be dicing at the inn and lost!"

Reba looked harassed. "I never lent you George's suit," she said. "What would I be doing with George's clothes?"

Carolina opened her mouth to tell all she knew about Reba's affair with the Marquess of Saltenham—and then thought better of it. Across from her Reba looked frightened and her russet eyes held a wild appeal. Carolina remembered bitterly how many times she had borrowed Reba's clothes—indeed this very dress in which she now stood belonged to Reba. Well, she would go upstairs right now and take it off!

"I have nothing further to say to either of you," she said shortly. "I will be taking my leave as soon as a coach can be brought to take me back to London."

"A coach has already been brought," said her hostess heavily. "It waits for you now and it will *indeed* take you to London." She clapped her hands and the door opened to reveal Carolina's boxes, stacked in the hall. Flanking the luggage was a very large scullery maid whom Carolina vaguely remembered having seen in the kitchen when Reba took her on a tour of the house, and by her side one of the big footmen, his muscular bulk dwarfing the pile of luggage.

"But you will not be staying there," Mistress Tarbell told Carolina. "I have no mind to let you loose in London to seek out your other school friends and tell them lying tales about my daughter and the hospitality you received here! One of my husband's ships, the

Flying Falcon, leaves London on tomorrow's tide. She is bound for Yorktown in the Virginia Colony and my inquiries have indicated that is near your home. Bertha and Thorpe here"—she indicated the grim pair who hovered near the luggage—"will see to your safe arrival on the *Flying Falcon* and will convey to the captain a letter detailing your behavior. That letter will be delivered to your mother when you arrive in Yorktown."

Carolina, who had been stunned by the pace of events and by her energetic hostess's swift actions, spoke up for herself.

"You cannot abduct me like this!" she cried. "I will not go with these people, nor will I set foot on the *Flying Falcon* or any other ship belonging to you!"

"Ha!" cried her hostess. "Will you not? Thorpe, Bertha, take her from my sight!"

Carolina tried to run but it was useless. Reba watched, shivering, as the pair of them caught her in the hall and dragged her out to the waiting coach.

BOOK II

The Belle of Yorktown

She dreams about him through the night—at plays, beside a
*   mill. . . .*
She sees his face in every cloud, his form strides every hill.
She swears she will return to him—by heaven, yes, she will!
And when she does, she has no doubt that he will love her
*   still!*

FARVIEW PLANTATION
OLD PLANTATION CREEK
VIRGINIA'S EASTERN SHORE

Spring 1688

Chapter 20

Carolina was home at last—and she was in disgrace.

She had been dragged protesting aboard the *Flying Falcon* and shut into the captain's cabin for safekeeping until the ship sailed. Later she was to learn just how handsome were these quarters, for she was removed to those occupied by the women voyagers. Already crowded in, they were not glad to see her. Many of them were married and would not be reunited with their husbands, who slept in a separate men's dormitory, until they reached port in the New World.

She had had no chance to send a message to Lord Thomas in London, much less to see him. But with every fiber of her being she had willed him to think of her and when at last they were underway and she was let out of the captain's cabin, she had rushed to the railing almost expecting Thomas to appear, waving from the shore, shouting that he would have her removed from the vessel, that he would pursue her by a faster craft, that he had miraculously found out about her plight, that he would rescue her!

Nothing of the sort had happened, of course. With

dismay Carolina had seen the skyline of London drifting by as the tide took them and the white sails billowed out overhead. She had almost hurled herself overboard in chagrin as they made their stately passage down the Thames, past Execution Dock (and Carolina felt herself no less a prisoner than those unfortunates who met their end there), past Wapping Old Stairs, past the Isle of Dogs, past the mighty pile of Greenwich Palace, toward the open sea.

But although her worried eyes combed the shore (and indeed she *might* have hurled herself over had she seen Thomas running along that shoreline waving at her) no small boat appeared, being manfully rowed toward the departing vessel, no lover hailed the ship commanding it to stop.

The flood tide was carrying her fast away from London, from Rye, from Thomas, from all her bright young dreams.

She wept. She called the captain an abductor—and worse. This brought instant punishment and she was confined below-decks to the damp creaking communal cabin where the women slept, to sit with her head in her hands and languish, pushing away her aching memories of Rye to focus instead on Thomas. She wondered what he must think of her defection. Would anyone even tell him what had happened? What would he surmise? That she had casually deserted him without so much as a goodbye?

And all the while Carolina agonized about him, handsome Lord Thomas was lazing away the time in London, changing mistresses almost by the week. He gave her not a thought.

In time the captain allowed Carolina out again upon the deck. She was thinner now and there were bluish circles beneath her lovely eyes. Her gaze at her captor was resentful, but she now knew enough to hold her tongue. She had had a long time to think in the stuffiness of that damp cabin below and it had come to her that between them, Reba Tarbell and Rye Evistock were the cause of all her troubles: save for Reba's pleading she would have told Rye the truth early on. Then she would never have got so involved with him, and *she would not now miss him so much!* And had Rye, when he learned the truth at last, only given her a chance, had he let her explain instead of trapping her in the maze and filling her hands with unasked for gold— then Reba's mother would not have come to her startling (but on the face of it, Carolina admitted, perhaps warranted) conclusions about their relationship—and forced her onto this ship bound for Virginia.

There had been a moment of ironic amusement when Carolina had learnt that the boxes she had brought with her, packed helter skelter by the servants at Broadleigh while she waited downstairs in the library, were stuffed with all the clothes she had borrowed from Reba, kept in the big press in her bedchamber, and worn at Broadleigh. Naturally the servants had assumed them to be her own! She had laughed harshly as she rummaged about, unpacking each item and staring at it in wonder before replacing it. There was Reba's fox-trimmed velvet cloak, her fox-trimmed hood and tippet and muff, there were all the dazzling gowns made in London for Reba but worn by Carolina, even—she had gasped when she saw it—that wonderful gray and silver creation.

Carolina had closed the boxes, intending to return them upon arrival in Virginia, but as the monotonous weeks of the voyage passed and her bitterness deepened, she decided that Reba—who would not really miss them anyway—deserved their loss, for she had not stood up for her and told the truth to her mother at Broadleigh.

Although at first she had blamed her troubles on others, later on, in the fresh salty air of the deck, with the white sails crackling above and the sea wind blowing her bright hair back, she stood by the rail thinking long thoughts. And realized that she herself was the author of her troubles. Reba had schemed and connived and lured her—true. But she had had no need to follow blindly! She could have stopped short of her own disreputable part in this shabby game! It was no wonder Rye had felt as he did, acted as he did. But that was no excuse for leaving her in the freezing maze to die. Resentment coursed through her at the memory. *She* could never have done that to *him!* Nor did the punishment fit the crime! She told herself that Rye could never have loved her or he would have come back to save her. His masculine vanity had been pricked when he learnt there was someone else, and any affection he had ever felt for her had vanished on the instant. A shallow lover!

She had been attracted to Rye, she admitted. But she had been wrong. It was Thomas who truly cared for her, Thomas who deserved her love. And she had treated him shabbily. What must he be thinking of her now? That she was false to him—as indeed she had so nearly been. . . . She winced at the thought.

More and more she began to feel that she had suffered at Rye's hands, and she began to hate him. One cold foggy day on the Atlantic, when her teeth were chattering as she stood at the rail looking out into chill white nothingness, she told herself he was to blame for everything that had happened—it was he who had caused her to be set aboard this ghost ship en route to nowhere! In her fury she grasped the gold locket which she had foolishly worn ever since he gave it to her and tore it from her neck, breaking its delicate chain. She glared down at it for a moment and then with all her strength she hurled it from her into the wintry sea. It disappeared silently into the fog—she did not even hear a splash. One glittering flash and then—like Rye himself—it was gone forever.

Carolina stared after it, peering into the white murk. And then, quite inexplicably, she burst into tears.

But throwing away the locket had seemed to break some bond that had bound her to Rye. It was easier to hate him when she no longer felt that locket lying around her neck! And as her rancor at Rye Evistock grew, so did her warmth toward Lord Thomas increase until he glowed almost godlike in her memory, larger than life—the perfect lover. She could not wait to be reunited with him. Somehow she would get back to London where she belonged, and to Lord Thomas, to whom she belonged. By choice. Her own choice.

So she reasoned as she stood upon the deck watching the gray-green waters of winter turn into the aqua blue of spring. So she reasoned as her heart filled with despair, for she envisioned a haggard Lord Thomas pacing about, asking himself why there was no word from her, no word at all.

Meantime she was going back to Bedlam, she told herself bitterly, and there would be an ocean between them.

And it was to Bedlam that the captain of the *Flying Falcon* conveyed her, casting anchor in Chesapeake Bay at Old Plantation Creek above Cape Charles and personally escorting her home by longboat to her astonished family.

Carolina had tried vainly to persuade him to tear up the letter from Reba's mother, arguing that it would only cause her harm, but the captain was too well aware of the power of Reba's father. If he failed to carry out Jonathan Tarbell's trust, he could well find his command taken from him. It was with a rolling dignified gait that he followed Carolina as she leaped out of the longboat and ran toward the now well-repaired house overlooking the inlet known as Plantation Creek.

They were met at the front door by Carolina's mother, who gave Carolina a startled look and then turned majestically to meet the captain and deal with whatever situation had brought her daughter home unannounced.

Rather stiff greetings were exchanged and the letter handed over while Carolina hovered anxiously in the background. Letitia tore the letter open, hastily perused it, and without comment offered the captain a glass of port which was not accepted as he "must get on" while wind and tide favored him, to make port in Yorktown.

As the captain turned, about to leave, Letitia Light-foot stood back and considered her daughter, whom she had not seen for many months.

"You are thinner," she said critically. "It makes you look older." *But perhaps not wiser,* she was thinking.

She might have said more but at that point Virginia came running out of the house and embraced Carolina with shining eyes. "Oh, how wonderful that you're back!" Virgie exclaimed, and Carolina, hugging her sister, thought privately how well Virgie's widow's weeds became her. Mother should not give up hope of marrying Virginia off, she thought. With the handsome background of Papa's new house, once it was completed, and a fat dowry, Virgie would be desirable merchandise on the marriage market and sought after by half the young bucks around!

Arm in arm, Virgie swept her into the house, and Carolina was surprised to find it almost devoid of furniture. "Oh, we've already moved all but the essentials," Virgie informed her. "But Mother was determined not to move in until the smell of fresh paint was gone from the new house—you know how she hates it!"

"Where are Flo and Della?" wondered Carolina, for the house seemed strangely silent without the sound of childish laughter.

"Oh, they're with Aunt Pet. Mother said it was too much trouble to have them underfoot while we're moving. They're to join us day after tomorrow at the new house—at Level Green. You won't believe how they've grown. They're practically young ladies now! Did I tell you we're moving tomorrow?"

"No, you didn't!"

Virginia rattled on throughout the day, bringing Carolina up to date on all the local gossip. Carolina was relieved for she was not eager to face her mother now that she had read that letter. But Letitia busied herself elsewhere. Meantime Virgie kept up a continuous flow of words: Did she know, Athena Weeds was married now but entertaining Ross Dwyer every time her husband went away to view his upriver plantation? And the Darburys had just had their *seventeenth* child—imagine! And the baby was a girl. That made *twelve* daughters to be married off—Amanda Darbury was almost in mourning over it. She swore she'd never let her husband into her bedroom again!

"What about Mother's cousin, Sandy Randolph?" Carolina inquired at dinner, for Virgie had not mentioned him. At the head of the table she saw her mother stiffen slightly—Letitia always sat at the head of her table when, as now, her husband was not expected home for dinner, and Carolina had already been told that he would be staying overnight at the new house and would meet them all there tomorrow.

"Oh, he's fine," said Virgie vaguely. "We haven't seen much of him lately. You can't imagine how busy we've been, Carol. Not only the drapers and the furniture makers, but all last week we were struggling with the Great Wash for Mother has decreed that everything we bring into the new house must be clean—laundered or scrubbed or polished!"

So her mother had exchanged those calls and drives with Sandy Randolph for the joys of moving into an elegant new house, thought Carolina, casting another glance at the head of the table. Her mother, even by flickering candlelight, seemed to be sitting very straight. Annoyed that Carolina had asked about Sandy, no doubt!

Not until after dinner when Carolina was called into the library did she face her mother alone. Letitia's thin rustling gown of watered wine taffeta had an elegant glaze and Letitia herself, standing straight and tall and imperious in it, was a formidable sight. She stood among boxes of already packed books—and the letter from Reba's mother was in her hand. Carolina felt a little involuntary thrill of fear go through her. Her spirited mother had had the ordering of her young life for so many years. . . .

For a long time Letitia stood facing her without speaking, studying her daughter by the light of the branched candlestick that reposed on the polished cherry table. Carolina found herself fidgeting beneath that calm appraising gaze. Then her mother lifted the letter negligently.

"The woman who wrote this, who is so high-handed that she ships you home without my permission, describes you as a whore," she said bluntly. "Are you become one?"

Indignation made Carolina's gray eyes snap silver. "Of course not!"

"She claims you lured away her daughter's intended."

"I did that," admitted Carolina shamefacedly. "Reba wanted to marry a marquess, you see, but he already had a wife, and it did not work out after all, even when his wife finally did die in Italy—"

"Spare me the details." Her mother raised a hand to stop this flow of words. "The daughter sounds like an upstart and a fool."

"The mother is worse," said Carolina morosely.

"I don't doubt it. She adds that you roamed London dressed as a man and spent your time gaming!"

"One night only," admitted Carolina.

The shadow of a smile quirked the corners of her mother's wayward mouth. "I always wanted to do that," she murmured. "And your headmistress, the letter speaks of her. . . ."

"What she says of Mistress Chesterton is probably true. All the parents have withdrawn their daughters from the school."

"Indeed?" Letitia pondered the letter in her hand. When she looked up her face was inscrutable. "I am probably beholden to the writer of this letter for letting me know about conditions at the school, but her accusations against you are such that I do not feel inclined to thank her. Try to avoid her sort in future." She tossed the letter into the fireplace where it burned merrily. She veered to a new subject. "I have had a chance to look at your wardrobe after Virgie unpacked your boxes and I must say that you have done remarkably well with the money I gave you!"

Carolina gave her mother a nervous look.

"Especially," added her mother casually, "since you had almost no money to buy anything with, having given it all to your sister so that she might elope."

Carolina swallowed. So her mother knew about that!

"So I think there is a good deal you have yet to tell me," said Letitia in a soft, almost menacing tone.

Yes, there was—that she was no longer a virgin and that she was committed to Lord Thomas no matter what the opposition! With a sudden feeling of panic, Carolina found her voice and explained about the clothes. Indeed she told the whole story—leaving out only Lord Thomas, and the reason for Rye's deserting her in the maze, saying only that he had overheard her tell Reba she would not continue leading him on.

Her mother listened, unmoved. "So you have nothing more to tell me?"

Carolina shook her head. Her feelings about Lord Thomas were too personal, too private—she would share them with no one.

And this very night, by candlelight, she would pen him a letter and give it to one of the servants when they reached Yorktown to be given to the captain of any ship leaving for the Port of London!

"You may go, Carolina," said her mother with a sigh. "The clothing is winter clothing. It will be packed away while I think about all this and decide what to do."

The next morning with the dawn they began their Great Move. By boat and wagon their goods were hauled to the new house. Level Green lay on the eastern bank of the York River several miles to the northwest of Yorktown. Laden with furniture, their boat crossed the Chesapeake, moved smoothly into the York's wide mouth and made its stately way up this shortest of the Tidewater's four major rivers. Carolina looked up at the long line of reddish rock marl cliffs. Along those bluffs, some fifty feet high, that rose above her, lay the village of Yorktown, paralleling the broad river, its short streets with their neat brick and frame houses bisecting the length of the main street.

303

And now the oarsmen were bending their backs as they passed other plantations. Beyond Yorktown they passed Ringfield, a solid two-and-a-half-story brick house with a roomy wing, lying on the peninsula where King's Creek and Felgate's Creek joined the York. Across from it lay Timberneck, where the Mann family had lived for so many years.

"But wait until you see *our* house!" cried Virginia proudly when Carolina turned to admire the buildings and the spring flowers, blooming from plants brought from England. "*It* will stun you!"

And indeed Carolina was stunned when she saw the house. She had not imagined anything so grand.

"It is the largest house in all Virginia!" Virgie told her merrily. "It has twenty-three rooms—there are three vast wide halls and no less than nine passages. Indeed each wing contains six rooms!"

Carolina stared at the splendid brickwork ("All Flemish bond," her sister declared proudly), at the elaborate masonry trim ("See the white marble lintels?"). And then her gaze rose in awe, up four stories (if you counted that high-windowed basement) to the soaring leaded roof with its twin turrets. ("All glassed in, don't they make excellent lookouts?")

"It will *beggar* Father!" Carolina gasped.

"So I have told him," murmured her mother, passing by. "Here, Josh, that table belongs in my bedroom and all that furniture goes to the wing over there." She nodded to her right. "We will be replacing it when the furniture we've ordered arrives from England," she added over her shoulder.

"Father named it Level Green," whispered Virgie. "But Mother privately calls it Fielding's Folly—but she is proud of it all the same!"

And then Fielding Lightfoot came smiling through the front entrance. At sight of Carolina he missed a step, cast a quick look at his wife, then strode forward to welcome her. There was little warmth in his greeting but she told herself it was the unexpected shock of seeing her there.

"Bring that table around to the side," he directed,

turning to the men just then carrying in a handsome trestle table. "I'll be wanting it in my office."

"No." Letitia hurried over to demur. "I have already decided that table should be set by the window just to the left of the—"

"It belongs in my office," he interrupted impatiently. "I wish to set my small writing desk upon it."

"Then what will support the tall brass candlesticks?"

"Anything you like can support them! A mantel will do well enough."

"Fielding, we have already discussed this and we *decided*—"

They were already quarreling.

Used to that, the girls left their parents outside and passed into the enormous hall paneled with polished mahogany.

Virginia gave a last look over her shoulder toward the sounds of bickering outside. "I don't understand it," she puzzled. "They both seemed so happy planning the house. I mean, they were getting along so well before you got home." She sighed. "Do you think it's the strain of getting moved in that's set them at each other's throats again?"

Carolina shrugged. It seemed to her that all her life her parents had erupted into dissent the moment she appeared. Now her gaze swung from the full-height pilasters of the hall to the upward curve of the grand staircase, its mahogany balustrade handsomely carved into wooden baskets of flowers and fruit. "I can't believe we're going to live here," she cried in amazement.

"Just wait till you see *our* rooms!" Virgie picked up her skirts and Carolina followed her in a dash up that stairway on treads so wide that eight people could easily have ascended abreast.

The rooms were spacious and they reflected Letitia Lightfoot's taste in their soft "Williamsburg" colors, the muted greens and calm blues. And the furniture, while much of it seemed too small for the vastness of their surroundings, was all of fine polished fruitwoods and cedar and walnut—for Letty had a great dislike for the pine furniture being produced in New England and shipped south. She would allow none of it in her new home.

"Mother has ordered Aubusson rugs sent out from England, and ever so much new furniture," Virgie told her. "She has commissioned Mr. Arbuthnot to buy it for her because she says he has such impeccable taste. Oh, doesn't my old fourposter look splendid there by the windows?"

Carolina looked about her thoughtfully. Virgie's room was indeed beautiful with its pale green painted walls and embroidered green and white coverlet and hangings. Her own room too was of a delightful simplicity, but elegant with walls of misty blue and dainty blue and white curtains and a white quilt with a large blue *fleur de lis* design worked into it.

Fleur de lis. . . . The very sight of a *fleur de lis* brought her painfully back to memories of Thomas, who wore them almost as a hallmark, embroidered on his cuffs.

"Mother is buying for your room a pale blue Aubusson carpet and a lovely pier glass," confided Virgie. "And for me a cheval glass and a French dressing table and a splendid green Turkish carpet!"

Carolina could not help but compare the simple elegance of her parents' new home to ancient Broadleigh—so old, so steeped in time and yet so marred by the ostentatious bad taste of its new owners. She was suddenly fiercely glad to be back in the fresh free air of Virginia. If only Lord Thomas could be here by her side . . .

She would have been astonished to learn that the letter she had penned last night and now waited to entrust to whichever servant went first to Yorktown, would never reach Lord Thomas. For even while she herself was aboard the *Flying Falcon* skimming across the blue Atlantic, Lord Thomas had run into trouble. He had seduced the daughter of Sir Perry Blaine and Sir Perry was, word reached him, quite wroth about it. Sir Perry would have him marry the girl, and was even now advancing upon London with a party of able gentlemen. Lord Thomas took this report seriously. He left word with his friends that he was off for Europe and promptly embarked on the first available vessel bound for the West Indies. He had distant cousins in Barbados and he was curious about the island girls. Reports had it that they were quick blooming and very willing—he would find out.

But Carolina, standing musing in the middle of her new bedroom, knew nothing of that.

"And we are to have excellent neighbors just above us across Carter's Creek," added Virgie triumphantly, as if to cap all she had said. "For Lewis and Abigail Burwell are constructing a manor house there called Fairfield. The brick arches and vault of the basement are already completed and the chimneys are to be tapering, like those of Bacon's Castle. The house will be in the shape of a rectangle with two wings attached at right angles—and one wing is to compose a ball-room. Oh, we will be in the very thick of things here with balls and parties—Williamsburg across the peninsula will have nothing to rival us!" She added more soberly, "Mother says it is too bad that poor Mr. Bacon is not alive to see this house. He told her as a child that she was destined for great things and she seems to have achieved them!"

Carolina was reminded that Bacon's Rebellion—with most of the planter aristocracy solidly behind him—had ended a little to the north, in Gloucester, at the house of a Mr. Pate—and many an aristocratic neck had been stretched by the hangman's rope over that affair!

"In England they are apt to consider us traitors if we speak out against the King's policies," she said bitterly.

"Well!" Virgie's affronted tone reflected the fact that Fielding Lightfoot had been one of the planters who, six years ago, when the government would offer no help, had taken to the roads by night, tearing up young tobacco plants in an effort at production control. Six of the "plant cutters" had been executed and the only result of the Tobacco Riots was that the rate of customs, already over 300 percent, was raised, as well as taxes in Virginia.

The girls, who were in sympathy not only with Bacon, who had stood bravely against outrages by the Indians when the government refused to do so, but with the Tobacco Rioters as well, frowned at each other— and then promptly forgot politics and paraded out to survey the rest of the house.

England and England's King seemed very far away. . . .

But when night came in their strange new enormous home, Carolina could not sleep. She rose and looked out restlessly upon this unfamiliar Tidewater landscape with the river and not the bay glistening below. The moonlight outlined little clumps and hummocks here and there on the lawn below, where Letty Lightfoot had already begun setting out her rose gardens and her rows of boxwood. It was beautiful here, but Carolina had left her heart back in England. . . .

She leaned against the open window and felt the night wind ruffle her hair and looked down at the letter in which she had poured out her heart to her golden lover, back in England.

"You must come and get me, Thomas," she had written. *"I promise to stave off all other suitors until you get here no matter how Mother coerces me!"*

She meant every word. And it could well have changed her life had that letter been delivered. For it was a very winning letter, the ingenuous outpourings of a girl lost in a dream of love—and it could have persuaded Lord Thomas to take a later ship to Virginia's Tidewater country instead of an earlier one bound for the West Indies.

But Fortune is a devious jade—and she had other things in mind for Carolina.

ROSEGILL ON THE YORK
TIDEWATER, VIRGINIA

Summer 1688

Chapter 21

On the wide lawns and sweeping gardens of
Ralph Wormeley's Rosegill plantation, its cluster of
houses dominated by the eleven-room brick manor
house his father had built in 1650, the second best
attended party of the season was in full swing. The *best*
attended party of the whole year would of course be the
ball held last week at Level Green, for not a family in
the Tidewater but had yearned to visit Fielding Lightfoot's new house, the largest in Virginia. The Eastern
Shore had arrived almost in a body. Everybody who
counted had come from the York and the James.
Indeed people had journeyed from as far away as the
Falls of the James and there had even been a spat-
tering of guests from the Carolinas. Virginia had been
ecstatic—Carolina less so, for she had noticed
an ominous matchmaking light in her mother's eyes of
late.

Now, a week later, at Rosegill in the summer afternoon, ladies in wide-skirted pastel gowns, their faces
shielded from the bright Virginia sun by broad-
brimmed hats or ruffled parasols, were strolling along-

side leisurely silk-clad gentlemen about the thirty acres of lawns that Rosegill, with its ten thousand–acre grant, could well afford to devote to pleasure. They laughed and chatted, they admired the myriad clumps of wild roses that had given the estate its name, and they wondered—the ladies behind their fans and the gentlemen in between pinches of snuff from enameled snuffboxes—whom Letitia Lightfoot's daughter would marry—the gorgeous one, the one with hair like spun silver and the fashionable London education.

Most of those speculating agreed that Ned Shackleford and Dick Smithfield were the leading contenders. Both had vied with each other in dancing Mistress Carolina around the room at that first great ball held at Level Green, and today at Rosegill they were still vying for her favor. An impromptu "tourney" had been arranged and the antagonists, their ladies' colors tied to their arms, were even now charging across the lawn on their mounts, lances fixed, spearing circlets that had been hung from the branches of trees that were saplings when a Virgin Queen ruled England. To ride the course of three and garner a dangling circlet from each was the goal. And the two main contenders, Ned and Dick, both of them peerless horsemen, had so far a perfect score apiece.

A ladies' finger ring had now been called for to break the tie, and from a window in Ralph Wormeley's famous library Carolina, who had gone there at her mother's request to collect her sister (both of them knowing well Virginia's love of books), was watching the show.

"Look at those two fools," she said to Virgie. "Now they're down to finger rings. They'll both spear the ring and what then? A duel through the rose bushes?"

"They only want to shine in your sight," laughed Virgie, closing one of the lovely leather-bound volumes with a sigh. "I had so hoped Mother would forget about me and I could spend the afternoon reading!"

"Nonsense, she didn't drag you out of mourning and into that blue gown to have you hide here among a lot

310

of musty old volumes—indeed she just said so for all the world to hear!"

Virgie joined Carolina at the window and her sky blue skirts mingled with Carolina's petal pink ones as they watched Ned Shackleford thunder down the grassy course, daintily catching the ladies' gold finger ring on the point of his spear. There was laughter and applause.

"Is that your scarf he's wearing on his sleeve?" Virgie asked.

"They're *both* wearing my colors," Carolina said with a sigh. "Ned has my scarf, and Dick has tied my white lace kerchief to *his* sleeve!"

"It must be fun to be a reigning belle," said Virgie seriously, "and have *two* men desperate to win you!"

"Well, it isn't," said Carolina in exasperation. "It's very confining. Both of them chase me into every corner, they interrupt my conversations—it's a very great bore to have them hovering over me all the time!"

"Ned styles himself Knight of Gloucester and Dick styles himself Knight of Accomack," murmured Virgie. "They've beaten all the other knights on the course."

"They aren't *knights*," scoffed Carolina. "They're only playacting! I do wish they'd stop."

"I rather like Ned," said Virgie with a sigh.

"Well, if you do you're welcome to him." Carolina was watching her champions take a second try at the ladies' finger ring. For the course must be ridden by both contestants until one of them lost out and a winner could be declared to crown a Queen of Love and Beauty. The whole thing was a relic of the great medieval tourneys, the memory of which these Virginia Colonists had brought with them to America—along with other bits of old England.

"It won't be so easy as that." Virgie gave her sister a slanted look. "Mother may make you marry the victor, you know."

"Will she?" asked Carolina restlessly.

"Yes, she will," was Virgie's soft but firm rejoinder. "I heard her say to Aunt Pet that Ned and Dick were

311

the two to choose between—that they were equally eligible and both head over heels in love with you."

Carolina gave a little start at her sister's words. They had brought back to her a terrible scene she had had with her mother this morning back in the gardens of Level Green. While Carolina was cutting roses for the breakfast table, her mother had come out and tried to pin her down as to which of her suitors she preferred.

"I prefer neither of them!" Carolina had insisted, stabbing her finger with a rose thorn and putting the finger to her mouth in a sulky childish gesture.

"You prefer, perhaps, someone back in London?" her mother had asked smoothly.

Finger still in her mouth, Carolina had turned slowly to regard her mother. The morning sunshine was very bright, the tangle of wild roses from which she was cutting sprays was heavy with dew. Nearby the sandy loamy soil was mounded around newly planted moss roses that had arrived by ship from England, and sprigs of boxwood that would someday be a towering hedge. From the tall oaks that had been saplings when Columbus discovered America came a burst of birdsong, and farther away the cooing sound of mourning doves.

"Why do you say that?" she asked slowly.

"And would his name be Lord Thomas Angevine?" pursued her mother, answering a question with a question.

The world about Carolina had seemed to hold very still. High above her a golden eagle wheeled and soared—free. As she was not. All her pleas that she be sent back to England, to some other school, had availed her nothing. Her school days were over, she had been told. A planter's daughter in the Virginia planters' aristocracy, she was chained to convention, to a certain way of life. But she would break her chains, she would be as free as that eagle!

"Yes." She moistened lips suddenly gone dry. "There *is* a man in London and that is his name." She took a deep breath. "I am betrothed to him. But how did you know? I have told no one."

For answer her mother held out a letter, held it

delicately between thumb and forefinger. Carolina could see that it was the letter she had written to Thomas on her first night home, a letter in which she had poured out her heart. "How did you get it?" she gasped, her face flaming scarlet.

"Very simply," said her mother. "When you appeared on the doorstep without notice, I alerted the servants to deliver any of your mail—outgoing or incoming—to me."

"Well, since you have read my letter to Thomas," Carolina said bitterly, "you know that we are in love and plan to marry."

"In love?" echoed her mother lightly. "I have since made inquiries about young Lord Thomas and I have discovered that he is a worthless rake and that he is always in love—with a succession of women—but never for long. I think it is your good fortune to have escaped him." She looked into her daughter's rebellious face. "Carolina, you should remember to wear a hat in this sun. You will ruin your complexion."

"Oh, the devil with my complexion!" cried Carolina, who was thinking that now she would have to write Lord Thomas again, that there would be a further delay in his knowing what had happened to her, a further delay in his coming for her.

"He won't come for you, you know," said her mother softly, as if divining her thoughts. "Men like him are not to be trusted. They flit from flower to flower."

Carolina's head came up indignantly. "How can you say that? You do not know him."

"No, but I recognize the type. Some men marry and settle down—quickly and quietly. But you and I would never be attracted to those." She sighed. "Some men" —was she thinking of Sandy Randolph, Carolina wondered?—"are always in love with the unattainable. They want most dearly what they cannot possess and will pursue it forever. But others—like your Lord Thomas—will never settle down. And even if they do, they will never be faithful." She broke off. "Now that we have moved into our new home and have properly

313

introduced you to Virginia society, now that you are being pursued by half the young bucks in the county, you must make a decision. I think it should be a quick decision. And whoever you choose will need to be in love with you for I take it from all this overprotesting that you are no longer a virgin?"

Carolina choked and did not answer.

Her mother studied her for a long time. Then, "I take it from your blushes that I am right," she said softly. "Well, you will not have been the first girl to make a mistake. I—" She cut off the words and made a sudden regal gesture of dismissal. "Wear your pink dress. No one has yet seen you in pink."

At any other time Carolina might have pursued that "I—" left hanging in the air. As it was, she was so filled with dismay that her mother had found out about Lord Thomas that she stumbled back to the house forgetting her roses. Once in the cool dimness of the hall she closed her eyes and leaned against the paneled wall and tried to get hold of herself. But she felt stripped naked —and humbled—by her mother, as she always did, for Letitia seemed to ferret out everything without even trying. *Except that one time when she had been taken in by Carolina's ruse of pretending that she was about to run away with Virgie's lover. . . .* How had her mother missed seeing through that?

Carolina was standing directly across from a mirror as that thought occurred to her, and as she opened her eyes she saw her own face reflected. In its way it was a face as determined as her mother's—and just as wild. And in that flashing moment she understood her mother's mistake. *Her mother recognized in Carolina a woman like herself, a woman who would take chances, make mistakes, suffer for them—as she herself had. She understood her daughter's wild nature, so different from her sister Virginia's. Which meant*—Carolina stood for a moment stunned by the realization—*that she could do it again!* She could escape this marriage her mother planned for her by pretending to go along with it, and then arranging passage on a ship that was leaving for

314

England—and making her mother believe that she had run off to the Marriage Trees with somebody else! And her mother would be fooled just long enough for the ship on which she sailed to make the open sea before some fast ketch could overtake her and bring her back to Level Green—and back to an unwanted betrothal and perhaps a hasty wedding ceremony in the new Bruton Parish Church.

It would have been so easy if only her friend, madcap Sally Montrose, had been here. Sally had nerve, she had sense, she was a kindred spirit. Sally would have thought it a wonderful escapade to help Carolina escape! But Sally had been away all spring and summer visiting relatives in Philadelphia and would not be back until sometime this fall. But—maybe it could be accomplished anyway, she told herself, planning rapidly. Maudie Tate, one of the women who had shipped over with her in those crowded barrackslike women's sleeping quarters aboard the *Flying Falcon,* had been hired as a scullery maid at Rosegill—and were they not attending a garden party at Rosegill this very afternoon? For money—or for something else she wanted— Maudie would clamber into one of the rowboats tied up at Rosegill's pier and slip away downriver. It was common knowledge that the *Fair Alice*—that ship that had brought so many fine fabrics to Yorktown to delight Virginia's feminine hearts—was sailing for England three days hence. And passengers would be few this time of year when planters were busy with their crops and the ladies busy with the summertime round of parties. Maudie could arrange for passage, pay part— and she, impersonating Maudie in a scullery maid's costume of coarse gray linen, her hair pulled up into a linen cap like Maudie's, could come aboard, look down shyly and plump the rest of her passage money into the captain's hand.

She could be gone before the week was out!

All this had flitted idly through her mind as she made her way on down the hall. It had been but a pleasant daydream—and that was all it could be, for she did not

315

have enough money to pay for her passage. What she had brought home she had already lavished on gifts for everyone in the shops of Williamsburg.

Now, standing beside the library window at Rosegill, leaving in haste suddenly seemed the best thing to do. She would not write to Lord Thomas—she would go to London and surprise him.

She stared out at the two young bucks on horseback, each so valiantly vying for her attention, and her gray eyes narrowed. Her mother would believe her just perverse enough to run away with one of them—or with somebody else. Indeed Letitia Lightfoot would probably just shake her head and tell all comers that Carolina had eloped for the sole purpose of depriving her mother of managing a big lavish wedding at Level Green, with the bride trailing down that wide majestic stairway, and roses everywhere, and the sun slanting down through the windows to shine on everyone who counted in Virginia.

"Virgie," she said rapidly, for she had just noticed that Ned had won and had dismounted. He was posing jauntily with his spear still conspicuously displayed and looking around for Carolina when his opponent, Dick Smithfield, chagrined but too well bred to show it, leaped off his bay horse to congratulate the winner. "Virgie, how much money do you have?"

"Why, naught but a few pence. I spent all my pin money on laces and a length of dress material from the shipment Captain Frobisher brought aboard the *Fair Alice.*"

Carolina sighed. Virgie could never be counted on where money was concerned—she would have to find some other way. Outside in the distance she could see that little Sally Majors had nearly finished weaving the circlet of roses and ivy for her "crown." She would be expected to come out and wear it.

She cast a quick speculative glance at Virgie. Virgie was loyal but she folded under pressure and she found it difficult to keep a secret. That was why Carolina had not told her about Lord Thomas—for had not Virgie confessed to her mother where she got the money for her own elopement? Still—such weakness could be useful.

She lowered her voice conspiratorially. "Virgie, would you help me make a dash for the Marriage Trees?"

"You're going to run away to the Marriage Trees?" gasped Virgie. "Oh, Carol, who *with?*"

But Carolina was already halfway out into the hall. Virgie ran after her, calling out, but when she reached the front door, Carolina had already picked up her wide skirts and run lightly over the lawn to join the others.

She passed the younger children, playing Blind Man's Buff on the lawn, and waved to flushed-faced Della and Flo. Had she ever been that young? she asked herself as she watched them. Had her world ever seemed that bright?

She was looking back at them, hardly noticing where she was going, when she stumbled. An arm shot out and righted her instantly. And she found herself looking up into Sandy Randolph's dazzling smile. He had detached himself from the others and she had blundered into him on his way across the lawn. Now he swept her a low bow and she made him a curtsy.

"'Tis a splendid vista here at Rosegill, is it not, Mistress Carolina?" he asked.

Carolina came up out of her curtsy and looked into a pair of glinting eyes. She murmured that yes, it was.

"So you will be crowned Queen of Love and Beauty this day," he added softly. "It is most warranted. You have grown up to be a beauty indeed."

Carolina gave him a sharp look, surprised at this sudden compliment from a man who had never paid her the least attention save that his gaze had seemed to follow her sometimes when he rode by and saw her strolling down the street near Aunt Pet's in Williamsburg, or again racing across the lawns during one of his rare visits to the Eastern Shore.

"They say I resemble no one," she said lightly, quoting Aunt Pet. "Not my mother, not my father."

He gave her a melancholy look. "Oh, I would say

317

there is some resemblance," he murmured. "To your mother at least. You have her light step, her graceful carriage, her low warm laugh. . . . I am leaving Virginia, Mistress Carolina," he added gravely.

Carolina was astonished that Sandy Randolph should have noticed so much about her. She was surprised too that he was leaving. She knew of course that he traveled a great deal—who would not with a mad wife at home, a wife who tore out tufts of her own hair and could not stop laughing hysterically for hours, a wife who had attacked him twice, once with a butcher knife and once with a pair of scissors? He bore the scars of both on his handsome face.

"We will miss you, sir," she said inadequately.

Again his melancholy gaze passed over her. "That is good to hear, Mistress Carolina," he said soberly. "For there are times when I have thought my life was wasted."

They were standing together, a little apart from the rest, while Ned waited impatiently for the crown to be finished, and Virgie—now standing beside her mother —watched them speculatively. Letitia Lightfoot's expression was inscrutable as she too watched the pair of them.

There was a faint rustle on the grass as a strolling couple passed behind them and the man's murmured comment was carried clearly to Carolina.

"They look like father and daughter, don't they?" he said idly. "All that white hair and pale eyes?"

And the woman's hissed, "Hush! They'll *hear* you!" silenced him.

Carolina, who had been standing there relaxed, stiffened suddenly. They meant *her*. And Sandy Randolph. She shot a look up at him. Apparently he had not heard, for his melancholy gaze was focused across the river to some far horizon. Almost in panic her gaze swept over his features. *She had his eyes . . .* long and wide and silver, dark lashed. *She had his hair,* so glistening pale it was like white metal in the sunlight. *She had his fair fair skin.* And Virgie had said, *They*

318

were getting along so well before you got home. . . .
Suddenly those words rang through her mind like a
great bell tolling.

And with every peal they brought the truth clanging
home to her.

She was Sandy Randolph's daughter!

And everyone—her face grew hot at the thought and
she hardly dared to look around her—*everyone* had
known but her! So many things she had never understood came flooding back to her now with diamond
clarity: little comments people had made, voices suddenly hushed when she came into a room, knowing
glances cast her way, Aunt Pet's commiserating sympathy that had always seemed overdone, Fielding Lightfoot's willingness to let her visit away from home while
he kept the other girls close around him, being sent
away to school in England—oh, it all made sense now.
Most stunning of all was the harsh realization that
everyone else had known while she herself had been
walking around in the dark.

How could she face them, all these people drifting
about on the lawn, waiting for her to be crowned
Queen of Love and Beauty? How could she face them,
feeling that all these years they had been talking behind
her back, laughing behind her back, nudging each
other, whispering, "There goes that poor little Lightfoot girl—the one who isn't really a Lightfoot at all!"

Beside her Sandy Randolph was talking, making
polite conversation—but she did not hear him. Her
head was awhirl as all the implications of being Sandy's
daughter and not Fielding's raced through her mind.

She was the reason for all the trouble at home.

Carolina could easily imagine how it had happened.
Her mother had found the one man who was right for
her—but she had been so young, she had been able to
make no impression on her dashing cousin. When at
last Sandy Randolph noticed that skinny little Letitia
had grown up to be a beauty—and that he desired
her—it was too late. He already had a wife and that
wife was mad—divorce was impossible. So even had

she managed to free herself from jealous—and wronged—Fielding Lightfoot, she could not legally have wed her lover.

What her mother must have gone through! thought Carolina in panic. For this sudden revelation made so many things startlingly clear to her:

It made clear the aversion of her Lightfoot in-laws, the trouble between them and her spirited young mother. And now she remembered something else— something she had heard Aunt Pet say once about a "visit" her mother had made to distant relatives in the Carolinas sometime before Carolina was born. A visit? Or had she been running away? Had she met Sandy Randolph there, lived with him for a while? Aunt Pet had always been reticent about that visit and her mother had never mentioned it. Perhaps Sandy and Letitia had both rebelled at a fate that meant never to let them be together, perhaps they had "skipped over the traces" and spent brief blissful days and nights together . . . and then realized that it could never be, that Letty had a husband in Philadelphia and two small children while Sandy had a mad wife to care for back on his plantation up the James.

Now that Carolina thought about it, trouble had always erupted between her parents whenever she had attracted her father's attention. And there was Aunt Pet's quick comment, "You should have done it long before, Letty," on being told Carolina was being sent away to school in London.

She had always sensed Fielding's antipathy—and now she knew why. Fielding was not her real father and he knew it. He had accepted Carolina as the price of getting Letty back—but he could not love her.

And her mother did not really love her either because . . . Carolina stood in the way of her having a happy life with Fielding. That was why Carolina had been kept in England with no discussion of when she would return home. Neither Fielding nor Letitia had wanted her to come home.

Facing it squarely as she stood poker straight upon the lawn at Rosegill, Carolina realized achingly that it

320

would have been better for them both if she had never happened. The thought shook her and she turned suddenly for comfort to the tall straight reed-slender man beside her, so fashionable in his ice gray suit. Ice colors—the kind she favored. Just as they both favored gray horses. Oh, they were alike, alike!

"Where will you go?" she asked, fighting for control.

"Oh—England perhaps."

She had control of herself now. "You will sell your plantation?"

"Not at first," he said. "I must first find a place suitable for Essie. Then I will return and sell my plantation."

Essie. His wife. He could not shuck her off; she must go with him to wherever he was going. And because of her, he could never have a son to bear his name—or claim a daughter, because to do so would be to shame another man's wife.

Carolina looked up at Sandy Randolph, so elegant, so debonair—so caught in a world not of his own choosing.

"I hope you will find happiness, sir," she said softly—and in that moment she wished him well with all her heart. "Wherever you go."

He was surprised and touched. "Will you stroll with me, Mistress Carolina?" he asked wistfully. "After you have been crowned? It seems to me that we have never truly become acquainted."

Carolina nodded silently. There was a lump in her throat. Over Sandy's shoulder she could see Ned walking briskly toward her. She could also see her mother studying them, her eyes shadowed beneath her wide sweeping hat. And just beyond, her father—no, not her father, that was the trouble—her foster father glowered.

It was like a weight pressing down on her to know that *she* was the center of all the trouble between them. Whatever her mother felt for Sandy Randolph now, Carolina did not know and would never dare to ask. But she herself was the living reminder, residing in Fielding Lightfoot's fine new house like a taunt, reminding him, endlessly reminding him of what had been. . . .

"Mistress Carolina!" Ned's happy voice interrupted her brooding. "'Tis true there'll be no great ball tonight where I could crown you properly, but since 'twas an impromptu tourney, 'tis to be an impromptu coronation! I'm to crown you on the lawn and all your maids will fall in behind as we lead you to your throne beneath yon large oak." He nodded toward one of the big trees that dotted the lawn. "If you'll excuse us, sir?" And Sandy Randolph gave ground to allow the tourney winner to claim the lady whose colors he had worn to victory.

Carolina gave Sandy Randolph a last look as he disappeared among the colorful crowd drifting toward the oak. *Oh, she was right to think of going—and so was he! Here they could only cause trouble for those they loved!*

It had been easy facing Sandy Randolph—for he had suffered too. But—now she had to face the crowd. Knowing what *they* knew. And nothing would ever be quite the same. For a moment she felt she could not do it and she stared down at the grass, asking herself miserably if she would be forever wondering what people were saying, whether they were talking about *her?*

Then as swiftly as the thought had come, the courage that she had inherited from both Letitia and Sandy— both of them brave as lions—came to her rescue. Her silver-gold head came up and her dainty jaw set stubbornly. She squared her slender shoulders and her silver eyes threw the world a challenge.

Let them talk! Everyone had always talked about the Lightfoots, about "Bedlam," let them talk about *her* too! What did *she* care what they said? She was in love with a man far across the seas, a man who would take her away from all this!

With her head held high as any queen's, she forced her features into as bright a smile as she could muster and let Ned proudly escort her to her "place of coronation," which was in the full glare of sunshine surrounded by the assembled company. Dazzled by the sunshine, shaken by the recent revelations, she still could see—and almost feel, in a detached sort of way—the envy of the other girls, several of whom had hoped to be courted by either Ned or Dick.

Ned was looking straight into her eyes as the circle of roses and ivy was placed upon her shining hair, and she read in his heated stare a determination to have her. She wondered if he had already asked Fielding for her. . . . It was so terrible not to know, to have others deciding one's fate!

Past Ned her gaze strayed to Sandy Randolph, who stood a little apart, watching. At one point she saw her mother turn to smile at him—and then turn crisply back and adjust her expression to one of unruffled calm. How awful to need constantly to mask one's feelings as her mother must have done all these years!

It was difficult but finally she managed to escape Ned when he fell into a discussion of horse racing with one of the other lads. As he had promised, Sandy Randolph appeared suddenly at her elbow and led her for a stroll beneath the trees.

She wondered if her mother was watching—and if she was, what she would think.

Once she even turned, but her mother's lavender form was nowhere in sight.

The tension of the afternoon seemed to press in upon her as she walked beside that tall straight figure. He was making courteous small talk but she felt his mind was not upon it.

If he really was her father—and she now felt certain that he was—she would dare to ask him for money. But she did not know him very well and she found it surprisingly hard to do so. They had gone some distance before she could get up her courage.

She took a deep breath and looked up at the tall man in ice gray who strode leisurely beside her.

"I need passage money—to England," she told him bluntly. "And I dare not ask my mother."

He broke stride to look down at her keenly. "Is one entitled to ask why you need passage money?"

She gave him a troubled look and tried to choose her words carefully. "Perhaps you who are leaving us can understand what it is like to feel—to feel unwanted in one's own home."

A hard line appeared around his attractive mouth as his expression froze. "And *who* does not want you there?" he asked silkily.

"No one," she said in panic, for she did not wish to cause a duel between this man and Fielding Lightfoot. They were both good blades—and good shots. They might well kill each other. And what would that do to her mother, caught in a situation from which there was no escape? "I only meant—my presence seems to trigger quarrels between my parents. It would be better for everyone if I were elsewhere."

"By 'elsewhere' can one presume you mean back in London?"

She nodded. "There is a man I love. I am betrothed to him. My mother has just found out about it. She has made inquiries and considers him a rake. She will not let me go to him but intends to marry me off at once to some good safe planter here in the Colonies."

Sandy Randolph looked down into that beautiful rebellious face so like his own—and looked away. In the blue distance, out beyond the tall old trees, beyond the shining river, he saw another day, another woman. He saw Letitia—his own Letty, age eighteen—fling herself down weeping upon the grass. "They will push me into a 'safe respectable marriage,'" she was crying. "When all the time I love you—and they know I love you. It is because you are married and they are afraid that I will make a scandal of myself."

He had failed her then. He had gone away. And while he was gone a desperate Letty had run away with Fielding Lightfoot. Returning, he had told himself it was for the best, that Letty should not fritter away her youth on a hopeless love, that she might even—he had winced to think it—come to love Fielding. The young Lightfoots had gone away to Philadelphia. Sandy had not seen Letty, had received no word from her. In time he heard that she had borne two children.

And then she had run away from Fielding. She had run all the way back to Virginia—to Sandy Randolph's arms. They had met at a nervous Aunt Pet's. And between them they had contrived that Letitia spend the Christmas season with relatives in Carolina. Her cousin Lysander Randolph would escort her there.

That was a holiday season Sandy would never forget. Letty had spent every moment she dared with him. They had been guests in the same large house and she had stolen down the hall to his bedroom and spent wonderful nights clasped in his arms.

And then with Twelfth Night sanity had come. Letty had put him from her, weeping. She had reminded him that she had two children left in Aunt Pet's care and a husband back in Philadelphia, and he had a wife back on the James. They must return, they must forget all this had ever happened. To do otherwise would bring calamity upon everyone.

The next day they had parted quite stylishly for Letty was going back to Williamsburg in the company of other guests while Sandy rode south to visit friends at a neighboring plantation.

He had bent down to kiss her a quick goodbye. "If something comes of this, Letty," he had murmured thickly, "I stand ready to carry you away wherever you desire."

She had flashed a look upward at him, her mind made up. "If something comes of this, and it is a son, I shall name him Chance," she told him recklessly. "And if it is a daughter, I shall name her Carolina for the site of our happiness."

And he had learnt that nine months later in Philadelphia Letitia had been delivered of a daughter—and had named her Carolina. It was as if she had sent him a message. . . .

And now he, who had so carefully stayed away from this fresh lovely young creature who was blood of his blood, flesh of his flesh, had been asked by her for passage money to send her winging to her lover.

What would have happened, he asked himself, if Letty had not let herself be shackled to Fielding, if she

325

had struck out for herself? What would have happened if he had left Essie in charge of others and gone away? He and Letty could have lived all these years together in some far place, these lonely years that they had spent apart. The thought tore at him.

"This lad, is he of good family?" he asked abruptly. For *someone* should ask these questions.

"He is Lord Thomas Angevine of Northampton," she said. "An old family."

The name meant nothing to him. "And he desires to marry you?" he pursued.

"Oh, yes! It is his ardent wish."

His voice hardened, remembering. "And is he free to do so?"

"He is. We were secretly betrothed back in England."

And sharing a bed, he guessed, for he knew his own hot blood and Letty's only too well.

"Would you prefer me to intercede with your mother?" he asked gravely.

"Oh, please do not!" Her rising panic showed in her voice. "For she is set against him even though she does not know him. She is even now deciding whether to give me to Ned Shackleford or to Dick Smithfield—and I want neither of them."

He snorted. Letty must have forgotten her own anguished feelings as a young girl when she had thrown herself on the grass and wailed to him about being forced into a "safe" marriage!

He took out a purse, weighed it in his hand and studied her. "How will you manage it?" he asked.

"I don't know," she said unsteadily, "but I *will* manage it."

Looking at this daughter of his, he had no doubt she would. Silently he handed her the purse.

"Consider it a wedding gift," he said softly.

BOOK III

=== ∽ ===

The Beauty and the Buccaneer

The Caribbean night's about to fall
And sweep away restraint from one and all
For under tropic skies one may yield to melting sighs
And a perfumed dusk is stealing over all. . . .

PART ONE

Christabel

The winds that blow across her heart, the footsteps blazoned there
    there
Are insubstantial as the mist that cloaks the evening air
And yet like chains they bind her to a love she can't
    forswear
And she has now convinced herself that she will always care!

Summer 1688

Chapter **22**

On the deck of the *Fair Alice*, one week out of Yorktown bound for London, a slim girl in a plain gray linen dress, its wide white collar and cuffs innocent of lace, was combing out her long fair hair. She had washed it in sea water and she was letting it dry in the bright sun. There was an amazing lot of it and it shimmered around her head and shoulders and swung about her slim waist in a manner that attracted the eye. The captain, striding by, could not recall ever having carried such a beauty aboard his vessel, yet there she was, signed onto the passenger list as "C. Willing."

The "C" stood for "Christabel"—for Carolina had decided that since she was going to change her life she might as well change her name as well. The dress she wore belonged to Maudie Tate. Maudie had traded it eagerly for one of Carolina's ballgowns—although Carolina had warned her that if she wore it in Williamsburg or Yorktown she might have to answer some stern questions from Letitia Lightfoot, who would not be pleased at being outfoxed by her runaway daughter. But Maudie had been glad to make the arrangements and it had all gone off without a hitch. Virgie was left believing that Carolina was off to a rendezvous in Yorktown with a mysterious lover (Carolina had steadfastly refused to name him) and from there would strike out across the Chesapeake for the Eastern Shore and the Marriage Trees. Virgie, Carolina knew cynically, would eventually break down and confess all to Letitia —but by then it would be a cold trail that her mother would have to follow.

And she would be away in England, safe in the arms of Lord Thomas!

There was one small problem: Aside from the dress she was wearing, she had managed to bring with her only a change of undergarments, for she had sped away in the night and when she boarded the *Fair Alice,* it was assumed that her boxes were already on board.

At first she had been afraid someone on board might recognize her. But Yorktown, though small, was a busy port, with people passing in and out, and this new grown-up Carolina had hardly been seen there. She had gone directly from the Eastern Shore to Level Green and except for one or two brief shopping excursions to Williamsburg her blazing beauty was known only to the plantation set. She had breathed a deep sigh of relief when she had not encountered a familiar face.

Her presence aboard had excited some notice on the part of the other passengers however: an elderly gentleman with a limp who said he was going home to England to die; a plumpish fellow with a bird-boned wife with small bright eyes who had been visiting a married daughter up near the Falls of the James; an assortment of agents and tradesmen off to London to negotiate or buy goods. For servant girls (and such, by her clothing, they presumed Mistress Christabel Willing to be) were more often bound *for* the Colonies than away from them.

"Did ye not like it in Virginia, lass?" one man had asked her curiously.

"I did, sir, but my father died a few days ago and so I'm on my way back to London to my betrothed." Carolina had her answer ready.

And in a way it was true, she thought. In some indefinable way, she felt as if Fielding Lightfoot *had* died. She had been an unwitting thorn in his flesh all along and she had now removed herself. She had found a new father who chose not to claim her. And her mother was interested only in arranging a quick marriage to some "suitable" lad and getting her gone.

But now she was free of them all—free to return to London. To Lord Thomas. She could hardly wait to see him.

But the sea air had cleared her brain. It was coming to her slowly that she had judged the warring Lightfoots with the harshness of youth, had seen only the black and white with no grays in between. Now she rested her comb and let the sea wind take her pale hair. She leaned upon the taffrail and realized that there was *something*, some unseen bond between Fielding and Letitia. Not the breathless magic Letty had known with Sandy Randolph perhaps, but a true fondness sprinkled with passion and filled with frustration and grief.

What lay between them was Another Kind of Love.

She was standing there brooding about her life when she became aware of a sudden flurry of activity going on about her. Seamen were running by, canvas was being piled on, the *Fair Alice* had come about and was suddenly scudding over the sea in the opposite direction.

Carolina looked about her in bewilderment. There was hardly a cloud in the sky. Could they actually be running back to the Virginia coast?

"What is happening?" she called to the old gentleman who was going home to England to die.

He hesitated, then limped toward her and joined her at the rail. He nodded behind them. "Did ye not see them? Three sails on the horizon. And I'm told the captain has looked through his glass and they fly the flag of Spain."

Spanish ships! And Spain the foe of England!

Carolina turned and studied the horizon. There they bobbed, those tiny ships. How had the captain made out their flags even with a glass? she wondered.

"What will happen if they catch up?" she asked nervously.

The old gentleman gave her a troubled look. "Our captain is not one to stay and find out."

Carolina had heard of terrible things the Spanish did when they caught an English ship venturing into "their" seas. Tales of terror and maiming had filtered back to Virginia—of ears cut off, of floggings, and of passengers who were dragged off to Spain to face trial by the dread Inquisition and death by fire—or release to that living death, the galleys.

But she was young and she could not believe they would be so unlucky. And anyway the wind was strong and the Spaniards had advanced only a little through the morning. But they were now close enough that by squinting she could see for herself the Spanish flag flying on their mastheads.

And then the wind failed them.

It seemed to die of a sudden and left the sea in a flat calm, an ocean of glass reflecting the sun like a mirror. The Spanish ships rose and fell upon the horizon, their sails dangling and drooping like those of the *Fair Alice*.

And then the Spanish ships began to move again. They were galleons, and as the afternoon dragged on, the great sweep of their long oars was steadily closing the gap.

Carolina watched with fascination the slow but inexorable advance of those distant ships. They were very large and their massive gilt foretowers and sterntowers rose high above the water. The sun glinted on that ornate gilt, making their advance a golden sweep. Those distant little ships grew larger and larger until to the watching eyes of the *Fair Alice*'s terrified passengers they seemed to fill the sky. All the stories she had ever heard of Spain's terrible Inquisition—some of them directly from her friend Ramona, and those at least *must* be true—coursed through her mind as she waited, along with the others, for the end to come.

All the passengers were on deck now, milling about uneasily.

"What will they do to us, do you think?" the little birdlike woman was whimpering.

"They should do nothing to us for we're a peaceable ship disturbing no one." Carolina heard the birdlike woman's husband's staunch reply.

333

"But if they'll do nothing, then why are they chasing us?"

Why indeed? Each minute brought the leader of the three ships closer to the steady beat of tired but powerful arms upon the oars. Bulky merchantmen like the *Fair Alice* were easy prey for the warlike galleons with their tall towers and heavy guns.

"A single broadside would sweep us from the sea," she heard one of the men mutter. "I've put my most valuable papers in my boots. Have you?"

"Yes, but little good 'twill do us," came his friend's laconic rejoinder. "They'll steal the boots!"

Carolina shivered. She did not really believe that. The Spanish dons, for all that was said of them, were civilized aristocrats—they would not stoop to pilferage.

And then, without warning it seemed, a single shot was fired across their bow.

"They'll be boarding us now," came a sigh.

And then it was happening. Carolina, who had prudently donned her change of underthings and so was wearing a double set, watched the Spaniards come aboard over the captain's huffy protest that he was a peaceable merchantman and not subject to search on the high seas!

There was no reply in English to that. The boarding party did not speak English—they were depending on guns, not conciliation.

Carolina stepped forward. "I speak a little Spanish," she volunteered. "Perhaps I could translate?"

Captain Frobisher gave her an amazed look. A strange servant girl indeed who looked like an aristocrat and spoke the language of the enemy!

Her Spanish was rusty and the officers of the *Santiago* spoke very fast. Sometimes she had to grope for words but generally she was able to make their meaning clear. The three galleons were part of the treasure *flota* that came in the spring to collect the gold and silver of Peru and carry it back to Spain. They were warships all, part of a larger group that had been scattered, some time back, in a storm. Their duty was clear: They had found an English ship sailing in *their* waters and must

334

dispose of it. The captain of the *Fair Alice* almost had apoplexy when this was translated to him; he growled that these were open seas and the English had as much right to sail them as anyone. Not so, replied the Spanish dons icily. The Pope in Rome himself had divided this entire New World between Spain and Portugal—and no other—and these were therefore Spanish waters. Their plain duty was to sink this English vessel and they would do so forthwith. This brought a wail from the passengers. The Spanish captain held up his hand. Ah, but they were merciful. They would not execute anyone, not even the captain of the *Fair Alice*. The crew would be impressed into service aboard their three ships for they had lost men during the storm. The strongest of the passengers would be required to replace the Spaniards' galley slaves who had been lost when their oars snapped in the high seas. And the ladies—well . . . he looked perplexed, then his face cleared. The ladies would be placed on board the smaller ship *Coraje* and dropped off at Havana. Arrangements to dispose of them could be made there.

Carolina duly translated this message, which was greeted with horror. Their ship sunk? Their goods all perished? And to row in the *galleys?*

It had been on the tip of Carolina's tongue to tell her captors haughtily, "I for one *do not choose* to go to Havana!" But the words were never uttered. Upon the deck of the *Santiago,* so close at hand, she now saw, as the wall of Spanish officers parted, something that she had missed before.

Tied to one of the *Santiago*'s masts and stripped to the waist was a man who sagged, unconscious, against his bonds. He looked to be English, she thought at first glance, for his hair was sandy and the skin of his back and shoulders was burnt red by the sun. And, she noted in horror, it was striped by the lash as well. Red welts crisscrossed where the whip had drawn blood.

In the instant that her mind took that in, a sailor dashed a bucket of water over the unconscious man to revive him and reached out and roughly jerked the man's head up so that he sputtered to groaning life. As his blue eyes snapped open he was looking full at Carolina.

For the space of a heartbeat her world stood still. *It could not be!*

"Thomas!" she screamed.

And Lord Thomas Angevine, coming to in a world gone mad, where Carolina Lightfoot, dressed as a serving wench, peered at him over the side of this Spanish warship that had sunk the ship that was carrying him to Barbados and taken him prisoner, saw her as in a dream, saw her, indeed, as an angel of deliverance come to effect his rescue. Hardly had her cry rung out than he gathered his voice in a wild appeal.

"Carolina!" he called hoarsely.

Transformed by the pitiable sight of him into the very avenging angel Lord Thomas, in a moment of madness, thought her to be, Carolina swung to face the tall dark-garbed Spanish captain.

"That is Lord Thomas Angevine!" she cried in a voice that rang with accusation. "Dear God, *what have you done to him?"*

Taken aback by her fury as much as by her imperious tone, Captain Garcia was hard put not to retreat a step. His thin olive countenance reflected his amazement. He turned in bewilderment to view the source of the wench's concern—ah, the insolent Englishman in the salmon breeches, of course, who was now desperately bellowing out the name of one of the English Colonies in this New World—God alone in his wisdom knew why, for the Englishman's ship had been headed for Barbados! But his interpreter, Mistress Christabel Willing, was young and pretty and she deserved an answer.

"We stopped another English ship on the way," he explained. "She was sailing our waters so we sank her. This fellow has given us perpetual trouble. He needs to be tamed."

Tamed! Carolina's hands were clenched.

"You are killing him, you murderer!" she shouted.

The Spanish captain, used to blood, looked even more amazed. "Before God, señorita, he has had only

336

ten lashes," he cried. "It was the scorching sun that caused him to faint."

The angry eyes that stared up at him flashed silver in that same blinding sunlight. Carolina's overwhelming indignation at seeing Lord Thomas thus so humbled and abused had made her forget how precarious was her own position here. "You must release him immediately!" she cried, and turning to that struggling figure bound to the *Santiago*'s mast, she called out with determination, "I am coming, Thomas, I will take care of your wounds!" She would have brushed past the dark frowning figure of the Spanish captain, whose officers looked dumbfounded by this turn of events, and leaped over the side onto the *Santiago*'s deck had not Captain Garcia reached out a long black taffeta-clad arm and caught her firmly by her sleeve.

"I think you would be a disrupting influence on board my vessel, señorita," he said severely. "But one of my sister ships, the *Valeroso*"—he nodded at another of the towering galleons—"has on board a lady bound for Cartagena. Doña Hernanda's maid was unfortunately washed overboard in the storm. She is in need of a maid, and I believe we will press you into service."

Carolina gave him a dangerous look and clawed at his coat. "I will not serve as anyone's maid!" she cried, trying to shake free of his grasp. "You must take me aboard and let me care for Lord Thomas!"

Captain Garcia shrugged and pushed this violent wench away from him. "I am sorry to lose you as an interpreter, señorita," he said grimly. "But your presence on my vessel is not desired." He made a jerking motion of his head and rough hands seized Carolina and dragged her into a waiting longboat. "Take the wench to the *Valeroso*," he called. "Let Captain Santos deal with her!"

"Thomas!" she called back futilely as the longboat pulled away from the *Fair Alice*, taking her to the nearby *Valeroso*. "Oh, Thomas, they are taking me away but I will be back to free you!" In her excitement, the unlikelihood of that event never crossed her mind. *She would do it!* "Thomas!" she wailed. "Thomas!"

And Lord Thomas, hearing her, set up such an uproar of anger and self-pity and denouncement of his captors that of the torrent of words he loosed only her name being called out was distinguishable to Carolina. Her nails dug into her hands as she imagined him back there—bare-backed, sunburned, lashed—but still unbowed. He would be struggling valiantly against the cruel ropes that bound him to the *Santiago*'s mast, fighting to free himself. He would be facing down his captors but they would never subdue him, never! Carolina's beautiful face was pale beneath the sunshine of her hair, her flashing silver eyes gone dark with anguish as his roars drifted to her heartbreakingly across the water. She was bent forward, her face was held in her hands, and she was sobbing when she heard his last desperate cries of "Carolina! Carolina!" suddenly choked off. She turned a face of fear toward the *Santiago*'s massive gilded foretower, seeming to overhang the *Fair Alice* demonically, like a cliff risen menacingly up from the sea. Choked off by what? Fingers grasping his throat? A hard blow?

How could she know that Lord Thomas, thwarted, thrashing about in rage, had collapsed in tears of frustration, great gulping sobs that precluded speech?

"They have killed him!" she cried, and would have tumbled from the longboat had not one of the swarthy sailors quickly reached out a callused hand to stop her.

"No, no, señorita," he tried to soothe her. "The Englishman has already had all the lashes intended. Someone will only have dashed a bucket of water into his face to quiet him. 'Tis nothing to be alarmed about."

But the girl in the gray servant's gown had collapsed into the bottom of the boat in despair and refused to be comforted. Above her the tall towers of the *Santiago* were replaced by the tall towers of the *Valeroso* and she might have given a care to her own fate, but she did not—she wept only for Thomas, murmuring his name. And her torment was the worse because her heart had flown to the instant conclusion that Lord Reggie had told Thomas she was in Essex, that Thomas had

338

descended on Essex to find her spirited away to America, that he had taken to the sea to retrieve her—indeed that he had been on his way to Yorktown to find her and bring her back to London as his bride when the golden galleons had intercepted him. It was a natural enough conclusion—though far from the truth—and it increased Carolina's suffering because she blamed herself for his present predicament. If she had not been such a fool in Essex, none of this would have happened. *It was all her fault!*

"Santa Maria!" muttered the sailor who had kept her from leaving the longboat. "It would be worth a few lashes to be loved like that."

"Rosita loves you like that," jeered his companion, whose taste in wenches ran to more buxom females than this one. "And so does Dolores. Think on them—for you'll have to decide between them one day!"

His friend gave him an impatient look for not understanding. "I meant a girl like this one," he muttered. "Made of moonlight."

"You'd best leave off your gabbling and get your backs into your rowing," advised a third companion cynically. He cast a quick uneasy look upward at the sky. "For there's a storm coming or my name's not Gomez!"

His prediction proved to be correct. A wild West Indian hurricane was on its way—and the days that followed were to be the strangest in Carolina's life.

THE SPANISH MAIN

Summer 1688

Chapter 23

The next few days were a revelation to Carolina—or Christabel as she was now called. Haunted by the hellish vision of Lord Thomas, alone and friendless and bound to the mast, tormented by the memory of his wild agonized cry of "Carolina!" she found herself now confronted by a new specter: In all her life she had never even contemplated the possibility of becoming a lady's maid.

Doña Hernanda was not an exacting mistress. She was of middle age and middle height and quite unfashionably plump—for to be fashionable in Spain one must be reed thin and flat-chested, a shape induced by iron stays that flattened the budding breasts of young girls unfortunate enough to be born into aristocratic families. Those who survived viewed their altered figures as proudly as across the world Chinese women viewed their tiny bound feet. But poor Doña Hernanda had always been too healthy a specimen for that. Her mother had died when she was a tot and her father had taken a peasant mistress who—when little Doña Hernanda had wailed at the pain of her iron cage—had

340

surreptitiously removed the iron grating that bound her young body. As a result Doña Hernanda was healthy and strong in her middle age and happier in the New World to which she was returning than in Madrid, where her unwelcome girth was a frequent subject of discussion. She had never quite mastered the floating walk of the thin willowy Spanish Court ladies, but she still had a light step—and, widowed now, a taste for dashing young men.

She viewed her new lady's maid with complacency. Such a beauty would be sure to attract all the young officers of the ship and Doña Hernanda could bask in their attention too. And she counted herself fortunate that this captured wench spoke Spanish—imagine being able to find a replacement for poor Maria, washed overboard, here in the middle of the ocean! She was not entirely lucky however for the fact that Carolina was not apt to become proficient in her new duties became immediately apparent.

On her first evening in the small private cabin that Doña Hernanda's rank entitled her to aboard the *Valeroso*, Carolina demonstrated that. Sick at heart over the sight of Lord Thomas being abused and with her mind only half on the task of garbing her new mistress for dinner in the captain's cabin (she was to learn that Captain Santos was Doña Hernanda's only surviving son, her elder having been lost in a mine disaster in Peru), she had reached out to steady herself when the ship rolled, her hand had caught in Doña Hernanda's black lace mantilla just as that lady lurched against the wall, and she had heard the lace rip. A moment later as the ship rolled again, sliding down into the trough of a wave, she felt herself thrown to the side and stepped on the hem of Doña Hernanda's fine black taffeta overskirt, tearing that.

Good-natured Doña Hernanda had only sighed and tottered to her bunk, narrowly missing a chair that slid toward her. She told Carolina there was another mantilla in the curved top trunk—no, not that large one, the small leathern one over there. And as Carolina slipped and nearly fell against the trunk, the ship having taken another violent lurch, Doña Hernanda suggested half humorously that she would require the services of a *costurera*—a sempstress—if the wind and Christabel continued in this vein.

"Christabel" was too miserable even to reply. She rummaged for the mantilla in silence and gave it to Doña Hernanda.

"Never mind, *niña,*" sighed Doña Hernanda. "I can understand how you must feel, to lose your ship and your friends. And besides, the wind is coming up—it makes the vessel sway."

Carolina felt comforted somehow when Doña Hernanda called her "child." Indeed she had felt as helpless as a child when, from the deck of the *Valeroso,* she had watched the *Fair Alice* set alight. Once all the goods the Spanish wanted had been removed from her, including some of her sails, the English ship was left to drift like a funeral pyre, burning down to the water line before she sank.

She was in enemy hands—but Doña Hernanda's hands did not seem like enemy hands. They were white and rather pudgy and helpless, for she had been cared for from childhood like a China doll and had never even had to comb her own hair.

"Oh, how could they do it?" moaned Carolina, and Doña Hernanda took that to mean not the punishment meted out to Lord Thomas but the firing of the *Fair Alice*.

"The captain of your vessel was breaking the law," she told Carolina severely. "His Holiness the Pope gave the lands of this New World to Spain—and therefore these are *our* waters."

"Who gave *him* the right to portion out a continent?" cried Carolina, and Doña Hernanda looked shocked.

"I had forgot you were a heretic," she muttered.

Carolina was brought up short. To say more might subject her to a trip to Spain to be tried before the Inquisition—and she could end up by being burned at the stake. It angered her that the *Fair Alice* had been summarily destroyed, and the forcing of her passengers

342

into menial service was surely inexcusable—but she managed to hold her tongue. She was on an enemy vessel running through what Spain had always claimed were Spanish waters, and a slip of the tongue might be her last. But she could not resist one parting shot.

"I worship God even as you do," she told Doña Hernanda defiantly.

The older woman sighed. "We will not continue this conversation, Christabel," she decided. "Bring me my fan and pour me out a small goblet of that wine. I would fortify myself before essaying dinner with my son. He was always a difficult boy and he becomes no easier—" She gave a small scream as the cabin floor suddenly took on an evil slant and a wooden table and two chairs glided toward her.

"I do not think you will be dining with your son tonight," predicted Carolina. "He will be too busy trying to keep his ship afloat!"

As it turned out, Doña Hernanda did not dine with her son that night or for many nights to come.

At first there were long slow swells into which the ship seemed to sink, only to rise triumphantly. And then as the wind gathered strength the seas appeared to pile up and pour down upon the vessel. The *Valeroso* seemed to shudder and fall down into deep troughs between waves, enduring great seas that crashed green across her decks. Trembling violently, the ship would shake off the onslaught of the waves, but each time more weakly.

The first night was bad but the next day was worse. Both Captain Santos of the *Valeroso* and Captain Garcia of the *Santiago* could see their sister ship of the *flota*, the *Coraje*, send them a distress signal. The *Coraje* had lost her rudder and was turning about wildly in the storm, heeling over in imminent danger of capsizing. But the strong winds were driving them apart, the boats that were put over the side to aid their sister vessel promptly capsized with the loss of their crews and soon the *Coraje* was nowhere in sight.

Her loss seemed to draw the two remaining galleons together as if for protection—and night found them drawing too close. There was a great crash, Carolina and Doña Hernanda were thrown from their bunks, there were shouts from the deck—the two ships had collided.

"*Madre de Dios!*" gasped Doña Hernanda, clawing her way back to her bunk. "Go see if you can find out what has happened! Are we sinking?"

Carolina fought her way to the deck and found it a scene of wild confusion. In the blinding rain the two great galleons had struck each other broadside and done some damage. Their rigging had become tangled and was hastily being cut away lest they carry each other to the bottom. She clung to the rail with the rain beating down in her face and watched the *Santiago* reel away from them—and then a great wave came over the bow and swept her back on a wall of water, back the way she had come into a passageway which, as the wave departed, was now awash.

The hatches were secured, an order bawled that the women were to keep to their cabin, and Carolina groped her way back, aided in getting her bearings by Doña Hernanda's plaintive cries.

"We are not sinking," Carolina gasped as she almost fell through the cabin door. "At least not yet." She tossed back her wet hair. "We collided with the *Santiago*."

"With the *Santiago*—oh, then we are surely lost!"

"No, no, the rigging was fouled but the ships have been separated now."

Doña Hernanda gave a frightened bleat. "We will never see land again," she wailed. "Oh, I was wrong to make a trip back to Spain even though my brother desired me to meet his new wife! I should have stayed in Cartagena and never ventured upon the ocean!" She gave a scream as the ship heeled over and all the furniture and trunks in the room crashed against the cabin wall. "We will not survive the voyage!"

And Carolina wondered bleakly where Thomas was tonight—and if he had been cut down from the mast and put in irons. . . . Like as not that was what had happened to him. And if the *Santiago* was lost he would have not even the slight chance of those who elected to swim—his chains would hold him fast and carry him, down, down to the bottom of the sea.

At the thought she gave a little moan and Doña Hernanda interpreted that as fear for their fate. "Do not worry, *niña!*" she cried in a sudden reversal of feeling. "My son is in command. He is a good sailor, he will not let us drown!"

But good sailor or no, the collision with the *Santiago* had shaken Captain Santos. He set himself to put some distance between him and his wallowing sister ship, and in so doing lost her altogether.

So it was with a damaged hull and with part of her rigging missing that the *Valeroso* fought her way free of the storm at last and found herself alone upon an empty ocean.

Carolina and Doña Hernanda—bruised and dazed from the ferocity of the storm—came up on deck. They were wobbly and had trouble keeping their footing in the giant swells that were the aftermath of the storm.

"It is a wonder we did not sink!" cried Doña Hernanda, breathing in great drafts of the clean-washed air. Her high-backed Spanish comb of carved tortoise-shell sat awry in her tumbled hair for she had been too frightened and banged about during the storm to demand that Carolina comb her hair. Carolina too was the worse for wear. Her fair hair, innocent now of pins, had come entirely loose and was cascading down over her shoulders. One of her sleeves had been rent when she had been tumbled along the passageway at the height of the storm, and her gray linen overskirt was ripped where it had snagged on a piece of skidding furniture the night before.

Neither woman cared at the moment how she looked. They were grateful to be alive. And Carolina, peering around her at decks swept bare of all the gear that had been piled about, then tripping over shattered timbers and trying to avoid cloth from fallen pieces of rigging, echoed Doña Hernanda's amazement.

But with the calmer seas, Doña Hernanda had become her regal self again. "Come, *niña*," she told Carolina. "We have had a bad time of it but it is over now. We will have my son send us some hot food and we will both sleep all day. I command it!"

Carolina felt sympathy for the harassed captain, who looked as if he had not slept in days, as his mother advanced upon him. He made a strangled sound in his throat, gave her a beaten look, and muttered something about "served in their cabin." But somehow aboard that sodden battered ship, a fire was started and before the women collapsed in their bunks they had both enjoyed bowls of surprisingly delicious steaming soup.

"It tastes the better because it is the soup of deliverance!" Doña Hernanda laughed and Carolina returned her a wan smile. Out there somewhere was Thomas, God knew where. . . . She asked herself whether the *Santiago* had survived these seas, and tried not to think what might have been Thomas's fate. Then, filled with hot soup and exhaustion, she fell asleep on her bunk and—like Doña Hernanda who was snoring musically on the other side of the room—slept for hours.

But the storm was not to be the last of Captain Santos' trials aboard the *Valeroso*. The following night a fog bank drifted in and the *Valeroso*, still searching for her sister ships, kept her stern lanterns lit and clanged a bell in an effort to find them.

It was to be his undoing.

Suddenly in the night there was a shout from the watch and the bleary-eyed captain bounded from his bed and staggered out on deck.

"'Tis the *Santiago!*" came an excited cry.

This was good news indeed for they had feared themselves to be the storm's only survivors. Captain Santos strained his eyes to see through the enveloping murk and suddenly, too close for comfort, the hull of a tall ship appeared. It was indeed the *Santiago* and he and the deck watch both shouted a warning as the *Santiago* hove up alongside, her wooden hull rising up

346

out of the mist to scrape against the side of the *Valeroso*.

Captain Santos' straining eyes had seen no one aboard, and the wild thought had crossed his mind that the *Santiago* had become a ghost ship, a derelict that had ridden out the storm without a crew, without a captain. But he had not the time to voice his fears.

Before he could grasp what was happening, from the *Santiago* grappling irons came flying. And even before the two ships were firmly secured, from the *Santiago*'s apparently vacant decks rose muscular men who had crouched there, waiting for the vessels to touch. Having seemingly materialized out of thin air, they now bounded silently over the rail, cutlasses swinging. The suddenness, the silence with which the whole thing had been accomplished, made the attack seem a hellish, unreal vision to Captain Santos.

"Pirates!" he shouted hoarsely and wheeled about in a desperate attempt to gain his cabin—and his sword.

"Buccaneers," corrected the tall sinewy leader of the first wave as he landed solidly on two feet upon the deck of the *Valeroso*. His long arm reached out and caught Captain Santos in mid-flight. Seized by the scruff, Santos was swung about. The buccaneer's smile flashed in his dark face but his voice and his hard gray gaze were deadly. "Ye'd be well advised to strike your colors and surrender your ship on the instant."

"Who are you?" asked Captain Santos faintly, swaying back from his formidable adversary as from a vision of Hell.

"Kells is the name," was the laconic reply. "Captain Kells. You may have heard of me."

Captain Santos shuddered. He had indeed heard of Captain Kells—as who had not? It was a name that resounded throughout the Caribbean. Resounded to Spanish ears like a death knell, tolling.

"I have women aboard," he cried hoarsely. "You cannot expect me to—"

"Well, they can wait," said the tall buccaneer mildly. "Meantime I'm taking over your ship. Order your men

347

to put down their arms and surrender peaceably and none will be killed. You have my word on it." The grim smile deepened. "My word as a buccaneer."

Captain Santos swallowed. To be taken—and with his mother aboard! Through his mind in that instant flitted everything he had heard about the formidable buccaneer who faced him. Many were the stories told, and some of them frightening enough—of night attacks and daring raids, of impossible escapes and quick reprisals. But none of those stories had suggested that Captain Kells had ever broken his word to any man.

"And the women will not be harmed?" cried Santos.

"I've never harmed a woman—Spanish or any other," was the cool rejoinder. The buccaneer's gray gaze raked over Santos. "Can *you* say the same?" he challenged.

Captain Santos winced for there had been an English girl once, taken from a ship in mid-ocean. He had kept her in his cabin, tamed her to his hand. Sweating, he wondered if Kells knew about that. Something in those cold eyes told him he did.

"Make up your mind," snapped his adversary, "if you don't want your men's throats cut!"

The Spanish captain's shoulders slumped in defeat. There was nothing for it but to do as he was bid. Numbed by events, he struck his colors and surrendered his ship.

So swiftly, so silently had the attack taken place that the first thing the two women knew of it was when a ship's officer knocked on the door of their cabin. He was very pale and he informed them in shaky Spanish that the ship had been taken by buccaneers and their presence was requested on deck.

Behind Carolina, who had opened the door but a crack, Doña Hernanda started up and grabbed at her heart. "Buccaneers? Did I hear him aright, Christabel? Did he say *buccaneers?*"

"He did." Carolina felt her own pulse begin to race. In any case, she told herself as she dressed hastily, she would be no worse off than as a prisoner of the Spanish who might on a sudden whim send her on to Spain to be

348

tried by the Inquisition. The buccaneers were reputedly gallant toward women. *But suppose . . . they were not?* A little thrill of fear went through her. She would have preferred not to have to find out first hand!

"My jewels," Doña Hernanda was gabbling. "Hand me that case, Christabel."

Carolina helped the older woman secrete a variety of rings and chains in her stiff black clothing. "They may search us," she warned.

Doña Hernanda blanched. "Oh, surely not that!" she gasped, looking as if she might faint.

It was Carolina's opinion that none of Doña Hernanda's jewels were very fine; she had obviously spent her wealth in other ways—perhaps on the career of the son who must even now be on deck surrendering his sword to the bitterest enemy Spain had in the New World—the buccaneers of Tortuga.

It was in the end not a Spaniard at all who escorted the two women to the deck but a rakish young buccaneer named Lindstrom. He had not an ounce of fat on his cordlike muscles, had Lindstrom, and he was carelessly dressed in a loose white shirt and leathern breeches. His shoulder-length yellow hair was held back by a wide band of black cloth that gave him almost the appearance of wearing bangs—the headband concealed a deep scar where a musket ball had creased his forehead and he wore it for vanity's sake, but Carolina was not to know that. His light blue eyes raked over them both and lit up at sight of Carolina. "My captain would like to know your names," he said in slightly accented English.

Carolina's head went up. To give her real name might mean that she would be sent back to Virginia—to marry Ned or some other lad chosen by her mother! She would prefer to take her chances on Tortuga or whatever other buccaneer port they set sail toward.

"I am Mistress Christabel Willing," she said firmly. "And this lady is Doña Hernanda, the mother of Captain Santos who commands this ship." She hesitated. "This ship that has taken us, is she English?"

That he at least was *not* English was the clear

implication. Lars Lindstrom smiled. It was a very infectious smile. "The ship that has taken you is a buccaneer ship. She bears no nationality. But *I* have the honor to be Danish. And my captain is Irish. His name is Kells."

"Kells?" Doña Hernanda spoke no English but her straining ears had caught the name. "Oh, we are lost! It was Captain Kells who last year sacked Cartagena. We made our escape in a cart with all our plate before the pirates burst through our defenses." She leant forward, wringing plump hands now completely barren of rings. "Christabel is my personal maid." Her voice rose to a hysterical squeak. "Do not hurt her, I implore you!"

She had spoken in Spanish and Lindstrom now responded in his waterfront Spanish. "We will hurt neither of you. Come."

Once on deck they found themselves in the midst of a scene of wild activity, carried out in the mist with the aid of torches and lanthorns. Guns and other weapons were being stacked upon the deck and the resentful crew—after all they had just been through a terrible storm and now to find themselves captured without so much as crossing swords with the enemy was really too much—were being herded down below decks, muttering.

She did not see the buccaneer captain who was doubtless occupied in the captain's cabin, gathering up the valuable maps and the ship's manifest.

Lars Lindstrom grinned as he boosted Carolina over the side onto the other ship that was now lashed firmly to the *Valeroso.* Even in the mist Carolina's startled gaze recognized it as the *Santiago.*

But that meant Lord Thomas was here! Nearby she saw Captain Santos, who stood unarmed with his arms folded, watching sourly. She turned to him.

"There was an Englishman tied to the *Santiago*'s mast for punishment just before you took me aboard," she cried. "Can you tell me what happened to him?"

Captain Santos had been watching his mother approach with some trepidation. Now he favored Carolina with a cold look. "All the prisoners save you were

350

transferred to the *Coraje* before the storm struck," he told her. "And we lost the *Coraje* in the storm—we do not know what has happened to her." He winced as his mother cried reproachfully, "How could you have let this happen to us? You could *not* have been watching!"

Disappointment at Captain Santos' words flooded over Carolina. Her hopes had flared the moment she realized she was stepping onto the *Santiago*'s broad deck—and now to find that Thomas was gone somewhere else, possibly lost . . . !

"Come along, Doña Hernanda," she said sadly, knowing that it would do no good at this point for the older woman to heap recriminations on her son. "Watch your step over those ropes." She steadied Doña Hernanda and added beneath her breath, "It would not do for you to fall—you would jangle!"

Doña Hernanda, mindful of her rings and baubles, paused to cast one vengeful glance at her son, who ducked his head and looked away. Then she moved on, treading carefully indeed as she and Carolina followed Lars to a comfortable cabin quite similar to the one they had so recently left.

"This cabin will be yours to share," he stated matter-of-factly. "But you must remain in it, you will not have free run of the ship. Captain's orders."

Carolina nodded.

"What will happen to the *Veloroso?*" she asked, for she had visions of a magnificent mountain of flames fading away into the ocean mist as the mighty galleon sank beneath the waves—even as the *Fair Alice* had done on a sunny afternoon.

Lars Lindstrom shrugged. "We will put a prize crew aboard her and sail her to Tortuga."

"I had thought you might—"

"Sink her? She is too valuable a vessel. Captain Kells may decide to outfit her and send her against the Spanish, just as he will do with the *Santiago* here." He patted the cabin wall.

And then he left them—Doña Hernanda to wring her hands and worry about her son, whom she alternately wept over and denounced as negligent, Carolina to sit wistfully upon the edge of her bunk and ponder the strange ways of fate. She the runaway, captured and now recaptured, was on her way to a buccaneer stronghold—and still she knew nothing of Thomas's fate.

A prize crew was hastily put aboard the *Valeroso,* and Carolina could feel the *Santiago* creak and hear her sails catch the breeze with a snap as they pulled away from the other ship. It was very late—near morning, she thought—when there was a discreet knock on her door. She opened the door a crack and found herself looking into the smiling face of Lars Lindstrom.

"Mistress Willing," he said, "did I understand you to say that the Spanish lady with you is Captain Santos' mother?"

"Yes, that is what Doña Hernanda told me. Is he all right? She is worried about his safety."

"He is well enough. Our captain wishes to know how you came to be aboard a Spanish ship, Mistress Willing?"

"Why, tell him that I had sailed from Yorktown on the *Fair Alice* bound for London and we were attacked by three Spanish galleons. The other passengers were put aboard the *Santiago* and later transferred, I was told, to the *Coraje.* But because Doña Hernanda's personal maid had been washed overboard, I was transferred to the *Valeroso* and ordered to take her place."

"As her personal maid?"

"Yes."

Did she see a flicker in those blue eyes? She could not be sure. "I will inform Captain Kells of what you have told me," he said tersely. As she was about to close the door he added, "Keep your door latched. Remember there are men aboard this vessel who have not seen a woman for some time and such a woman as you— never!"

With this parting complimentary warning, he was gone, leaving Carolina to report to Doña Hernanda in Spanish what had been said.

A short time later Lars was back. "Captain Kells,"

he told her laconically through the door, "will see you now."

So they had been summoned to an audience with the buccaneer captain! Some of Doña Hernanda's alarm was communicated to Carolina as Lars led the way to the great cabin in the stern.

He knocked, there was a booming "Come in!" and he flung wide the door. Carolina took a step inside. Before her stretched a more luxurious cabin than any merchant ship was likely to boast. It was very spacious, handsomely appointed in the severe Spanish style with tall-backed mahogany chairs, heavily carved, a large and heavy mahogany table, and a bank of windows at the stern. Her gaze passed over the rows of books with Moroccan leather bindings, the crimson velvet cushions, the heavy maroon velvet draperies that seemed to be everywhere—and focused on the giant who stood opposite her.

He was the very picture she carried in her mind of a buccaneer. By size alone he seemed to dominate the room. His thick curly black hair bushed out from beneath a battered black tricorne hat, set slightly askew, and ornamented with tarnished gold braid. A gold earring dangled from one of his ears. She thought his eyes were gray—or possibly blue, but they looked out at her from beneath thick lowering black brows and were at the moment too narrowed to tell what color they actually were. He was wearing loose-fitting leathern breeches and the remnants of what had once been a wine velvet coat with the sleeves torn out. It hung open to the waist and since he wore no shirt, it revealed a deep barrellike chest covered with coarse hair almost as thick and curly as the black beard that bristled from a massive square jaw.

A formidable fellow indeed! Doña Hernanda shrank against her.

"Captain Kells," said Lars, and she noted that his manner was more formal than it had been before; indeed there was something military in it as there was in his bearing. "I have brought you the ladies from the *Valeroso*. The younger one"—he indicated Carolina—

"is Mistress Christabel Willing, who was taken off her ship against her will when the dons attacked."

"A Spanish captive?" the giant echoed in a cavernous voice, and his great head seemed to sink into his massive shoulders as he looked down at her. "I am told you were forced to become this Spanish lady's personal maid, Mistress Willing."

"That is true," said Carolina, feeling inadequate before this huge man who seemed to dwarf even the massive Spanish furniture.

"As buccaneers we band against Spain and give insult for insult," he rumbled. She thought he was saying these words by rote, as if he had said them many times before. Now his big head came out of his broad shoulders and he seemed to rear up. "This Spanish lady who reduced you to serving maid will find the tables turned. Henceforth she shall be *your* serving maid, if you like."

So truculent was his mien, so surprising his words, and such was her relief that this powerful buccaneer seemed to be on *her* side, that Carolina felt laughter bubble to her lips. "Poor Doña Hernanda isn't up to it," she chuckled. "And besides she was kind to me. She did not even chide me for tearing her mantilla and stepping on the hem of her gown and ripping it."

That formidable countenance looked taken aback, and Lars swiftly intervened. "It would seem that Mistress Christabel came in fighting, even though her captain did not," he said dryly. "I have learnt that he surrendered his ship, the *Fair Alice*, without firing a shot."

"No, it was not that I attacked Doña Hernanda—it was the storm that made me so awkward," Carolina felt called upon to explain. "You see"—she smiled ingenuously at them both—"I have had no practice at all in being a lady's maid. And the ship lurched and rolled and threw me about the cabin. It is indeed a wonder that I did not fall against poor Doña Hernanda and bear her to the floor with me! As for the *Fair Alice* surrendering, we were becalmed and those great galleons simply rowed across the glassy water and took us. Not to have surrendered would have been madness." She didn't know whether it would have been madness or not but she wanted to defend Captain Frobisher whose poorly armed merchantman could not have been expected to stand up against three Spanish warships!

"You will both be my guests in Tortuga," boomed the big man. "Meanwhile, Lars, put a padlock on their door. These latches will not stand up against the shoulder thrust of a buccaneer." Looking at *his* shoulders, Carolina could well believe it!

As they were leaving, a slender buccaneer whose cutlass, Carolina thought, looked too big for him, hurried up.

"The dons had three buccaneers they'd captured somewhere chained to the oars," he cried in an excited voice. "Would you tell Captain Kells the doctor says they're in a bad way, two may not live, and they have messages for their families before they go."

"Tell him yourself," said Lars. "He's in there." He nodded his head at the cabin they had just left.

At that point the preoccupied young buccaneer seemed to discover the ladies. He gave Carolina a dazed look and his breath came through his teeth in a silent whistle. "I didn't know we'd captured a wench like this one!"

"We didn't," said Lars, shoving past him. "We *rescued* this lady from the Spanish, Nat. She's to be a guest of Captain Kells on Tortuga."

"Who was that?" asked Carolina as Lars hurried them away to their own cabin.

"Nat Larkin—he assists our ship's doctor. He's learning his trade."

"Ship's doctor?"

"Aboard the *Sea Wolf*, Captain Kells's flagship."

"Is the ship as large and formidable as her captain?" asked Carolina humorously, for she now felt that she had not landed in bad hands and that she would soon be freed.

"The *Sea Wolf*'s not large, as ships go," said Lars

355

dryly. "But she's formidable. She's a sleek gray ship, is the *Sea Wolf*, and she's devoured many a galleon and proud galleass." His engaging grin flashed. "Ye may feel safe from the dons on any of Captain Kells's ships, Mistress Christabel—he's never lost an engagement yet!"

"You make him sound like an admiral with—with a navy!" she protested.

"And so he is regarded among the Brethren of the Coast, Mistress Christabel. Ask anyone. He's an admiral without the title. Lord Admiral of the Buccaneers!" He laughed. "And though we all be men without a country now, there's many a lad among us has done naval service before deciding to turn buccaneer."

Of which he himself was one, she suspected, considering his military bearing!

"If Doña Hernanda and I are so safe," she said, turning to glance at the Spanish lady who trudged along beside her, looking tired and worried, "why do we need a lock on the *outside* of our door as well as a latch *inside?*"

"Ah, that's just for *your* protection, Mistress Christabel," Lars told her with a roguish inflection. "The captain's of the opinion that you're too pretty for mortal man to gaze upon without desiring you—and it could be that he's right. So he'll be locking you in just like the jewels and plate and coin we found upon the Spanish vessels!"

Carolina gave Lars an indignant look. *It was all very well to be treasured, but to be locked in—!*

"What did he say, Christabel?" Doña Hernanda asked anxiously once they were back in their own cabin and listening to the heavy lock being hammered into the door from outside. "Captain Kells looked to me a very devil—I was afraid to speak!"

"He isn't a devil," sighed Carolina. "Just an invincible fighter. And we're to be his guests in Tortuga, which seems to be where we're headed."

The older woman shook her head and shuddered. "Tortuga is a terrible place, I am told. We will be lucky

356

to survive it. I've no doubt Captain Kells fancies you," she added gloomily. "Else why would he be putting a large lock on our door?"

Carolina caught her breath. That was one thing she wasn't prepared to face—that Captain Kells might have become enamored of her!

PART TWO

Kells

"There are many wounds of which a man may die,"
He said, and looked her squarely in the eye,
"But love gives no such wounds to such as I."
Her mocking smile said, "I will prove you lie!"

THE ISLAND OF TORTUGA

Summer 1688

Chapter 24

Carolina found Tortuga full of surprises, but the greatest surprise of all awaited her at Captain Kells's rambling masonry house, its whitewashed walls starkly bleak in the molten tropical sun.

She and Doña Hernanda were not allowed off the ship their first day in harbor. They chafed as they heard through their locked door all of the activity of a vessel being unloaded of both its human and its nonhuman cargo. Their only contact was through a towheaded cabin boy who seemed struck dumb by Carolina's beauty. He never took his wistful gaze from her as he served them their meals and always seemed to leave the room walking slightly aslant. He responded to questions with confusion as if caught out in some underhanded endeavor.

"He fancies you," Doña Hernanda told her.

Carolina wished Doña Hernanda would not tell her that every man and boy they ran across "fancied" her. She was beginning to feel very nervous about going ashore to what she privately considered a "pirates' lair," and this constant harping on the effect she had on the male population did not help!

They finally disembarked in bright sunlight on their second day there and Carolina was amazed to see that

the rock-bound harbor with its tall cliffs rising sheer
was filled with French and Dutch and English ships.
Commerce was being carried on briskly along the quay,
where merchants inspected great piles of confiscated
Spanish goods. And above the town, which was mostly
a ragged collection of taverns and brothels with an
occasional white-painted residence baking in the afternoon sun, brooded a formidable-looking mountain fort
of stone construction where captured Spanish guns
guarded the entrance to Cayona Bay.

Their passage through the quayside crowd caused
some excitement for hot bathwater had been brought to
the ladies on board ship and they had had time to bathe
and to mend the clothing that had been ripped during
the storm. Their hair was carefully dressed and although Carolina had refused to wear the black lace
mantilla that Doña Hernanda, in an excess of generosity, had tried to thrust upon her, she almost wished she
had it to help hide her blushes as loud admiring
comments reached her ears.

"Now there's a little lady who could share *my* bed
any day!" exclaimed a half-drunk buccaneer whose
sheathed cutlass clanked against his leg as he shouldered his way toward her.

"Ripe, ain't she?" came another awed voice.

"Be ye here to work for one of the madams?"
rumbled another male voice. "Speak up, little lady—
I'm talking to you with the blonde hair!"

"Ye'd best not let Captain Kells hear you ask her
that, Deke," warned Lars Lindstrom, who was leading
the two women surrounded by an honor guard of four
slouching buccaneers, across the quay. "For she's on
her way to his house as his guest."

"Ye might have known Kells'd cream off the best o'
the lot!" groaned an inebriated fellow who rocked
unsteadily on his feet. "Just like he does o' the Spanish
ships that sail these seas!"

" 'Tis the luck of the Irish," laughed Lars. He gave
the speaker a good-natured cuff on the shoulder as he
went by. "They're famous for it—and what better proof
could you have than this wench?"

On they went, shouldering their way past merchants who gave Carolina curious glances, and bold-looking men she took to be buccaneers. She was surprised at the number of women, many of them quite young, some dragging young children, who sidled through the crowd, occasionally fixing her with an envious stare. One even stopped to glare at her and spat.

"Harlots," muttered Doña Hernanda with a shudder. "We are in Hell, I tell you, Christabel."

"Oh, they can't all be harlots," objected Carolina. "There must be some honest wives and daughters among them!"

Doña Hernanda gave an expressive sniff and kept her mantillaed head high as they left the quay and set out through the narrow streets of the town.

"Where are we going?" asked Carolina.

"Up," said Lars promptly. "Where the air is better."

Soon they had left the jumble of taverns and brothels and were walking over a road of pitilessly white coral that led upward through a grove of lemon and avocado trees.

"All this belongs to Captain Kells," Lars told her, waving a hand expansively. "And see, there is his house—that is where you'll be staying."

She had not expected anything so large. It seemed to be a sprawling medley of buildings, all whitewashed and with green shutters but set on different levels and yet connected.

"Is there more than one house?" she asked doubtfully.

"There was," said Lars. "But Kells bought out his neighbors and connected the houses with passageways built by captured Spanish stonemasons. The ironwork" —he indicated the heavy black-painted grillwork that from this distance looked like black lace over the windows and doors— "is Spanish too. It was destined for Porto Bello and other Spanish towns when Kells took it off the ships. Here, you'll be down here—in his guest quarters."

He led the women to a high-walled courtyard which they entered through a green wooden door. Inside they found themselves in a riotous though somewhat over-grown tropical garden. Bougainvillea tumbled over the wall, spilling brilliant red flowers, and on another white wall a climbing pink rose vine was blooming its heart out.

Lars nodded toward the green door. "Captain Kells bids me tell you you'll be quite safe here, Mistress Christabel," he told Carolina. "This wing of the house is where he keeps his guests. And now that you're here, that garden door will be kept locked—and at night the other doors will be locked as well so that you may sleep sound."

"This wing? Will we not have free run of the house?"

"I'm afraid not," Lars said regretfully. "Although the central portion of the house is Kells's private quarters, the far end of the house is occupied by his officers, and not all of us"—he grinned roguishly—"are so peaceable when we're drunk! He thought it best that a locked door be kept between such a morsel as yourself and carousing buccaneers."

She was to be a prisoner then. . . . The thought sobered her.

They moved on through a heavy iron grillwork door into a short dim passageway which led through yet another similar door into an inner courtyard floored with stone, where a stone fountain tinkled. Beside it were a pair of blue-tiled stone benches and even here the tropical flowers had fought their way up through broken patches in the stone, making the air fragrant. The courtyard was shaded by an enormous pepper tree through whose branches the hot West Indian sunlight filtered down to make patterns of light and shade upon the stone flooring. Several stout wooden doors opened onto the courtyard and there were windows as well but Carolina, coming out of the brilliant sun, could not make out the dim interior of the rooms beyond. Across the far end of the courtyard stretched a roofed gallery supported by arched pillars and beneath that roof what appeared to be an outdoor dining room, for there was a stone table, its top covered with blue tile like the benches, and several heavy wooden chairs. From one

of the arches dangled a large hoop and clinging to that
hoop a large red and green and gold parrot squawked a
greeting. "Pieces of eight, pieces of eight!" it cried, and
beside Carolina, Doña Hernanda jumped nervously.

Lars laughed. "Yon bird knows what counts!"

"Kells! Kells!" screamed the bird, suddenly swinging
upside down from the hoop and peering at them over
its hooked beak—and even in this island paradise,
Carolina felt a little shiver of apprehension go through
her at the name. Doña Hernanda's, *He fancies you . . .*
came back to her.

Her attention was attracted then by a sturdy girl in a
cool white cotton dress cinched at the waist by a little
blue linen corselet that emphasized her abundant
breasts and wide swinging hips. Her bright yellow hair
hung down in two long fat braids. She gave them all a
graceful curtsy but her smiling blue eyes rested on Lars.

"Katje is bidding you welcome," said Lars. "I hope
you speak Dutch for that is Katje's only language."

"Is she Captain Kells's wife?" asked Carolina in
bewilderment.

"No, she's his housekeeper." Lars's gaze kindled as
he looked at the abundant Katje.

Perhaps she was his mistress then? Carolina gave
Katje a doubtful look.

Lars caught that look and laughed. "Katje is an
impregnable fortress," he told her, answering her
unspoken question. "Many have tried, all have failed!"

Carolina blushed. She saw that Katje was giving her
a puzzled look.

"The vessel that was taking Katje to Curacao—that's
a Dutch island—to join her betrothed struck a reef and
most of the passengers were lost. Katje was lucky. She
was discovered clinging to a spar after drifting for hours
at sea. She said that God must have been looking out
for her, for those were barracuda waters where the *Sea
Wolf* found her. She would have been sent on to
Curacao but she learnt quite by accident that her
betrothed had married somebody else and she refused
to go. Kells would have been glad to give her guest
quarters in his house but she insists on working for her

364

keep." He began speaking rapidly to Katje in Dutch. She beamed at him and bobbed her golden head. Carolina had a feeling from the way the girl smiled at Lars that Katje would never reach the Netherlands Antilles—she would move into the arms and bed of this handsome buccaneer.

Unless of course she was already warming Captain Kells's bed for him and Lars did not know about it!

Which brought her mind squarely back to bedrooms and Doña Hernanda's insistence that the huge buccaneer captain "fancied" her. She frowned when Lars handed them over to the smiling girl with a shrug: "Katje will take care of you."

Katje led Doña Hernanda into a pleasantly appointed bedroom to their right. Instead of following, Carolina paused and turned to Lars.

"Will we see you again?" she asked wistfully, for she liked the attractive young buccaneer.

"I doubt it," was his blithe response. "For the *Sea Wolf*'s being refitted and Kells will be taking her out soon. But," he added as an afterthought, "you two ladies will have some company at least." He nodded his head toward the center door leading in off of the gallery.

"You mean Captain Kells has another guest?" asked Carolina quickly. At this point another face would be very welcome!

"Yes, an English gentleman." Lars grinned. "But you'd best enjoy him while you can—Kells is trying to persuade him to join us!"

An English gentleman, someone who was not a buccaneer! Carolina's face brightened and she cast an expectant look at the door, which remained uncompromisingly closed, before she shot a last question at Lars, who was just taking his leave. "Why is this English gentleman not out here taking the air on the gallery on a hot day like this?"

Lars shrugged. "Because he's out taking the air on the quay, is my guess."

Her senses quickened. "You mean he has the freedom of the town?"

"Oh, yes. Although now that you're here, he may find himself locked up like the two of you!"

"For our own protection, of course," murmured Carolina ironically.

Lars laughed and was gone.

Carolina would have followed Doña Hernanda into the bedroom that she assumed they would share but that Katje, just coming out, grasped her arm, said something in Dutch, and pointed toward the door at the other end of the gallery. Her grip was surprisingly strong and brooked no resistance when Carolina demurred, insisting first in English and then in Spanish that she would prefer to stay with Doña Hernanda.

Swept irresistibly along over the stone flooring by Katje, Carolina found herself propelled past the "English gentleman's" door and into an even larger bedroom than the one into which she had just peered. It had big windows covered with thick iron grillwork that opened onto the gallery they had just left. Katje smiled and departed, disappearing down the hall.

Left alone, Carolina explored her room. It was large and square and very clean. The walls were whitewashed like those on the outside and there were wooden interior shutters to keep out sun and rain. The room was comfortably furnished with a bed and a table and chairs that looked as if they might have been made in Spain, and there was a dressing table with a mirror and a trunk with a curved top.

Curious about that trunk, since she had sailed without baggage, Carolina went over and opened it—and its contents sent her flying out onto the gallery to burst in upon Doña Hernanda, who was sitting in a cushioned chair fanning herself with a palm leaf fan.

"Does your room contain a trunk?" she cried, and broke off as she noted there was indeed a trunk. She rushed over and threw it open. "Oh," she said, feeling a little foolish. "I suppose it is all right then." She turned to Doña Hernanda whose lifted brows seemed to demand an explanation. "I found a trunk in my room that contained stockings and underthings and a lacy nightrail and I thought—" She broke off in embarrassment. "Well, now that I find that a trunk was left for you with even more undergarments and night things, I suppose it is all right."

"But that is my own trunk!" protested Doña Hernanda. "Do you not recognize it from the ship? *Both* my trunks were brought in right after you left—the other one is over there in the corner. See? I have been sitting here in amazement. One would feel that we were actually *guests* instead of captives of sea robbers!"

So the trunk of underthings in her room had been collected especially for her. . . . Carolina did not know just what that suggested. She told herself uneasily that this pirate chieftain was merely being remarkably civil.

"You will be fortunate if they fit you," said Doña Hernanda in a practical voice. "Why don't you go back and try them on?"

When Carolina returned to her room she found another surprise waiting. Plainly Katje had been here in her absence for on the bed was spread out a neatly pressed thin voile dress of a soft Chinese yellow that made her catch her breath—that color would turn her hair to palest gold, she knew. She wondered suddenly if Katje had chosen it, for it was hard to imagine that big blustering buccaneer appreciating such fine nuances of color harmony.

Still her gaze was troubled. The selection of the dress showed so much special attention. . . . But when she put it on, all doubts fled and she reassured herself hastily that this gesture reflected merely kindness—surely had his motive been lechery, he would have given her clinging silk or satin! The dress was a nice fit, snug around the waist and molding her supple torso and fine young breasts. Indeed it had a carefree but elegant styling that might have come from France. Suddenly she wondered if it had, and if it had been preceded by one of the tiny exquisite fashion dolls Paris was always exporting. She sat down thoughtfully, wondering whom this gown had originally been intended for and what had happened to her.

Katje brought her a bath—or rather she supervised the bringing of it. The actual warm water and tub were carried in by a shy, barefoot island girl with long black hair and golden skin and soft dark eyes who didn't speak a word of English or any other language Carolina was familiar with. Katje strode along after her carrying fresh towels and a large round sponge and a washcloth and delightful scented soap. It had been a long hot day since she had bathed this morning but two baths in one day was an unheard of delight!

Carolina marveled at all this attention. She tried to ask Katje about it, but Katje's English was as nonexistent as Lars had claimed. Katje smiled, shrugged, said something unintelligible in her native tongue and vanished. Carolina was left to bathe alone.

It was near dinnertime when she strolled down to Doña Hernanda's room. The Spanish woman was suffering the aftermath of so much worry and strain. Now that she seemed for the time to be relatively safe, she had collapsed upon the bed and refused to leave her room.

"I am not hungry," she told Carolina faintly. "Bring me any word of my son, and if my absence is inquired about, say that I am very tired and would prefer to dine in my room."

Realizing how exhausted the older woman must be, Carolina strolled restlessly onto the gallery where she saw that the blue-tiled table had been covered with a spotless white linen cloth and set with silver trenchers and cutlery. It was set for three and she wondered whether the buccaneer chieftain was going to favor them with his presence—if so, she might have a hard time explaining Doña Hernanda's absence.

She was just meditating on that when she heard a step behind her and turned. A tall man was striding toward her. Unlike the buccaneers she had seen on shipboard, he was wearing the ordinary dress of an English gentleman—in this case gray with silver buttons. Despite the heat he was sporting a light broadcloth coat, the wide cuffs of his sleeves decorated with silver braid. He was very fashionable up to his neck, where a froth of white lace was held in place by a piece of jet set in gold—but there fashion stopped. The sardonic face that rose above the lace was fringed by his own hair, not by one of the big curly wigs that were making the wigmakers rich and all over Europe causing peasant girls seeking money for dowries to cut off their long hair and sell it. It was a head of thick gleaming dark hair that he had, and although carefully combed, it was carelessly cut and rested upon his broad shoulders, swinging as he walked.

But even in the dimness of the gathering tropical dusk, the fitful shadows of the great pepper tree's swaying branches, that lean purposeful face, that swinging walk, that light step, were all unmistakable— and indelibly imprinted on her memory.

"Rye!" she gasped. "What are *you* doing here?"

"I might," was his cool rejoinder, "ask you the same question!"

Chapter 25

Carolina was unprepared for the sudden rush of feeling that came over her as she saw him, realized that he was actually *here* standing before her in his somber gray, looking momentarily as startled as she. It was as if her world had gone atilt. Over the thunder of her heartbeat she heard her own voice, sounding breathless, explaining.

"I'm a guest here—of Captain Kells. He saved me from the Spanish. But *you*, Rye"—she sounded incredulous—"you *can't* be the English gentleman they hope will join them?"

"Even so," was his laconic answer.

It was a relief that the same soft-footed island girl who had brought Carolina's bath earlier chose that moment to come out onto the gallery bearing food.

"It would seem," said Rye, who had got control of himself first and now seemed as calm as Carolina was flustered, "that we are to sit down to dinner. I was told there was another lady who is a 'guest' in this house. Will she be joining us?"

Carolina was still fighting the tumultuous feeling in

her heart that had overwhelmed her when first she saw him step onto the gallery. "Doña Hernanda is very tired and would prefer to dine in her room. Do you think that could be arranged?"

He shrugged. "I am sure Katje can arrange it." He turned and spoke to the island girl in some fluid dialect Carolina did not understand—and she was reminded that he was an island planter; he would know these dialects. The girl nodded and left them.

As debonair as if they were still in Essex and not in some godforsaken pirate's lair, Rye pulled back Carolina's chair with courtly grace. She sank into it, smoothing down her yellow voile skirts. He dropped into the chair opposite and smiled at her across the table. It was a smile that made her very nervous.

"You must try the conch soup," he told her. "It is delicious."

Carolina had hardly been aware that there was a bowl of soup in front of her, much less what kind it was. She dipped her spoon into it and her hand shook a little as she lifted the spoon to her mouth. Rye seemed not to notice. He finished his soup slowly, as if giving her time to think.

"And now tell me," he said as he poured her a glass of wine, "what it is that brings you to Tortuga?"

"Did they not tell you?" She recounted how her ship had been taken by the Spanish. But her mind was not on what she was saying. Indeed, under the calm pressure of that gray gaze, she was having trouble making sense of her narrative. The feeling persisted, interfering with her breathing, making tasteless the food upon her trencher.

"My story is somewhat different," he murmured, studying the ruby liquid in his glass. "A tale of rescue at sea. It seems I had sailed in an unseaworthy vessel. She was breaking up in a storm when the *Sea Wolf* chanced upon us. Captain Kells was kind enough to convey me here."

Carolina was gaining confidence at the normalcy of his tone.

"Lars Lindstrom—do you know him?"

Rye inclined his head. "I know the fellow."

"Lars tells me that these buccaneers seek to have you join them," she shot at him. "Are you going to do it?"

"Oh, it is not myself they want so much as my cove," he told her with a grin—that attractive grin she remembered all too well. It still had the power to move her, and she fidgeted uncomfortably in her chair. "My property in Barbados abuts the ocean. It lies along a remarkably well-protected cove. These buccaneers seek to enlist my aid in giving them signals with a light as they pass by, telling them whether it is safe to land—and other information."

"So you would not be fighting aboard their ships?"

"No."

Somehow that pleased her. "What do you know about this Captain Kells?"

"Only that he is successful—and Irish."

She gave him an uneasy look. "When I arrived here I found a trunk containing underthings, then a dress was laid out on the bed—and everything fit!"

"Perhaps Katje—"

"No, the underthings were already there when I arrived. Katje could not have known my size unless someone told her."

Rye shrugged. "Perhaps Kells has a good measuring eye for women."

"Tell me"—her face was intent—"is Katje his mistress?"

Rye seemed amused. "Would that make a difference?" He gestured toward her plate. "But you aren't eating. This fish is excellent—a triumph of the cook."

"It would make me feel safer if Katje *were* his mistress," said Carolina frankly. "I would sleep better if I were certain that *I* am not his target. And," she added thoughtfully, "it might help me to understand this strange household." She gave her trencher an impatient look and took a quick stab at the uneaten fish. "Did you stay in this wing alone before we came?"

"No, I was quartered with the *Sea Wolf*'s officers at the other end of the building."

She pounced on that and paused with a bite of fish

halfway to her mouth. "Why do you think you were moved over here to the guest wing?"

"I think some large plan is afoot," he told her frankly, leaning over to refill her glass. "And until I agree to join them, these buccaneers do not wish me to know too much of the enterprise which they no doubt discuss at night in their quarters."

"We should escape," she said firmly, ignoring the wine.

"There is no need for desperate measures," he told her in an easy voice. "Are you then so hot to get back to school?"

She reminded him of Mistress Chesterton's downfall. "So the school no longer has any students," she said. "I am sure Mistress Chesterton must be rather glad for she hated trying to be conventional when she wasn't conventional at heart!"

"Then you weren't being sent back?" He pondered on that.

"Oh, no," said Carolina. "I ran away."

"Why?" he asked bluntly. His gray eyes were very intent.

Carolina sighed. "Because my mother was about to marry me off to the nearest suitor—she was certain I'd got myself into trouble in England." She had blurted that out before she thought; the gray eyes were studying her.

"And had you?" he asked softly.

Carolina flushed. "Of course not! But she confiscated my letter to Thomas and now he doesn't know where I am or why I left or—or anything." She moved restlessly, toying with her knife. "Do you think you could get a letter off from Tortuga?"

"I could try. But do you expect him to come here to get you?"

Carolina gave him a level look. "I expect Lord Thomas to understand that I was shipped away from England against my will and that I have been trying to return to him ever since."

If he winced at that, at least the slight motion escaped her.

"You would seem to be very loyal to this Lord Thomas," he said with raised brows. "Despite a certain lapse in Essex."

She flushed again. "I realize that you have much to reproach me for, Rye," she said. "But surely leaving me trapped in a maze to freeze to death should have evened the score."

"I stayed to make sure you got out safely," he told her pleasantly.

She gave him an uncertain look. It had not occurred to her to look about for him that night. She had assumed that he had departed instantly.

"You were very harsh with me that night," she complained. "You said terrible things."

"I was feeling harsh." He smiled, fingering his glass. "A wench I fancied had just played me false. But"—he shrugged and lifted the glass—"we will let bygones be bygones. There is naught to be gained by our quarreling here."

"Rye." She leaned toward him in a supple gesture of appeal. That gesture brought into view the loveliness of her pale bosom in the low cut-voile bodice. "As a planter on Barbados you must know sea captains who ply between Barbados and Tortuga? Merchant ships?"

He nodded warily.

"Could you not manage to procure passage for me with one of them? I am told you have free run of the quay."

"Passage to Virginia?" he asked in a thoughtful voice. "That might be arranged."

"Of course not back to Virginia!" she interrupted impatiently. "It was Virginia I was running away from. But could you not take note of the ships that arrive and when you find one with a captain you know, persuade him to take me along?"

"So you are still set on England?" he said slowly.

"Of course! Will you do it? Oh, I promise I would pay him for my passage when I arrived in England."

"You mean, Lord Thomas would pay him?" he shot at her.

"Yes—well, no. But his family will, when I tell them

374

that Thomas is being held somewhere in a Spanish prison and will need ransoming. And that would be better than writing to them." She put from her firmly the thought that Thomas might be dead. He *could not* be dead, she told herself fiercely. The other two galleons had survived the storm, so must the *Coraje!*

Rye leaned back, considering her. His face was in shadow. Night had fallen as they talked and the palm fronds swayed and rustled in the moonlight. "More coastwise vessels from the Colonies reach us here than vessels from overseas," he murmured. "I have been watching the shipping. But tell me," he said curiously, "how do you plan to get away?"

"Oh, I will think of something," she said with a careless shrug.

He chuckled. "I don't doubt you will," he said appreciatively and his suddenly merry gaze told her he was thinking of London and the inn roof.

She gave him a quelling look and recounted how pitiful Thomas had looked when last she had seen him, lashed to the mast with Spanish stripes on his back.

"Ten lashes?" said Rye, when she repeated what Captain Garcia had said. "He will not die of that. And his family will no doubt hear from the Spanish ambassador in London in due course. You will only unduly alarm them by telling them he is imprisoned somewhere but you do not know where."

Plainly Rye had not enough sympathy for Thomas's plight. She tried a new tack.

"Besides, it is *dangerous* for me here." Her voice grew plaintive.

His ears seemed to prick up. "How so?" he demanded, suddenly alert.

"Well"—she could feel a blush stealing over her cheeks—"I find myself a virtual prisoner in the house of a pirate captain—"

"Buccaneer," he corrected her softly.

"A man who has looked at me hard enough—though he has laid eyes on me but once—to memorize my measurements!"

"Many a man must have studied you hard enough to

375

guess those," he told her whimsically, draining the contents of his glass.

"Yes, but *this* man has power over me, Rye!"

"I haven't a doubt," he said dryly, "that you could bend this 'powerful' buccaneer captain to your will if you set your mind to it."

"How can I?" she asked helplessly. "He doesn't even dine with us!"

He laughed. "So much for his being hot for your body! It is said he is taking the *Sea Wolf* out soon. Then you will lose your apprehensions, no doubt."

"I will breathe the freer," she affirmed. "But then, who will be left in his place? The situation could be even worse!"

"Oh, he'll leave Lars in charge probably," he told her in a careless voice. "Lars seems to be his second in command."

She stole a speculative look at him. "Perhaps I should ask Lars to help me," she ventured.

He frowned. "Perhaps," he said shortly and was silent for a long time, twirling his empty glass in his fingers. When finally he spoke, it was to reassure her. "I would not worry too much about Kells. If he has not troubled you thus far, you are probably safe from him." And when she gave him the scathing look she felt that airy assumption demanded, he added thoughtfully, "Kells will be allowing Doña Hernanda to visit her son, I don't doubt, and you can ask to go along. It will give you a chance to see the town."

"But surely Captain Santos will be allowed to come here and visit his mother? It would be very fatiguing for Doña Hernanda to walk abroad in this heat!"

The tall man lounging across from her poured himself another glass of wine before he spoke. "No," he said with decision. "Captain Santos will *not* be allowed to come here. This is Kells's home and since he took over the premises I'm told no Spaniard, whatever his rank, has ever crossed this threshold—save as a workman."

"But Doña Hernanda is Spanish and *she* is being treated as an honored guest!" protested Carolina.

376

Rye shrugged. "Kells has no quarrel with Spanish women. He treats them as he treats other women— with courtesy. But you must understand that Kells is at war with Spain. It is a personal war with him and he does not care to entertain his bitterest enemies under his own roof."

"Then Captain Santos is in some danger here?"

He quaffed the wine. "I did not say that. Kells observes all the conventions of civilized warfare. He has demanded ransom for Captain Santos, which will in time be paid, and Captain Santos will walk away unharmed. Meanwhile he is in protective custody."

"But suppose he has not the money to pay the ransom?" she cried.

Rye's broad shoulders moved in an indifferent shrug. "Then Captain Santos—like any captured Spanish seaman—will be required to work out some three or four years of endeavor in lieu of ransom. He might have to load and unload goods at the quay or, if he has skill as an artisan, he might be set to build a building." He nodded about him at the massive house walls that surrounded them. "I am told that captured Spanish labor built all of this." He leaned forward. "I see you are frowning at me. Let me tell you that if the shoe were on the other foot, it would be very different. If Captain Santos were an Englishman captured by Spaniards, he would—had he not been summarily hanged from the yardarm as often happens—have been cast into a dungeon, chained and left for the rats to gnaw on. There is a slight possibility that he could be ransomed out, but if he were unable to pay, then he would most likely be tried for heresy by the Inquisition and burned at the stake at the first auto-da-fé. Like thousands before him."

"But surely not to have money is not heresy?"

His short harsh laugh seemed to crackle in the evening air. "In Spain it may be! In Spain I will have you know that for a child to defy its parents or a wife to defy her husband can be called heresy and subject one to the Inquisition! We are all heretics in the eyes of Spain."

Carolina suddenly remembered Doña Hernanda's muttered words, *I had forgot you were a heretic.* She shivered. The warm night air had suddenly gone cold.

Rye was quick to note that. "But you have led a sheltered life—you cannot be expected to know these things. I only explain them to you so that you may understand the passions here and why these men feel as they do. Most of them have suffered at Spanish hands—or have relatives who have been ground beneath the Spanish heel. Nevertheless you will find that Doña Hernanda will be treated with all respect. Even as you are yourself."

They talked a bit more. He drank moodily. Carolina, disturbed by his presence, rose after a while and declared she was for bed.

"I will walk you to your door," he volunteered, rising, and the sound of their light footsteps blended as they moved over the smooth stones of the gallery.

She had turned to say good night when Rye suddenly swept out a long arm and pulled her around to face him.

"It is good to see you again," he muttered thickly, and his lips came down on hers even as she was gasping "No!"

The pressure of those urgent lips was long and sweet and wonderful. All the music that had sung through her veins all evening at finding him a guest here soared about her, dimming her senses. Dizzily she let herself melt into those arms so that she seemed fluid, malleable, a molten ingot to be cast this way or that to suit his pleasure. His lips traced fire along her uplifted chin, along her pulsing throat. His strong arm cradled her back as he bent her backward. All that he had meant to her in Essex was coming back to her in force. The world was slipping away. . . .

Abruptly that world came back to her. *This* was the man who had tricked her into a freezing maze and left her to die in Essex! Regardless of what he said now! He was not worthy of her love and never would be! It was Thomas she must hew to, Thomas to whom she had given her heart and her body in keeping before she even met Rye! It was treachery to Thomas to melt against this hard chest and listen to the uneven beating of her own heart! Poor Thomas, who might even now be languishing in a Spanish prison!

She broke free from Rye's arms so violently that her back collided with the whitewashed wall.

"You will not make free with me!" she panted. "For you well know that I belong to someone else!"

"Do you?" He had moved forward and now he placed both hands against the wall she leaned upon, making an effective cage with his arms. His lean face was dangerously close. And as he leant forward the skirt of his coat, hanging free, brushed against her quivering thighs and the buttons lightly abraded the nipples of her firm young breasts, tingling through the thin voile of her bodice. She gave a quick involuntary shudder of desire, and heard his voice soften. "Has no one ever told you that beauty belongs to the man who can take it?"

"No, and I do not believe it!"

He laughed then—and there was self-mockery in his laugh.

"Perhaps you are right," he said. "Perhaps beauty is a free spirit and slips through our hands like moon-beams."

He stepped aside to let her pass.

She went by him with a toss of her head and opened the door of her bedchamber. "In Essex," she said severely, "you promised not to pounce."

"Oh, but that was in Essex," he told her in a leisurely voice, hinting of things to come. "And this is Tortuga where anything may happen."

"Not to me!" She slammed the door in his face and stood with her back against it, trembling. She closed her eyes to shut out the vision of him laughing down at her, holding her, kissing her.

This was a purely physical attraction, she told herself, this *tendre* she had for Rye. She belonged with Thomas—and she would find him. Despite Rye, despite Kells, despite dons or buccaneers!

She almost tore out the hooks of her bodice so

violently did her shaking fingers endeavor to unhook them. And when she was free of the tight-bodiced yellow gown at last, when she stood there in her thin chemise with the light ocean breeze reaching in through the shutters to caress her hot body, she tried to push away from her the thought that perhaps Rye was right.

This was a tropical world, a buccaneers' world; here there were different standards.

Perhaps things *were* different on Tortuga—even for her.

Chapter 26

At least some of Rye's words of last night had rung true. The next day a remarkably uncommunicative but courteous English buccaneer named Hawks showed up and said simply that he had come to take Doña Hernanda to see her son. Doña Hernanda was overjoyed—especially when Carolina was given permission to accompany her.

"I am afraid of this wild place," she whispered to Carolina just before they left. "Indeed I feel that on this cursed island we are safe only behind the walls of this house. Don't you sense that, *niña?*"

In truth Carolina did not. Despite Rye's reassurances, she was uneasy about Kells for she was in his power. And after last night she did not trust herself with Rye. On the whole she thought she might feel safer on the quay overlooking blue Cayona Bay, where merchant ships from friendly nations dropped in to buy captured Spanish goods at bargain prices, and merchant captains and their crews strolled companionably about.

She was glad when Rye did not put in an appearance

at breakfast. At the moment she felt she could not face him.

After breakfast they started out, walking over the white coral rock, escorted by the big buccaneer Hawks, down toward the town. Doña Hernanda was puffing before they had gone halfway.

They found Captain Santos decently quartered in a low rambling white building surrounded by palms, some distance from the quay. He was wearing clean clothes and his beard was trimmed but he was very low in spirit. His cubbyhole room overlooked a small courtyard, but he showed no wish to leave it.

"God has forsaken me," he told his mother gloomily when she tried to comfort him.

"Could we not leave them alone?" Carolina asked the heavyset buccaneer who watched mother and son impassively. "I think it would cheer them up if we were not here to listen to what they have to say."

Hawks nodded and they left the dimness of the room for the sunlight of the small courtyard. It was full of strolling men, taking the air.

"Are these all Spanish prisoners?" she asked.

"Yes, and there are more of them over there." He jerked his graying head toward a long low building she took to be a barracks. "And there are others quartered about the town."

"What of their sick? Their wounded?"

He shrugged. "They are here too."

"Without a doctor? But this is barbaric!"

Hawks looked at her for a long time. Then he spat. "They have Spanish doctors, mistress," he said. "Captured along with them."

She felt that she had spoken in haste and tried to make up for it by giving Hawks one of her dazzling smiles. The effect was immediate. Hawks squared his heavy-muscled shoulders and when she asked sweetly, "Could I visit the sick and the wounded?" he led her with his long rolling stride into the barracks.

She spoke with some of the prisoners, assuring them that she had learnt much about their captors and that they would not be hurt. And then, quickly, she asked about Lord Thomas and what had happened to him. But she learned nothing. None of them knew the fate of the *Coraje*, but presumed she had reached Havana.

And if she had, then Lord Thomas should still be alive and in a Spanish prison!

She left the prisoners, promising that she would come again soon and bring them fresh fruit. Hawks watched her speculatively.

"Why does an English wench take such interest in the Spaniards?" he asked in wonder as they went back through the sunny courtyard.

"Why, because they are human beings," she replied, astonished. "Men like yourself. I presume that if *you* were captured, some Spanish lady would show you kindness!" And as he thought about that, she said, "I have not really seen the town. Would it be possible for Doña Hernanda and me to walk back by way of the quay?"

Her pleading smile melted the big buccaneer. He cleared his throat. "I reckon so, mistress."

Doña Hernanda protested that they were going the wrong way, but Carolina overrode her protests. She wanted to get to know her surroundings, to get her bearings in case the strange buccaneer captain who had captured her suddenly changed his tactics. She wanted to know the direction in which to flee in case flight became necessary.

Hawks walked them down to the quay, where they moved about between piles of bananas and mangoes and lemons and limes alternating with stacks of captured Spanish goods—Spanish muskets and Toledo blades, tall candlesticks and powder and shot, fine wines and Moroccan leather, frothy mantillas and pearls and spices—all the things the towering golden galleons transported back and forth between Spain and the New World.

"Piratas," muttered Doña Hernanda, glowering at a stack of high-backed Spanish combs just being unloaded from a buccaneer vessel. "Robbers!" She was about to shake her pudgy fist when Carolina grabbed her arm. She had just seen, past a mountain of coco-

nuts, the golden hull and tall gilded towers of the *Santiago* anchored in the blue waters of Cayona Bay and it brought back to her stabbingly the sight of Thomas bound and whipped, and the memory of Thomas calling to her.

"Remember," she told the older woman severely, that vision of Lord Thomas sharpening her voice, "that you are a guest of one of these *'piratas'* and so far he has offered you only courtesy!"

Doña Hernanda subsided, muttering, and if Hawks heard he took no notice, but Carolina, looking around her at the men who swarmed about, dickering over the goods, decided that she would do better without Doña Hernanda's smoldering company.

She turned with a rueful smile to Hawks. "I am used to taking long walks every day but it seems that Doña Hernanda finds it too fatiguing. Do you think," she added wistfully, "that you might sometime walk with me down to the quay—just for exercise?"

Walk—with *him?* Hawks's lounging shoulders swung the straighter. "I'll ask the captain," he told her in that laconic voice that was a feature of the man.

"Oh, yes, please do."

Carolina had been conscious of admiring glances turned her way, but as they were leaving the quay she heard for the first time the name that was to ring throughout the Caribbean. Quite near her a young buccaneer nudged his companion with his elbow. "See, Jack?" he said. "There goes the Silver Wench the crew of the *Sea Wolf* were all talking about last night."

And his companion gave a long low whistle and watched Carolina until she was out of sight.

That night, as they waited on the gallery for Doña Hernanda to appear for dinner, Rye asked Carolina if she had enjoyed her outing.

"Very much," she told him, steeling herself against the attraction she felt for him. "I am used to exercise, and being cooped up behind a garden wall is too confining for me."

An outdoorsman himself, Rye gave her a sympathetic look. "Perhaps Kells will allow you to walk about more," he said.

"Hawks is going to ask him for me. And next time Doña Hernanda visits her son, I want to take some fruit to the Spanish prisoners. Would you ask Katje about that?"

The slight smile that had been playing about his mouth deepened. "Of course. Is there any special place you have chosen for your walks? I will endeavor to join you if these fellows ever leave off haranguing me and dragging me off to where they are careening their ships."

"Yes, the quay."

"I suppose that would be interesting to you," he said. "Shipments of laces and fabrics and fans piled up among the coconuts and mangoes!"

"Oh, it is not the goods," she said instantly. "But I must study the island if I am to make plans for my escape."

For a moment his smile wavered. *"Escape?"* he echoed in surprise. "Faith, a man might attempt it, but a *woman?"*

"Nevertheless," she said firmly.

"Have you a plan?" he asked with interest.

"Yes—and so should you have. Suppose you do not agree to go along with these buccaneers? Suppose you anger them? What do you think your life will be worth? *I* am going to—somehow—meet English captains and officers of English ships who put in here. They will be more sympathetic to my plight."

"For the life of me, I cannot understand your haste," he murmured. "Captain Kells has offered you no incivility, has he?"

"No, I have not even seen him since arriving here but it is not my intention to stay here as his 'guest' eternally!" She smiled at his inscrutable expression. "Oh, Rye, I treated you badly—I admit it. But I promise that if I am able to arrange for my escape, I will find a way to include you."

His fingers drummed restlessly on the table and what

he might have said then she was never to know, for Doña Hernanda came out dressed for dinner and there were introductions. Rye spoke excellent Spanish. She commented on it.

"I have spent some time in Spain," he admitted.

This brought a happy exclamation from the Spanish lady who must needs know where. Carolina listened to his easy answers, but her expression was skeptical. She did not believe a word of it. Some Spanish girl had taught him the language, she guessed—perhaps the wife of some Spanish don who had chosen not to be shipped to Havana immediately, but to linger on Tortuga for a while—and had found a planter who came here occasionally from Barbados.

"Do you have a wife at home?" she interrupted to ask, in English.

He turned to her with a startled look. "But you know already that I am not married. I told you so in Essex."

She shrugged, thinking of Reba back in Essex and her married marquess. "Perhaps a wife in Barbados does not count when one is in England?"

He followed then the drift of her thoughts. "Or perhaps I might have a Spanish mistress tucked away on my plantation? No such luck, I am afraid." He laughed. "You are a suspicious woman, Mistress"—he cast a thoughtful look at Doña Hernanda, not following this sudden exchange in English, but certainly able to hear and perhaps remember proper names—"Christabel."

Carolina's warm smile thanked him for remembering to call her that. "Virginia's shores are not very far away," she told him in justification.

"But England's are," he said lazily and she felt he was talking about last night and her too warm responses.

"It would be easy, I suppose," she mused, "to fall into the relaxed way of life of the islands."

"And what do you know of their relaxed way of life?" he wondered, leaning back and eyeing her.

"Not a great deal," she admitted. "But one hears

386

engaging stories of beautiful native wenches who rule their masters' plantations—such things as that.''

He grinned at her. "You have a romantic nature, Christabel. Plantation ownership in the islands is not so entertaining as all that. Mostly it is just endless hard work to break the ground and get it planted with inexpert labor, nurture the crop—and then hope to God that a West Indian hurricane doesn't destroy it as it stands, or marauders burn it, or the ship that carries it to England sink before it can be sold, or overabundance and overproduction drop the price below what it cost to produce—all the same things your father must face back in Virginia.''

"Plus one more—being kidnapped by the buccaneers.''

His grin widened. "That happens but rarely. As I told you, it is my cove and not my body they desire.''

They went back to speaking Spanish and Doña Hernanda told them how worried she was that she would not be released soon enough to be present at the birth of her first grandchild, for her daughter was expecting a baby not three months from now in Cartagena.

"Why did she not accompany you to Spain and have the baby there?'' wondered Carolina. "Spain must have excellent doctors.''

"I did not learn until I was in Spain that she was expecting and she was judged to be too frail to travel,'' Doña Hernanda told her. "Her health has been poor and I would not have left her at all save that my brother was so insistent in his letters. He said how simple it would be—I could return to Spain and sail back with the *flota*. And now see what has happened? I am a captive, and who knows when I will be sent to Havana for eventual voyage back to Cartagena? I may miss the birth!''

"That would be a pity,'' said Carolina slowly. "Surely if someone spoke to Captain Kells . . . ?''

"*I* will speak to him about it,'' promised Rye. "He is a reasonable man and there is no reason for him to

387

retain Doña Hernanda—he is not holding her for ransom. Perhaps she could be sent along the next time Spanish female prisoners are sent to Havana."

"How do they do that?" asked Carolina curiously. "Surely no buccaneer would sail directly into Havana harbor?"

"No, the guns of El Morro would blow such an impudent fool out of the water," said Rye frankly. "But the authorities in Havana are even more desirous of getting their women back than the buccaneers of Tortuga are to be rid of them. So when the weather is clear, a ship is sailed to some point near the Cuban coast, the women captives are loaded into a longboat, Spanish prisoners who have worked out their ransoms are set to the oars, and they row to shore in Cuba, eventually to be reunited with their families."

Carolina's eyes sparkled as she tucked away that bit of information, which might prove useful.

Rye was watching her in amusement. "You cannot plan to effect your escape by that method?" he said politely. "Your Spanish is certainly good enough, but your face—now that you have strolled along the quay— has been remarked and will be remembered by every buccaneer who saw you. Besides, if you did manage it, remember that you would be a heretic in Havana and very possibly subjected to the Inquisition which is no respecter of women or children. Small children and old women are tortured to death by the Inquisition to wring from them 'confessions' which will only allow them an easier death than the fire."

He had been speaking in English but still Carolina frowned at him. "You will upset Doña Hernanda," she chided.

Rye shrugged. "The truth will sometimes out," he said.

Chapter 27

Carolina's request of Hawks had borne some fruit at least. After that day, with few exceptions, the big buccaneer proudly escorted her through the crowded quay every morning. Soon the "Silver Wench" became a familiar sight there. And sometimes in the heat of the lazy tropical afternoons he allowed her to accompany Doña Hernanda and bring the Spanish prisoners big baskets of fruit. Always she sought to question them as to the fate of the *Coraje*, which, she told them sadly, had had her lover aboard when the storm struck—and they, quick to sympathize with the heartrending loss of one so young, so lovely, tried to comfort her by telling her how sturdy a ship was the *Coraje*, how fine a sailor her captain. The *Coraje* would have reached Havana safely, Señorita—indeed at this moment her lover's ransom would already have been settled and matters proceeding toward his release. And who knows, he might even at this moment be strolling along Havana's harbor front—under suitable guard of course—before the palace that faced the Plaza de Armas. He might even have stopped there and turned his face toward the sea and be dreaming himself once more in her arms!

Carolina was not such a fool as to imagine that Thomas would be allowed to prowl the town even "under suitable guard." He would be stashed away somewhere in forbidding Morro Castle. But even in the depths of El Morro there was hope for him—if he was still alive. And listening to these men telling her so earnestly of the skill of the *Coraje*'s captain, she could not but believe that the *Coraje had* fought her way through the storm and made Havana harbor in all her gilded splendor. And that Thomas, her golden Lord Thomas, was languishing there now, awaiting rescue.

The thought gave her buoyancy and hardened her resolve to be gone from this place. Nor was she likely to forget Thomas's plight even while strolling Cayona's exotic quay, for the tall towers of the mighty *Santiago*, glinting gold from the blue waters of Cayona Bay, were ever there to remind her!

She grew to like the Spanish prisoners, most of whom beamed at the sight of her and showed her every courtesy. Once or twice she heard them call her *"palida,"* "the pale one," and once from a Spanish sailor who watched her adoringly as he bit into the fragrant peach and gold mango she had brought him, "the pale madonna." And once she heard the word *"argentina"* murmured as she passed and guessed that here too she was called the "Silver Wench"—but in Spanish. Word got around, she thought whimsically, and Rye was right—the buccaneers were getting used to her. Some—although she had never met them—had become familiar faces to her as well. Many of them now bowed to her as she walked by and she returned their greetings with a blithe nod.

Before the week was out she had met two of the island's most famous womanizers: Captain Shawn O'Rourke, who as a child had been called "Tawny" for his Celtic red-blond hair, and Captain Bourne Skull—who might have been named for the dead men he had piled up, for the brawny Skull was famous with the cutlass and his specialty was chopping off his opponent's head. O'Rourke was a lighthearted fellow, known for his blarney, while Skull was a brooding hulk of a man whose head usually seemed sunk in his enormous shoulders. They had little in common save a love of wenches and gold—and a shared birthplace, Ireland.

It was inevitable that their gaze should fall on Carolina, for "Christabel," as she was known here, was watched for on the quay. Men who had never known a truly patrician woman paused in their dickering to watch her walk by with her light yellow voile skirts seeming to float behind her and the brilliant tropical sun turning her hair to spun white metal.

On this particular day she was strolling between great piles of coconuts wondering if she could reach a group of officers who had just rowed in from an English merchantman anchored in the harbor—Hawks usually steered her away from such as these—when Shawn O'Rourke and Bourne Skull sighted her. On the instant they stopped their haggling over price with a saucy prostitute fresh from the Bristol docks. Copper-haired O'Rourke grinned. "Later, wench—we'll talk about it." Bourne gave her such a smack on her plump bottom that she let out a little squeal of dismay. And both sauntered as one man in Carolina's direction.

It was O'Rourke with his long stride who reached her first. He planted himself firmly in front of her, blocking her way between a pile of bananas on one side and a small mountain of wide-brimmed straw hats on the other.

"Sure, 'tis a fair colleen ye have with ye, Hawks," he said to the big buccaneer who had come to a halt at having his way barred. "I think we'll just be introducing ourselves. I'm Captain O'Rourke of the *Talon*—but you can call me Shawn. And this ugly fellow here"—he grinned at black-bearded Skull who was about to shoulder him aside in his impatience to get a better view of Carolina—"is Captain Skull of the *Claw*."

"I take it your ships were named to terrorize the

Spanish?" Carolina dimpled for she thought O'Rourke had merry eyes. Certainly they were a brilliant shade of green.

"And ye can call me Bourne," rumbled his black-bearded companion.

"I am Christabel Willing," said Carolina, her forward progress thus impeded, and amused by Hawks's discomfiture.

"Mistress Christabel is staying at Captain Kells's house," said Hawks warningly.

"Oh, we're well aware of where the Silver Wench is staying," said O'Rourke lightly. "The question is, will she be staying there long?"

"I don't really know," said Carolina frankly. "If ever I get a chance to speak to Captain Kells, I intend to ask him."

"If ever—?" An expression of disbelief spread over O'Rourke's handsome face. "Ye mean ye've not met him?"

"Oh, yes, I met him aboard the *Santiago* after he had rescued me from the Spanish, but I've not seen him since. Although," she added hastily for Hawks's benefit, seeing him frown, "I lack for nothing in his house."

"She's not seen him, Bourne, did ye hear her say that?" said O'Rourke.

"I did," rumbled Bourne. He looked Carolina up and down until she felt stripped naked. "But I find it hard to believe."

"So do I," laughed O'Rourke. "I think you're making sport of us, Mistress Christabel!"

"Oh, no, I'm not!" she said tartly. For she had twice asked for an audience with the elusive captain and twice been refused. "Captain Kells must be the busiest man on the island—at least he has no time for *me!*"

"Will ye gentlemen let us pass?" cut in Hawks, who was looking very perturbed.

The eager pair gave ground reluctantly and when Carolina and her cutlass-carrying chaperon were out of earshot, Hawks cleared his throat.

"Mistress Christabel," he began uneasily. "Those two men—"

"Oh, come," she interrupted, laughing, for she did not want to be forbidden to speak to people. "Half the men along the quay nod to me now. Why should you mind if a few words are exchanged?"

Hawks cast a look at the sky as if pleading for assistance, received none and said, "I think we'd best go home, mistress."

"Oh, Hawks—not till I've looked at those lengths of cloth over there." Carolina was advancing upon the pile even as she spoke, and a smiling buccaneer proudly lifted up a silvery silk that gleamed like metal in the sun. "Oh, it's beautiful!" She fingered it, still watching out of the corner of her eye the puzzled faces of the two men she had just left. Plainly they were astonished that Kells had not at once sought her out. It should be, she supposed, a blow to her vanity, but she could almost hope the situation remained that way, even though she would like an opportunity to plead her case with Kells.

"Are ye finished now?" asked Hawks abruptly. He too was aware of the concentration of two dangerous buccaneer captains upon his charge, and sharply aware of how outnumbered he'd be if they chose to stroll up and demand her company for a drink in one of the nearby taverns!

"Yes, I'm finished now," said Carolina with a sigh. "And the sun *is* rather hot. I'm losing my fair complexion, Hawks—I should have one of those straw hats over there."

To her surprise he promptly guided her to the pile of hats and insisted she select one. Carolina was touched.

"I'm grateful to you, Hawks," she said, adjusting the pale wide-brimmed straw she had selected over her shimmering hair. "I wish I could pay you back but I've no money, and no prospect of any!"

"Never mind that," muttered Hawks. "Captain Kells will pay for the hat."

Carolina gave him a look of surprise. She could not know that Hawks was less interested in preserving her complexion than he was in shadowing her beautiful face and her gleaming hair from the hot gaze of buccaneers who, if they chose, could easily surround him and take the lass away—and what would the captain say then?

That night as she came to supper, to her surprise she saw that the entire length of cloth she had admired, what seemed like yards and yards of it, was lying on the blue tile bench beside the tinkling fountain.

"Katje brought it," explained Rye, who was lounging against a pillar watching her. "She said it was a gift from Captain Kells." He gave her a sardonic look. "You must have charmed him."

"Kells, Kells!" screamed the parrot, upending and hanging upside down from its hoop to regard them with bright eyes.

Carolina gave the parrot a reproving "Shush!" and turned to Rye. "No, it was two other captains I charmed," she laughed. "Their names were O'Rourke and Skull."

"Hawks told me about that," he said. He gave her a curious glance. "Were you impressed by them?"

"Well, Skull is a bit too fierce for my taste, but O'Rourke is charming."

"So say the ladies," agreed Rye pleasantly. "You were in some danger, you know. O'Rourke is all right, but Skull is not to be trusted. He might have cut Hawks down and dragged you off."

"Well, doubtless *then* Captain Kells would have come to get me!"

"Oh, he'd have come for you, all right." His gray eyes glinted. "Tell me, Christabel, is it your intention to cause a riot on the quay?"

She flushed and would have given him a sharp answer but that Doña Hernanda joined them at that moment. Doña Hernanda was overjoyed because she had learnt that she was to be sent to Havana with the next group of Spanish women—perhaps sometime this week! She broke off to go back to her room for a fan and while she was gone Rye and Carolina resumed their sparring.

"What do you plan to do with all that material?" He jerked his head toward the pile of shimmering gossamer cloth.

Carolina had gone over to it and was running her palm along its silvery surface. "I don't know—unless Captain Kells has some captive Spanish sempstress eager to work out her ransom by making me endless dresses of this lovely stuff!"

He ignored her levity. "You could send it to Barbados or Jamaica along with your measurements and one of the fashion dolls they sell down at the quay, and have gowns made up for you."

Carolina shrugged. She felt somehow that the gift was unreal—as insubstantial as the man who, seen once, had disappeared forever. "That would take a long time and I won't be staying that long," she said flippantly. "Besides, I can't accept it. It's one thing to have a dress replaced that's half torn from my back—or a hat to keep my nose from peeling in this sun. That's generosity and it's welcome. But this is—" She hesitated, groping for a word.

"A bribe?" he asked softly.

She looked up and met his gaze squarely. "I feel that it's payment on account for something," she said with characteristic frankness. "Something I don't mean to give. And I won't accept so fine a gift under false pretenses."

"A woman of principle," he murmured.

"If you want to call it that," said Carolina calmly. "I may at the moment be staying in the house of this buccaneer and eating the food at his table, but I do not belong to him and do not intend to. And to accept this"—she gave the light material a contemptuous flick of her slender fingers—"would be to—to—" Again she sought for a word.

"To let him move closer to you," supplied Rye thoughtfully. "That is how you view it?"

"Yes." She flushed. "Isn't that the way *you* view it?"

"Not necessarily." He sighed. "Remember Kells is a rich man. This small extravagance means nothing to him. Perhaps in a way it's payment for something already given. He may enjoy the notoriety of having it known that the Silver Wench sleeps in his house. Every man on Tortuga envies him the position of being your host!"

"A position I jeopardized today?" she hazarded. "That's what you're really saying, isn't it? By telling O'Rourke and Skull that I never see Kells? Well, shouldn't I say so? It's true, isn't it?"

"The truth, like gold, should be guarded well," was his whimsical comment. "Both can be used against you!"

Carolina sniffed. "You talk in riddles."

The discussion was abandoned when Doña Hernanda rejoined them. They began to talk about her life in Cartagena. Rye asked her many questions about the town and she seemed to enjoy telling him about the life there and the setting. Carolina was not paying much attention. She toyed with her green turtle soup and listened to the rustle of the palms. It had come to her uneasily that if she *had* offended Captain Kells by her idle remarks on the quay she might well have endangered not only her own future but Lord Thomas's chances of rescue as well.

When Doña Hernanda had retired with a swish of stiff black skirts to her own room and she and Rye were alone on the empty gallery, she rose.

"I think I shall take a turn in the garden, Rye," she said restlessly. "Would you care to join me?"

He rose with alacrity and adjusted his long stride to her shorter one, as he accompanied her into the lush overgrown tropical garden with its locked green door that led to the outer world. Strange flower scents drifted in the night air and a light breeze rustled the fronds. It was a soft intimate sound like sheets rustling.

Carolina, lost in her own brooding thoughts, had never felt more alone.

Rye was watching her keenly, seeing in the moonlight the sad expression of her face, her drooping shoulders.

"Tortuga has offended you," he said softly. "I was afraid it would. But there is an island more to your taste. I am an expert sailor. I could steal us a boat and sail you to my plantation on Barbados."

His secret cove . . . where these buccaneers would come after him and kill him!

"Oh, Rye, I couldn't ask that of you."

"You could ask anything of me," he told her, his voice deepening, growing in intensity.

"Could I? Could I, Rye?" Her lashes were wet as she looked up at him for in the last few minutes she had felt herself very much a prisoner and very much alone.

For answer his arms went round her. It was not like that other time when he had seized her for a good night kiss at her door. That had been passion—this was compassion. After that first attempt and her sharp rejection, Rye—although he had looked upon her sometimes with yearning—had not again tried to touch her. As the days passed there had developed between them a sense of comradeship, a oneness of the spirit. *Companions in misfortune,* she had called them whimsically, and Rye had smiled. And his smile had deepened as he realized how she had begun to rely on him. Did she need something? Rye would be her go-between with Katje or the little island girl who served her. Did she wish to convey a message to busy Captain Kells, always out somewhere provisioning or having the barnacles scraped from the *Sea Wolf's* rakish hull? Rye would carry the message and bring back an answer. And it was to Rye that she turned now.

The arms that enfolded her were strong arms, warm arms, loving arms—if she would let them be. But she must be true to Thomas, she told herself, even as she felt, through the thin broadcloth of Rye's gray coat, the steady rhythmic beating of his heart, as steady, as reliable as the sea. They were comforting arms that held her, but—they were the wrong arms.

"Oh, Rye!" Her treacherous heart was beginning to race again and she twisted away from him in haste—before her breathing grew so short that he would realize the effect he had on her.

He let her go easily—even though he would have given worlds to keep her there, resting against his chest.

"I can't go with you to Barbados," she said breath-

397

lessly. "These are desperate men, these buccaneers—they'd find you and kill you if they thought you'd tricked them! And besides"—her voice broke on a little sob—"it's not to Barbados but to England that I must go if I'm to save Lord Thomas. How else can I arrange his ransom?"

His face was in darkness against the moon. She could not see his suddenly changed expression, how bleak it had become. "Surely a letter could be sent by some merchant ship that will eventually call at an English port?"

"Yes, but how would I know it ever reached Northampton? How would I know it wasn't lost somewhere along the way? I must go *myself* to make sure Thomas's family knows what has happened to him. Oh, Rye, you didn't see him as I did, tied to the mast of the *Santiago*, hanging there limp and unconscious—and then coming to and calling out to me! I must save him, Rye, I *must!*" Tears of frustration spilled over her lashes.

She looked very forlorn in the moonlight with her pale hair gleaming against the dark backdrop of the rustling palms. Very dainty, very feminine, very desirable. Rye's heart went out to her instantly but—she was weeping for another man.

Had she not been blinded by those tears she might have seen his strong hands clench white and his jaw harden.

"I will see you to your room and bid you good night then," he said in a voice he kept well controlled—indeed with a note of what she took to be finality, an acceptance of the fact that she would not be accompanying him to Barbados. "For they will be coming with the keys to lock the grillwork doors."

To lock out the night. . . But you couldn't lock out the night here, the perfumed languorous tropical night. It permeated everything—the wine, your restless bed, even your heart. . . .

Rye saw her to her room and then, instead of returning to the door that marked the "English gentleman's" quarters, he strode restlessly back to the courtyard. The trade winds rustled the palms about him and

398

above his head, the night was still lovely. But for him it had lost its magic, for *she* had gone.

He studied the black velvet night sky with haggard eyes. There hung the Big Dipper and there Orion the Hunter. Why could not his course be as steady as theirs?

Chapter 28

Rye did not appear at breakfast the next day and when Carolina tried to ask Katje where he was, all she got was a shrug and a blank stare. She supposed the buccaneers must have routed him out early and that he was off somewhere, perhaps at the careening of one of the captured Spanish vessels to make her fast and fit.

Doña Hernanda chose that day to have one of her migraines and Carolina was left alone after breakfast with nothing to do, for Hawks did not appear to take her strolling through the town, as he usually did.

She wandered into the garden, drinking deep of the tropical perfume that filled the air. Bursts of red and purple and pink blooms lighted up the bougainvillea vines that tumbled over the whitewashed walls, and the stones underfoot felt hot through the thin soles of her shoes. The sky was its usual diamond-hard blue and a land crab clattered by her, scuttling into the bushes at her approach.

She felt bored and restless. Even her nagging worry about Lord Thomas's fate was stifled by the heat and the inactivity. It was as if time stood still in this exotic place and the clock of her life had stopped ticking. She asked herself in sudden despair if she would be condemned to stay forever on this brawling island, living in seclusion, the perennial guest of a busy buccaneer who so far had not deigned to notice her.

Which was very surprising, considering that he had looked at her keenly enough to have guessed her measurements. . . .

Curiosity about Captain Kells suddenly overwhelmed her. At that moment she would have given a month of her life to have had the answers to all the questions about him that flooded her mind. And she felt one thing very strongly: If she could only confront him face to face, she could make him see how unfair it was to keep her locked up here. She could tell him about Lord Thomas—surely a buccaneer would be sympathetic to the plight of anyone seized from a ship by the Spanish and cast promptly into a dungeon, for such *must* have been Lord Thomas's fate. She thought of that vast forbidding fortress, Morro Castle, which Doña Hernanda had described to her. Was Thomas even now lying there, in some dark forgotten hole?

She shivered. Even the merciless tropical sun could not seem to warm her as she thought of what Thomas might be enduring. And here she was, helpless, being walked out like some pet poodle and then returned to her enclosure! It was galling.

Anger made her stride back toward the courtyard, as if to beard the lion in his den—and it was an opportune time. Katje was just emerging from Carolina's room with a pile of rumpled linens in her arms—she must have been changing the sheets. She did not see Carolina observing her from the garden. Instead of carrying the sheets through the heavy locked door that was opened only to serve meals and to admit her and the little island girl, she turned into Rye's room and closed the door.

Carolina stepped forward and just as she did, from the gallery Poll the parrot swung gymnastically on the big hoop and screamed "Pieces of eight, pieces of eight!" Poll's sudden squawk caught Carolina off guard

401

and the toe of her slipper found and tore a tiny portion of the hem of her yellow dress. She looked down at that tear with a frown. There was still a chance that Hawks would come to take her walking and it would be annoying to spend the entire walk holding up her skirt lest it trip her. She walked past Poll, who was ruffling his feathers and beating his elegant green and yellow wings. Perhaps Katje would be able to find her a needle and thread.

With that in mind, she flung open Rye's door, for she was certain he would not be in there while Katje was collecting the sheets—and stopped in surprise.

The room was empty. Katje was nowhere in sight.

She took a turn about the room, half expecting Katje to materialize. The chamber was Spartan in its plainness. It contained a bed and a bedside table—no personal articles at all.

And then she noticed a door set into the wall across from her. It was ever so slightly ajar.

Certain that door must lead into the main part of the house, which was off limits to her, Carolina walked across the room and opened it cautiously. And found herself viewing the same stone-floored corridor she had glimpsed when the island girl brought in food or cleared the dishes.

There was no one in the corridor. This was her chance to explore, and to satisfy at least a part of her curiosity about Captain Kells's domain—and she could disappear back into her own quarters very quickly by the same route through which she had come. Carefully leaving the door barely ajar, just as Katje had left it, she moved down the empty corridor.

Its walls were whitewashed like the other walls and there were spearlike arrangements of iron set into the wall to serve as torches by night. Her soft footsteps made no sound. Around her in the heat the house was silent. Katje must have carried the linens into some outer courtyard, perhaps off the kitchen, where they would be laundered in big iron pots.

To her right through an open door she saw a room

that contained maps. To her left was a locked door that looked very stout. A treasure room perhaps? She had heard that buccaneers had them. She kept going and suddenly entered another courtyard much grander than the one she had left. This one had a far larger stone fountain with several tiers and a gallery that went all around. She judged herself to be in the middle of the main house—and this courtyard too was unoccupied.

Burning with curiosity about how this buccaneer lived, she chose at random one of the closed doors that opened off the gallery and carefully opened it. The room beyond was small and barren of furniture save for a single stout wooden table but there were linens and dishes stacked neatly in a cupboard that stood open. She judged it served Katje as a storeroom.

The next room was a dining room and it had character. It might almost have been a room in England instead of tropical Tortuga. The furniture was Spanish but there were English touches everywhere—no tilework here; the walls were solidly paneled and the windows were glazed with small panes, unlike the jalousies she had seen so far. She walked across the thick Oriental carpet that might once have graced a handsome house in Toledo or Barcelona to open those windows and gaze out.

There was no view. A thick whitewashed wall soared up before her—perhaps the wall of one of the other buildings that Captain Kells had added to the jumble he already possessed. It was a kind of compound, she supposed, a little like the palisaded forts of the early settlers in Virginia.

But why had the Captain chosen this room to panel? And why no view? Why indeed this bit of old England in lawless Tortuga? The only answer that came to her readily was that this was the private domain of an exile, a man who longed for home.

But that was ridiculous. Captain Kells was Irish, not English. Or did they have rooms like this in Ireland? She supposed they did. So he longed for Ireland, did Kells. She thought about that, wondering how she could turn it to her advantage, for her mind was made up—she was leaving Tortuga, with or without his permission!

Quickly she closed the windows and left the room, to try the next door. This turned out to be a bedroom and she thought it must be a woman's room for there was a beautiful gown of pale orchid silk lying across the bed as if for inspection. Katje's? Carolina fingered the silk. It was a lovely gown, simple but in perfect taste—lovelier even than the handsome gowns Reba Tarbell had worn back in England. And it made Carolina wistful to see it for here on Tortuga she had been wearing only the one gown, the modest pale yellow frock Captain Kells had given her. She looked about her. The room had other women's touches as well. There was a dressing table with a French mirror and a cheval glass to twirl before. Little sweet-smelling jars and pomades sat upon the dressing table top. The furniture was more delicate here—she suspected it was French. Everything, it seemed, found its way to Tortuga.

The room puzzled her. There were other clothes, lovely clothes, hanging in the big wardrobe of hard island mahogany. And a stout curved-top chest with brass fittings that opened to reveal all manner of delightful feminine gear from fans and slippers to chemises and petticoats. But they could not be Katje's —the shoes were too small, the dresses made for someone more slender than Katje.

Some woman was living here—or at least *had* lived here, someone not Katje. But who was she?

She saw that there was an adjoining door and opened it hesitantly, wincing as it creaked. But her luck held— Katje did not suddenly appear, nor did any stranger confront her. She was again in an empty bedroom, only this was an eminently masculine room. Instinctively she knew it must belong to Captain Kells.

Just as the dining room might have been somewhere in England, so this room might have been somewhere in Spain. Handsome iron sconces stood ready for lighting on the plain whitewashed walls. The furniture

404

was heavy and Spanish, deeply carved, with an enormous square bed. It had once, no doubt, boasted a heavy canopy but it was innocent of one now. In this heat one could not endure a canopy. The room was richly appointed. A pair of massive gold candlesticks rested on a table inlaid with ivory that must have been brought from the Far East and taken to Spain. Beside the candlesticks lay a brace of pistols and standing in their scabbards in one corner of the room was an assortment of swords and cutlasses. She hurried to the large wardrobe and threw open the door. The masculine clothing that hung there was all of the dark and somber Spanish style, very elegant, made for a tall man. Several pairs of boots rested on the floor of the wardrobe and—this shook her—there was a golden rosary hanging from a nail inside the wardrobe door.

Spanish clothes, a rosary—oh, no, Captain Kells could *not* be a renegade Spaniard turned to buccaneering! She had heard him speak and at the time she had judged him to be a Yorkshireman by his accent, which was vaguely like that of one of her London schoolmates who hailed from York. But he was Irish— the world agreed on it.

There were other things in the room: some well-thumbed leather-bound books, a small brass chest she believed to be a money chest, a pitcher for water that appeared to be made out of gold, a pair of jewel-encrusted goblets, a couple of carved chairs supporting rich tangerine velvet pillows that looked comfortable.

Oh, this buccaneer lived well!

And then she noticed what she had somehow overlooked before, perhaps because it was so ordinary looking in this opulent room. Tossed carelessly over the back of a chair was a coat she recognized. Why, it was the plain gray broadcloth coat worn by Rye Evistock! There could be no doubt. She had faced that coat across the table at breakfast and dinner ever since she had been here!

What could it be doing in this room? she asked herself. Could the Englishman, like herself, have gone a-spying and taken off his coat to look more inconspicuous as he climbed out the window and went down into the town? Could he have taken it off and—surprised by someone in the next room—have melted away into the corridor, leaving it behind?

Her mind was full of speculations—and then she heard the murmur of voices coming down the corridor. Panic filled her. She was trapped. She ran over and stood behind the door, hoping whoever was there would go on by.

To her horror, the voices paused outside the door, and she could hear them plainly. And one of the speakers was undoubtedly Captain Kells.

"I tell ye," that voice she recognized as belonging to the huge black-bearded buccaneer she had met aboard the *Santiago* boomed out, "that even if this latest story be not true—and mind you, I believe it is—all Cayona is alive with gossip about her. It don't do no good to try to quiet it, it just begins again every time she walks across the quay. Indeed"—the big voice sounded aggrieved—"there's even some as say she's a Spanish spy."

"A Spanish blonde?" laughed another voice she recognized. "Hardly, with that silver coloring—too pale, I'd say!"

They were talking about *her!*

"I tell ye only so ye'll be giving it thought," rumbled the big voice.

"That I will," was the lighthearted reply.

The door swung open. Carolina shrank back behind it.

It closed to reveal a tall man's back. His broad shoulders were encased in a flowing white shirt, his narrow hips in typical leathern breeches, and a scarred basket-hilted sword slapped against his lean thighs as he moved into the room.

Carolina stared at that broad back—and gasped.

At the sound he whirled, his long sword instantly drawn, his shoulder-length dark hair swinging back with his catlike movement.

It was Rye Evistock—but a different Rye Evistock from the one she had known.

406

"Who *are* you?" she whispered.

He sheathed his sword and stared at her for a long moment. Then he made her a sweeping bow from the waist.

"Permit me to introduce myself. I am Captain Kells."

Chapter 29

Carolina felt as if her world were tilting. *Rye could not be—!*

"But Captain Kells is an *Irish* buccaneer!" she gasped, as if to refute his statement.

"The better to keep my real identity a secret." His smile was grim.

"No." He was fooling her. Whoever he was, he wasn't Kells. "You forget I've met Captain Kells," she said stubbornly. "I met him aboard the *Santiago!* And you were talking to him in the hall just now. Don't deny it, I recognized his voice!"

"Oh, I don't deny it. But it was Doncaster you met aboard the *Santiago*—and Doncaster in the hall just now, warning me that you're the talk of the island and coveted by all. He played out a charade for your benefit on board the *Santiago*—they all did. At my request."

Lars, Hawks, Katje, this man Doncaster, Rye himself—they all had tricked her. Her head seemed to be spinning. The man she had danced with in Essex and near lost her heart to, the "good catch" Reba's mother had schemed to obtain for her daughter, Lord Gayle's third son, so popular among his neighbors in Essex—Rye Evistock was Kells, the notorious buccaneer!

"I can scarce believe it," she muttered, for her own deception as "Christabel Willing" paled before the enormity of this deception. "Lars, all of them, they should be on the stage," she said bitterly. "And to think," she marveled, "I *trusted* you!"

"And I have been worthy of that trust." He crossed the room and poured some wine into one of the jewel-encrusted goblets and proffered it to her. "Nor am I the only one who sails under false colors," he reminded her. "You told Lars you were Mistress Christabel Willing."

She waved the goblet away. "It was a name I—I took not to embarrass my family," she said in a stifled voice.

His cynical gray eyes mocked her. "I too," he said airily.

"But—but that is different," she sputtered. "I am not doing anything illegal. I am merely running away!"

"Perhaps we are all running away," he said morosely, and downed the wine at a swallow. As his dark head lifted she could see the sinewy muscles of his neck and was aware again of the strength of that clean-shaven jawline.

The shock of her discovery had subsided a little now but it had left her resentful. She looked at him more penetratingly than she had ever looked—and she saw much:

He was younger than he had seemed in Essex, where his countenance had been so often grave. When first she met him, she had thought him swarthy, but now she saw that his skin, so fair beneath his tan, had been burnished to bronze by the hot Caribbean sun. His polished manner had concealed the steely inner strength of the man. For there was a hardness in him, and she had never felt it more than now—cold, impervious, unbreakable, and yet resilient. As if he had been tempered by life's hard blows like a fine Toledo blade—he would bend if it became necessary but he would never break.

"How do you like my house, now that you've seen more of it?" he asked, almost wistfully.

"It is very strange," she said in a sulky voice. "And very lovely," honesty compelled her to add.

Her last remark seemed to please him. "Would you like to see more of it?"

"No," she said coldly.

He gave her a penetrating look. "Oh, come now," he said in a bantering voice. "Matters could be worse. You could have fallen into other hands—some other ship could have taken the *Valeroso,* wandering through the ocean with that mother-ridden fool at the helm!"

So much for Captain Santos! "That *other ship's* captain would have returned me." She stated it as a fact with no idea whether it was true.

"To Virginia? Perhaps."

"No, to England!"

"To England? Doubtful." His gaze passed over her in a leisurely way, seeming to caress her lightly heaving bosom, seething beneath the thin yellow voile of her bodice. "The more I look at you, the more I doubt that any man would return you, Carolina."

"Christabel," she corrected him.

He gave her a droll look. "Very well—Christabel."

"How did you know I was aboard the *Valeroso?"* she demanded.

"I did not know. Lars told me."

"But I told Lars my name was Christabel Willing. How could *he* know that I was really Carolina Lightfoot?"

"Lars told me we had bagged a silver wench. From the way he described you I knew there could not be two such. I went with him and listened when he spoke to you through the cabin door. It was your voice, I was certain, for your voice is as hard to mistake as your face. So I arranged for Doncaster to substitute for me and watched you from behind the draperies in the great cabin of the *Santiago."*

Those heavy maroon hangings! She remembered them well.

"Doncaster seemed a likely choice," he added, and

amusement curved the corners of his mouth. "I was sure you would be impressed by his monstrous size."

Carolina flushed because she had indeed been impressed by Doncaster's monstrous size—she had never doubted for a moment that the black-bearded giant was Captain Kells!

"But you are not Irish!" she protested angrily. "You don't even *sound* Irish!"

"There are those who will swear that I am. And my brogue has been lost, I say, from being so long abroad. You see, I have brought with me several men from Essex—men who worked on my father's estate or neighboring estates, who are loyal to me. Two have elected to be from Kerry, one from Cork, and so on. All will swear they knew me back in the Old Country."

"Your friend Hal," she guessed suddenly. "The one who died two winters ago—*he* was one of them?"

He nodded, his face gone suddenly bleak. "Cut down by a shot from a Spanish culverin. It was one of my reasons for returning to England, to make sure his father got Hal's gold."

"You waited rather late, didn't you?"

He shrugged. "The same culverin shot near did for me. Convalescing gave me time to think."

He had set up his cover well, she realized. His operations in the Caribbean were as well cloaked from English eyes as if he were indeed invisible!

She had underestimated Rye—no, Kells; she must think of him as Kells. To do otherwise might cloud her judgment of what he was capable of.

But his words about the culverin shot had chilled her. "You've chosen a dreadful profession!" she mumbled.

His mood must have changed because he flashed her a sunny smile. "Sometimes a man's profession chooses *him*." His voice was light but it held a tinge of malice. "But now that we're dealing with truth for a change, we can effect a trade. If you'll endeavor to overlook my choice of profession, I'll endeavor to overlook your error in judgment in preferring Thomas Angevine to me."

"My *error in judgment?*" Her eyes flashed. "Kindly

411

remember that I am *betrothed* to Lord Thomas Angevine!"

He sighed. " 'Tis a folly I have tried to forget. Indeed I had hoped that time and distance would have shown you your error. Thomas Angevine may have more charm but at heart he's my brother Darvent all over again. Marry him and within a year he'll have run through whatever fortune you possess and—"

"I have no fortune," she cut in.

"The worse for you then. You'll have no chance at all." He was gazing upon her kindly. That look enraged her.

"Oh, don't be so superior!" she cried. "You—you pirate!"

"Buccaneer, if you please," he corrected her softly. "Call me all that I am and welcome, but do not label me what I am not."

"Very well then, *buccaneer!* It is one and the same, is it not?"

"Not to me," he sighed. "But then you do not sail the seas against Spain."

She sniffed.

"Nor," he continued inexorably, his dark brows grown straight and his wintry gray gaze very level, "are you in a position to stand in judgment, Mistress Willing —or are we back to being Mistress Lightfoot now?"

"I will thank you to refer to me as Mistress Willing," said Carolina, biting her lips. "For I would rather that my family should not find out where I am." But her glance wavered for he had brought home to her what she had forgot: They were *both* flying under false colors—he as the Irish buccaneer Kells, she as the English servant girl Christabel Willing.

There was a flurry of footsteps outside, a quick knock, and Katje flung open the door. At sight of Carolina standing there conversing with the debonair buccaneer captain, an expression of dismay flooded her countenance and she loosed a torrent of Dutch.

Kells gave her a grim smile and turned to Carolina. "She had come to tell me that she had lost you," he said, then spoke to Katje in Dutch. "Katje will escort

412

you back to your room, Christabel, in case you cannot find your way."

She was being dismissed!

With her color very high, Carolina stalked after Katje back to the closely guarded "guest wing" of the house where a disapproving Katje saw her into her own room—and to Carolina's indignation, promptly locked the door on her.

Carolina flung herself down to think. Every man had *some* weakness—but what weakness had Kells? He seemed so impervious to the arrows of fate. But if she could only ferret out a weakness, she would have a better chance of bending him to her will—which meant, of course, aiding her in leaving the island instead of holding her here.

She puzzled and puzzled but she could come up with nothing. After a while she drifted off to sleep in the heat and when she woke, Katje was unlocking the door. It was time for dinner.

She flounced out onto the gallery to find Rye Evistock dressed as usual in his neat sober gray English clothing. She gave him a disparaging look. "You should be wearing a gold earring and have a rag tied around your head," she said with a sniff. "So one could identify you for what you are!"

His expression, which had shone with pleasure at sight of her, lost its radiance. "Some of us lead double lives not entirely of our own choosing," he said politely.

"Bah!" was her rejoinder.

"Others, like your unfortunate self," he continued smoothly, "have double lives thrust upon them. How could you be expecting to travel under your own name, alone and unchaperoned, on a runaway journey to meet a rakehell who has few equals?"

"You do not know him!" she cried.

"Ah, but I have heard of his exploits with women. His fame precedes him. And look, he has caught you in his snare as well. He is to be congratulated, is our Lord Thomas."

Carolina thought of Lord Thomas as she had last

413

seen him, hanging limp from the ropes that bound him to the mast, and that memory sharpened her voice. "I would have thought that you, a buccaneer, could have had more sympathy for Lord Thomas, taken by the Spanish and lashed to the mast and whipped!"

Kells remained imperturbable. "Oh, I have no lack of sympathy. Indeed, had I chanced upon Lord Thomas, I assure you I'd have offered him aid!" At her doubtful glance he added, "I have news for you. Doña Hernanda is being shipped off to Havana tomorrow."

"She is? Oh, I must tell her—she will be so happy!" Carolina turned toward Doña Hernanda's closed door.

"She was told earlier, while you were"—he drawled the word—"*exploring* my house. She spent the afternoon visiting her son and has been packing ever since. I expect we'll have to wait dinner for her."

"But I thought you said there were not enough Spanish ladies gathered in Tortuga to make the voyage feasible yet?"

"I am escorting her myself," he said gravely. "In your honor. I will sail her close to Havana and send her ashore rowed by those seamen from the *Valeroso* whom her son Captain Santos has designated as the most reliable."

"You are foregoing their ransom?" she marveled.

His white grin flashed at her. "My men would take a dim view of that. No, Captain Santos has elected to pay their ransom along with his own."

"Rye," she said wistfully, "take me along. Perhaps Thomas is there and—"

He shook his head. "It is not safe to sail too near to Cuba," he told her briskly, ignoring her reference to Lord Thomas. "Havana harbor bristles with warships. The only reason they do not pay us a visit is the mountain fort yonder, whose guns sweep the channel." He nodded carelessly toward that fortress which lay now shrouded in darkness protecting this wild buccaneer stronghold. "Should I find myself outnumbered and outgunned by rashly sailing too near Havana, I will have brought it upon myself. But I will not expose you to possible capture again by the Spanish."

"That is not the reason," she insisted. "You are making yourself appear noble, but your real reason is that you fear that if you take me along, I will suddenly throw myself into the longboat and try to escape you!"

"The thought had occurred to me," he admitted. "For I think there is no end to your folly. I tolerate it only because you know so little of the world."

That calm pronouncement left her gasping. "How dare you treat me as a child?" she flared.

"Because you insist upon acting like one, Christabel." His gaze softened. "But such a pretty child. . . . It makes you easy to forgive."

Somehow the caressing note in his voice was more irritating than his insulting words.

"I wonder what Doña Hernanda will say when I tell her that she has been dining every night with the infamous Captain Kells?"

That brought a frown to his lean face. "You will *not* tell her who I am," he told her sternly. "She is already frightened enough about making this short voyage."

Carolina gave him a rebellious look.

"If you tell her," he added softly, "I will change my mind about sailing her to Cuba. I will let her wait here until Captain Santos' ransom comes through—and that may take a long time."

"But then she would not be able to reach Cartagena before her daughter's baby is born!" Carolina was indignant.

There was a ruthlessness in his gaze that told her he had already thought of that. "The choice is yours," he murmured.

She knew she was beaten and her resentment surfaced when the parrot suddenly squawked, "Pieces of eight! Pieces of eight!"

"You might at least have taught that bird to say something more Christian!" she rebuked him.

Kells shrugged. "I have taught him nothing." He regarded her calmly. "The bird's education was already complete when an old buccaneer gave him to me. He was dying, we were trying to pull him from the wreckage where part of the rigging and timbers had fallen on him when Spanish shot clipped off one of our masts, and his last words to me were, 'Take care of Poll, won't you, Cap'n?' He'd fought beside me well and Poll has swung on that hoop in my courtyard and screamed out 'Pieces of eight!' for three years now—and may scream for as many more if he cares to. Are you saying you object to the bird?"

"Of course not! It's the bird's owner I object to!"

"Oh, that's already been made clear," he said with a sardonic grin.

Carolina was still smoldering when she heard Doña Hernanda's door open.

"Remember what I said," Kells warned.

And even though it galled her, Carolina knew she must keep silent about the lean buccaneer's identity.

Doña Hernanda had so much on her mind she did not even notice the tension at the dinner table. She enjoyed talking to Kells for his Spanish was fluent and courtly and so, after greeting Carolina with a brief, "How splendid you look, Christabel—your cheeks are so pink!" she turned to Kells and said in a conspiratorial whisper, "Do you think you could have Katje get me some thread? For I must needs sew my jewels tightly into my clothing—indeed they nearly fell out when I disembarked here in Tortuga!"

Carolina glared at Kells. Poor Doña Hernanda was innocently telling the "Lord Admiral of the Buccaneers" that she had secreted treasure in her garments!

But Kells rose to the occasion. "I think I may be able to manage it," he told Doña Hernanda gravely. "I will send it to you by Christabel here." He smiled. "You should caution her not to reveal where you have hidden your treasures."

Carolina choked. Oh, the man was really too much! She yearned to rise to her feet and scream, "Doña Hernanda, *this* is Kells!" But her fear that he would make good his threat and hold Doña Hernanda here in Tortuga kept her silent while the older woman finished her meal and announced she must be early to bed for she feared tomorrow's voyage.

Once Doña Hernanda's door had closed behind her,

Carolina also rose. "I too am for bed." She gave him a dark look. "And if you use what Doña Hernanda has told her to take her jewels from her—!"

"Oh, haven't they told you about me?" he asked carelessly. "I never take ladies' jewels away from them. It is the treasures they wear beneath their jewels that interest me."

Carolina gave a lofty sniff and stalked toward her room. She could almost feel his appreciative stare as he stood and watched her haughty departure.

He had bested her, damn him!

Sleep, for the American beauty, was hard to come by that night.

PART THREE

The Silver Wench

They sing of her in Trinidad, they sing in Port of Spain
Of silver eyes and swaying hips—her kind won't come again
To shores like these. They say of her that she'll find
*   wedding bells—*
And turn away, preferring far the arms of Captain Kells!

1688

Chapter **30**

Doña Hernanda departed before breakfast for the ship must catch the outgoing tide. Katje and two buccaneers came to get her. The older woman hugged Carolina before she left. "I do hope you reach England safely, *niña*," she told the girl. "Ask that nice Englishman to take you. *He* will get you out of here."

Carolina gave her a weary look. Had Kells been present she might have been tempted to denounce him on the spot, but since he was not she kept silent. Indeed she felt she had made a devil's pact with him—she would not tell his secret if he did not tell hers.

"I promise you I will make my escape, Doña Hernanda," she said in a low voice, for even though the buccaneers were out of earshot there was still Katje— and who knew what smattering of languages the girl had picked up even though she pretended she could speak only Dutch! "And please"—she leaned forward and her voice increased in intensity—"please do find out where they are holding Lord Thomas Angevine and try to send word to me here through your son, for I will be visiting the Spanish prisoners as often as they will let me. And tell his captors"—she was twisting her hands together—"tell them not to hurt him, that his ransom will be forthcoming if only they will name the sum."

Doña Hernanda gave her a pitying look. "I will do all I can, *niña*," she promised. "Meantime, bring fruit to my son and try to cheer him for he looks far too pale."

"I will do it." Tears stung Carolina's eyes and she hugged the older woman. "Captain Kells will keep you safe," she promised.

Doña Hernanda's dark eyebrows rose and she crossed herself. "I pray God I do not see him on the voyage!" was her fervent rejoinder.

Oh, you will, you will! thought Carolina grimly. *Even though you may not know it!*

Then the buccaneers were picking up the trunks and Katje indicated that Doña Hernanda was to walk ahead of them. But when Carolina would have accompanied them, she waved her back.

Carolina stood and watched her Spanish friend go. She was glad for Doña Hernanda but she could not help feeling despondent as she watched those black skirts sweep down the whitewashed hallway. She would miss her.

She sat down at the table on the gallery to wait for breakfast and watched the parrot swing upside down from its hoop. The bird was like everything else here, she told herself glumly—a little out of kilter.

Food was brought, but only one trencher.

So she was to eat alone. She felt vaguely disappointed and realized that she had hoped that Kells would not make the voyage but would send someone else.

There was a great deal of noise elsewhere in the house, she noted as she ate. It sounded as if heavy objects were being dragged about. When the little island girl came to clear the dishes away, Carolina thought she looked excited. Through the open door she could hear the sound of boots, then a crash as something dropped and a curse, but she could not see anything.

The little island girl had no sooner cleared the dishes than Katje closed and locked the door.

Rebuffed, Carolina walked across the sunny courtyard where the stones felt hot underfoot and reached the entrance to the garden. To her surprise there were two stout fellows lounging against the wall by the green-painted door that led to the outer world, and both were heavily armed. They looked up alertly at sight of her, then bowed politely.

"We were told to stand guard here, mistress," one of them volunteered at her puzzled expression, but when she asked "Why?" he only shrugged.

Carolina turned and went back to the gallery. She whiled away the time trying to teach Poll to say "Christabel."

She had no more luck with the parrot than she had had with the two buccaneer guards.

In the afternoon she undressed and took a restless siesta, lying upon the hot bed fanning herself with a palm leaf fan. And then when dusk came and she knew that dinner would soon be ready, she dressed and came out on the gallery.

To her surprise, Kells joined her there. He strode in armed to the teeth with a brace of pistols stuck in his belt and wearing not only a cutlass but a dagger whose hilt stuck out of his boot top.

"But I thought you were sailing Doña Hernanda to Cuba!" she exclaimed.

"There has been a change in plan. Lars is taking her there," he said, and his gaze was not upon her but upon the courtyard wall through which could be glimpsed the garden with its wooden door to the outside world. "Bring the piece out here and set it up facing the gate," he called back over his shoulder. "And now," he turned to Carolina abruptly, "I think we might dine together in my private dining room."

As opposed to the bigger dining room that doubtless existed in the wing which housed his officers, she thought. She rose—and then stepped back in alarm. Four men were wheeling a small cannon down the hall and onto the gallery.

"In one moment I will join you," Kells told her, and went out to make sure the cannon's mouth was lined up precisely facing the garden's wooden door.

Hawks was one of the men who had brought the

cannon out, and as he came back past her, sent by Kells to bring shot for the cannon, she caught at his sleeve. "What is happening, Hawks? Why is a cannon being set up in the garden? Are the Spanish attacking?"

Hawks cast an uneasy look over his shoulder at the entrance to the garden where he could see his captain supervising the other buccaneers. "There's ugly talk in the town," he told her briefly. "The captain can't afford to take chances with you here, so he's set up that gun in case they storm the gate."

"They? Who are they?"

"That Portuguese captain the Spanish call El Sangre —I don't know no more name for him than that."

El Sangre—The Bloody One. . . . Carolina felt as if a cold wind had passed over her face. The small bronze cannon and its little crew suddenly looked very cozy. She stepped back and Hawks hurried on past her.

"Is El Sangre planning to attack the house?" she asked Kells bluntly when he came back and coolly offered her his arm.

He looked at her sharply. "What do you know of El Sangre?"

"Nothing. I have never met him."

"You have not spoken to him on the quay?"

She returned him a look of pure astonishment. "Not that I am aware of!"

"Perhaps you've seen him—heavy red beard, food-stained coat and the filthiest breeches on the island? Anyway, it would seem he's been watching you stroll about the quay and your beauty has inflamed him."

Carolina gave a nervous laugh. "Surely you're joking?"

"I hope so," he said gravely. "But there were nasty rumors floating about Cayona last night and I couldn't afford to ignore them." He paused to speak to an efficient-looking fellow hurrying past. "Tim, did you deploy the men as I told you?"

The fellow nodded. "And with cannon taken from the ships to command all the entrances." He flashed a grin at Carolina. "We will sell our lives dear if they overwhelm us!"

423

"Tim—that's enough," said Kells with a swift look at Carolina. And Tim shrugged and swaggered away down the corridor.

Carolina found herself growing excited. "Perhaps we should not take time to eat—perhaps we should stand watch!"

"There are others standing watch," said Kells. "And I would have a word with you. While we dine is as good a time as any."

She regarded him apprehensively as he led her to the room that she privately considered "a little bit of England" and seated her at the massive polished table.

"This room should have a calming effect upon your nerves," he observed. "Familiar surroundings give one confidence."

"Do not try to soothe me," she said. "Tell me what is happening."

"I intend to." He turned as Katje herself hurried in with their dinner on a tray. A sharp conversation ensued and Katje hurried away. "She was telling me that some of El Sangre's men have been seen drifting up this way, so it is best that I eat fast for I may be called away. You may eat at your leisure."

Carolina looked down at her trencher without interest. "Are you saying this assault upon your house is just to abduct me?"

"Oh, not entirely," he told her cheerfully. "Although that is partially his object, of course—and his excuse as well. El Sangre is a renegade Portuguese who has always attracted around him the most lawless elements of this island. When he is in port, which fortunately is seldom, there is always turmoil. He has received word—erroneously, I may say—that I took a large treasure off the Spanish galleons who attacked you, and he has gathered around him some riffraff from the town as well as the men from his own two ships."

"But you should not have sent Lars away this morning!" she cried. "He and the men with him would have been a help in any fight!"

His smile was melancholy. "I would not break my word to a lady," he said softly. "And I had promised

424

you that if you held your peace, Doña Hernanda would go free this morning."

She was amazed. That he should hold her in such regard! She who had scorned him! What a strange and complex man he was. . . .

"You did not need to do that," she said, troubled.

"I wanted you to think better of my character," he told her wryly, "which my profession of buccaneering had so totally destroyed."

For a moment she was conscious of some magic between them, a kind of bond, perhaps the bond that brings together the lost. . . .

The moment was dispelled as Kells stood up. "I have left five men to guard you," he said. "They are among my most trusted friends on this island. Two of them will stay in this room with you—the other three at the door." He hesitated, then handed her a large pistol. "Do you know how to use this?"

She looked at it doubtfully. "No. My father disapproved of firearms for women. My mother took a shot at him once. She missed him of course."

Kells laughed. "I can understand his feeling. Nevertheless. . . ." From a nearby cabinet he produced a long dagger with a carved jade hilt encased in a delicately worked scabbard. He drew it out and she ran her finger along the shining edge of the blade. It was incredibly sharp.

"Careful," he cautioned. "You'll cut yourself." He sheathed the dagger again and presented it to her. "I doubt there'll be any danger. But this will make you feel more comfortable. . . . Hawks will be with you," he added.

"We could be trapped here," she whispered, looking around her fearfully at the paneled room.

"No, there's a tunnel. Hawks knows about it and so do the others. That's why I've left you here. If worse comes to worst, there's a way out that will lead you straight to a cove and a waiting boat. You'll be all right, Carolina."

She noticed that in this extremity he had called her by her right name and was somehow absurdly pleased.

It came to her that it would have been very easy for him to have sent her away with Lars and to have made it known that she was gone. Then perhaps this attack would have dissolved.

"Rye." Her voice arrested him as he reached the door. She went around the table quickly and reached up and took his face in both her hands. "Thank you for protecting me." She kissed him softly, full on the lips—and was surprised at the sudden shock that went through his hard body.

He stood looking down at her for a moment with his face darkly flushed and an unfathomable expression in his eyes. Then, as if he could not help himself, his long arms went round her and she found herself held in a dizzying grip while his lips wandered hungrily over her cheeks and lips. It was a very tender moment and when he pulled himself away he looked shaken.

"Have no fear," he told her hoarsely. "This house is a fortress—I have made it so against just such an event."

He strode through the door and immediately Hawks and another man came through it, then shot the bolt. She helped them remove the dishes from the table and they turned it over on its side so that its thick wooden top presented a shield.

"El Sangre's men are surrounding the house now," explained Hawks laconically.

Long moments later a quiver went through Carolina as she heard a crash, the sound of splintering wood— and almost immediately the deep-throated boom of a cannon.

"That will have been our lads greeting El Sangre's men as they broke through the wooden door into the garden," said Hawks with satisfaction. He grinned. "They won't have expected to be met by cannon. Those cannon're from the *Valeroso*—Captain Kells had them hauled overland through the jungle and brought in from the back." He looked proud.

But what if they bring up their own cannon? was Carolina's silent troubled thought. *What then?*

There was pandemonium outside now, dimly heard but seeming to come from many sides. There were more resounding cannon booms—which must mean that El Sangre's men were pouring in through the different entrances—or attempting to. The battle raged on.

And then suddenly there were shouts, the clashing of cutlasses erupted in the corridor outside. She could hear running feet, shouts and curses. Hawks, who had been resting on the edge of a chair, sprang to his feet with cutlass bared.

"Go out and help them," cried Carolina desperately. "*Help Kells!* Don't stay here with me waiting for El Sangre's men to burst through that door!"

Hawks and the other fellow looked at each other and shifted their feet uneasily. It was plain they yearned to be in the thick of it.

"I'll be all right," she cried. "Just show me how to get into the tunnel in case I must."

"It's right over here, mistress," Hawks told her, indicating a large heavy cupboard. "You press right here." He threw his weight against one side of the cupboard and to her surprise it began to turn. Hastily he put it back. "Tunnel's right behind there and it'll take you clear to the beach that way." He jerked his head. "But you don't want to go in there unless you have to."

"Why not?" she demanded.

"It's full of rats from the ships. Big ones. They might attack you. If you have to go in there, take along a cutlass." He nodded at an unsheathed blade that stood in the corner.

Carolina shuddered. "I'll be all right," she insisted, but with a bit less bravado. "Go out there and help Kells!"

He listened a moment at the door and it seemed to Carolina that the fighting was moving on down the hall.

"You stay at the door," Hawks told the other man as he shot the bolt. "And yell like a banshee if they come at you. I'll be helping out the lads—"

Another cannon burst blotted out whatever else he might have said and they were gone, closing the door behind them.

Left alone, Carolina bolted the heavy door, took a cord from one of the wall hangings and girdled her waist with it, then slipped the sheathed dagger inside. She laid the large pistol down on the table beside her and took up her position behind the large upended table.

The next hour was perhaps the longest of her life. Around the outside there was a chorus of shots, yells, screams, a rattling sound as God knew what missiles landed on the roof, a crash or two from the nearby courtyard as thrown items went entirely over the roof and crashed down near the fountain. Twice she heard the clashing of cutlasses and thought the battle was again surging down the hall toward her. Intermittently and less frequently there came a boom of cannon.

Then, abruptly, silence fell.

Minutes later there was a knock on the door. "Christabel, it's over. Unbolt the door."

It was Kells! Joyfully she let him in. She had never been so glad to see anybody in her life. She felt weak with relief and almost sagged into his arms, save that he held her at arm's length.

"Careful," he warned. "You'll get blood on your dress."

She realized then that one of his sleeves was slashed and there was blood on his shirtfront. She drew in her breath sharply.

"Somebody else's blood," he said casually. Her gaze flew to the long gaping slash in his sleeve.

He shrugged. "A scratch." Indeed aside from the condition of his clothing he looked quite jaunty and entirely wild. Now he flashed a glance about him. "Where is Hawks?" he demanded.

"Gone to help you," she said sturdily. And then with a defiant look she added, "I *insisted* he go." And hastily, to wipe that stern expression from his face which boded ill for Hawks, "What happened out there?"

"El Sangre has gone to his reward," he told her in a casual voice. "And when he was cut down, his men scattered. They won't band together again—they're already rowing out to their ships, and with the tide going out, they'll be making for the open sea. It seems El Sangre got word I was going to take the *Sea Wolf* out—he thought to attack the house in my absence, abduct you, ransack for treasure and be gone before I could return."

Carolina drew a deep shuddering sigh. "Kells," she said, using the name they had agreed upon just as he called her Christabel. "Do you really have a plantation in Barbados?"

"Yes," he said. "With a cove such as I described. But it's not much of a place. I've no time for it and the plantation is overgrown, the house run down."

"Why don't you take me there?" she asked suddenly. "Away from all this turmoil here on Tortuga?"

He hesitated, studying her—then he gave her an answer that, chagrined as she was, she realized was completely truthful. "I was tempted to do that once but now I know that you would not stay," he said frankly. And as she was about to demur, "Oh, I realize you *think* you would, now—in the aftermath of battle. But you are young and subject to whim. You would change your mind about staying—you would be gone the first chance you got."

There was a grimness to his jaw as he said that, and Carolina sighed. That brief magic between them, that perfect understanding, was gone. They were back to their old footing—mistrust. "Were many hurt in the raid?" she asked.

"A few. The doctor is here and Nat Larkin and Katje are assisting him."

"But I thought you said your ship's doctor was isolated with some fever patients in his house some distance away through the grove and would not come out for fear of spreading contagion?"

Kells hesitated. There was no reason for her to know that Ives Grenoble, his ship's doctor, had been roaring drunk for three days now and would have been no use

429

to them in any event. Indeed, drink was poor Grenoble's only vice and it had cost him everything: his wife, his family, his practice back in England. It had brought him at last to the beach at Cayona where Kells had discovered his talent and enlisted him to serve upon the *Sea Wolf*, for he could control Grenoble's drinking while at sea by the simple expedient of having his possessions searched before he was hustled aboard. No need for Carolina to know these things—indeed she would like Grenoble, who had been in his day a gentleman.

"Yes," he said evasively. "I told you that. But we have got Dr. Cotter up from the town. He is a good doctor, although why he chooses Tortuga to set out his shingle is anybody's guess."

He is one of the lost—like you, she thought with a pang.

"I need to speak to Dr. Cotter," he said, turning toward the door.

"I'll go with you," Carolina offered, thinking she would volunteer to help Katje tend the wounded.

Kells gave her an approving look and led her to that wing she had never seen, where his officers were quartered. One of the rooms there had been turned into an infirmary and wounds were being stanched and bandaged. One prone figure on a cot appeared to be dead. She looked questioningly at Kells.

"Not dead," he said, interpreting her look. "Unconscious from a head wound. He'll come round." Even as he spoke the fellow groaned and reached up gingerly to touch his head, which she could see now was matted with blood.

A moment later they had reached the English doctor who looked up from his work and cheerfully congratulated Kells on how cleverly he had deployed his men. "And lost none," he added complacently. "All should be well and flourishing in a matter of weeks."

Kells looked relieved and she guessed this was what he had come to ascertain—how his men had fared.

"But I can see three dead men from here!" protested Carolina, interrupting. "They are in plain sight out there in the hall." She waved a hand toward the sprawled bodies.

"El Sangre's men," said Kells easily. "They left their dead behind as they charged back down the hill." His lean face hardened. "Tomorrow morning those bodies will be ceremoniously carried through the town, rowed out to where the *Santiago* lies at anchor in the bay, taken aboard, and in full sight of shore, carried aloft and flung from the rigging to feed the fish."

Dr. Cotter nodded approval.

"It's barbaric," whispered Carolina.

"It's an object lesson," Kells pointed out gravely. "A warning to any others in Cayona that to attempt to storm my house is to die. Afterward we send a few kegs of rum down into the town and invite all comers to toast our victory!"

Stunned by this—to her—remarkable aftermath of the battle, Carolina began to understand why to the Brethren of the Coast the lean buccaneer lounging beside her was "Lord Admiral of the Buccaneers." He kept abreast of rumor in the town of Cayona; his best men were conveniently quartered in his house and personally loyal. And besides being a dangerous blade and a good shot, he had a dramatic flair that kept this unruly island afraid of him—and a winning personality that made even the envious grudgingly admire him.

He ruled here—and yet he was homesick. She knew that from the loving way he had set up "a little bit of England" in his dining room.

Kells had turned to speak to Hawks, who was looking a bit sheepish, and Carolina asked Dr. Cotter if he did not need some help.

"Between Nat and Katje, I have help enough," he laughed. He turned to watch Katje, some distance away, expertly tying a bandage, and shook his head. "Katje should have been a man—she belongs on a buccaneer ship. What a ship's doctor she would have made!" Jovial and bouncy, he beamed at Carolina. "Not a man on this island could have handled this difficult situation so well as Kells. When he heard the gossip in the taverns that El Sangre planned to attack

431

the house as soon as the *Sea Wolf* sailed, he fortified the house. Then he and his ship's officers walked boldly through the town with the Spanish lady, boarded the *Sea Wolf,* up anchored—and then as soon as they were out of sight all but a handful poured over the side into longboats and returned by way of Cutlass Point—dragging cannon with them—to defend the house." He shook his head in admiration. "Quick, efficient, successful—that's Kells." He chuckled. "And now his reputation will increase tenfold, for it'll be said in the taverns of Tortuga that he's superhuman—able to be in two places at the same time!"

So the world was not to know how the urbane buccaneer chieftain had returned so quickly.

Quick, efficient—and deadly. "What about the wounded on the other side?" she asked. "Where are they?"

The little doctor looked at her in some surprise. "If they could run, they took to their heels. If not, they were carried or dragged away by their comrades. They are the concern of some other doctor who has by now received them and is binding their wounds—but not of mine."

It was her first view of casual warfare as practiced in the West Indies. They used cannon routinely, did these men—culverins, port pieces, twelve-pounders. They were as much at home slashing with cutlasses on slippery decks as firing their big pistols across the white beaches. They gained treasure, or they lost their lives. And after it was over everything went back to normal—the wenching, the drunkenness in the town. Except for a man like Kells, an exile really, who watched the scene from his high eyrie and dealt with it as needed.

She felt an enormous tug of sympathy for him, living always atop this powder keg that was Tortuga! And now she saw that he was moving about the room, speaking to the wounded one by one.

"Well, at least let me help you with that one, Dr. Cotter." Carolina indicated the young buccaneer whose wound the doctor had been bandaging when they arrived.

432

"I'll give you a lesson," volunteered the jovial doctor. "This is the way—here, you can bandage it yourself." And Carolina bent gravely to bandage the slight leg wound of the sturdy young buccaneer whose face glowed with embarrassment but who would forever brag that the Silver Wench herself had saved his life "the night he had near lost his leg" in a desperate fight that had raged at Captain Kells's house in Cayona.

Kells had returned to her side.

"I must take her away from you, doctor," he said cheerfully. "Mistress Christabel is tired and 'tis time she supped." As they strolled back he said, "On a hot night like this I thought you would prefer to eat outdoors. Unfortunately the guest quarters . . . that end of the house was somewhat damaged by the assault. The battering ram that crashed through the gate did some damage and later a cannon shot that went wild shattered one of the colonnades. I thought you would prefer to eat in the inner courtyard rather than view so much destruction."

She shuddered. "Was the parrot hurt?" For in the excitement she had forgotten all about Poll.

Plainly *he* had not. "No, I removed Poll myself and he is now once again swinging on his hoop, only somewhat ruffled by the disturbance."

Carolina smiled at him. A trustworthy man, one who looked after his own. No wonder his men worshipped him!

She let him lead her back to the inner court where a table had been laid in the white moonlight, although there was also a flickering orange glow from the torch that flared up on the wall beside his bedroom door. The torch glittered from behind the palms, casting seductive shadows that wavered as a light breeze ruffled the lacy fronds. After all the turmoil it was now remarkably quiet, as if all the world had gone to bed. She could hear the sonorous sound of the surf foaming in over the white beach from Cayona Bay.

Kells seated her with great formality, then excused himself briefly. When he came back she saw that he had changed his clothes and was now dressed Spanish fashion in clothing he had captured from the dons with whom he warred. She supposed that in a way those rich garments, as well as this basically Spanish house, were badges of his victory—his way of telling the world that he had won. Certainly he looked very elegant in rich black taffeta coat and trousers, black silk stockings and silver-buckled shoes. His coat had black velvet cuffs edged with gold braid, a heavy gold "money chain" hung around his neck, and a pigeon's blood ruby flashed from the burst of white lace at his throat. She knew he had gone to this trouble for her, and gave him a wan smile.

"I am sorry," he apologized as he joined her at the table. "I did not think to ask you if you might care to change your gown."

Carolina, who had been glad to sit here and collect herself after all that had happened, shook her head. "I am much too tired for that." Indeed now that it was over, she could feel her entire body begin to tremble.

He gave her a kindly look. "I think some brandy is in order. You are unused to battles."

"I hope I may *stay* unused to them," she said fervently. But with shaking fingers she took the glass he filled, swallowed and promptly choked.

"Drink it slowly," he counseled. "It is liquid fire but on such a night as this it restores the spirit."

Sputtering, she did as she was bid and life did seem to come back to her faltering limbs, strength to her tired arms.

"Your men are brave," she commented. "When their wounds were being cleansed, I would have expected many of them to shriek yet the most I heard was a groan."

"Buccaneering is not a profession that lends itself to cowardice," he said dryly. "The timid are left behind, the cowards quickly die."

And only the strong are left, seemed to be the echo of his words. *As he was strong. . . .* She accepted another glass of brandy.

He watched her finish it. "And now at last we shall have our dinner," he said, as the little servant girl who usually served Carolina came in carrying a large tureen with an enormous pewter ladle.

Carolina watched as a stewlike concoction was ladled into the silver bowl before her.

"We will not have many courses, I am afraid," he told her, "for tonight all will eat the same fare. But you will find this a very good stew. It is called salmagundi and is a great favorite among the buccaneers."

Carolina tasted it cautiously. She found it hot and spicy and filled with strange exotic flavors. "What is in it?" she asked.

"Almost everything," he laughed. "Fish and pigeon and turtle meat—perhaps even chicken or pork—marinated in spiced wine."

"But there are other things as well," she insisted, tasting the stew thoughtfully.

He shrugged. "Palm hearts, grapes, cabbage, olives —and yes, I distinctly taste mangoes—all well peppered and salted, with garlic and mustard seed and vinegar and oil."

Dutifully Carolina forced down a bit more. But she was not very hungry. The excitement of the evening had left her tingling and keyed up and the brandy was having its effect, as well as the wine he had poured for her.

"You are very lovely," he murmured. "I had never thought to see you sitting at my table, here in this place."

If that remark was meant to woo her confidence, it did not. She gave him a slightly blurred look. "Before you say more," she told him, "I would know one thing: *Who occupies the bedroom with all the pomades and women's clothes?*"

"A fair question," he said. "No one occupies it."

"Who *did* occupy it then?"

Did she imagine it, or did his hard eyes soften? "No one has occupied it," he said. "I began furnishing it idly, after I returned from England. And have added the cosmetics and the scents and the clothing since."

"Did you really mean to marry Reba?" she challenged him.

He gave her a brooding look. "I toyed with the idea," he said with bitter honesty. "I had come home to Essex to find that nothing had changed, that my brother Darvent is still a wastrel and my sister still a fool and my father too old and sick to care. I had wasted on them what seemed to me rivers of gold—and now I had returned once again to find them barely afloat on a sea of debts. It occurred to me then to chuck it all, never to return to the Indies. I would marry me a fortune and settle down to a comfortable life of riding to hounds and managing the estates that would come to me by right of my wife when I married." His lip had a wry curl to it. "And when Reba's father spoke to me, I gave his proposition some thought. Oh, yes, when I came down to London to get back a part of what my brother Darvent had lost gaming, I had every intention of marrying me an heiress."

"But you did not. . . ." she murmured.

"I met a wench," he said.

Something tingled warningly in her veins and her silver eyes leaped to shimmering life. "A—wench?"

He gave her a derisive look. "Do not tell me you do not know who it was, or you make fools of us both."

"And yet you searched for me none so long in London!"

"I searched the better part of two days," he admitted —and glanced away. He did not want her to see his eyes just then; they might give him away. She might see in them the naked truth—that for him she burned like a star in heaven.

"That long?" she whispered, fascinated.

He nodded gravely.

"Would you really have gone through with it?" she asked softly. "The marriage to Reba?"

"Not after I met the Silver Wench again," he said, and winced at the triumph that flamed in her eyes. She was seeking power over him, he guessed, and she already had too much.

"And yet you left me stranded in the maze?"

"I counted you lost to me," he said moodily.

"So you went back to buccaneering. . . ."

He shrugged. "It is what I do best."

From across the table she stared at him, turning her wineglass about in her hand. He was attractive, he was urbane, he was perhaps the most dangerous man in the Caribbean, the mightiest nation in the world feared him—and he desired her. It was written in his eyes.

"Christabel," he murmured—and his tone made the word a caress. "It is a lovely name."

The fountain tinkled. The red and green and yellow parrot seemed to hang motionless on its big hoop.

"I do not believe you," she said stubbornly. "Those clothes in the bedroom you furnished for a woman looked to be of one size. The pomades and scents all seem new, unused."

"That is true." He was smiling. "I chose them for *you*. It is *your* room, Christabel. You can sleep there tonight, if you wish."

For her? And yet, had she not known it all along? Had she just refused to face the truth about this wily and dangerous buccaneer who was even now playing a cat and mouse game with her? Still, to hear it baldly stated suddenly took her breath, and her face grew hot beneath his steady scrutiny.

"I—I think I would like another glass of wine," she said unsteadily.

Here in this exotic place where the only law was might, where men carved out their futures with pistol and cutlass, here in the aftermath of the battle with the night air soft and mellow and the sea moaning softly on the beach its age-old lullaby, she felt her senses waver just as they had when she had believed him to be Rye Evistock—and not Captain Kells, the notorious buccaneer.

She shook her head to clear it, telling herself the strong Caribbean sun had dazzled her eyes and addled her senses, but the lure of the night was too strong.

Kells poured the wine and his teeth flashed white against his dark face, etched in shadow against the moon. The ruby set against the lace at his throat flashed too, like a drop of blood against snow in shadow. His was a dramatic figure, his a life steeped in drama. Even across the table she could feel the pressure of his masculinity. In silence he held out the glass to her. In silence she took it, and sipped.

"I give you the future," he said in a timbred voice and their glasses clinked.

But a buccaneer's future was the gibbet and the hemp and an unmarked grave between the high tide and the low. . . .

Somehow tonight in this unreal place it did not seem to matter. She drained her glass. She was not used to drinking so much strong wine—and especially not after brandy. The room reeled slightly, righted itself.

Kells poured her another.

"To steady you," he recommended. "You have warring thoughts."

She voiced one as she took the glass. "Buccaneers *have* no future," she said in a low voice.

He shrugged. "To a short future then." He lifted his glass to hers. "But a happy one."

She sipped the wine soberly, considering him. And then she tossed it off, uncaring. The future . . . he talked about the future as if it was going to happen some other time. The future was here, the future was now, they were drinking it up—like the wine.

The room revolved slowly and she rose and took a dizzy step around the table toward him.

"I think you have drunk enough," he said sharply, rising too.

She gave him a blurred look. "Yes, I think I will go to my room." She took another step, wavered.

He stepped forward and caught her as she fell.

PART FOUR

The Scarlet Wench

Scarlet wench she seems to be, scarlet she does appear
Before a town agape to see her with her buccaneer!
A lovely prize of silver-gold—and he displays her here
But nothing yet that she's been told says that he holds her
*   dear!*

Chapter **31**

Carolina woke to a crash of timbers. It sounded very close. Of course it was Spanish workmen already repairing the house, but for a moment her mind did not work and she stared around her, recognizing nothing. This airy bedroom with its handsome Spanish furniture and jalousied windows open to the sunlight, those windows with their iron grillwork—this was not the room she had waked up in yesterday!

And then she remembered and tried to sit up, even as a sharp pain split her head. *This* was the room Kells so amazingly had told her he had furnished for her. That dressing table that looked so inviting—all those puffs and pomades and scents, the spicy jars, the silver comb—all that belonged to her.

His gift.

Everything had happened so fast, and with her head fuzzy from all she had drunk in the wake of last night's attack upon the house, she felt confused. She sat up gingerly, trying to sort it all out, and when the light sheet that had covered her slender body fell away, she realized that she was looking down at her own naked breasts, pale pink in the sunlight.

With a gasp, she threw off the sheet and discovered that she was sitting there in her chemise and that the riband that held it had come loose in the night and allowed the light lacy garment to float down gracefully around her hips. Had it come loose because she had tossed and turned? Or had she not been alone in the big bed? Had the chemise riband been urged off by probing fingers, had her woman's body been plundered by the lean buccaneer who took what he wanted from this part of the world?

The thought made her breath come fast and her pulse race. Her eyes grew wide and dark and she leaped from the bed regardless of the pain that seemed about to split her head, threw on a light yellow silk robe that lay across a chair conveniently near as if placed there for just such an occasion, and went out into the courtyard.

A breakfast table had been laid for one, and at that table Kells was just finishing his breakfast. Gone was the somber Spanish finery of last night. Today he was a typical buccaneer in loose white shirt and breeches with a cutlass swinging at his thigh.

"I was afraid that last crash would wake you," he sighed. "One of the beams must have fallen at the far end of the house." He nodded in the direction of his officers' quarters, which last night had served as a hospital. Now his appreciative eyes roved over the thin silk robe that outlined her figure in an inviting way. "Faith, you look very fetching this morning."

Fetching or not, she stood there staring at him in an agony of doubt, hoping it did not show on her face. Had she or hadn't she? She would have given years of her life to know.

He rose and pulled back a chair for her. "I had thought to let you sleep late after last night," he said. "But since you are up, you can share breakfast with me."

After last night. . . . Oh, God, what did he mean? She sat down rather abruptly in the chair he proffered.

"Do you like the fit of that robe?" he asked, and when she nodded: "The first dress I sent you was a guess, but Katje took the measurements of the gray linen dress you arrived in, and the rest were made or altered to those measurements. I trust she took them well?"

441

"I have not yet tried any of them on," said Carolina nervously. "But they do look as if they will fit me." She jumped as the little island girl came softly up behind her, bringing another trencher.

He gave her a sympathetic look. "You are entitled to be edgy this morning," he said. "After all it was your first."

"My—first?" she faltered.

"Battle," he said absently.

"Kells," she burst out. "I must know. Where did you sleep last night?"

"Sleep? Ah—I see." His eyes grew shuttered but beneath his lids the gray irises glittered; he looked angry. "What would you like to hear me say?"

"The truth, of course!"

"The truth?" He gave her a mocking look and rose lithely. He cut a dangerous figure with his cutlass swinging against a narrow dark-trousered hip. "I can see that you will not be good company today, but if all El Sangre's men have left—as I expect they have— Hawks will take you walking down to the quay and that should restore your good humor."

"Kells!"

He had begun to walk away but now he turned, his expression inscrutable. "Can you really not remember last night, Christabel?"

"No. Would I ask you if I did?"

"I am not sure. You might."

"Kells, answer me!"

"I will leave you to think upon it," he said wistfully. And then his wicked smile flashed. "But I will say this: that last night I found you irresistibly charming."

She sat back, dazed. She *had*—oh, God, she had!

Worse, she now began to remember vaguely a dream she had had last night, a dream that she had pushed away from her as she woke. A dream of a lover who had carried her in his arms to the big bed and there had laid her down and joined her. Her cheeks burned as she remembered the hot caresses of her dream, how her very flesh had burned as his questing hands wandered beneath her flimsy chemise . . . and she had

442

waked in that chemise with the dream still fresh in her mind.

And now she knew it had not been a dream! It had been reality.

Unable to eat, she shoved her trencher away and walked restlessly back to her room. Her mind was aswarm with thoughts, but paramount among them was the thought that she had betrayed Thomas. Inadvertently, of course—she must hold onto that belief. To believe anything else would be to admit she was a light woman, unworthy of such a man as Thomas.

Did sinners absolve themselves if they fled from their sin? she asked herself in panic. *If they changed?* Would she cleanse away the stain of her faithlessness if she fled this place, found Thomas and was true? Her mind whirled with such thoughts.

It was with relief that she heard a knock on the door, heard Hawks's laconic voice say that he had come to take her for a stroll if she cared to go.

"Yes—just give me a minute to dress, Hawks," she cried, and reached for her usual yellow gown which lay across a chair. And then her hand stilled. This was not the day for modesty, for simple unassuming clothes. This was a day for dramatic elegance and startling effects. For *this* was the day she was going to make her escape from Tortuga! Before last night's slip could become a habit. Before the overwhelming physical attraction the lean buccaneer had for her became an obsession that would sweep all before it. Before she could be found out and ruin Lord Thomas's life!

And there was no other answer but to run. For to stay was surely to court disaster. Last night Kells had taken her without her permission. But *next* time—ah, the next time she might melt in his arms and never count the cost.

A hot sense of guilt almost overcame her.

She could not do that to Thomas.

So today she would somehow—*somehow* make her arrangements to escape this island and the too attractive man who ruled it. A man who, if she stayed, would lure her down paths she had no wish to follow.

And with that decision to leave, a kind of peace descended upon her, a cold inner calm, and her nervous fingers lost their tremble. With cool decision she chose the gown she would wear along the quay, and with considerable cunning made her plans.

The dress she chose was a dress to be reckoned with. It was the flashiest of the lot: of brilliant scarlet silk, low cut and with its neckline and its elbow-length puffed sleeves edged in glittering silver threads. Beneath it she wore an almost transparent black silk chemise whose lace spilled as delicately as spider webs from her elbows across her slender forearms. She found a pair of black satin slippers with high red heels and a pair of black silk hose. She put both on, fastening them artfully with the rosetted black garters set with brilliants that she had found amidst a pile of garters of all colors in one of the chests. She rummaged through the available petticoats until she found one dramatic enough to wear this day: a sensuously rustling sheer black taffeta garnished with silver threads and sprinkled with occasional brilliants. She tucked up her scarlet skirts into wide panniers, piled up her hair fashionably high and then let several fat gleaming curls cascade down to rest seductively upon her white shoulders—they would bounce and attract the eye every time she took a step. A ruffled parasol of scarlet silk completed her costume and she twirled in satisfaction before the mirror.

She needed no rouge—her cheeks were already flushed with excitement, indeed with desperation, for she felt that she must make her escape now or she never would—and she would bite her lips to make them redder. Yes, and she would carry her skirts daintily high with one hand—not just the better to clear the dusty coral streets but the better to display her trim black silk ankles and smart red heels!

She recalled that Hawks had told Kells she usually attracted too much attention when she strolled along the quay—well, she would garner *twice* the attention this day!

Hawks looked taken aback at sight of her. He chewed on his lip with worry, but she walked proudly on, chatting with him as airily as if she were not a red and black and silver vision to startle the eye.

Down into the town they went and Carolina's advent upon the quay was all that she could have wished. Not a masculine head but turned as she passed. She twirled her parasol so that the scarlet ruffles danced in the sunlight. Buccaneers jostled by, stumbling into each other as they craned their necks to see her. Harlots from the town gave the lady in scarlet resentful glances. Hawks viewed his charge with great disapproval as she picked her dainty way among the piles of merchandise, stacked up against a backdrop of the blue-green waters of the bay.

As she walked, Carolina considered narrowly the field presented: The quay contained a great variety of men—on whom should she take a chance? Sea birds wheeled above her: a ragged line of pelicans, and a cloud of gulls that swooped and squalled and occasionally darted down to secure a piece of food discarded by some buccaneer who munched as he sat upon a pile of plunder. An admiring crowd gathered behind the dazzling beauty, but fell back every time Hawks turned a menacing look upon them and fingered his cutlass. She was straining his good humor to the breaking point, she knew, but—her cause was desperate.

And then her questing silver gaze found the target she sought: the pair of captains she had met once before on the quay—Shawn O'Rourke, the Irish buccaneer, and his friend, the black-bearded Bourne Skull. They stood together, talking earnestly in the brilliant sunlight. O'Rourke's hair flamed copper in the golden rays. Carolina eyed him speculatively.

A moment later she indicated a pile of silken scarves. "I would like this one," she told Hawks, picking up a yellow one so sheer it was almost gossamer. While Hawks haggled over the price with the grinning one-eyed buccaneer who was selling the scarves, Carolina twirled her parasol and O'Rourke, looking up, came to attention. Skull, turning to see where O'Rourke was looking, straightened up too.

Hawks was concentrating on the purchase. Carolina

445

gave O'Rourke a winsome smile. Across a pile of barrels she saw his chest expand. A moment later both he and Skull were heading in her direction.

Promptly Carolina attracted Hawks's attention by asking him about one of the ships in the bay—was it a French ship or was it English? Hawks, asked such a reasonable question, squinted into the sun—and while he was thus occupied, Carolina watched the two buccaneer captains approach.

When they had almost reached her she lifted the light scarf in the breeze and let it float away from her. The wind caught it just as Hawks pronounced the ship a "Frenchie." Carolina gave a little cry of dismay. "My scarf!" she cried on an anguished note. "Hawks, it's blowing away!"

Hawks made a snatch for it, but the wind was capricious. He took off after it, floundering into a pile of kegs. The scarf had come to rest atop a pile of mangoes but as Hawks reached for it, the breeze snatched it away again.

O'Rourke had reached her now.

"Captain O'Rourke," she said rapidly, "I would speak with you. Can you keep Hawks occupied for a few moments?"

Shawn O'Rourke had not reached his present eminence as a buccaneer captain by being dim—he was nothing if not resourceful. He cast about him and saw a small boy playing nearby with a hoop. "You, lad!" He flipped the boy a coin. "Keep yon big fellow who's chasing that scarf occupied for a while. Trip him up if ye have to!"

The boy, who had grown to his present size knowing nothing but the life on this island, grinned and ran toward Hawks, rolling his hoop.

"What is it ye want of me, mistress?" asked O'Rourke curiously.

"I want to leave this island and Kells won't take me!" she pouted.

His reddish brows raised. "Faith," he murmured. "Where is it ye wish to go? London?"

A week ago Carolina would have answered feverishly, "Yes!" But now she had another plan, a desperate one.

"I wish to go to Cuba," she said.

"Did you hear that, Bourne?" O'Rourke murmured to the hulking black-bearded buccaneer who had come up and was almost jostling his shoulder. "The lady wants to go to Cuba!"

"Why?" rumbled Skull.

"I have business in Havana," said Carolina airily.

This time two pairs of brows shot up.

"Business in *Havana?*" repeated O'Rourke incredulously.

"Yes."

"There's a small buccaneer settlement on Hispaniola," rumbled Skull. "'Tis near enough to reach Havana easily."

"But it's—" began O'Rourke, and Skull raised his big hand to quiet him.

"Mistress Christabel wants to go to Cuba, Shawn," he rumbled. "Are ye saying we won't take her within striking distance?"

"No, I'm not saying that." O'Rourke, who had been about to protest that the little group of lean-to shacks built along a secluded cove by the buccaneers and occupied on occasion could not really be called a *settlement*, subsided. He warmed to the idea. "And a lady dressed in black with a black mantilla to hide her hair and her face would not be much noticed in Havana, if she wished to visit there."

"I do wish to!" said Carolina fervently. "You'll be well paid for taking me there," she added on an anxious note.

The two buccaneers exchanged glances.

"Well paid, the lady says, Bourne," murmured O'Rourke.

"In gold," interposed Carolina. For was not her old friend Ramona Valdez wife to the governor of Cuba? And even if she could not reach such an exalted personage, she could hang about and waylay Doña Hernanda on her way to church for that pious lady would never miss mass, and surely Doña Hernanda

447

would help her! She was sure—well, almost sure—that she could get the gold.

"Silver will do," murmured O'Rourke. He was studying the gleaming spun metal of her hair. His bold eyes raked her speculatively. *"I'd* sail ye anywhere, Mistress Christabel, and welcome. Whether it be Philadelphia or Port Royal—or Cuba, if you please—the *Talon* would take you there. But Bourne here, he wouldn't like to be left out. Indeed, I think he'd fight me for the privilege." He gave her an impudent grin. "Would you accept a *matelot?"*

Out of the corner of her eye Carolina was aware that the boy with the hoop had managed to collide with Hawks just as he had grasped the flying scarf. Hawks had gone over in a heap against a large pile of oranges, which had collapsed from the sudden assault, raining oranges impartially down upon them both.

"Matelot?" she murmured, casting about for what the word meant.

"Aye, *matelot,"* rumbled Skull. "I'd settle for that!"

Matelot, thought Carolina, keeping an eye on Hawks, just now extricating himself from the oranges. That must be Spanish for—let's see, *"lote"* meant "share," and *"matel,"* that must mean "metal" . . . their pronunciation might be vile but obviously Captain Skull wanted a share in the venture, a share in the gold and silver coins. And Havana was dangerous territory; it was reasonable that O'Rourke would want a sister ship with him. Obviously that sister ship was to be Captain Skull's.

Hawks had by now dusted himself off and was striding back toward her.

Carolina did not pause to make sure what *matelot* meant.

"Yes," she said quickly. "I would indeed."

O'Rourke pulled a large silver *daalder* from his pocket. "Call it, Bourne!" He flipped the coin in the air.

"Tails," cried Skull.

O'Rourke slapped his palm down on the coin he had just caught on the back of his hand. For a moment he stared down as if afraid to lift his palm. Impatiently Skull seized him by the wrist. "Well, let's see it, Shawn!"

O'Rourke's palm came away and a lion rampant gleamed up at them from the coin.

"Ye've lost," laughed Skull.

"No, I've won," murmured O'Rourke, and triumph lit his green eyes, making them shine like green glass when the light is behind it. Swiftly he pocketed the coin.

Carolina had been taken aback by the exchange and by the flipping of coins—obviously they were deciding who should transport her to the vicinity of Havana in his ship. For although O'Rourke seemed clean-cut, she had not envisioned voyaging anywhere with Skull—and she was relieved that O'Rourke and the *Talon* had won the toss.

Perhaps O'Rourke sensed her relief for he was suddenly very attentive. "Perhaps ye'd rather wait until the *Sea Wolf* sails?" he asked politely and Skull snorted.

"No," said Carolina nervously, for Hawks had almost reached them, winding through piles of bananas and coconuts and those who haggled for them. "I will have to send you word when I can get away."

She turned abruptly to accept the scarf from Hawks. His face was very grim at his finding her deep in conversation with two buccaneer captains.

"Good day to you, Captain O'Rourke and Captain Skull," she said, dismissing them both with a twitch of her shoulder. "I will remember our conversation." She turned quickly away, fingering the scarf. "I am sorry I have caused you so much trouble," she told Hawks.

"What was that about, mistress, those two tossing a coin?" Hawks asked, frowning after the departing pair.

Carolina shrugged. "Oh, were they tossing a coin?" A touch of insolence had crept into her voice and Hawks's frown deepened.

"I think we'd best go home," he told her. His uneasy gaze took in not only the swaggering backs of the two buccaneer captains, but several of the prostitutes who

449

frequented the quay and who were standing nearby. Indeed they had listened avidly to the conversation between O'Rourke and Skull, and now one of them was saying rather loudly to the others, "I wonder if blonde hair pulls out as easy as dark hair? What d'you think, Nan?" And Nan shrugged and said, "Why don't we find out?" Hawks had no desire to separate fighting wenches here on the quay—he'd seen too many of them. A man could not but come off second best, with a scratched face and torn clothes. He might even get knifed in the bargain.

"Yes, I would like to go home now," Carolina surprised him by saying.

She had done what she came to do. For her the die was cast. She accompanied Hawks home through the afternoon heat with the sun glaring down upon the white coral stone of the path. It was a relief to reach the shade afforded by the dark waxy green leaves of the lemon and avocado trees.

She usually kept up a bright conversation with Hawks as she walked, but today she was silent, full of plans for reaching Lord Thomas, for using influence in lieu of ransom—even if they were holding him in the deepest hole of Morro Castle! And she was still puzzling over ways and means as they reached the sprawling green-shuttered whitewashed house that was just now being swarmed over by Spanish workmen repairing the scars caused by El Sangre's assault.

Hawks escorted her not through the green garden door which had been shattered, but through the front entrance, a more imposing portal. The heavy iron grillwork had been carted away for repair but the massive inner door of heavy wood was only scarred. Its locks had burst open beneath the assault of the battering ram but they had been given temporary repairs and now the door swung open on well-oiled hinges.

Her plans to escape had occupied her mind outside these whitewashed walls, but once enclosed by them again, once she was walking through the inner courtyard where she had breakfasted with Kells, where he had taunted her—yes, taunted her! about last night, for

had he not called her behavior "irresistibly charming"?
—her indignation mounted.

She flounced through the empty courtyard and into that bedroom furnished for her alone—or so Kells claimed.

Across the Caribbean the shadows were lengthening. Night would soon be coming to the emerald green islands of the Indies—among them the buccaneer stronghold of Tortuga.

And with the night Tortuga's most celebrated buccaneer captain would be coming home . . . home to claim as his right what he had last night taken by guile.

Chapter 32

An early moon rode the sky when Kells came home. She knew he had been busy with the careening of the *Valeroso* at Cutlass Point and guessed that he had stopped by some tavern on the way home to have a drink with friends. She dined alone, fidgeting beneath Katje's speculative glances. But she was not hungry, she only toyed with her green turtle soup and grouper and citrus.

Her mind was on the night—and what it would bring.

At first she determined that she would ignore him. She would go to bed. She would push a chair against her door first of course—and then she would go to bed.

Still she hesitated. At last she took off her fiery red dress—glad to be rid of it, actually, for she had only kept it on to provoke him in case he should hear of the comment she had caused down at the quay today.

Outside the trade winds rustled the palms seductively. Fitful shadows raced across the moon. The night air from the Caribbean was filled with magic.

It was then that Kells strode in.

She had heard his step in the hall and tensed,

expecting his knock. But she was unprepared for the sudden way her door burst open. She was caught standing there clad only in her thin chemise—more than sufficient for the heat—before her dressing table. She had been about to comb out her long fair hair but as the door opened she whirled and dropped the fan with which she had been fanning her damp skin.

"Get out!" she cried, outraged. "Can't you see I'm not dressed?"

"Indeed I can see that." His raking gaze passed over her, but he made no move to go. "I have just come from the town," he said. "You are the talk of it. Faith, since you came here, men speak of little else! It is true that a woman can cause more havoc than a battle!"

"If you are speaking of my red dress," she said haughtily, "I will remind you that it was you who gave it to me!"

"I am not speaking of your red dress, even though I understand that it is being vividly described, along with every detail of your figure and your flaunting walk, in every tavern on Tortuga. What devil is in you, Christabel?"

He advanced upon her and she retreated behind a carved high-backed chair.

"Kells," she warned him, "go back." And then her resentment overcame her and she burst out, "How dare you speak to me of devils, you—you despoiler of women!"

"Despoiler of—!" For a moment amazement blanked his countenance of expression. As he paused, the moonlight that poured through her bedroom window in a pale golden shower struck full upon his face, etching the hard lines and the steady narrow gray eyes. He cut a handsome figure, tall and dark, his white shirt with its flowing sleeves open to the waist, his cutlass hanging carelessly from his belt and slapping against his lean thighs in their dark trousers. But his saturnine countenance, deeply tanned from the tropic sun, did nothing to reassure her. "Despoiler of women, am I?" His sardonic grin flashed. "And why should *I* be left out?" he demanded insolently. "Why should I not share you too? Since you promise yourself so recklessly to others?"

Clinging to the chairback, she gave him a bewildered look. "What are you talking about? I have promised nothing."

"What of your dealings with O'Rourke and Skull? They have tossed coins for you!"

Her color heightened at his knowing manner and she answered with heat. "They tossed coins only as to which one would take me where I wished to go. Since *you* will not!" she added bitterly.

He had taken another step toward her across the stone floor and she caught her breath. His face was again in darkness but she could see the gleam of his strong white teeth, flashing in a smile that held no mirth.

"Kells, you cannot blame me!" she cried in sudden panic at the looming anger she saw in his face. "They promised to take me wherever I wished to go."

"Promised to take you. . . ." he murmured. *"And you believed them?"*

Her heart was hammering harder in her chest. Not only his commanding presence but something dangerous in his tone frightened her.

"Should I not?" she asked stiffly.

"You agreed to accept *matelotage* from them!" he exploded. "Don't you know what that means?"

In truth she did not, but she would not have admitted it for worlds. "Of course I know." She tossed her fair head and the moonlight struck it into a cascade of spun white gold that poured down upon the rounded gleam of her shoulders. "It is—oh, some Spanish word that means 'to share metal' or some such. I had promised them gold—"

"Whose gold?" he cut in.

"Why—why, Doña Hernanda's, of course!"

His expression grew incredulous.

"She may not have it but she can get it!" cried the girl whose lovely face looked back at him indignantly from over the top of the tall carved chairback. "And since they had both offered, they felt entitled to share the

454

gold—to share the metal, I suppose," she added lamely. She was wishing with all her heart that when O'Rourke had mentioned the word *"matelot"* she had asked him what it meant instead of so blithely assuming its meaning.

"Share metal," he murmured and for a moment she thought his expression was bemused. "So you thought they wanted coins?"

"Yes!"

His face broke into a sardonic grin. "Let me enlighten you, Christabel. Buccaneers know the words for 'money' in any language. They do not speak mysteriously of coin of the realm."

"Then . . . what?" A frightened feeling was creeping over her. Even in this heat she felt a shiver.

"Matelotage is a French word, Christabel, not a Spanish one," he informed her grimly. *"Matelotage* is an old custom among the buccaneers, who have long suffered from a shortage of desirable women. It means to take a wife 'sailor fashion.' Two buccaneers toss a coin as to which one will marry the wench, and the loser goes through with the ceremony."

It rang now in her head, Skull's snorting laugh, *"Ye've lost!"* and O'Rourke's triumphant, *"No, damme, I've won!"* as he pocketed the coin he'd tossed—and all the while his hot green gaze had roved over her lissome body in the low-cut red silk dress she'd worn down to the quay.

She was looking at Kells now, dazed. Dear God, did these buccaneers think she had actually promised to *marry* one of them?

"Tell me, did O'Rourke lose the toss?"

"Skull said he did," she admitted in confusion. "But O'Rourke insisted he'd won."

"I don't doubt O'Rourke felt he'd won," said Kells heavily. "For that meant he would get you first. O'Rourke would go through with the ceremony with you—and as part of the bargain take you to any convenient location you chose. By the way, what place *did* you choose?"

"Havana," she said sulkily.

455

"Havana?" He looked at her in wonder.

"I chose Havana because Lord Thomas is imprisoned there—he must be! And . . . they laughed."

"A Spanish stronghold? I don't doubt they laughed!"

"But they told me there was a small buccaneer settlement nearby on the island of Hispaniola from which Havana could easily be reached—"

"Oh, Havana can easily be reached from there—but did they tell you that this small 'settlement' appears and disappears? It is subject to raids by Spanish ships."

She gave him a bewildered look. "Then they weren't really going to take me to some safe place near Havana?"

"Not as near as you would like!" He returned her gaze coolly. "I see you still do not fully understand, Christabel. When two buccaneers desire the same woman and that woman is willing to accept *matelotage* —as you have declared yourself willing—one will wed her and stay with her for a time whilst the other is at sea. The other buccaneer then returns and takes the husband's place and lives with the bride as if *they* are man and wife—until the husband returns, when they trade places again. The one to whom she is *not* wed is called the *matelot*. It is a custom time-honored among the buccaneers. In this settlement on Hispaniola which you have selected, O'Rourke now believes you will live with him as his wife—a natural assumption since he intends to marry you. And when he feels the call of the sea again, Skull will take his place, move in and live with you until O'Rourke returns. Skull was telling you that he would be your *matelot*—your 'other husband.' And to this you have agreed!"

As the full import of what she had gotten herself into, down on the quay, sank in on her, she thought her knees would buckle. Those two buccaneers thought she had promised to—! She clung to the chairback, staring at him in horror. "Oh, no, I never intended—Rye, I did not understand. I—"

"Call me Kells," he interrupted ruthlessly. "Or we will terminate this conversation."

"Kells, I did not understand what they meant." She was shrinking back as if trying to disappear behind the chair.

A contemptuous expression played over his face. "You did not wait to understand, you did not ask what a *matelot* was! You are hot to depart with O'Rourke or Skull—and they intend to share you!"

"But they cannot!" she cried. And it was Carolina Lightfoot, the reigning Colonial belle, who was speaking, not this other self she had become—Christabel, the Silver Wench of the buccaneers.

"Who is to stop them?" he asked softly.

"Why, you must, of course! You must explain to them that I did not understand!"

"*I* must explain?" He gave her a mocking look. "O'Rourke is a friend of mine, he's a hot-blooded Irishman—as he believes me to be—and a dangerous man with a blade in his hand. Skull is a master of the garotte and some other things too harsh for your tender ears. And you wish *me* to take on this disappointed pair who will believe you duped them? Faith, you've little regard for my life!"

"But *you* must have regard for my honor," she wailed. "For you are a gentleman! You cannot forget that fact."

"I can in these waters," he said grimly. "Here I live the life of a buccaneer, abandoned by God and man."

Her breath came shallowly. Her fingers gripped the chairback and it was hard to keep her voice steady. "You mean—you would not stop them?" she whispered. "Oh, Kells, you would not let them take me?"

A muscle in his hard jawline worked for a moment as his steely gray eyes considered her. She felt she saw doom in their hard glitter, but she could not know the torment within him. *Let them take her? They would have to cut him down first!* Indeed, for her sake he would chop them both down like trees—but she was not to know that, for it would give this arrogant silver wench a power over him that he did not wish her to realize she possessed.

He fought for control and when he spoke at last his answer was cool. It was flung in her face and it struck her like a slap.

"You are saying that you are mine?" His hard gaze swept over her.

"No—no, of course I am not saying that!" Regardless of what had happened last night, she was suddenly terribly conscious of her state of undress, that she was standing here facing him in the tropic night, clad only in her chemise. "I am saying—" She swallowed nervously. "I am saying that you could *pretend* that it is so."

"I will not pretend." The words rang like metal cast upon stones. "If I do this thing, it will be *true in fact* that you prefer my bed to theirs. Make your choice, Christabel. It is to be them—or me. I am telling you that I will deal with this pair on your behalf—but only if you come willingly to my bed."

Her whole world spun round. She was not debauched, not willingly at least—not yet. But soon to be. Kells's face, she thought, looked almost demonic in its intensity as he brutally named his price for saving her.

"After all," he told her in an offhand manner. "Better myself than O'Rourke and Skull. Skull has never known a lady and O'Rourke gets drunk as a skunk every night and has been known to manhandle his."

She was not listening. A tormenting vision rose up in her mind of Lord Thomas with his hands tied, dangling unconscious on the sun-baked deck of a Spanish galleon, and other visions even more frightening—of Lord Thomas locked away from the sun, deep down in a Spanish dungeon in Havana's Morro Castle. Chained, eaten by rats. . . . There was only one way she could save Lord Thomas, she told herself with a surge of rather splendid feeling, and that was to appease this dark buccaneer who stood scowling down at her, determined not only to ravage her young body but to make her come willingly to his arms! If she would save Lord Thomas, she had no choice but to agree to his disgraceful bargain!

She drew a deep shaky breath.

"I will do as you ask," she said faintly.

Around them the stillness was suddenly deafening. It was broken only by the sound of the sea breaking over the beach. The moon, being old and wise in the ways of lovers, with sudden delicacy retired behind a cloud and left them together in scented darkness in that wildest place of all—Tortuga, stronghold of the buccaneers.

Had Carolina not been looking down at the floor at that moment she would have seen an expression of shock pass over Rye Evistock's face. Not for a moment had he believed she would do it. He had only been baiting her, tormenting her for all the sleepless nights she had caused him. He had been paying her back, he realized that now.

And now she had agreed to share his bed. Mixed emotions flooded him, mixed emotions so powerful he was afraid she might see them writ plain upon his face. "Very well," he heard himself say gravely. "I will accept your word on it. Come out from behind that chair, Christabel, that I may see you."

She seemed to drift away from the chair, forlornly, like a child. She did not look up, but gazed instead miserably down at the floor, overcome by a sense of shame.

He might have let her out of her bargain then for he felt a rush of sympathy for her plight, alone and friendless in this barbaric part of the world.

But of a sudden her silver blonde head was lifted and a pair of level eyes shooting silver sparks transfixed him. "I take it," she said bitterly, "that you will not demand your payment now and then go back on your word?"

He flinched as if she had struck him.

"No, I will not go back on my word," he told her almost lightly. "Nor will I demand payment in advance."

You have already had that, she thought resentfully. *Last night! But I was unconscious then—and now you mean to bend me to your will with my eyes wide open!* She averted her head, hating to look at him.

She expected him to turn away, to head for the door.

459

Instead he suddenly stepped forward and pulled her to him, pressed a hungry lingering kiss upon her flinching mouth. His hand strayed down her back as she struggled, tracing the length of her backbone in the thin chemise all the way to her softly rounded buttocks. She struggled against him, gasping, sure he could feel the tumultuous pounding of her heart against his broad chest.

As suddenly as he had pulled her to him, Kells let her go.

"A little something on account," he said dryly.

"Damn you!" Her voice trembled. "You would bargain with my honor!"

"There are those who would bargain without it," he said with a shrug, turning away. "And you would like them even less." At the door he paused and turned to her with a crooked grin. "Take heart," he said softly. "One of these buckos may kill me—and then you will have to pay me no price at all!"

Real terror flared in her eyes at his words. He saw that terror and laughed as he went out, closing the door.

Carolina's fingers did not unclench until she heard the sound of his boots receding down the hall. Then she looked around her at this handsome high-ceilinged room built by Spanish labor, this luxurious corner of the buccaneer's stronghold that had become her prison.

What did her reckless promise make of her? she asked herself—and did not care to answer.

Chapter **33**

The night passed—alone. Kells did not return. Carolina slept fitfully. And woke at last with a restless start to see the sun beaming through her jalousies. But it was only Katje's knock that had waked her, informing her that breakfast was ready.

She breakfasted alone in the spacious stone-floored courtyard. And told herself she was glad to rid herself of his infuriating company. But she found she was lonely and ate little, hardly touching the tasty little pancakes or the blushing mangoes, the papayas and oranges that were piled into a huge earthenware bowl to serve as an edible centerpiece.

The rest of the morning she spent prowling restlessly about the house. She would have wandered out into the cool rustle of the lemon and avocado grove if she could, but she found the front door guarded by a scarred buccaneer who looked at her gravely and silently. Indeed he kept a watchful eye upon her as if he felt she might suddenly dart past him and try to bolt through the door. *Kells must have told him she would try it,* she thought wryly. She strolled out to the hot kitchen but the burly cook, at sight of her, frowned and made a point of going over and bolting the kitchen door which stood open to let out the heat from the cavernous stone fireplace where a great stew was simmering in an iron pot. Carolina took the hint and returned to the courtyard.

There was no use going toward the wing that contained Kells's officers' quarters—even if she managed to penetrate it, it would be full of men in varying stages of undress for there were some still recuperating from their wounds of the other night. And the guest wing where she had slept when she first came here was barricaded and still aswarm with Spanish labor, for in this heat men took a siesta at noon and worked in the cooler morning and late afternoon until dusk closed down.

Afternoon came—a still afternoon with almost no wind. The heat was oppressive. She tried to recline in the hammock stretched between two palms in the courtyard with the rustling palm fronds above her for shade, but it was no good. After a while she jumped up and paced the stones of the courtyard until the hot sun drove her back into the cool dim interior. She went to a window and stood looking down through the open jalousies at the sprawling town below, then turned her troubled gaze toward the massive pile of the mountain fort bristling with stolen Spanish guns that could sweep the channel of blue Cayona Bay.

Panic settled over her as time passed. Why wasn't Kells back? Why did she not hear his firm booted step in the hall? Hear that deep resonant voice speaking to Hawks, settling some household matter with Katje? Every moment increased her foreboding. She could not rest, she paced about as restlessly as a caged tigress. Something *must* have happened to him! Dear God, she would be to blame for that too!

Eventually her anxiety grew so intense that she could not stand it. Unable to find Katje, who seemed to have disappeared forever, she went back to the front door and spoke to the big silent buccaneer who guarded it.

"Can you find Hawks?" she asked. "I must speak to him."

He studied her, then beckoned her toward the passage that led to the officers' quarters. "Hawks!" he bellowed.

Carolina waited what seemed an interminable time and then Hawks appeared.

"Where is Kells?" she demanded.

He thought a while before he answered her. "The captain's gone to settle some personal business in the town."

"I know that! Has he been hurt?"

"Not as I know of," said Hawks cautiously. His puzzled gaze said plainly, *Would you care?*

Carolina flushed before that gaze. She read reproach in it. After all, it had been kindly Hawks she had tricked in her effort to arrange her escape.

"Could you take me walking down into town?" she asked plaintively, hoping that somehow she could still straighten out this mess and no one would be killed.

Hawks gave her a look of total amazement. "No," he said in such a definite tone of rebuke that she made a hasty retreat. Once she looked over her shoulder and saw him glowering after her.

Time dragged by, the shadows lengthened, and the dying sun sent its last long bolts of gold across the sea. The bay shimmered its last hot reflection before dusk settled—and still Kells had not returned.

Had he not been able to find O'Rourke and Skull in town? she wondered. Was he tracking them down, relentlessly combing the twisted streets, alley by alley? She shivered, thinking of the whisper of the cutlass in the night, the sudden plunge of cold steel, the scream. And *she* was the cause of it. Alarmed, growing more tense with each passing moment, Carolina felt dismayed—and then ashamed of her dismay. Surely she was not *anticipating* the lean buccaneer's return!

She walked restlessly in the courtyard, she paused to eat a bite at the table that was set at dusk—but she was too excited to swallow. She went back to her bedroom, determined not to undress, not to seem to be *awaiting* his pleasure! She tried to lie down, to rest, but she could not. She leaped up and continued her pacing. *Where was he?*

And then when the soft black velvet night of the tropics had fallen, when the cool moonlight shimmered upon the dark waters of Cayona Bay and bathed the red tile-roofed town with a magic it never knew by day, she heard at last his step. It was unmistakably his, that ring of boots on the stone floor, for his stride had a certain easy rhythm hard to duplicate. Carolina stopped pacing and stood tense as the boots stopped outside her door and she heard his knock.

"Come in," she whispered—for a bargain was a bargain.

The door opened and Kells stood there. To her frightened gaze he seemed to fill the doorway with his presence. There was blood on the flowing white shirt that fell open to the waist and a wicked look to his dark face.

"What, still dressed?" he said.

"You're wounded," she said, staring fearfully at the bloodstains.

"Oh, this?" He looked down casually at the dry red stain. " 'Tis not my blood. I killed a man for you this day. A man with whom I had no quarrel."

He had killed—! She had clung to the belief that it would not go this far. She had overlooked how quickly violence flared in these men, how lightly they counted human life.

Her throat felt dry and she spoke through stiff lips. "Not—not O'Rourke?" she asked shakily, for she had liked the lean Irishman with the wicked twinkle in his green eyes.

"Skull. When I stated my case, he seemed to acquiesce—and then as I turned to go he tried to garrote me. I took exception."

"And O'Rourke?"

"Stormed out calling me vile names and went somewhere—to get drunk, I presume."

464

"Then—then it's over?" she whispered, hot with shame that, along with guilt, relief should flood her.

"Yes," he said roughly. "It's over—as far as you are concerned. For me, there may yet be a reckoning."

He meant, no doubt, Skull's friends. . . . The whine of a musket ball some day when his back was turned, the whisper of a knife in some dark alley. . . . She felt a shiver of fear go through her.

"I never expected it to end like this," she told him miserably. "Did Skull have a wife? Children?"

He forbore to tell her that Skull had fathered numerous children by rape and had claimed none of them. She was looking so troubled that for a moment he almost weakened. Then his eyes glinted.

"No. But you cannot inflame men like these and expect them not to fight for you," he told her flatly. "And now," he added, "having taken care of the situation, I expect to be rewarded."

He turned and called to Katje, and they had a murmured conversation in Dutch. Then his cold gaze returned to Carolina. "I've ordered us each a bath. To be taken here."

She gave a violent start. "I'll not take a bath with you in the room!" she protested.

"You will," he said grimly, unbuckling his sword belt and flinging it aside. "Skull wasn't much but *I* had no quarrel with him. And Shawn O'Rourke will not soon forgive what he called my 'meddling.' If you want me to cut down those you embroil, you must pay for it!"

There was no mistaking his dangerous mood; it would brook no restraint.

Carolina backed away from him, hoping the water would take a long time to heat. Then she remembered that this was a luxurious household, water was kept hot at all times. One-eyed Jesse, who helped Cook in the kitchen, brought a big container of hot water and emptied it into a metal hip tub that was hastily set down by the soft-eyed island girl who accompanied him. Kells was silent and watchful, keeping his tall form between Carolina and the door while another tub and another container of hot water were brought. He waited until the barefoot island girl had deposited washcloths and big linen towels and scented soap and sponges upon a small table and padded out—then he closed the door.

"Now," he commanded. "Strip."

Watching him with a wary eye, Carolina began to clamber out of her dress. The hooks eluded her nervous fingers and she could hardly get her bodice free. Kells stood leaning against the wall, arms folded, and watched her insolently.

At last the light yellow fabric slid to the floor and she emerged in her chemise. It was daintily sheer and lacy. She felt naked in it, realizing that its almost gossamer thinness revealed the pulsing pink tips of her breasts and every outline of her figure—for the white moonlight beaming in through the open jalousies was as light as day. Kells stood watching her appreciatively. Then, "And now the chemise—unless you mean to bathe in it."

She made no move to take it off, but faced him defiantly.

"Or perhaps," he added evenly, "you would prefer me to rip it from your back?"

"That is what you will have to do," she flashed. "For I will not disrobe for your pleasure!"

"A promise forgot so soon?" he murmured. And before she could more than turn away he had crossed the room and seized her by the wrist.

"A promise dishonorably wrung need not be kept!" she panted.

"Indeed?" He almost smiled but his teeth were clenched, and his grip on her tightened.

She writhed in his grasp but he held her inexorably. The most she was able to manage was to turn about so that her back was to him—and even then her soft hip collided with his hard thigh in an intimate way. With his free hand he now scooped up the flimsy material that comprised the back of her chemise. There was a sharp ripping sound and with a single hard wrench the light garment parted company with her body. He flung the

466

offending chemise away from him and it floated down into a little pile, like foam upon the sea.

Only then did he release her. And now she reeled away from him, clad only in her stockings and shoes.

"Kick off your shoes," he commanded, advancing a step and letting his hand fall upon her bare shoulder.

His hot gaze angered her—he was *enjoying* this! For answer she kicked at him, but it was not a very effective kick for she was half turned away from him in an attempt to shield her slender body from his bold gaze.

His grip on her shoulder tightened and he spun her around to face him. A slow measuring smile spread over his taut features as his hard gaze stroked her up and down. She could feel that gaze like a firm but caressing hand exploring every curve of her tense young body. She felt herself tremble.

"Remove your shoes," he advised her. "Unless of course you wish to get them soaked."

The indifference of his tone nearly drove her to frenzy. Run away from him she would, she promised herself—but not in sodden slippers. Sullenly she kicked off her shoes and the slight effort it took to do that made her soft breasts bounce. His hard gaze took that in too.

"Will you have your stockings pulled off wet or dry?" he asked dispassionately.

She gave him a murderous look but she bent down, ungartered and tore off her stockings. He kept his grip on her meanwhile and stepped lightly aside as she aimed another kick at his shin.

"You'll hurt yourself," he warned her, "if you bang those dainty toes against these jackboots of mine. They were made to withstand a harder blow than you're likely to give!"

It was undoubtedly true but Carolina was past caring. She tried again to kick at him even as she attempted to win free from that vicelike grip on her shoulder.

"If you force me to hold you any tighter, I'll leave prints on your flesh," he observed in a remarkably calm

467

voice, considering that he was, at the moment of speaking, lifting her up by her buttocks with his free hand and depositing his squirming burden in one of the two metal tubs.

Carolina arrived in the tub with a splash that drenched his clothes. He grinned as she sank down into the water, drawing up her knees in an attempt to cover her breasts and hugging those wet knees with her arms even as she glared up at him.

Kells never took his eyes off her as he began to undress. Furious, she sat crouched in the tub with the white moonlight gleaming on her pale hair and silken shoulders, on her shining wet knees. Silver sparks seemed to flash from the dark-lashed eyes that returned his rapt gaze.

He had already removed his flowing white shirt when he turned to shoot the bolt on the door. Her gaze left him then and fled for a moment to linger speculatively on the bolt.

"I'd reach you before you could ever unbolt it," he answered her thoughts laconically, and tossed her a sponge.

She caught the sponge deftly with one hand. But it annoyed her that his gray eyes had brightened as her uplifted arm gave him a sudden glimpse of her bare round breasts. Quickly she tucked the sponge between her knees and her breasts and as a further barrier to his sight, wrapped her arms about her knees. Her gaze now flicked murderously at the big cutlass in its scabbard that he had tossed carelessly to a chair.

"Abandon that thought too," he advised, tossing her a bar of the scented soap. "It's quite heavy, you'd find. And before you could draw this one from its scabbard I'd be taking it away from you. I might even spank your bare bottom with the flat of it if you were so foolish as to try it!"

But not if he had soap in his eyes! she thought. *That* would give her a few precious moments to seize her clothes, unbolt the door, dash through the empty courtyard, break through that temporary barricade set up by the Spanish workmen who were repairing the guest wing—and she would be out into the night! The wall into which the green door was set would not deter her, for there was such a pile of stones and tiles that she could clamber over. It would be noisy but what would noise matter then? Once she had gained the lemon grove she could find a patch of moonlight and dress and be gone before the buccaneers could sort themselves out enough to follow her and search the grove. And in the town there were honest traders, captains who *weren't* buccaneers and whose ships were anchored in Cayona Bay. She had only to reach one of them, to explain her plight! So she reasoned. . . .

So now she took the soap—which she'd been about to throw back at him—and lathered the wet sponge, began sulkily to wash her smooth white shoulders with it.

Appreciatively Kells watched her bathe as he tugged off his boots and then—she averted her gaze in embarrassment—his trousers. He was quite immodest, she thought resentfully, as he strode over to open another window and let in the sea breeze that had picked up and now rippled the tendrils of her hair. Lord Thomas had *never* let her see him naked. Indeed he had been quite adroit about it, while Kells seemed simply not to care. That Lord Thomas's adroitness might have come from long practice with easily frightened maidens had quite escaped her—even as had the cool masculine indifference to nudity of a dominant male about to take his woman in his arms. Lord Thomas had been amusing himself with a succession of women. The lean buccaneer—although Carolina did not know it—was this night taking a mate. A woman who would be his until the end of time.

None of that reached her as she felt the warm water curling up around her bottom, swishing gently against her private parts, rippling the soft golden triangle of hair at the base of her hips.

Out of the corner of her eye Carolina watched Kells take his bath in swift businesslike fashion—a quick soaping, a quick rinse, whistling all the while. And then he stood up, a magnificent figure, handsomely muscled,

469

gleaming and wet. Careless that she was watching, he toweled himself dry, stepped out of the tub, bent to dry his calves and feet, tossed away the damp towel and strode toward her.

"I'll wash your back," he offered and bent over in what was meant to be a friendly fashion.

For answer she rose with a screech and dashed the heavily soaped sponge into his astonished face. She had hoped to get enough soap into his eyes temporarily to blind him. But the reflexes of this man accustomed to instant combat that could overtake him anywhere—in a dark alley, on a sunlit street—were too fast for her. His eyes had snapped shut before the soapy sponge splattered against his face, and he was dashing the soapy water from his eyelids even as Carolina sprang from the tub.

He caught her long before she made the door and held her fast, looking down at her with a boyish excited light in his gray eyes.

"What, finished bathing?" he mocked.

Carolina gave him a murderous look but deigned no reply.

"Then shall we towel us both dry? Or perhaps a rinse first?" He seized a pitcher of rinse water and poured it over his face to remove the soap. Then deliberately he held her at arm's length and poured water over her breasts and back, careless that it ran down upon the floor.

She flinched as the cool rinse water poured down over her soft breasts, over their summits, down the valley between them, making the pale pink nipples come alive and harden.

"You're getting water over everything," she protested as her foot slipped.

"So I am," he said absently, his eyes never leaving those inviting twin peaks that seemed to wink at him as she tried to shrug her body away from him. "But then 'tis my house and this floor is my floor and I can dash water upon it if I choose." Still holding onto her, he set the pitcher down and took up a large towel. "Hold still," he instructed.

But she did not choose to hold still. She fought him as he tried to dry her wet back and hips and stomach. She clawed at him, enraged, as he essayed to dry her thighs—and that interesting space between them.

"Stop!" she cried, striking at his hand, and he gave her a heated look that was an answer in itself. He seemed to enjoy her struggles, she thought bitterly.

But she was tiring from her efforts at trying to fend him off. After all it had been a long day, fraught with anxiety. It was still very hot and she was not only tired but very distraught. And something else drove her—she thought it was animosity for this arrogant fellow so bent on bending her slim body to his will, but it was more than that. With every touch of his competent fingers she felt weakened. She felt as if she were being driven onward by some irresistible force, and that no matter how she struggled she would be pinned like a butterfly before his will.

Abruptly she ceased to flutter.

"What, dry enough?" he asked genially, and tossed the towel away.

With its removal, once again naked before his sight, she quivered again.

"Let me go, Rye," she said tremulously.

"Rye no longer," he told her. "In this part of the world I'm Kells the Buccaneer, remember? I'm a man with taking ways and faith, I'll act the part!"

"No," she panted, putting both her palms flat against his chest and pushing against him. "Don't do this, Kells, you'll regret it."

"Will I?" he asked hoarsely, for the soft pressure of her delicate hands upon his chest had fired him even more. "Then I'll regret it in the morning instead of tonight! I'm holding you to your promise—Christabel!"

Christabel . . . He had called her by that other alien name, that name she had taken for her sea venture, a name that had seemed to have no connection with her at all. Suddenly she crumpled—it was as if being called by that other name had set her free. She was not Carolina Lightfoot any longer—Carolina Lightfoot would have fought to the death to save her honor. She

471

had become Christabel Willing, a woman who had but one goal in life—to save her imprisoned lover! She would give this lean buccaneer what he wanted—the pressure of her silken body against his own, the melting softness of her lips and thighs, the sweet crushing of her breasts—yes, even though she shrank from it, she would do it.

For hers was a high purpose: She must save Lord Thomas!

Kells felt this instant change in her. He looked down at her, puzzled, then leaned over to peer into her face below the silver blonde hair that had come loose from its pins and cascaded down, catching the moonlight. "You have changed your mind?" he asked softly. "I am not such a blackguard after all?"

"You *are* a blackguard," she said in a voice that trembled. "But"—her arms stole round his neck and her body twisted against his in a way that made his flesh ripple—"I desire you."

There, the lying words were spoken! The words that would transform him from an opponent into an ally. He could not refuse to help her now!

She desired him. From her own lips he had heard it! Any hesitancy he might have felt at taking to his bed a reluctant woman was flung away on the instant. He swept her up and carried her triumphantly to the bed.

"Wait," she whispered. "I have but one favor to ask of you—and you must grant it. Lord Thomas is imprisoned in Havana and I would have you secure his release."

His muscles jerked as if he had received a savage blow. So this was what the wench wanted, this was the price of her acquiescence—to have Lord Thomas back again! Such a flood of disappointment and anger and frustration engulfed him that his voice was thick and savage as he flung her upon the bed.

"You've made me one bargain, wench," he rasped. "I'll not be cozened into making another!"

And with that he took her. It was as if devils were driving him. He had forgotten for the moment how young she was. He had forgotten that she was a virgin—and then was astonished and somehow hurt to find that she was not. Overwhelmed by his own frustration, rage—and grief that she did not truly desire him—he drove straight and true within her and felt her soft shudder as she tried now to resist, to ward him off.

And then with a convulsive shudder—for she was in his arms at last, her female softness pressed against his hard loins—he relaxed and took her more gently. He began to make love to her then, exciting her, tempting her. He moved within her rhythmically, luxuriously. She lay tense beneath him, fighting against the powerful sensations that roused her, lured her, lulled her as he played delicately with her body. He bent his dark head and his thick dark hair spilled in a shining mass over her white skin in the moonlight as he nuzzled her breasts, tickling her pink nipples to flaming life with his tongue.

She trembled beneath him, trying to fight back the warm feelings that were flooding over her in an irresistible tide. She told herself desperately that it was only because it had been such a long time, that she was not responding to him but to her own urges. She told herself, even as her senses swayed and righted and swayed again, that it was the tropic night and the scent of strange exotic blossoms that drifted on the trade winds, that it was the glitter of the stars against a black velvet sky that produced this magic. She told herself it was the aura of danger that surrounded this man, his fascinating reputation—and the fact that she knew his secret, knew that, renegade though he was, he was still a gentleman born and bred and that . . . sometimes, as he had done last Christmastide, he returned to that life. But all the while her passion was flowering as little waves of excitement danced and crested within her. Her heart thumped so wildly that she was sure that he must hear it. She tried to resist but she could feel the sudden unbidden ripple of her stomach muscles, the fiery involuntary tremors of her inner body responding —indeed her whole slender frame seemed to vibrate softly as he did wondrous things with his lips and fingers.

And then she gave up the unequal struggle and sagged beneath him, let her arms twine around his neck, and with a little moan low in her throat surrendered herself to joy.

Kells was not the man to miss such a signal of surrender. More confident now and feeling a kind of bittersweet triumph that at least he could have her body if not her heart, he gathered this loved woman to him and increased the pace of his lovemaking. He was infinitely clever now, thinking ever of her enjoyment, driving her to sobbing bursts of passion when her nails dug into his heavily muscled back, so fervent was her grip. He lifted his dark head to watch her face in the moonlight, and though her eyes were closed with their fringe of dark lashes resting against the peachbloom sheerness of her cheeks, he saw her smile despite herself, heard the little gurgling laugh that caught in her throat as he tickled her almost to madness.

But this buildup of shared caresses had taken its toll on him and now, thoroughly aroused, with his hot blood throbbing a drumbeat in his head, he held her tighter and took her with him on a dizzy climb to passion and beyond, into deep driving moments of white hot ecstasy that made them seem alone and triumphant in a lost and beautiful world past all mortal enduring, bright scalding moments that would leave footprints across their memories, trackless ecstatic moments that lifted them up and seemed to have no end. . . .

It was with a soft lingering sigh that Carolina came down from that lofty ledge of bliss on which she had been poised, drifted down from it in total exhaustion, spent in mind and body. Drained by the fires of strong emotion, unwilling to face whatever lay ahead, she fell away from him like a tired child and—as if to hide her troubled emotions from him—she threw an arm across her face and bent her body away from him in the bed.

She did not see him rise on an elbow and study her tenderly, although she did flinch as he gently brushed away a wandering tendril of fair hair that clung to her hot cheek in the moonlight. Had her arm not been

clasped tightly over her eyes, she would have been
amazed at the softness of the lean buccaneer's expression and how boyishly young it made him look.

Ever since he had first met her he had been haunted
by the thought of that wondrous body pressed to his,
close enough to feel the beating of her heart. The silken
way he had imagined her smooth skin beneath her
chemise, all her enchanting feminine secrets were even
lovelier in reality. She seemed to him a creature of
wondrous design, endlessly fascinating, abrim with
delights to be tasted with every touch, every sigh—
heady wine indeed. . . .

And—her body desired him, if not her soul. At least,
there was some comfort in that to a man who loved her
passionately and without reserve.

Now in the moonlight he forced himself to consider
her critically. Her beauty was wonderful, challenging, it
overwhelmed him. But in his heart he knew that it was
not her winsome face, not her thick gleaming silver
blonde hair, not her dainty alluring figure that attracted
him so much as something else.

Being with her was like being on the leading edge of a
storm. From the first he had felt excitement race
through his veins at the very sight of her. Every sense
seemed to come alive, his whole body grew taut and
strained with desire every time she walked toward him.
Her every graceful gesture seemed to him a marvel, her
every slanted look held a deeper meaning. He had been
tormented with dreams of her that woke him sweating
and unsatisfied in the night, and even by day, out
careening his ship, he had found himself falling into a
reverie that brought her lovely face tauntingly up
before him.

And there was more to it: He had divined in her the
hurt child, although he did not know just what it was
that had hurt her. Something left over from her childhood perhaps, some deep scar that had never quite
healed over. Someday she would tell him about it,
someday . . . For surely what he had felt in her just
now was more than a mere physical response to an
experienced lover. Surely that wild passion with which

she had returned his every kiss, his every caress, lay somewhere along the shallow shoals of love, if not the deeps. . . .

Certain she had fallen asleep, he bent down and pressed the lightest of kisses upon the soft bare nipple of the rounded breast nearest him.

But Carolina was not asleep. She was lying there with her spirit cringing at what she had just done.

It would have been one thing to have faked a response, to make him believe she cared—so that he would help Thomas. Her conscience could have endured that. But her response to this buccaneer had been as overwhelming as it was unpredictable. By its very violence it had shaken her—and made her afraid of what she might do in the future. She felt as if her body was a battlefield and it had been overrun and plundered.

Now, bitterly, the realization of how treacherous she had been washed over her in a great wave. It was to Thomas that she owed her loyalty! And she was overcome with hot shame by her wild response to this man who had taken her against her will, driven her into his arms by his unfair bargain!

"Go away!" she gasped, striking his face away from her breast. "You have no right here!" She was voicing a revulsion of feeling against her own infidelity, flaying herself—but she did not realize it.

Her words struck Kells like a sword thrust, and gashed not only his vanity—for she had seemed indeed to respond to his lovemaking—but his heart that ached for her to return his love. The wound was sudden and deep and he wanted to strike back.

"No right," he murmured. "But then I take it I was not the first?" he said ironically.

She sat up violently. "No—did you expect to be?" she cried.

She had said it rudely, before she thought, and was oddly surprised that he flinched. In truth he *had* expected to be the first.

"Lord Thomas?" he murmured and at her vengeful nod, "I might have known. First in love, first in

476

war—you told me he was a redoubtable duellist, did you not?" His face darkened. "Would you like me to find him, to pluck him from his 'prison' and show you what kind of duellist he is? Would you?"

"I would like for you to rescue him!" she shouted. "Is that so much to ask?" And she turned her angry face away.

He stood up, studying her. "Perhaps it is. . . ." he said. "In any event, you can sleep on it." He had reached the door, swooping down and picking up sword and clothing as he went, and his parting shot held an edge of bitterness. "I promise you will not be disturbed further this night, mistress," he said grimly and went out, shutting the door firmly behind him.

Carolina lay there tingling and trembling, her mind wavering resentfully between what was pleasurable and what was right. Her teeth nearly met through her soft lower lip as she thought of how fully she had enjoyed having her body plundered by this buccaneer—and how well he must know it!

But, she told herself quickly, it was all in a good cause—the best of all causes: Setting Thomas free! For she would make Kells do this for her—*she would make him do it!*

Still her mind was roiling so that dawn had pinked the sky over Cayona Bay before she got to sleep.

Chapter 34

The sun was high when Carolina's door burst open. She, who had not slept much, sat up to face a man who had not slept at all. He had sat alone in the courtyard drinking moodily, listening to the night birds' cries and the sighing of the palms, feeling his resentment building as the trade winds blew upon his scowling face.

"Get up!" he commanded. "Up!" He went over and seized the light coverlet, tore it from her indignant grasp. "Dress!" His voice was a little slurred, his eyes bloodshot. Carolina retreated from him in fear, easing her back up against the headboard.

He turned away from her, reeled a little unsteadily toward the tall wardrobe where her elegant dresses were hanging. "Wear this." He flung toward her the scarlet dress she had worn to the quay. "Wear every damn thing you wore when you plotted with O'Rourke and Skull to leave me!"

And when still she did not move, but sat there paralyzed, watching him, he strode to the bed, seized her and spun her out onto the floor, held upright only by his steadying arm.

"Katje!" he roared. "Katje!" And when Katje appeared, he loosed such a torrent of Dutch that the girl, her usually calm face showing alarm, went into violent action. She helped Carolina in such disastrous haste that the first pair of stockings to be slid over her legs were ripped—they had to be discarded and new ones found. Carolina's feet were summarily jammed into her black satin slippers with the high red heels, and the black chemise dropped over her head.

Kells thrust his face into hers—just a breath away and smelling strongly of spirits.

"I have killed enough men for you," he said thickly. "Men who doubted you were really mine. Today I will prove to all Tortuga whose woman you are! You will walk on my arm and smile and bow pleasantly to those who speak to us. You will turn to me and ask my opinion, you will lean toward me—by God, you will show everyone on this cursed island once and for all to whom you belong!"

Carolina, who had just gartered the newfound pair of black silk stockings and who had just had the sheer black lacy chemise pulled summarily over her head by an anxious Katje, gave him a baleful look.

"I will not do it!" she cried. "I will not be put on display like a pet Pomeranian dog for your pleasure!" She pushed away the glittering black and silver petticoat that Katje held out. "Nor will I wear these clothes!" she added hotly.

He leaned toward her with a wolfish expression. He was a little unsteady on his feet but somehow it made him all the more menacing. His bloodshot gaze was fixed on her with what she thought was a murderous light.

"If you are not dressed in five minutes," he warned her, "I swear before God that I will parade you through Tortuga dressed as you are—in your chemise!"

Carolina recoiled from him and grew a shade paler. He would do it, she knew he would! Oh, that she should be the prisoner of such a man! He would not hesitate to shame her! In sudden desperation she lunged for the petticoat which Katje quickly tied about her and then held out her arms in angry silence so that Katje could slip the vivid red silk dress over her head. Dressed at last, she gave him a resentful look and hitched up the neckline of her low-cut silver-edged bodice.

"I prefer it worn low," he said through his teeth. "The way all Tortuga remembers!" He reached out and gave the low-cut neckline a jerk downward that stopped just short of ripping the fabric. The tops of her white breasts gleamed pearly white—even as they had when she had worn this dress down to the quay—and a slow flush spread over her face.

"My hair," she cried, when he would have taken her arm. "I have not combed it! And my parasol—in this sun, I will need my parasol."

"I prefer your hair streaming down," he said coldly. "It makes you look as if you have just been tussling with me between the sheets, and that is exactly the impression I wish to convey."

Her flush deepened. "You were never a gentleman," she said bitterly. "How wrong I was to think you were!"

"Wrong indeed." He gave her a tipsy bow. "But now your vision is righted, you see me more clearly? Will you precede me, mistress, or must I drag you along?"

She lifted her dainty chin. In courage she was not lacking. Head held haughtily high, she swept from the room. Behind her Kells snapped his fingers. "Katje, the parasol," he said in Dutch and Katje whirled around to bring it.

Hawks was standing guard at the door. "You are taking her into the town?" he demanded in wonder.

"Aye," said Kells grimly. "I want all Tortuga to view my prize!" His long body came to a rocking halt. "Wait—keep her here, Hawks. If she tries to bolt, bring her down." He stalked away, leaving Carolina seething and Hawks looking alarmed, and when he returned she saw with shock that he was wearing a red band tied around his head and was sporting a single gold earring.

"This is how you told me I should look, I believe," he said, leering at her. "So I'd be recognized for what I am, was the implication, I believe."

Both Carolina and Hawks looked taken aback. In his loose flowing white shirt open to the waist, with a pistol stuck into his belt and the big cutlass slapping against his leathern trousers, he did indeed look like what all the world knew him to be—a buccaneer chieftain, armed and dangerous.

Hawks shook his head. He called to someone to take his place at the door, loosened his cutlass warily in its scabbard—for who knew what a stroll into the town would bring!—and trailed after them in wonder, keeping some distance behind. Hawks had known Rye Evistock since his boyhood in Essex, he had followed him to this godforsaken island and watched his transformation into the feared buccaneer captain whose name rang throughout the Caribbean—Kells. For himself Hawks had chosen not to become "Irish" for he never could master the brogue or remember the names of Irish towns, but his loyalty to Kells was such that he would have let his throat be slit before he would have revealed Kells's true origin, that he was an English gentleman—something anyone would have found hard to believe could they have seen him at that moment swaggering down the white coral rock path with a reluctant Carolina, in her scarlet silk dress and twirling her parasol, clinging perforce to his arm.

They were a handsome pair—but not to Hawks.

"Many a foolish thing I've seen ye do, lad," he murmured to himself. "But none more foolish than to lose your heart to this slip of a wench who won't have you!"

Kells walked more steadily now and his grip on Carolina's arm was less punishing. The fresh breeze that swept in from the ocean was clearing his head. By the time they had cleared the grove of dark waxy-leaved trees in their descent into the town, his step was as crisp as ever, his eye as keen.

Beside him, stiffly erect, walked Carolina. *No*, she told herself bitterly, *it was Christabel who walked*

*beside the lean buccaneer captain—Carolina had been
lost somewhere, perhaps never to be found.*

It was early but already the quay was alive with
traders. Indeed the quay was busier at this time of day,
before the burning sun made walking on the hot sand
and pitiless white coral rock almost unbearable.

Unwavering, Kells walked her through the crowd,
nodding occasionally to those he knew. Curious stares
followed them everywhere. Sometimes scarred men
sporting cutlasses sidled closer to get a better look at
the disheveled beauty in scarlet strolling beside her
buccaneer.

Twice Carolina would have turned back, but the
pressure of his left arm that held her right arm pinioned
to his side carried her irresistibly forward.

"You are holding me too tight, Kells—you are
hurting me," she said under her breath.

"Then cease to struggle," he muttered and immediately nodded to a passing trader from Holland.
"Smile!" he said beneath his breath.

Dead center of the quay there was a little knot of
men, and in that group Carolina could see O'Rourke.
The sun was shining on his coppery hair and he looked
very dissolute in the penetrating rays of sunlight that
dazzled the eyes and glittered upon the blue-green
waters of the bay.

"You are not—you are not going to speak to *him?*"
she gasped.

"I am," he told her grimly. "It seems he has made
your acquaintance. You should not ignore a friend!"

She ignored that taunt and, color high, twirled her
parasol arrogantly as he dragged her along. She could
hardly keep up with his long booted stride.

They came to a halt directly before O'Rourke, from
whom the others seemed to fall away as if they expected
cutlasses to be drawn.

"Shawn," drawled Kells. "A good morning to you."

"A good morning to you," said O'Rourke warily. He
had been sitting on a keg but now he came to his feet.

"I believe you've met O'Rourke here, Christabel."

"Yes," Carolina admitted in a stifled voice. "We have met."

"Mistress Christabel." O'Rourke swept her a low bow. There was a tinge of regret in the green gaze that passed over her as he rose from that bow.

"Mistress Christabel is about to take a sea voyage with me," Kells told O'Rourke.

"Is she indeed?" murmured O'Rourke. He was regarding Kells from narrowed green eyes. "I thought it was Havana she wished to visit," he added with a trace of humor.

"Mistress Christabel has changed her mind," Kells told him. "She no longer yearns for Havana. She wishes to accompany me wherever I go. Is that not true, Christabel?"

Carolina yearned to kick him. But his grip on her arm was crushingly tight—tight enough that he could swoop her up in a moment and carry her away with her feet dangling. She preferred to avoid the ultimate humiliation of such a moment, which she could all too easily bring on herself. "Yes," she agreed in a choked voice. "It is true."

O'Rourke studied her silently. He would never understand women.

"We will bid you good morning, Shawn." Kells swung Carolina around and walked her away to O'Rourke's growled, "Bid ye good morning."

But Kells was not done with her yet. To a pile of dress lengths of shimmering silk he led her—silk that had come from the Philippines on Spanish galleons, been transported overland across Mexico, loaded again onto other galleons and snatched from them at gunpoint by buccaneers roving the Florida straits. Silk from the Orient that now lay ready for bartering on the quay of Tortuga.

Carolina thought he wanted her to select a length of silk—as further proof to the quayside crowd that he owned her. But he had something worse in mind than that. Beside the pile of silks lay another pile—of women's clothing, garnered from captured ships carrying buttons and buckles and leather flasks and kegs of gunpowder to Spain's colonies in the New World. And atop that pile of women's clothing lay several chemises, sheer and black, meant for some Spanish beauty in Lima or Cartagena.

To her dismay, he stopped beside the chemises and held up one to the light, studying its flimsiness. "Oh, no," she whispered, as very deliberately, he turned her about and measured its width against her shoulders.

"It seems about the right size," he told her in a cheerful carrying voice. And then he bought it, counting out the coins with deliberate slowness while Carolina looked down, sure that her face must be as scarlet as her gown.

"Stuff it in your pocket," she whispered, certain that everyone was looking at them and chuckling inwardly. "Or here—let me tuck it into the pannier of my gown."

"No need," he said carelessly. "'Tis a light burden. And now I think we have done with shopping for the day."

Firmly he took her arm again and marched her away, with Hawks trailing along behind, still marveling at his folly. Kells's step was jaunty as he led his Silver Wench back through the town—she on one arm, the lacy black chemise billowing sheer over his other arm.

He could not more firmly have declared her his woman had he shouted it from the housetops.

Carolina, dragged along beside him, told herself she hated him.

"Are you done with me?" she panted, when at last they reached the house.

"Yes." He gave her a bleak look. "I have done with you for the time being." And he strode away from her to hurl himself upon his bed and sleep the clock around.

She did not see him at supper, and although she started awake nervously at every sound, he did not visit her bed that night.

She awoke from an uneasy sleep to find him fully dressed and standing with his back to her, staring out the window at a green chameleon with a pink throat that peered back at him timidly over the giant blossoms of a red bougainvillea.

"Why are you here?" she cried, aware that it must be morning and that Katje had not chosen to wake her up. "Am I to have no privacy?" Her voice was laced with resentment for she had returned from her humiliating walk along the quay yesterday to discover that someone —undoubtedly on captain's orders—had removed the bolt from inside her door.

He turned toward her then. She saw that he was clean shaven and that his hair was carefully combed. His white shirt was spotless—for all that it was tucked into a wide leather belt that sported a cutlass.

"I behaved very badly yesterday," he said tersely. "You have every right to scorn me."

"I am surprised that you would have second thoughts," she said on a bitter note. "First you took me when I had had too much to drink. Then—"

He gave her a tormented look. "There was no such taking," he interrupted. "I never touched you—not then. It was Katje who put you to bed."

"But then why lead me to believe—?"

"That I took you then?" He sighed. "There was something in your manner that goaded me. Faith, you drive a man to excesses! You were so ready to believe the worst of me that I let you think what you wished. Had I known where your belief would lead you, I would have disillusioned you then and there as to my character, which had been rather good up to then, where you were concerned."

"But all that has changed now," she pointed out spitefully.

"Yes." He looked weary. "All that has changed. When you began conniving with O'Rourke and Skull, you drove me too far and I determined that since you had given me the name, I would have the game as well. It does little good to say that I am sorry."

"No good at all," she scoffed.

"I feared you would think so."

"Well, what else could I think?" she burst out. "You keep me here, locked up—oh, I realize that I am

485

allowed to stroll about the town under guard, but what kind of a life is that?"

"A safe one where Tortuga is concerned," he said bleakly.

"It is one I do not choose!" She tossed her head. "And now I suppose you will double my guard?"

He gave her a lingering look. Her lower lip was thrust out, her hair was an unruly mass of silver-gold that tumbled down over her bare white shoulders, her gray eyes snapped rebelliously. She was so beautiful it hurt to look at her. He averted his eyes.

"No," he said. "I will not double your guard."

"Indeed?" Hope sprang into her voice for she had escaped Hawks once, and she could do so again!

"There will be no need to double your guard," he told her tersely. "For you will no longer leave this house except in my company." He gave her a twisted smile. "I have already killed too many men in your behalf, Christabel. Would you have me decimate the entire male population of the island?"

She ignored his levity. "You mean Hawks will not—"

"You are too much for Hawks. You might get him killed. In future you will remain at home unless I accompany you."

He was walking toward the door as he said it, and her fury caught him midway.

"Oh, damn you, damn you!" She choked. "You would keep me here for your pleasure!" She reached down to snatch up a shoe from beside the bed and fling it at him.

The shoe bounced harmlessly off his broad shoulder. He did not seem to feel it. He was not looking at her but at some distant vista, endless and empty.

"You have no need to damn me," he muttered as he strode toward the door. "I was already damned before you met me. But as for your virtue, Mistress Christabel"—he turned and gave her a straight look—"henceforth it will not be assailed by me." Bitterness tinged his attractive voice. "I prefer willing women."

Her other shoe hit the door as he left.

Chapter 35

That exchange marked a change in Carolina's relationship with the lean buccaneer. True to his word, he came not to her room by night. She slept alone, tossing and turning, hating herself for missing him, mourning her lost virtue, yearning for Lord Thomas and a relationship that she could understand—not the sword-edge relationship she shared with the strange complex man whose captive she was.

Kells was very busy these days, outfitting the *Sea Wolf* to prowl the sea lanes again and harry Spanish shipping. The refitting of the *Valeroso* was now completed and she had been renamed the *Sea Shark,* but now it was the *Sea Wolf*'s turn. The lean gray ship was being careened down by Cutlass Point and Kells went there every day, supervising the removal of the barnacles and the calking and greasing of the hull, for a sleek hull made for speed—and speed was his ally.

But behind the whitewashed walls of his lair on Tortuga, the "Irish" buccaneer underwent a sea change —he became for the space of a few hours an English gentleman again. And when the sun went down on his red tile roof, when the green shutters were changed by the last rays of the western sun into a greenish gold that darkened, just as the waxy leaves of the nearby lemon trees darkened into the deep silver green of the tropical night, the world that lay behind the elaborate wrought iron entrance to his courtyard was an English world, moving to the dignified pace he had known as a youth in Essex.

"A buccaneer with a butler!" Carolina had scoffed, for Katje had announced one day with blushing cheeks that she intended to marry Lars sometime next month and Kells had pressed one of the buccaneers from Essex into taking charge of the house.

Kells smiled at her. "After the rattle of cutlasses, I find it relaxes me. Will you not take a seat at my table and dine with me?"

They were, as usual with them now, facing each other in the "English" dining room.

Kells had changed to the sober gray broadcloth which he had been wearing when she first met him, and it was Rye Evistock, gentleman of Essex, who pulled out her chair with courtly grace and smiled at her across his table as the food was brought.

They had struck up a truce, these two. He came home to her now with news of the Colonies, news of England, gathered from the sea captains who prowled the quay. And she, bored with her inactivity—and having read half a dozen times *The Nunnery of Coquettes* and *Harriot, or the Innocent Adulteress* and all the other novels Kells occasionally thought to bring her from the quay—tossed her books aside and took to supervising Cook, who, after a first skirmish, now accepted her domination with tranquillity and served up dishes that would tempt even a Williamsburg palate.

"This duck is very good," Kells remarked, savoring it.

"We prepare it so on the Eastern Shore," she told him absently.

"You live well on the Eastern Shore," he smiled.

"Yes," she agreed, but there was a tinge of sadness in her voice. For it was a shore she would never see again, she felt. She had always been an embarrassment there, although she had not understood why. The girl with the wrong father. . . .

One night she told Kells about it, and found him a surprisingly good listener. "Any man should be proud to claim you as a daughter," he told her with more vehemence than he cared to show.

"Not *any* man." Her voice caught. "Fielding Lightfoot did not feel so. You see, I was to him a reminder of his shame."

He studied her with heartfelt sympathy. *This* was the scar he had guessed at, the one that had marred her childhood. His heart went out to her—and it grieved him that his was not the heart she wanted.

"It is as well that I have lost myself somewhere far from Virginia," she told him frankly. "Best all around."

How many times he had thought the same thing—about himself! He lifted his glass to her and their eyes met above the ruby liquid flashing in the goblets. Hers were damp with unshed tears. He wanted to embrace her, to comfort her, to tell her that nothing that had happened to her before mattered now or would ever matter.

He did not.

"I drink to your eyebrows, Mistress Christabel," was all he said, and they drifted back into the gossip he had heard along the quay that day.

These were the good times, the close times, the times when they shared a common bond and felt they shared a common fate, the times that brought them close, that might even one day make them lovers again.

But there were other times as well—times when they clashed.

"I suppose that now that you have worked your will on me, you imagine that I will still keep your true identity a secret?" She shot the words at him one day when she had been brooding long over Lord Thomas and what might have happened to him.

"No," he said quietly, studying her across the long board of the dining room. "I do not suppose it."

She laughed. She wanted to strike at him. "You are right not to suppose it! Unless—Kells, you *owe* it to me to let me go!" she burst out. "If you let me go, if you will send me to England, I promise that I will never reveal to anyone who you are."

Did she notice a sudden ripple in those broad shoulders beneath the gray broadcloth? His voice, when he spoke, sounded strained.

"I cannot do that, Christabel." It jarred her now that he called her by that name, for it somehow kept up this farce of a buccaneer and his wench when they were really something quite different. "I cannot let you leave."

"Why not," she cried, "if you have my word?"

"For myself I could trust your word," he said wearily, running his long fingers through his dark hair. "But there are others here who came to this calling at my behest. Like me, they sail these seas incognito. If *my* identity is discovered, Essex might be looked at more closely, and they could be found out too—traced through my friendship with them. And then they could never return home."

Those other men who had trusted him, given him their loyalty—some of them, like Hawks, from his father's estate in Essex, others from neighboring estates—these were the English contingent, and sometimes one or the other of them joined them at table. These were men going about under false names just as their ships flew false colors, pretending to be Irish when they were indeed English—as English as Rye himself.

This was the stumbling block, these men with ties back in England, men to whom he owed an allegiance that far preceded her entry upon the scene.

Her voice sounded dull to her own ears, deadened, hopeless. "So you will not let me go?"

"No." There was a ruthless certainty in the way he said it. "I will not let you go."

"Then I am to be forever confined, a prisoner?" she burst out despairingly. "Shut up as if I had committed some great crime? *You* are the buccaneer but *I* am to suffer the punishment? Faith, that's justice!"

"They hang buccaneers," he told her in a noncommittal tone. "There's a difference between your rather luxurious confinement and a damp jail cell with rats gnawing at the toes of your boots!"

"I wish they *would* hang you," she mumbled, and for a single wild moment of frustration she almost meant it. Her voice when she spoke again was colored by grief. "Then I am not to be allowed out? Ever?"

His face showed the strain of the warring forces within him. Almost he relented. Almost. . . . Then his jaw hardened. There were others besides himself to think of, and Carolina had proved herself to be rash.

"I will take you walking tomorrow," he promised shortly. "You may wish to buy some things along the quay."

"You will flaunt me as your doxy!" she cried, rising from her chair.

"That too," he said with a sigh.

"You are a devil!" she cried, and ran from the room sobbing.

It was one of their worse nights, he told himself gloomily after she had gone, and he fixed his mind on going to sea again. Perhaps he would get himself killed and solve all this—for he had instructed Hawks and the others of the English contingent that should anything happen to him, Mistress Christabel was to be sent to London with a letter to his London agent, who would provide for her handsomely. Now, left alone in that room that reminded him so bitterly of home and all that he would never know again, he pondered his fate. Better far to get killed, better to be out of it than to have his lacerated feelings rubbed raw every day by a woman who held his heart in keeping, but who would never love him.

Carolina was still angry the next night, for it had been a bad day. Cook had overturned the great stew Carolina had been at such pains to supervise preparing and they must needs eat fish again. The girl who was ironing her favorite gown had turned from her work when a lizard had scurried through the iron grillwork and run beneath her feet—and the iron had burnt a shield-shaped hole in the fabric. It had rained last night after midnight and somewhere the red tile roof had leaked—its slow drip-drip had kept her awake. And to top it all, Hawks had asked her to give Kells a message that properly aged water casks had been found and were ready to be filled for the voyage—which meant of course that the *Sea Wolf* would soon be sailing and she would be left here, trapped in this supposed paradise like a bird in a cage!

He knew she was ready for him when he sat down to dinner, for her silver eyes were shooting sparks. She was wearing one of the many dresses which he had showered on her—this one of pale blue Oriental silk with a whisper of lace at the elbows and a cluster of brilliants marking the cleavage of her bosom.

"Excellent fish," he commended her, and added appreciatively, "Pale blue becomes you."

"I did not cook it," she said woodenly, ignoring his comment on her gown.

"Nor did you catch it or clean it," he elaborated for her. "Still it is excellent fish."

She gave him a withering look. "I am delighted that you like it," she said, sounding not at all delighted. "I take it you will be sailing soon?"

"Yes," he said moodily. "Soon."

"You intend to sail away and keep me locked up here?"

"So we are back to that again," he said.

Her silver glance narrowed. She leaned toward him. "I wonder what your men—those who do not come from Essex, that mixed bag of buccaneers of many nations who follow you—would say if they were to learn that you are not an Irish rover turned buccaneer at all but an English gentleman late of Essex?" she purred.

The dark face into which she gazed hardened perceptibly. "To begin with, they would not believe you," he drawled (and she had learned to her sorrow that when his voice drifted into a drawl he was at his most obdurate). "For there are many here who would swear they have known me in Ireland."

492

Some madness drove her on. "Your English followers would say that, of course. But if *that* were somehow exploded? What then?"

His gray eyes were cold but his hard smile deepened. "Then you would learn another 'truth' about me," he said flippantly. "You would learn that I am a renegade Spaniard, sentenced to death for heresy but my sentence mitigated to life as a galley slave. And I can prove *that* too, if I wish."

Her eyes widened. "You have actually rowed in their galleys?" She knew this sometimes happened to unfortunate Englishmen, but she had never met any who had survived it.

"For four months, seven days and six hours," he told her grimly. "I counted every hour of it. And knew stripes such as Lord Thomas will never know. So be not so fast to spread tales about me, Christabel—you will only be considered a jealous woman whom I am discarding. There have been others before you."

The momentary sympathy she had felt for his plight as a sometime galley slave fled before that last taunt. "I will be careful to make certain that all who come to this table know that there is naught between us," she said frostily. "Naught," she corrected herself, "that is in any way important."

"Yes," he said in a bleak voice. "By all means, save yourself for Lord Thomas." And he pushed back his chair and strode away before she could add a crushing rejoinder.

But always there were—like sprays of flowers—the good days between them. Like the day he took her riding in the hills and they threw themselves down beside a stream and picnicked on what Cook had packed for them in their saddlebags. They had lain on a cliff top and looked upon all Tortuga stretched out below—at the town, at the fort, at the ships that rode at anchor in Cayona Bay. It had looked beautiful from up here, fresh and new—a whitewashed town with red tile roofs splashed against the green, and in the blue bay, white-sailed wooden ships from many countries, looking like children's toys at this distance.

Kells had taken a swallow of wine from his flask and then, in mellow mood, lain back upon his arms and stared up at the flawless blue sky while she dropped pale green grapes into his mouth.

"I would we could have met another time, another place," he sighed.

"I too," she murmured, tossing up a grape and catching it deftly between her small white teeth. "When we were young."

He was moved to laugh. "And is seventeen so very old?" he twitted her.

"I feel I have aged years since being here," she admitted frankly. "It is something about the town, about the people, a—a worldliness perhaps." She was floundering, trying to explain what it was about this buccaneer town that somehow made one feel older than one's years.

"I know." He nodded moodily. "I have felt it too." *I lost my youth here,* he was thinking. *I did not lose it in the galleys—I was young then and my anger soared into the topsails of the galleon where I was chained to the oars.*

"How old are you, Kells?" she asked, tossing away the rest of the grapes and watching him sideways with her head resting on her drawn up knees.

"I am twenty-seven."

"You look older."

"Buccaneers"—he grinned, rolling over, his mood changing to one of lightness—"live a hard life, do they not?"

She sniffed. *"Your* life is none so hard! Servants to wait upon you, the best house in Tortuga, women sidling up to you on the quay!"

So she had noticed that, the few times he had taken her there. . . .

"They mean nothing to me," he told her quickly.

"Did any woman—ever?" she asked sadly.

He looked on her with yearning. At the moment she was staring out to sea and she looked very young and fragile in her thin white cambric bodice and soft yellow linen skirt. He would give her a gold chain to wear with

494

this costume, he decided. Something that would glitter in the sun.

"*Any* woman ever?" she prodded.

"There was a Spanish girl once." He did not elaborate and she did not ask him. *The rosary,* she thought suddenly, *that I saw hanging from a nail inside his wardrobe door—it must have belonged to the Spanish girl.*

"Spanish," she murmured. "And you are at war with Spain. . . . So you can never return to her."

"No." It was not so simple as that, and it was all so long ago, but the scars of that long lost love affair had never quite healed. No need to dredge it up now.

"Then we have both lost someone," she said, and she sounded so sad that it struck at his heart.

For a while they sat there in companionable silence—not captor and captive but two mortal beings caught in the web of fate, their lives being spun out in ways not of their making.

She smiled at him gently as they rode home, and he almost thought she had forgiven him for kidnapping her and holding her.

"Kells," she sighed, brushing aside a palm frond that flicked her face as she rode, "whyever did you become a buccaneer?"

"Because of a woman," he told her frankly.

She turned on her mount to give him a sharp look. "The . . . Spanish girl?" she asked, bewildered.

When he answered, his voice had gone harsh and he was staring straight ahead of him, looking into some dark and distant past. His eyes were windows of Hell. "I loved her—and because I loved her, they killed her. I have wrung a reckoning from the dons of Spain ever since—and taken a toll of their blood and their treasure."

So forbidding was his countenance that she did not probe further. She felt that he had retired within himself, to some dark inner vision, and that he would not answer her even if she asked.

Vengeance without end, she thought with a shiver. And then, almost with a twinge of jealousy, *He must have loved the Spanish girl very much.* But she was dead—he could never return to her. And anyway he was a different man now, the years would have changed him. Just as she was changing. No longer was she entirely Carolina Lightfoot, the lighthearted belle of Williamsburg. Something of Christabel, the Silver Wench of the buccaneers, had entered into her, never to leave.

Tortuga had changed them both.

But as the days passed, days when too often the heavy tropical rains drummed against the nerves, his leaving drew close upon them—and for some reason that made her angry with him too.

There came a day when, passing by on silent feet, she overheard Hawks talking moodily to someone at the front door.

"Aye, 'tis true the voyage has been put off another day." He spat.

"How so?" came another voice she did not recognize.

"Truth is, it's been put off because Captain Kells cannot bear to leave the wench. And he will not take her with him because he won't risk letting a musket ball crease her pretty hair."

Carolina, who had paused at the mention of the "wench," listened to those words with astonishment.

"Well, you'll have to admit she's a beauty, Hawks," was the rejoinder.

Carolina had not waited to hear Hawks's gloomy answer. She had stolen away quietly.

Was it true? she asked herself. *Had she really some power over this man after all?* And then she thought of Essex and Reba and the snowy maze and all the lies and deceit that had passed between them since she had been here—no, he was only holding onto the Silver Wench because she was a symbol of prestige in this wild community—and because at night, when he returned to face her across the long shining board of his "English" dining room, he could pretend that he was English gentry once again.

"Why do you stay here, Kells?" she taunted him that

night. "You—the misplaced Englishman? Why do you not return and marry someone like Reba?"

"I might have," he admitted frankly. "Had I not met a silver wench."

"Bah!" she said. "You are a buccaneer, it is in your blood! You would have returned to the sea in any event!"

It was not true, and perversely she knew it was not true, but she wanted to goad him. She was wearing the scarlet dress that she had worn during her most dramatic ventures down to the quay. She had worn it tonight, thinking to irritate him.

"Why do you not return me?" she snapped at him. "Is it not obvious we have no future together?"

He rose and seemed to tower over her. "I would return you to the Devil," he grated, "if I thought you belonged to him."

She threw back her fair head. "If I belong to anyone, I belong to Lord Thomas Angevine!"

It was the wrong thing to have said to him just now.

"Do you indeed?" His voice was cold but his eyes were hot.

She divined his intention and made to dart around the table but he caught her, pulled her to him. His lips were hot upon hers, his arms held her motionless while he explored those lips, and then quested over her cheeks, her lashes, her eyebrows, wandered down to caress her throat. When he let her go, they were both shaken and she fell away from him as if her knees were butter, clung for a moment to the table while she glared at him.

"What you have of me you must take," she declared bitterly. "For while I am still your captive I will give you nothing of my own free will!"

"You drive me too far," he said thickly and turned away as if he could not bear the sight of her.

But once she was gone, once that shimmering gown of scarlet silk had swept from the room, once the last rustle of her whisper-thin petticoat had faded away, he stood staring wistfully before him, trying to quiet the heat of his blood. For an unguarded moment there, as he held her imprisoned in his arms, he had imagined her loving him as he loved her, imagined himself settling down in some place where Kells and Christabel would vanish back into Rye and Carolina, imagined spending the rest of his days in the bright sunshine of her smile. She would have wonderful children, he knew, shining like herself. . . .

He was frowning now, for she had made him think on marriage. And marriage—especially to this uncaring silver wench—was not his intention.

He sighed. He was lost, he knew, but at least he could hope to keep her from knowing it.

He sat alone that night, in the dark, sat long and drank, staring at nothing, seeing a world that could never be.

And Carolina, more stirred by his kisses than she cared to admit, tossed her shoes at the wall as she tore them off and plunged into her bed to smother her tears.

For even though she tried to blind her eyes to it, she knew what was happening—inexorably, every day. She was falling in love with this damned buccaneer! She belonged to Thomas—and she was being untrue to him. She was as faithless as her mother! The thought made her wince. It was the first time she had ever admitted to herself that she considered her mother a faithless wife—trapped by fate, but faithless nonetheless.

It was the harsh judgment of youth, and it would temper with time, but for now she put her head in her hands and rocked with shame and grief. She had betrayed Thomas. She felt she had committed adultery, for as she lay in Kells's arms that night, her whole body had rejoiced. She had not meant to feel so—oh, God, no, she had meant only to feign passion—but the passion had become real and honest and soul-shattering. And here she was, confusing it with love!

Her head was bowed and hot tears fell upon her tightly clenched hands. What lay between her and Lord Thomas might not be a marriage in the eyes of the world, but she had plighted to him her troth—and she was not a faithless woman, she was not! That night in

London that she had gone into his arms—and oh, it seemed half a lifetime and more than a world away— she had committed herself to him forever. She felt a bitter inner grief, and a horror of herself that she could prove so unworthy.

Was she never to know peace? Was she never to face herself squarely in the mirror and see there an honest woman, one who had no secrets, nothing to hide?

She dashed away her tears and of a sudden she decided that she would escape Kells, she would escape him *now* before she got in any deeper.

And of a sudden, she knew just how.

Chapter 36

The tunnel! Why had she not thought of it before? (Perhaps because of Hawks's remark about the rats, but she put that firmly from her mind.) She would take a candle—no, she would take an entire branched candlestick, enough to light a dozen tunnels!—and a very large pistol, and she would make her way from the sheltered cove at the tunnel's end back to the town. And once there she would scour the taverns until she found a sea captain who would take her away with him. (That few might be willing to risk the enmity of the notorious Kells was another thought she put away from her.)

Having made up her mind, she felt suddenly energetic. The large pistol—well, that was easy to come by. There was one in the chart room. True, she would have to pass Kells's bedroom door to reach it, but she could steal by as silently as a shadow.

And her clothes—she would dress as a Spanish lady, for it might be that she could persuade one of the freed Spanish prisoners who roamed the waterfront to steal a small boat and sail her to Havana. It would be worth his while for he would not only be reunited with his countrymen, but Doña Hernanda would undoubtedly reward him with gold—if she was still in Havana. If not, there was always Ramona Valdez. Yes, that would be even better than seeking out an English sea captain because it would not only get her off Tortuga, it would put her within striking distance of Thomas!

The clothes were not hard to come by. Black satin slippers, black silk stockings. In the big sea chest that stood in one corner there was more than one gown suitable for a lady of Spain. Bearing in mind the heat, she chose one of thinnest black taffeta—and she regretted its rustle, but the only alternative was a gown of heavy black bombazine, richly braided. A black lacy chemise, a black brocade petticoat—and most important, a drifting black lace mantilla to hide the fair hair by which anybody in Tortuga might recognize her. It would not do to have the Silver Wench reported seen down in the town! With nervous fingers she swept up her hair and set in it a lofty tortoise-shell comb of intricate design. The black lace mantilla was richly worked and concealing—it would do well as a disguise.

She was so excited that she could not bear to sit down, but paced about. She forced herself to wait until she was sure Kells had gone to bed, and then she stole down to the chart room and secured the large pistol. It was very heavy, it would make her wrist ache if she had to carry it for long but she was determined to persevere—and she would need that pistol in the town, she had no doubt.

The branched candlestick she took with her on her silent path to the dining room. She could light it there from the single candle she took with her. For she had no desire to make such a blaze of light that Kells, who slept lightly and might be still awake, would see it through the crack beneath his door. Silently, clad in the rich black clothing of a lady of Spain, she made her way to the dining room, and opened the door without so much as a sound.

The room looked as always: the long gleaming table, the big high-backed chairs, their velvet coverings rich

501

against the carved wood of the arms. Her candle made strange wavering shapes against the paneled walls. The shadows cast by the chairs seemed like crouching animals. She forced herself to pay no attention, but laid the big pistol down on the table—and even as she did, a bird flew against the jalousies and she started, stifling a scream.

Keeping her attention now focused on her immediate pathway to the big cupboard that concealed the tunnel, she moved toward it—and put her shoulder against it, just as Hawks had done.

It did not budge.

"It takes a bit more strength to move it," said a grim voice behind her.

Carolina started so violently that she almost dropped the candle. She whirled and saw just rising from the big chair in which he had been lounging, his body hidden in the shadow—Kells himself.

"I—" she began, confused.

"Don't bother to lie," he cut in impatiently. "You were attempting to leave by way of the tunnel. How did you learn where the entrance was?"

"Hawks showed me how to open it when he thought the fight was going against you," she said sulkily. "I told him that he should go out and help you—and he thought so too."

He sighed. "I might have known. Hawks considers himself my guardian angel," he added by way of explanation. "He was my father's groom back in Essex. So now there is one more door that I must lock against you."

"It will do you no good!" she flared. "I will escape you if I have to break out through the roof or dig my own tunnel to freedom!"

He studied her tense form in the candlelight, took in the flashing eyes, the rebellious mouth.

"What have I ever done," he murmured, "that you are so hot to leave me?"

"Need you ask?" Icily. "You forced yourself on me!"

"Oh, yes," he sighed. "There was that." He gave her a crooked smile. "But I have been very good of late."

502

"Good? You keep me locked up!"

"And suppose I said that I would no longer keep you locked up?" he asked softly. "Suppose I said that if you would walk beside me—willingly—that I would take you anywhere you liked, that I would sail you to Havana, that I would sail you to Hell?"

She sniffed. "I would not believe you."

He lifted his head and his bitter laugh rang out. "Spoken like a true woman," he said. "Ever evading the question." He went to the door and called "Hawks!"

Hawks was obviously on guard duty at the front door. He quickly appeared. "Yes, Captain?"

Kells spoke to him rapidly in French—a language of which Carolina knew only a smattering. She guessed he was ordering Hawks to barricade the end of the tunnel in some way so that she would not be able to penetrate it, because Hawks threw her a sudden curious look.

"You might have spoken in English," she complained.

"Yes, I might," he agreed, coming back after closing the door and pulling out a chair for her. "But Hawks is a little rusty on his French. I have agreed to give him practice."

She gave him a disbelieving look as he sat down and poured her a goblet of wine.

"What am I to do with you?" he mused.

"That's easily answered! You can let me go." She tossed down the wine and gave him a resentful look. "And do not pretend that you love me for I will not believe it—a man who takes a woman against her will and then throws at her her lack of virginity!" Her voice was filled with indignation.

He rose.

"I do not think you understand me," he said slowly, coming around the table toward her. "I never 'threw at you' your lack of virginity when you first gave yourself to me—I only regretted that I was not the man." And at her slightly rebuffing shrug, he took her by the shoulders and lifted her to her feet. "No, hear me out—this once," he said, looking down into her face with great intensity. "And then we need never speak of any of it again. You do not understand the nature of my love."

"Do I not?" she said scathingly.

"No." His voice was suddenly sharp, a sharpness she had heard sometimes in Fielding Lightfoot's voice when he was exasperated with her mother. But the words were such as she had never heard Fielding say. He looked deep into her eyes as he spoke. "I would love you, Christabel, if you had had ten lovers—twenty. I would love you if you had had none." His voice grew rich and deep and fraught with meaning. "I would love you no matter what had happened to you, or what later came to pass." And when she would have spoken, he held up his hand to silence her. "But it is not Carolina Lightfoot of the sulks and moods that I love."

Her gray eyes widened, staring up at him. There was no sound in the room save their breathing and the light rustle of the palm fronds blowing outside their window.

He smiled, a slightly ragged smile, and she had a flashing vision of what she had put him through all these months when he was trying to fight off his love for her. "It is Christabel that I love," he said simply. "A girl who would throw away everything for her lover—and I only regretted that I was not that lover." He shrugged. "But now you will find him again and I will go my way and let you be happy." He smiled down on her wistfully, and she could not fathom the expression on his face.

But she caught his meaning clear—and held her breath. He was going to let her go, he had said as much!

Outside, somewhere across a silver sea, her future waited—with Thomas Angevine.

Here, inside this mock English room in this dangerous tropical place, there was only confusion. She studied that dark mocking face before her, puzzled, wondering if she could believe what he had just said. Those gray eyes, that dark face, were suddenly quite unlike Fielding Lightfoot's—they were Kells's alone, and she would never confuse the two of them again.

"But before I let you go," he said softly, "I will take some small token to remember you by."

"What—what is it you want?" she asked raggedly. "You can have anything . . . if only you will let me go."

"Anything?" His smile deepened. "Then I will take with me a memory to warm me on cold nights in Essex, for that is where I am going." And he wrapped his arms around her.

"To—Essex?" she faltered against his chest.

"Yes," he muttered. "I am tired of the Caribbean. I intend to live in England."

But he was a wanted man! In Essex, he would be found out, betrayed. It was one thing to snatch a visit as he had done at Christmastide, but not to try to live there—never that!

And then she was dizzily lost in the touch of him, the slightly tangy masculine scent of him, the warmth that exuded from his big body that sent a glow of desire through every fiber of her being.

"Kells, don't," she said faintly. She put the palms of her hands against his chest to push him away. "Please don't."

"Can it be that you feel something for me?" he wondered, letting his long fingers trail down her fair hair with its lacy black mantilla, to caress the curve of her neck.

"Yes, I feel something for you," she said in a strangled voice. "But it is wrong for me to feel so. I am not a faithless wench. I belong to someone else."

"Do you now?" He took her hand and pulled her unresisting body into the courtyard. She went with him as if she had no will, a leaf blown by the wind. He took her into the chart room which had a view down the hill of the town below.

"Consider me a magician," he said ironically. "Observe, I will produce Lord Thomas Angevine right before your eyes."

She gave him a troubled look. "I do not find that amusing," she said stiffly.

"I do not expect you to. Come, look out the window,

Christabel. You will see that he is strolling up the road."

Despite her disbelief, the compelling note in his voice drew her to the window.

Before her the white moonlight was beaming down upon the silvery green fronds of waving palms, and upon a roadway of white coral rock, in some places no more than a path, crushed and spread by Spanish prisoners. And upon that roadway, beneath those waving palms, being urged along by a dour-looking Hawks, Lord Thomas Angevine in the flesh was indeed strolling toward her.

"But—" She gasped. "It cannot be! Thomas lies imprisoned in Havana. How did you effect his release?"

"He was never in Havana. He was here all the time."

Her head whirled. "Here?" she said faintly.

"Yes. In Grenoble's house."

In Dr. Grenoble's house! Ah, now it was clear! Thomas had been one of the fever victims that Dr. Grenoble feared to leave lest he spread the contagion. And Kells had not told her because he knew she might manage to go to him, contract the fever and die!

"He has been ill?" she asked tentatively, for verification.

"No." His voice was cool. "Lord Thomas has been in excellent health save for several lashes the Spanish gave him on board the *Santiago*."

"Then you *did* take the *Coraje?*"

Kells shook his head. "No, I missed her. But it seems that Lord Thomas has a way with women. It was because he had been so bold as to speak to a Spanish lady aboard the *Santiago* that he had received several lashes. And this lady, half mad with love for him, had managed to bribe two Spanish sailors with a large emerald cross. In the night they released Lord Thomas from his bonds, set the two of them into a boat, and the pair set out for Havana, where the lady had a brother who would do anything for her. I chanced upon them on their way there—before I took the *Santiago*. And it

506

was as well I did, for understand the ways of the sea he does not, and they were about to be swamped."

So Kells had captured Lord Thomas! But with a lady?

"I do not believe you!" she cried. "A Spanish lady? I would have seen her—or at least heard about her!"

"Few knew," he said dryly. "And I promised death to anyone who told you. In any event she is a provable fact for she too is a guest of the good doctor."

Her head spun. "You mean—they were together?" she asked in an altered voice.

He nodded affably. "In one room."

In one bed, he meant!

He shrugged. "It was their own desire. Dr. Grenoble is no keeper of other men's morals!"

So they had been the "fever victims"—Thomas and this woman!

"I do not believe you," she accused coldly. "You have invented this terrible story to confuse me. But Thomas will be here in a moment and he will explain all!"

"Will he now?" Her captor gave a short laugh. "Would you care for the lady to tell you herself? She speaks only Spanish but fortunately you know the language."

This was surely some trick of this devious buccaneer! Her angry gasp gave him her answer.

"Before he gets here," Kells said coolly, "would you not care to ask me why I did it?"

"Yes!" she cried. "What did you intend by this charade?"

"I meant to gain myself a silver wench," he told her somberly. "I had thought that when you learned your perfect Thomas had been spending his days and nights with another woman it might change your mind. As it is, I have changed mine."

"What do you mean, you have *changed your mind?*"

"Just that," he told her calmly. "I have decided not to let you go so easily. I have decided to let Lord Thomas fight me for you, buccaneer style, with cutlasses—or if he prefers a more gentlemanly weapon, with rapiers. If he wins"—he gave her a sardonic look—"you are both free to go. But not until I lie dead upon the sand."

She could hear the big iron grillwork front door clang shut even as she tried to grasp all this. Her own face beneath the drifting black lace had gone white. "Why would you do that?" she demanded in alarm. She could hear Lord Thomas's boots along with Hawks's ringing on the stone flooring. "Why would you kill a man who has never harmed you?"

"Can it be that you do not know I love you?" he marvelled. "Well, hold your tongue and you will learn something." He stepped out into the corridor, leaving the door ajar behind him.

"Ah—Thomas." Kells's voice was casual. "And how is Doña Margarita today?"

"Complaining," was the prompt response. "She yearns for Toledo. It is very tiresome being cooped up with her all day long."

"I can well imagine," the buccaneer commiserated with him. "But then at first you did not seem to mind."

From behind that half-open door Carolina raked her fingernails into her palms. She could almost see Thomas shrug. "Well—you know how these things are. Passion waxes hot at first but then it wanes. I am glad at last to have the freedom of the town. Dr. Grenoble advises me that the contagion here on Tortuga has waned. I am eager to be out and about. There is a Silver Wench, Dr. Grenoble tells me, who is worth the viewing—although he does say she belongs to you," he added with a drawl.

So Kells had tricked them both! He had told *her* there was a contagion in Dr. Grenoble's house and he had told Thomas there was a contagion abroad in Cayona! He had kept them both prisoners of his lies!

She could hardly contain herself as Lord Thomas added, "Your hospitality has been much appreciated, but I was a little surprised to be wakened in the night and told to scramble into my clothes. Tell me, has some

508

great event transpired that I should be apprised of? Are we at war perhaps?"

"Not yet," said Kells. He swung the door wide. "Lord Thomas," he said sardonically, "I bring you your lost lady—Christabel."

Lord Thomas looked with surprise at this apparently Spanish lady who confronted him. The single candle that Kells had brought with him and set upon the chart room's long table cast its golden glow upon an elegant black taffeta gown and a face obscured by a heavy black lace mantilla held up by an intricately worked tortoise-shell comb.

"My lost—?" He peered at her in the dim room without recognition. "Do I know this lady?" he inquired courteously.

A slow astonishment washed over the lean buccaneer's dark countenance. Abruptly he began to laugh.

"Christabel," he said, choking back his mirth. "Your late lost love does not remember you. And it is strange," he added, cocking his head to view her. "For *I* would know you anywhere, no matter how much lace you draped over your head!"

Nothing so deflating had ever happened to Carolina. She ripped off her mantilla and her burning silver eyes were turned accusingly upon the English lord. "*Now* do you remember me, Thomas?" she demanded in a voice that quivered with wrath.

Lord Thomas had the grace to look astonished. "Carolina!" he marveled. "Have you been languishing in this fever port too?"

Carolina's pretty teeth ground slightly. To have been rejected would be bad enough, but not even to be *recognized!* No matter that she was wearing a disguise —he should have known her! Instantly! She looked with distaste at Lord Thomas. He was more tanned than when she had last seen him—from lying about in a sunny hammock with his Spanish lady, no doubt! And he seemed to have grown shorter. Suddenly she did not like his curly hair. It seemed coarse and thatchlike. "The fever was just in our minds, Thomas. We have both been duped. By this blackguard here."

The blackguard bowed slightly to acknowledge his regard. "The lady is understandably ruffled," he told Lord Thomas gravely. "She has been put to some trouble on your account. Believing you to be incarcerated in—I believe I quote her correctly—'the deepest dungeon in El Morro,' she has been trying to reach Havana in a vain attempt to rescue you."

Lord Thomas's elegant mouth gaped open as he regarded with awe this pseudo-Spanish lady who was at the same time Carolina Lightfoot. "I cannot believe it!" he muttered.

"She was ready to risk her life on your behalf, Lord Thomas." Kells's voice was crisp. "I think you might suspend your disbelief long enough to thank her."

"Oh, I do, I do thank her," cried that gentleman hastily. "But I cannot understand why. I mean, I cannot understand how—"

"Oh, damn your misunderstandings!" cried Carolina.

"But now that I have found you again, Carolina," he began quickly, "you and I—"

That did it, that easy assumption that she would *resume* her relationship with him!

"Not 'Carolina,'" she jeered. "Rather call me 'Christabel' as all in Cayona know me. You are looking at the Silver Wench you say you yearn to view!"

If Lord Thomas had looked astonished before, he now looked thunderstruck. "*You?* The Silver Wench?" he gasped. "But the Silver Wench belongs to—" He cast a look at Kells before his voice faded away.

"She is indeed the Silver Wench." Kells's hard voice, keen-edged as any rapier, cut into his words. "And you are right, she *does* belong to me."

"Oh, I'd not contest it," said Lord Thomas quickly.

"Would you not?" cried Carolina, outraged. "You who swore undying love but last December in England? *You would not contest it?*" Her voice rose.

"Carolina," he said unhappily. "This is not the time for recriminations. I would remind you that we are both in a buccaneer stronghold—"

"Ah, so that is it!" Angrily she pounced upon his

words. "We are to grovel before these buccaneers, are we? Well, *I* will not, and I will not let you grovel either!" Recklessly she turned to Kells. *"Fight your duel!"* she cried. "Let the blood of the loser stain the sand!"

Aghast, Lord Thomas turned to Kells. "What is she saying?" he stammered.

"I have just told her that I would fight you for her," drawled Kells. "To the death."

Lord Thomas paled visibly. "We can surely settle this matter peaceably between us," he began. "There is no need of a duel."

"And what of your lady of Spain?" jibed Carolina.

"Ah, she must be returned to Havana," he said promptly, sensing that this was a sore point. "She was but aiding in my escape, Carolina," he added beseechingly.

"And no doubt intended to marry you into the bargain!"

"We will let Lord Thomas be the judge of what she intended," said Kells. "It is my intention to release both you and Doña Margarita." He was speaking directly to Lord Thomas. "If you choose that she accompany you back to England——"

"Oh, no!" Lord Thomas put up his hand almost with a shudder. "She talks incessantly. Never stops. Indeed the lady and I have been constant companions ever since I reached these shores and I would be delighted never to see her again."

How shallow he was! Carolina regarded her late lover with contempt. And she had once loved this man, loved him desperately, with every fiber of her being! It galled her that she should have flung herself at him, that she should have turned and tossed so many sleepless nights, wondering where he was, in whose arms he might be lying. *What did it matter in whose arms Thomas was lying, so long as they were not hers?* And to think that she had been about to sail to Havana to find him! Why, he was not worth crossing the grove to find!

"Then I will arrange for Doña Margarita's return to

Havana," decided Kells. "Perhaps you would be good enough to inform her?" He glanced at his watch. "Well, we will not keep you, Lord Thomas. Dr. Grenoble will be up and eager to hear how you fared at my hands, and no doubt the lady will be grateful for the good news that she will be rejoining her brother in Havana."

Thus dismissed and free from the threat of immediate annihilation at the hands of this daunting buccaneer, Lord Thomas hesitated and cast a miserable look at Carolina. It was a look that pleaded with her for understanding. She returned him a frosty glance.

"Goodbye, Thomas," she said firmly. And she thought, *Everyone was right about you,* and marveled that she had not seen it before.

After Lord Thomas had left them, after she—standing now looking out the window with her back to Kells—could see him striding somewhat less jauntily down the moon-washed coral roadway, this time without escort, she waited to hear Kells speak. The moments dragged by. Then:

"You are free to follow him, you know," said Kells in an altered voice.

She turned slowly and looked at him in wonder. She had just learned one of the bitterest lessons in life—that there are some men no woman can hold. Then why should she feel so free, and all at once, so happy? "You would release us *both?*" she murmured.

He ran a hand through his dark hair and she could see that his face, which had looked so keen and young and vivid when he had faced Lord Thomas, now looked very haggard. "Yes." His voice roughened. "Yes, I will set you free. I will do better than that." He seemed to be warring within himself as he came toward her and took both her shoulders in his hands. "I swear that if you wish to go with him, I will set you both upon a ship bound for England."

How he must love her, she marveled, *that after all that had transpired, all her refusals, all the lengths he had gone to win her, he would actually let her go with Thomas if her heart desired it!* And of a sudden, all the

512

clashing, all the troubles between them melted away and she felt tears start at what he had said.

"Oh, Kells," she whispered, and her heart was in her voice. "I don't want to leave you, *don't you know that?*"

She felt him stiffen slightly and he held her back away from him so that he might look down into her face. Steel glanced on silver as his gaze found hers and for a moment there was a flicker between them that burned like molten metal.

"How I have waited," he said softly, *"to hear you say that!"*

"So now you can take more than a memory with you to Essex," she choked in a voice gone husky with love for him. "You can take all of me."

"I wanted to hear it from your own lips," he said simply. "For at heart I am no buccaneer—I want only what is freely given. But I can tolerate no wavering, for you have near broke my heart already. I doubt I could survive another such buffeting. Are you truly certain? Christabel would be, but what of Carolina, that creature of high resolve who would rather break than bend? What of Carolina of the already given heart?" His voice had gone wry and he watched her tensely. "Will we be meeting her again?"

The silver blonde beauty in the elegant black dress gave him back a winsome smile. "I think I am more Christabel than Carolina," she admitted.

"Good," he said and gathered her within the circle of his arms. "For you may have noticed from the sounds you hear that trunks and gear and plunder are being stacked at the front door to be carried down to the quay for loading. We sail this morning."

"This morning?" she gasped. For in the heat of these last moments, with her very soul swinging this way and that beneath the pressure of that strong masculine gaze, she had given little thought to the flurry of activity in the house around her. Now she did indeed notice, and realized that there was a fresh breeze blowing—good sailing weather.

"We will sail away," he told her, "while Lord

Thomas languishes on shore. He will be taking another ship no doubt. Back to London presumably. Do not worry about your things. Katje is packing them now. They will precede you aboard the *Sea Wolf.*"

She began to laugh. "So you meant all the time to carry me off?"

"Carolina Lightfoot I might have been persuaded to leave on the quay," he said, brushing her forehead with his lips. "But Christabel—never! She belongs to me and I will fight the whole world for her." Tenderly he gazed upon his Silver Wench.

"Then I will remain Christabel," she decided, leaning against him. "But Christabel is a part of *this* life, Kells. She is part of the blue Caribbean and the white beaches and the trade winds and the tropics—Carolina is part of that other life. Oh, do not go to Essex, Kells, do not chance it—stay here with me!"

The elusive expression she could not quite fathom was playing around his lips again. "Then you would share this buccaneering life with me, with all that it entails? All the hardships, the dangers, the never knowing when the end will come?"

"Oh, yes," she said breathlessly. "I beg you to let me share it—and I promise that I will never ask for more!"

For a moment a flaring triumph lit his gray eyes, savage, untamed. It was as if he had won a great battle. She stared at him in puzzlement.

"I wanted to hear you say that too," he said quietly. "And share my life you shall. But not here in the Caribbean—there is no longer any need to do that. We will both set sail for Essex. Ah, Christabel, had you not heard? There is a general amnesty proclaimed, and any buccaneer can sail in and claim it! I will have me a King's pardon for my buccaneering deeds and we can settle down in Essex and look any man in the face!"

"Tell me it's true," she cried. "Tell me you are not joking!"

"I am not joking and it is true," he said, smiling.

Her face was radiant and she threw her arms around him. "To Essex then!" she cried. "To our new life together!"

514

His face was buried in the hollow of her throat but now he lifted his head and saw the glittering promise in her luminous silver eyes. He swallowed, for he was shaken by what he saw there—more than he had ever dreamed of, all the courage, all the love, all the loyalty that he had hoped for in his wildest dreams was there beckoning in her smile.

"We have a little time before the tide changes," he told her hoarsely. "Not much—but enough."

She was laughing softly, triumphantly, as he carried her back to her airy bedroom, that bedroom he had planned for her, furnished for her, in the days when he had thought her lost to him. He had been living out a fantasy and she had been his dream girl, but now the fantasy had become real and the dream girl was alive and pulsing in his arms.

And for Carolina, all the frustrations, all the guilt, all the remorse were gone, vanished with Lord Thomas down a coral roadway that led down to Cayona. She no longer felt she had to hold back; she could accept him unreservedly and lavish on him all the delights of her love. Silently, dreamily, raptly, she let him remove her clothing with tender fingers and sighed with him in the depths of the big bed as his naked form descended upon her own.

And there in his arms—the right arms at last—her heart seemed to hear music, and her blood sang with an ancient singing that rippled on the magic of a sigh. Then the music swelled and burgeoned and the song grew feverish, frenzied, it wailed and dipped and moaned—even as her own voice moaned low in her throat—and it was a lovesong that she heard, sighing on the tropic wind, pouring over her in the moonlight, making her one with the night, one with her lover.

The time of torment was over and the time of joy had begun. The blissful moments flew by, a time of touching and laughing and playful lovemaking, of warm fiery embraces and mounting passions that crested in waves and spilled over into magic, of feelings so intense it seemed that they would tear the lovers apart, of soft endearing moments that would be remembered for a lifetime. And the wild ageless song that consumed them seemed to gather its forces and culminate in one great triumphant chorus.

They had never been so close, they had never loved each other as they did in those velvet moments, with dawn pinkening the night sky over Tortuga.

EPILOGUE

He came winging out of nowhere, her very heart to snatch,
Found the pulsing woman in her waiting breathless by the
*   latch,*
Then the door was bursted open and throughout a night of
*   sighs*
Her reckless heart went winging past the rooftops to the
*   skies!*

They missed the tide of course. But their reasons were compelling—and heartfelt for them both.

"Captain!" Hawks had pounded resolutely on the bedroom door, interrupting their rapt concentration on each other. "Captain, ye'll have to hurry if ye don't want to miss the tide."

Kells, caught up by the magic as desperately as she, lifted his dark head. "There'll be another tide," he called. "We'll catch the next one—no matter, we'll sail tomorrow. And that will give you time to say goodbye in proper fashion to that wench you're so fond of in the town, Hawks."

Carolina couldn't hear Hawks's mumbled response, she didn't need to. She lay there smiling, lost in love.

Eventually they rose, of course. Eventually they ate—a quickly concocted breakfast, mostly fruit, and Carolina felt a sudden pang of loss that this was the last meal she would ever eat in this picturesque courtyard with its blowing palms. She would miss the parrot, but Poll would prefer the tropics to the colder climate of Essex, Kells told her, and besides Katje loved the parrot and Katje wanted to stay. Just as Lars had elected to stay. And next month—perhaps sooner,

517

Carolina sensed—Lars and Katje would marry and Lars would move into Kells's old quarters and he and Katje would breakfast in this sunny courtyard, even as she and Kells were doing now. Meantime, the house would be kept open for the remainder of the "English contingent," those who, for personal reasons, chose not to take the King's pardon but to stay on here, buccaneering to the end.

Hawks had returned imperturbable from his last bout with the red-haired Yorkshire wench he fancied but whose hatred of the ocean was so great that she had declared she'd never trust her body to the sea again—she had refused to sail with him, and he was too homesick for England to stay in Cayona.

"Captain." Hawks had just come into the courtyard and stood chewing on his lip. "Have ye forgot the American gentleman? I've got him cooling his heels in the chart room now."

Kells, lounging back, just finishing his late breakfast, looked startled. "By heaven, I had!" he cried. "I had more pressing things on my mind. Thanks for reminding me, Hawks." He got up, unwinding his long legs, encased this morning in elegant Spanish breeches, and reached out a hand to lift Carolina from her chair.

"Who is it who comes to see you?" she wondered, trying to match her shorter stride to his long one as they approached the closed door of the chart room.

"Oh, he does not come to see me. He comes to see you. He arrived last night. Hawks has been entertaining him on my behalf in the officers' quarters. I have kept him waiting for my own reasons. I am puzzled as to just how to greet him."

Her curiosity was aroused. "But who is he?"

Kells's voice was ironic. "I am not sure. It would seem a Virginia gentleman has come to Tortuga to effect your rescue."

Visions of Ned and Dick vying with each other in that impromptu tourney on the lawns of Rosegill flashed through her mind. Had one of them, egged on by her mother—?

"He says he is your father," announced Kells coolly.

Had Fielding Lightfoot really come all this way to find her? He must care something for her after all then! Her mind was in confusion as Kells threw wide the door to the chart room and a tall man rose from a seat at the table.

Not Fielding Lightfoot—it was the tall elegant form of Sandy Randolph that seemed to fill the room with its presence.

"I bring greetings from your mother," he said in his courtly way. "She has commissioned me to bring you home to her."

Kells raised an eyebrow. "That will be difficult, sir," he said pleasantly. "For you will have to go through me to do it."

There was a catch in Carolina's voice as she spoke. "Kells, allow me to present my real father—Lysander Randolph of Tower Oaks. And this gentleman who claims me is the Lord Admiral of the Buccaneers." She hesitated, wondering if she should call him by his real name.

Kells saved the day for her by stepping forward and extending his hand in greeting. "Rye Evistock, late of Essex. Here I'm known as Kells."

"Your fame precedes you, sir." Sandy Randolph took the proffered hand but his attention was focused on Carolina. "Your mother told me you did not know," he said softly. "She made me swear never to tell you."

"I guessed," said Carolina simply. "And besides, I *look* like you. Anyone seeing us together would assume us to be father and daughter. And I think"—she considered him critically—"I really am like you. Tell me, did Mother really send you for me or did you come on your own?"

His taut smile relaxed and his white teeth flashed. "I will admit that I came on my own," he said. "Although your mother would have sent me had she not thought me already gone to England. I heard you had run away and learned that a certain Maud Tate was wearing one of your gowns and bragging she'd helped you. It was Maud who told me you'd gone to London, so I sailed for England and in London learnt a deal more about you from a certain wild young woman who once had a school where now she operates a fashionable gaming house."

So Jenny Chesterton had come into her own! No more dull meetings with parents of proper young ladies. She could pursue her light loves as she pleased—and keep afloat financially as well!

"What she told me about a certain Lord Thomas Angevine, and what I learnt of a certain ransom being demanded from Tortuga—"

Carolina interrupted, whirling on Kells.

"You were demanding ransom for Thomas?" she gasped.

"I sent a demand for ransom intending it to be your dowry in case you would not have me," he admitted with a wry grin. "But it seems it won't be necessary after all."

She was left speechless. He had not only swept her off her feet and into his heart, he had devised for her an escape route in case she chose to leave him and Thomas again proved false!

"You understand," Sandy Randolph was saying somewhat sternly, "it is only in this far place that I can claim you, Carolina. To do so in Virginia would be to cast shame upon your mother. And because you are so patently my daughter"—his gaze fell significantly upon her silver blonde hair, her silvery eyes, that coloring so identical to his own—"I tried to keep my distance from you in Virginia, lest we excite notice."

Carolina nodded. Her eyes had gone suddenly misty. "I understand," she said.

"But that will not keep you from giving the bride away on the deck of the *Sea Wolf,* where Carolina has chosen to be married?" Kells's uncompromising expression said that if the Virginia gentleman wanted to speak out against the marriage, the time was now.

"It would do me honor," said Sandy Randolph with a sweeping bow to the daughter he could never claim before his friends.

And so on the deck of the rakish buccaneer ship,

poised like a painting on the glassy waters of Cayona Bay, Rye Evistock claimed his bride—and her natural father gave the bride away. The bride wore ice blue satin, the fetchingly tight bodice above drifting skirts all set with brilliants that sparkled like stars in the moonlight, and her fair hair, encircled with a chain of sapphires and diamonds, shining like finely spun white metal. Discordant, clamorous, all the church bells rang in Tortuga. There were drunken cheers from the shore and the flash of cutlasses raised in salute from the assembled buccaneers drinking the bride's health in rum and stolen Spanish wines. Small boats dotted the dark glittering waters of the bay, rowing round and round, their crews calling out encouragement to the Silver Wench who was even now walking beneath an arch of cutlasses held aloft, to reach her smiling bridegroom.

"The Wench! The Wench! The Silver Wench!" came half-heard shouts from shore, drifting out across the water. And then on board ship several violas struck up at once and were quickly joined by other stringed instruments.

The din was deafening. The minister had to shout. And a man who was unmistakably the bride's father and who had all the courtliness of a prince of the blood roared in a voice that echoed in the rigging that it was he who gave this woman in marriage.

"We'll be married more fashionably in a church back in Essex," Kells bent to shout in her ear and Carolina nodded, her eyes abrim with laughter. Then her buccaneer straightened and glared about him for the minister had just howled, "If any man knows reason why these two should not be joined together in holy wedlock, let him speak now or forever hold his peace!"

Into the sudden comparative silence rose the voice of a massive buccaneer whose forehead was tied with a bright red rag and who had a scar that reached from his eyebrow to his chin. "And if ye speak ye'll indeed hold your peace forever," he chortled. "For Kells will surely split your gullet for you!"

There was general laughter at that and loud festive

singing as the ceremony went on—and a wild round of applause as they were pronounced man and wife. And then both bride and groom were lifted to eager shoulders and paraded about the deck while the crowd on shore went wild.

It was a raucous ceremony but Carolina forgave that. This was their leader up here, and he was taking a bride. Those rough-looking men who were waving tankards and cutlasses and dancing jigs and shouting their names were wishing them a season of happiness— and they would surely have it.

She looked up at Kells, waving now to those on shore, and her heart went out to them all—they were losing him but they were taking it like men. Their cheers would speed him onward to his new life—in Essex.

"Do you sail for England with us?" Rye asked the bride's father courteously as they drank a toast to the bride after the ceremony.

Sandy Randolph gave them both a restless look. "No, I'm for Virginia," he admitted. "Once I was gone, vowing never to return, I found a yearning in my heart to go back to my plantation on the James. My roots are there in Virginia."

My mother is there, thought Carolina. *He cannot have her but he cannot forget her. And perhaps it is the same way with her.* She gave him a misty look.

"I thank you for coming to rescue me," she said softly. "But as you can see, I am far from needing rescue!"

"That at least is true." He sighed and clapped Rye on the shoulder as he left. "But if ever you have need of me on my daughter's behalf, you have only to ask. And for both of you the doors of Tower Oaks are ever open."

Rye nodded and wrung his hand.

"Your father is a good man," he murmured as he watched the older man depart, his hair as frosty blond as Carolina's in the moonlight.

My mother always thought so. . . . "Yes," she said wistfully. "A good man. I am proud he has claimed me

522

at last." *And prouder still to be claimed by you,* her radiant look told him.

"You would like to see the Tidewater country again, would you not?" he asked her suddenly.

"Yes," she sighed. "I suppose I would."

"And so you shall." He called after Sandy Randolph, who turned questioningly, with one foot over the rail. "Come back, I'll sail you to the James!"

Quite readily, Randolph turned back. "I am glad you have made this decision," he said. "Rye here can accept his pardon in Williamsburg as well as elsewhere —and I'll be there to see that nothing goes amiss."

Carolina swallowed. *You are a wonderful father,* her eyes told him. *And I've missed you all these years!*

Suddenly she thought of something that would please him and she leant forward impulsively. "My mother despairs that all her daughters are runaways," she said. "Would it not be a kindness if we were not to tell her of this ceremony which we have just held here aboard the *Sea Wolf* and let her launch at last a virgin bride down the main stairway at Level Green?"

He looked startled for a moment and then he smiled. "I think it is what she most desires," he said softly. "And kind it is of you to think of it."

"And we can have a third wedding, if you choose, before all your friends in Essex," Carolina told Kells.

He laughed. "I'm a marrying man, but two weddings will be quite enough!"

"Then a toast to the bride's eyebrows!" cried Sandy Randolph. "May your lives sail as sweetly as this ship and cut the water as cleanly! May you find safe harbor!"

Kells smiled at him across his glass. "I take it you're a sailing man?"

"In my youth," said Sandy Randolph modestly. "I sailed a hitch with Morgan once," he added. "Now best forgot."

"And where was that?" wondered Kells.

The silver eyes so like those of the wench at his side glimmered for a moment with amusement. "To Panama," he said.

Kells threw back his dark head and laughed. Then he clapped the bride's father on the back. "A welcome to you, sir!" he cried. "For you were in the greatest venture of them all!"

"Now best forgot," reminded Carolina with a view to her father's safety. "Perhaps you'd best ask for the King's amnesty too," she told her father with a frown.

"Oh, all is forgiven where I'm concerned," he told her with an easy smile. "And long ago forgot. No need to tell it around the Tidewater however—although Letty knows of course."

Of course—Letty would know. Carolina wondered how many brave secrets her mother kept locked in that courageous but divided heart. Suddenly she longed to see the Eastern Shore again, to walk the streets of Yorktown, to throw her arms about Virgie and Aunt Pet, to show her lean buccaneer the beautiful Tidewater country—the great plantation of Sandy Randolph, lightsome rake and sometime buccaneer, and the elegant new seat of Fielding Lightfoot, who had, after all, put up with her all these years! She would do something at last to please her mother—she would dress herself in white and silver, or perhaps palest ice blue, and float down that wide stairway at Level Green that would take eight abreast and acknowledge the man who had let her wear his name all these years by letting him give her away as a bride to her buccaneer lover!

Her mother would have her cherished great wedding, and she herself would have one last long look at home.

And then she would begin her life's long journey beside the man who in all the world meant most to her—Kells or Rye Evistock or whatever he chose to call himself.

And then at last they were alone. Alone in the great cabin of a buccaneer ship with the moonlight streaming down through the bank of slanted stern windows. Beside them, untouched upon the heavy carved Span-

524

ish table, the Scottish cook had set out "a meal to give the captain strength—for he'll need it with such a lass!" as he had jovially told the sleepy cabin boy who sat nodding while it simmered.

The night was fair and the water that fled by them was silver with phosphorescence—*like her eyes,* Rye thought, *like her hair washed in moonlight, lit by stars.* Behind them lay the mountain fort with its captured Spanish guns overlooking the bay; behind them lay Tortuga and the life he once had led. And now the rakish gray *Sea Wolf* was cutting cleanly through the waters of the Spanish Main—for the last time, he hoped. All about them the tropical night was velvet soft and velvet black. There was not a sail on the horizon. They might have been passing alone through the perfumed night on a vast empty sea with love to fill the sails and love to steer their ship.

On some more formal tomorrow they would become their other selves—those aristocratic selves they had left behind them somewhere outside the buccaneer stronghold that so recently had been their home. And back in Essex—just as in Yorktown—they would again become Carolina Lightfoot and Rye Evistock, country gentry. They would melt into the English countryside. They would ride to hounds and give elegant balls and rear handsome children and spend glittering seasons in London.

But for tonight the past—all that they were in those former lives or had ever been—was stripped away. Tonight they were Kells and Christabel—a dangerous Irish buccaneer and his American love.

They passed the table of food as if it were not there.

As one they swayed together, as one fell upon the bunk, as one breathed and sighed and caressed and merged into a perfect joining, savoring an earthly paradise that would leave them sated and smiling and forgetful of all the world.

They were caught up by the night and the magic, by the silvery moonpath on a midnight sea, by a wide-eyed moon that looked down uncaring. Tonight the laws of

God and man seemed very far away. There would be no reckoning, and death was something that would never reach them.

Tonight they were lovers—and theirs would be a never ending lovesong.

In wild Tortuga many times they'll quench
With ale their stories of the Silver Wench
Who captivated such a man as he,
Stormed his defenses, swept him from the sea!
And ponder how it was a man like Kells
Was lured so readily to wedding bells. . . .

Tapestry
HISTORICAL ROMANCES

_____	544276	**NEVADA NIGHTS**	
		Ruth Ryan Langan	$ 2.95
_____	52626X	**TANGLED VOWS**	
		Anne Moore	$ 2.95
_____	544268	**LOVING DEFIANCE**	
		Joan Johnston	$ 2.95
_____	543962	**CAPTIVE HEARTS**	
		Catherine Lyndell	$ 2.95
_____	526774	**SECRETS OF THE HEART**	
		Janet Joyce	$ 2.95
_____	528432	**SILVER MOON**	
		Monica Barrie	$ 2.95
_____	523465	**AN UNFORGOTTEN LOVE**	
		Jacqueline Marten	$ 2.95
_____	530151	**WHISPERS IN THE WIND**	
		Patricia Pellicane	$ 2.95
_____	546066	**ARMS OF A STRANGER**	
		Lydia Lancaster	$ 3.50
_____	546864	**MIDWINTER'S NIGHT**	
		Jean Canavan	$ 3.50
_____	530178	**BELOVED ENEMY**	
		Cynthia Sinclair	$ 3.50
_____	546406	**FOX HUNT**	
		Carol Jerina	$ 3.50
_____	530194	**RIVER JEWEL**	
		Ann Cockcroft	$ 3.50
_____	543970	**VOWS OF DESIRE**	
		Catherine Lyndell	$ 3.50

Prices subject to change without notice.

 BOOKS BY MAIL
320 Steelcase Rd. E., Markham, Ontario L3R 2M1

Please send me the books I have checked above. I am enclosing
a total of $_____. (Please add 75 cents for postage and
handling.) My cheque or money order is enclosed. (No cash
or C.O.D.'s please.)

Name_____

Address_____ Apt._____

City_____

Prov._____ Postal Code_____

(LTM1)